PRAISE FOR BEAST MOM

"Imas pairs a brilliant premise with a highly memorable narrator, and together they should find a wide readership."

—KIRKUS REVIEWS

"For any woman who has been slighted, overlooked, and under appreciated, *Beast Mom* will have you cheering. In this humorous and warm-hearted novel, Kim Imas deftly portrays the everyday lives of mothers. By the end of the novel, you'll be wishing that beast moms were real."

—IVELISSE RODRIGUEZ, author of PEN/Faulkner Award for Fiction finalist *Love War Stories*

"In her delicious novel *Beast Mom*, Kim Imas infuses laugh-out-loud humor with an eff-the-patriarchy attitude, introducing us to an exhausted mom on the verge of discovering she has superpowers. As sarcastic as it is smart, *Beast Mom* is a wild literary ride that left me wanting more."

— JENNIFER KLEPPER, *USA Today* bestselling author

"*Beast Mom* is an audacious, timely, and darkly funny novel about the things moms think but do not say. Equal parts Simone de Beauvoir and Kafka, written with swagger and a keen eye. Harriet Lime's story will resonate with any parent who has hidden their rage under smiles for too long. You'll never look at a PTA meeting the same!"

—AMY MASON DOAN, bestselling author of *Lady Sunshine*

Beast Mom

Kim Imas

Beast Mom

Copyright © 2023 Kim Imas

Published by Mudlark

Paperback: 979-8-9882464-0-4
eISBN: 979-8-9882464-1-1

Cover illustration: Maggie Stephenson

For readers everywhere

CONFIDENTIAL MEMORANDUM

To: Special Agent T.J. Fullerson
From: Harriet Lime
RE: Weirder than usual happenings in Straussville, Oregon

Attached please find the report you asked for. But first, a few disclaimers.

I didn't write it for you, asshole. I only documented what happened to me in that strange run of weeks—starting with the first time I turned into, like, a total monster—so that in the event I don't survive your next little visit to town, my voice and my words will.

I tried to be professional. I do know what expository writing is. But as soon as I got to typing, my boss texted me with a "marketing crisis," LMAO. Then our smoke alarm went off, whereupon the dog went off. By the time my kids got into a bare-knuckle brawl in the next room, I'd decided that since my life is part improv-class, part battle-royale, this document should reflect that: Jokes will be made. Punches (and cuss words) will *not* be pulled. Some details are for color. But again—you can suck it, mister. You're a liar and a thief and I owe you nothing.[1]

You might run into more "vaginas" and "feelings" here than in other FBI reports, I don't know. Reproductive stuff and female emotions are central to this story. I hear a lot of men don't care to read about such things, so I fully expect you to squirm at the first whiff of estrogen and that is a thing that brings me much joy.

Lastly, this is more than an account of how my life went gaga for Kafka this year, and it's more than the furious yowl I've been holding inside myself for decades. Above all else, it's a warning, and a precursor; it's the storm surge before the hurricane. Because even though it's my own white, cishet,

---

1   I also jotted my grocery list in the middle of some paragraphs. Because a mom's gotta *oranges Cheerios pads* multi-task when a mom's gotta *zip-ties hydrochloric acid* multi-task!

middle-class-ish rage that seethes along these pages, I know that women of all stripes and in all places are raging right now.

But Harry, you might say, *women have always raged.* Indeed we have, sir. It's just that now, we can better see and hear each other. There is so much more to come.

1

It wasn't the first PTA meeting where I wanted to kill somebody, but it was the first time that the cops showed up.

I arrived even later than usual. All the chairs had been taken by parents who managed to get places on time, and the smattering of sleepy, slouchy kids they'd dragged along. I munched on the loose almonds I'd found in the console of my 2013 Grand Caravan and scanned the gymnasium for standing room. That's when I saw the officer, standing in the back. He wore a wide-brimmed hat—a cowboy hat, really—and the sole of his shiny black boot rested on the wall behind him, his thumbs in the belt loops of his crisp black pants.

"Thanks for hanging in there, folks," our PTA president, Mr. Terrence, announced through the speakers. "I'll let you get home to your Netflix—and your chill, if that's on the agenda in your house—right after this last bit of good news, about your long-awaited statue!"

The crowd clapped fervently at this—even letting out a few whoops—but my whole body sagged. I was so late that I'd missed everything I cared about, like updates on winter-break camps, and from the safety committee. I spied some free space along the side wall and trudged over, cursing the deli employee who'd held me up at New Seasons on the drive over, stepping in front of me with her magical, extroverted ways and her tantalizing free samples.

I squeezed in among the other parents and pulled out my phone. I was determined to check at least a half-dozen things off my to-do list so I wouldn't be up until one or two in the morning, grudgingly searching the web for an affordable party venue for fifty preschoolers. I pressed *Search* and glanced up again. The cop-guy hadn't moved, but his presence had nudged me a bit off-center.

"I'm thrilled to report that we'll be able to finish installing the statue in time for the big unveiling next month. And since I'm just a retiree," Mr. Terrence went on, to some empathetic titters from the crowd, "and the guys on my crew are teachers and lawyers—we've even got one nurse, folks—the board has kindly voted to hire some professionals to finish the job . . ."

This was met with full-throated laughter, although I had to quash the frown that snuck its way onto my face. Mr. Terrence had announced the donation of this statue a year earlier. He and his wife were friends of the reclusive Hoffman clan—the descendants of our schools' namesake, Jeremiah Hoffman—and their family foundation wanted the identity of the statue to be a surprise. Mr. Terrence had volunteered to manage the installation with a group of dads he'd handpicked for the construction. But by then, there'd been months of setbacks. I was scanning through work emails when Sue Bamford, or "Sooby" as I'd long called her, bopped over and squeezed in next to me.

"Why is that cop here, Soob? Did something happen?" I looked up from my phone and nodded toward the man in the back, while my brain composed a few images, as it often did, of what it might be like if an "active shooter" ever came to Hoffman. I pictured a pimply gunman—gunboy?—fumbling with a military-grade weapon, skulking his way down a hallway lined with construction-paper pumpkins put up by our kindergarteners.[2]

"Oh, no," Sooby replied, taking a bite from something in her palm. It looked like congealed tar but was probably a vegan brownie from the snack

---

2   They were more red than orange in my mind's eye, however, as I could never stop myself from imagining all the blood and human tissue splattered onto them.

table. "I'm not sure why that guy's here." She was a member of the board, and had a clipboard tucked under one arm and her daughter Satchel's pilled, pink hoodie under the other. She organized everything about these nights, from the refreshments to the speakers.

"Is he from the county or something?" I asked, suddenly remembering the pants I had tucked under my arm. I'd hemmed them for Satch, who also happens to be my goddaughter. I handed them over and Soob—a white woman like myself—mouthed an exaggerated *THANK YOU* before hugging them to her chest.

I don't know why I fixated on the guy. The elementary had a full-time security guard and so did the high school next door, where my daughter Bret was a freshman. At Healthy Start Preschool just across the road, where my twins Jojo and Frankie went, they had a part-time guard. And all of them were part of the campus scenery more or less, their cheap, gray uniforms blending in well with the cinder block walls. This guy, though? This guy seemed different.

"I think he got lost on his way to a *Gunsmoke* convention," I went on when Sooby still hadn't answered. I elbowed her in the ribs and moved on to the next item on my to-do list: making yet another list—this one of all the things that had broken recently in our house. *Front step, fridge, power button on dryer, oven smoking again (?), window (kitchen).*

"Harry, I don't know anything about that guy," Soob replied, sounding playfully irritated.

"You should probably go over there and offer him some spurs or something. Maybe a spittoon. Help him feel welcome."

"Are you done?" she asked as she licked the last of the brownie from her palm. "Look, I didn't invite any law enforcement here tonight. If I had, you'd be gawking at a cute firefighter over there instead."

Sooby and I had been friends since the fourth grade, when we'd held each other's ankles for sit-ups in that very same gymnasium. Back then, we'd been knobby-kneed and cocksure, our backs straight and our bangs sprayed into crisp half-pipes. Our friendship had been auspicious for many reasons, one being that all of us prepubescent girls were about to need a ride-or-die female in our lives—someone who'd whisper in our ear, for example, when our tampon string was hanging out from our gym shorts. Sooby was shorter than me, then and now, and a lot more practical in her leggings, fleece pullover, and neat, bobbed hair that she no longer cared to spray into unnatural shapes.

She held out her clipboard, with the sign-up sheet for Q&A. But I shook my head; I didn't want to keep everyone there past nine o'clock, and I could wait to share my ideas for new activities at the pool at some other meeting. Instead I went back to my phone—and my list—and typed *dog itches butt on carpet scooting prevention reasons* into the search bar.

"So just to wrap this up, folks," Mr. Terrence continued, "earlier tonight your board voted to redirect funds from three of our smaller afterschool programs, to make it possible to hire a crew to finish the statue. Remember, moms, this artwork was given to this body to honor *you*. It's for *you*, Bethany Haupt. It's for *you*, Lisette, and *you*, Tara. It's for . . ."

I let out a low groan. I mean, I had to: Mr. Terrence was actually jabbing his finger at those poor women, like he thought of himself as some kind of white, male Oprah—nicotine-stained mustache and all. Although when Sooby flung a ratty facial expression my way, I shut up.

Here's the thing about Mr. Terrence: Before retiring several years earlier, he'd been a beloved science teacher and the head volleyball coach at Hoffman High for decades—funny, devoted to the school, and a two-time winner of Oregon's Teacher of the Year award. He was even kind of handsome, in a Sam Elliott kind of way, if you didn't mind the smoker-stache. But he also "had a temper," as people liked to put it. Although "a predilection for assaulting people" is how I liked to put it, at least in my own head.

No one knew for sure how many times he'd exploded at students. And not just yelling at them, which I'd witnessed many times in his physics class back in the day, but also shoving things around and throwing stuff. In one outburst, legend has it, a huge blackboard fell off the wall, smashing through six shelves of the science department's only glassware.

But Mr. Terrence's best talent was in smoothing over such incidents. He'd gently approach the students he'd reamed out—who were all boys—and bestow clever nicknames on them. He'd tell them wild stories and jokes that were rumored to border on the inappropriate, and promise them an extra privilege or two at their next science competition.

When one of his grandchildren enrolled in our kindergarten the year after he retired from teaching, the PTA elected him to its board. He was our first-ever "grandparent" member, and it seemed like everyone I spoke to about him could only gush in admiration, and offer me their assurances—unsolicited—about how he'd "mellowed" over the years. I once made the mistake of telling another mom, during a conversation at our daughters' volleyball tournament, that our avuncular PTA president "has issues with women." And I'll never forget how she looked back at me in horror, as if I'd said "I grilled and ate my children" while slurping the last bits of one off my fingers. Once she'd gathered her wits she replied, "All three of my girls *adore* him and so do I. Maybe he's not the one who has issues." Sooby was one of his biggest fans.

"All right—let me have it, ladies!" Mr. Terrence again. "And Brad, of course. Remember, there's no such thing as a dumb question."

"Hello! Testing!" A new voice came through the overhead speakers, drawing my attention from the calendar entry I was making for Frankie and Jo's upcoming vision test. The parents who'd signed up to speak—Dianne, Christy, Ellen, and Brad—had lined up in the center aisle.

"I don't want to sound ungrateful, Mr. T. The sculpture is a wonderful, generous gift, and we appreciate you volunteering so much time to it," Dianne Chu began, her high, wavy ponytail swaying with her as she rocked her new kiddo—her fourth—from side to side. "It's just that . . . we spent all that time raising money over the summer, and now we're cancelling programs. At what point do we say, 'enough is enough'?"

I'd once complimented Dianne on her distinctive style—her funky, locally made jewelry and creative way of braiding her hair, for starters—but she'd batted the comment away with the back of a hand. They were just her "armor," she'd told me with a flash of a grin, some stuff she layered-on before facing the onslaught of each new day. But she looked especially wearied that night at PTA. She had an autoimmune disorder, I knew, and had gone back to work just weeks after adopting baby Ella. It was the kind of feat that Hercules himself would've taken one look at and said, "Nah, I'm good."

"Ma'am, let's not put words in my mouth," Mr. Terrence replied, pushing his fingers up under his glasses to rub at his eyes. As was often the case, the air in the gym was thick with moisture—and chlorine—thanks to the pool across the hall. "We're just *shelving* a couple of things for the year. Next?"

Something flared in my chest right then, as he motioned the next parent forward. I had all sorts of pains and tingles I could trace back to my two pregnancies, but this thing radiated from my heart in a terrible and searing pulse. Which was *new*. I clutched at the area above my left boob, alternately pressing and squeezing it. I thought I knew all of heartburn's manifestations—its sneaky belches and slow-motion corrosions—but I'd never felt it like that before. I'd never felt *anything* like that before, as if someone had sprayed shot all through my chest, from the inside out.

"Mr. T, I know you've chosen to cut—sorry, *shelve*—the programs with the fewest kids. But some of those provide benefits that will be difficult to replace. The Gay-Straight Alliance, for example," Dr. Christy Holmes pointed out. Christy was a leading surgeon, and a veritable Mom-Unicorn: She had kids and a pair of champion show dogs at home, yet still managed to appear in public in neat, well-fitting clothes. *Clean* ones! When she pushed some blond hair behind her pale ear, I noticed she was wearing a wrist brace of some kind and made a mental note to check with her about it. "The cuts you're proposing will harm the students most in need—"

"Let me stop you right there, Chris," Mr. Terrence butted in. "If there are students who want that sort of thing," he continued as an unpleasant buzzing sensation started up in both my ears, "you're welcome to put together a list of resources for them. *Next.*"

"Hello, sir—how are you doing tonight?" Dr. Ellen Stout was the next to step forward. She'd pulled her long twists into a low chignon, and wore a blouse with elaborate embroidery across the shoulders. She always wore clothes with fine, sometimes hidden details. Now, she looked at the chair in front of her and briefly rested a hand on her hip before pulling it away again. "I want to speak up for some of the parents who can't make it to these meetings," she began. She had a sunny voice, and in spite of what appeared to be a case of nerves—she held a piece of paper in her other hand, and rarely looked up from it—her perennial cheerfulness still came through. "Oftentimes, those parents—the ones who do shift work, or have irregular schedules—rely on our afterschool programs to keep their kids enriched and supervised, on a consistent basis."

Sooby elbowed me in the ribs. "Dude, we have a lot of mom-doctors," she whispered, pointing at the last two names on her sign-in sheet. "We are so awesome."

"Ellen's a PhD," I replied, pressing a forefinger into one ear then the other, wiggling it around as I went. "She works over at Hind Labs." I knew this because she'd come to my semi-regular walking club, the Walking Bred, a couple of times. We'd wandered the pathways around the K-8 and high schools, chatting mostly about movies. We joked about trailers we'd managed to catch, neither of us chastising the other for having missed a big block-buster or "important" film, knowing all too well how many things conspired to keep parents at home.

"Is there a plan in place for kids that suddenly find themselves idle in the afternoons?" Ellen continued, looking up with a buoyant smile. She seemed relieved to be done speaking.

"I'm afraid that falls outside my responsibilities, Mrs. Stout. But I recently came across an article on nanny-sharing—perhaps that's an option."

I snorted—I couldn't help it—and plenty of other parents laughed at that suggestion, too. Ellen gave it little more than a gentle huff, but it was enough to cause the AV system to squawk with feedback. She cringed and reached for the mic, calling out, "Oops—so sorry!" through the noise. I took the opportunity to type *ear chirring lesser-known symptom heart attack?* into my search bar.[3]

"Mr. Terrence," Ellen continued, gesturing as if unsure what to do with her free hand, "a lot of families can't afford additional childcare. Regardless of their schedule."

Yes. Amen. The crowd clapped at this, and I tucked my phone under my chin and joined along. *Way to push back on him.*

"Mrs. Stout, I've said all I can on that issue. So unless you have some additional complaint, I think we can move on."

The hell? I gave Mr. Terrence the stink eye as I rummaged around my bag for some Tums. *And that's Dr. Stout to you.* A number of people shifted in their chairs, setting off an unpleasant din of creaking hinges and squeaky rubber soles, and when I looked over at Sooby, even she was raising a brow. I popped a few of the antacids and went back to pressing a fist into my chest.

"Mr. Terrence, all I'm asking is whether we can find—"

"Let's keep moving," he said, interrupting Ellen again and glancing at his watch. "I know you care a great deal about the time of other parents, Mrs. Stout, so let's consider the folks waiting in line behind you."

Something tickled the back of my hand then, and I glanced down, expecting to see the gossamer strand of a spiderweb, or a stray hair perhaps. So I was stunned to see a ripple move across my skin instead, as if it were a viscous liquid of some sort. I jerked backward, accidentally banging my head on the wall. I lifted my hands high and examined them in the overhead lights, relieved to see they were simply trembling—nothing more. I lowered one and rubbed at my crown with the other.

"What I'm hearing tonight," Ellen said after a quick nod to Brad, the one person standing behind her, "is that there *is* such a thing as a dumb question. Or at least, a kind of question you don't feel a need to answer."

---

3   I also Googled "nanny-sharing," by the way, and soon regretted it. Let's just say some of the search results were inappropriate for polite society, and I had to stab at the little "X" on my screen like a jackhammer on the fritz, trying to close the offending window as quickly as possible.

Mr. Terrence shot abruptly to his feet, sending his chair backward with so much force that its metal legs screeched against the floor. The swishing of nylon and snapping of buttons in the audience came to a perfect standstill, like finches in the trees when a hawk is about. He yanked up on the waistband of his pants and called out, in the phlegmy, uneven voice of a person who's been caught off guard, *"I beg your pardon, ma'am!"*

I was so distracted by Ellen's courageous comment—and the thrum in my head, and the gurgling in my torso—that I almost missed it: I almost missed the nod Mr. Terrence gave to the back of the room. I followed his gaze, just in time to see the Gunsmoke Guy nod back, then push himself off the wall with that shiny black boot of his. I nudged Sooby and nodded toward the man, who began pacing back and forth behind the last row of chairs.

"That," Mr. Terrence went on as he shoved his glasses up his now-red face, "is not at all what . . . it's not . . . Mrs. Stout, that's a very inappropriate *tone*." His eyes and chin were firmly set now, and I knew that look; most of us knew that look, although probably not Ellen, who hadn't gone to school with us. She'd only moved down from Seattle about five months earlier, and she, her husband, and their sons were among the few people of color in the Hoffman community.

"OK, sir, but now that I have your attention," Ellen went on, now with a noticeable tremor in her otherwise upbeat tone. Some of the shuffling noises resumed, and I get it: Dragging one's tired, surly kids home and dealing with bath and bedtime drama is typically a lot more important than PTA drama. But something about the guy in the black hat and uniform, and the ridiculous way that this white man—one known to erupt at students, no less—was asking a Black mother to watch her tone? These had cranked my heart rate up to eleven, so I stayed put.

Ellen raised her hands, as if asking for—and offering—a peace of sorts, "I just wanted to point out some possible consequences of these changes. Consequences that are likely to fall on moth—"

"No—no, we're done here," Mr. Terrence interrupted. "Brad, please take your turn."

But it wasn't Brad who came forward; Brad just stood there like the proverbial deer, recognizing its maker in the oncoming headlights of a Mack truck. No, it was the Gunsmoke Guy who proceeded toward the microphone. Or rather, toward Ellen.

My eyes bugged out. *The* cop *is getting in on this? Seriously?*

Sooby clamped a hand on my forearm. "Is that guy, like, planning on dragging Dr. Ellen Stout away from the microphone?" she whispered.

"I . . . think so?" I replied. I scanned his torso for a holster but couldn't make out any details on the dark, monochrome uniform. I turned and watched Ellen turn toward the front again, then take a very slow, very deep breath. She must have seen the guy coming, although judging by the checked-out expressions on the faces of the parents around me, most of the room had missed it.

And again, that creepy bubbling thing happened on the backs of my hands, and up both wrists and forearms. My skin moved in a way that it shouldn't—as if there were something underneath it that wasn't just alive and kicking, but trying to get out, too.

I glanced around, my breath suddenly short. Sooby had left my side and was making her way toward some dad who'd waved her over, and many other parents were putting on coats and whispering commands to their kids. The rest remained focused on Mr. Terrence, however, who was still standing at the front of the room with his hands on his hips and his brow slung low over his eyes. I, meanwhile, shook my head like a wet dog, trying to recover my senses. The drone in my ears had approached the pitch and intensity of a fire alarm, and I began to think I should go to the emergency room.[4]

"I need ORDER, folks!" Mr. Terrence barked, banging his gavel. Ellen picked up her bag and turned toward the back of the gym, passing briskly by the cop-guy as her silk scarf and trench-coat billowed around her petite frame like battle flags. The guy spun on his heel and took a few steps in the same direction, then slowed, as if trying to pass off his actions as casual. But I didn't see anything casual about it, and decided to go after her, too. I

---

4   I was also wondering how I'd get my kids' lunches made, and all their forms signed, if I did.

stepped gingerly over the backpacks and trumpet cases still strewn about on the high-gloss floor, and when a few other moms reached out and grabbed my arm as I passed, I said hello as quickly as I could and kept moving. Still, by the time I reached the lobby, Ellen was gone.

The cop-guy was there, however, standing with a second officer I hadn't seen before—this one speaking into a radio pinned to his shoulder. I wanted to approach them, but the heat in my chest was flaring in a steady rhythm by that point, like a second pulse. I was resting my hands on my knees and dry-heaving when Sooby trotted up beside me.

"I'm fine," I told her between gulps of air. "It's just . . . it's just the usual crap. Mom-bod crap." I waved her forward and she jogged off toward the officers, who were heading for an outside exit.

"Excuse me?" I heard her call out. "Officers, can I talk to you a sec?" But less than a minute later, she tromped back to me. I looked up and saw her roll her eyes, the cops nowhere to be seen.

"They said they got an emergency call. They wouldn't stop to give me a card."

I nodded and swayed a little. To my immense relief, the burning and buzzing had tapered off somewhat. Even better, nothing seemed to be wriggling under my skin anymore like it was auditioning for a Ridley Scott movie.

"Did you see any . . . badges, or patches, on their uniforms?" I asked between gasps of air.

She shrugged. "Neither of them had a name tag on. I thought I saw a patch, but couldn't make out any words on it," she replied as she pulled out her phone. "That was kinda weird, right? For Mr. T to just stand there like that? While that cop went all John-Wayne on Ellen?"

I stood upright, my hands resting on my hips, and gave her as flat a look as I could manage. I wasn't surprised that she had missed—or chose to deny, perhaps—how Mr. Terrence had actually *sicced* the cop on Ellen. For decades, she'd been blind to all kinds of incidents in which Mr. Terrence treated women or girls as an afterthought. Hell, Sooby had been the one who picked me up when I was sixteen, freezing and alone on the front steps of the high school, after the van heading to a Science Club event left without me one miserable January afternoon—with Mr. Terrence at the wheel. I'd gotten there just five minutes late but apparently, they couldn't wait. The other members, all boys, told me later how he'd turned purple during the Rube Goldberg Contest, and paced the floor during Trivia Time, both events in which I often got the highest score on our team. But I'd be wasting my breath trying to get Sooby to see things differently, and I had to save my breath so that I could waste it on my kids and coworkers instead. Besides, *Sooby had been the one who picked me up, then and every other time.* Well, almost every other time.

"I'll mention it to Mr. T tomorrow," she went on, staring at her calendar. "He asked me to meet with him, anyway. I was going to postpone, because Satch felt sick earlier, and who knows if she'll go in tomorrow, and . . ." Her words turned into mumbles, then trailed off completely. But she continued to poke around her screen, and I knew what she was thinking because it's the same thing I thought roughly three thousand times a day: *What can I skip, in order to have time for this new thing that's landed on my plate? And how will that mess up my whole week?*

"You sure you're OK, Harry?" she asked as she slid her phone into her back pocket. "Do a sarcasm, so I know you're OK."

"What?" I asked as I popped back a few more Tums. "It's not like I turned green or anything."

1.2   SUNDAY, 9:00 P.M.

Hubba . . . HUBBA.

That was my thought when I opened our front door and saw my husband's profile, illuminated in blueish light from the television and from his laptop, in our otherwise dark family room.

I am married to a babe.

"Justin's in his driveway again, wearing nothing but jean-cutoffs and flip-flops," I said as I put down the groceries and shrugged out of my jacket, letting out a whooshy exhale. We had a new next-door neighbor, a retired Marine in his sixties, who seemed to dress for equatorial temperatures regardless of the conditions on the ground. "Do you think he's, like, confused about what people mean when they say 'climate deni—"

I stopped talking when I looked up and saw that Theo had turned toward me, his eyes big and his index finger pressing frantically against his lips. He pointed to the corner, at the portable crib we kept there. I tiptoed over and discovered the reason for his silence: Frankie was fast asleep on the thin mattress at the bottom, his rainbow-striped footie-pajamas damp with sweat.

"What happened?" I whispered as I turned around and headed toward the couch, crane-walking through the hundreds of Legos and approximately three-billionty Matchbox cars that littered the floor. I moved a basket of unfolded laundry from the sofa so I could sit next to him.

"He had another night terror," Theo replied, giving me a quick kiss on the cheek before turning back to his laptop. "He wouldn't stop screaming, poor guy. I brought him down here so he wouldn't keep Jojo up."[5]

I nodded. "Three-year-olds are a scourge," I whispered as I rubbed my eyes.

I waited for Theo to react—to joke, maybe, that he'd always thought of Jo and Frankie as more of a plague, or that fourteen-year-olds were stiff competition when it came to the Scourge Awards. But he just kept staring into the spreadsheet on his laptop, the mute television still flickering its ever-changing light on him from the corner of the room.

"So, hey," I said quietly, "I had some epic heartburn tonight." I got up and went to the kitchen, which was open to our family room and arguably

---

5   Normally, Rule #1 for Surviving Young Twins is to make sure they always—and I do mean *always*—sleep at the same time. That way, you get a little time to wash the pieces of your breast pump or whatever, before you start up another round of parenting. But ever since Frankie started waking up with terrible nightmares a few nights a week, Theo and I agreed there were times it was better to let Jo sleep. Because while one overtired three-year-old is a shit-show, *two* of them is a punishment I wouldn't wish on anyone. Well, I might wish it on Mr. Terrence. But only him.

the real scourge in our house. We found the "open plan concept" terrible when it came to wrangling two toddlers, and there was hardly ever any quiet in the place. There was also a constant, low-level odor of stale urine, thanks to all the potty training going on.

Theo didn't look up as he pulled a tortilla chip from the bag he'd propped between his thigh and the armrest.

So I started putting away the groceries, and also the food that had been left out from dinner, hours earlier—throwing away wrappers and wiping up crumbs and spills. My phone beeped, reminding me to finish the forms all three kids needed for school picture day tomorrow, so I pulled those from my bag and filled them out. I was grabbing our checkbook out of the junk drawer to make a payment for Bret's new volleyball uniform when I finally said, "Babe? Did you hear me?"

"Mmmm?" Theo replied. He was hunched forward, staring into his screen.

"It was like . . . like somebody had cracked open my chest, and poured Bengay inside," I said as I picked up the bath towel I'd laid in front of our incontinent refrigerator that morning, to sop up the half-gallon of water it leaked every day. Then I replaced it with a dry one from the laundry basket. "And then performed CPR on me, poorly."

I knew Theo needed time to himself in the evening, especially now that our workdays were capped with long nights of parenting. And I hadn't forgotten the way he'd confessed—in a mumbled rush, during a commercial break in a Seahawks game the previous winter—that his boss and coworkers didn't seem to need his input as much as they used to, and that it worried him. But that heartburn at the PTA meeting had been un-freaking-real, and if I postponed telling Theo I'd just forget about it, as soon as some new crisis appeared and demanded its own space on the ever-crowded front burners of my mind.

"It was really weird, Theo. I thought it was—"

"Do we have anymore snacks?" he asked, interrupting me. He looked up at me for the first time, holding up the near-empty tortilla bag. He even shook it a little, the way a person might do when they want the attention of their dog or cat. "I'm starving."

Frustration and hurt swelled up in me, the way the ocean does along the Oregon coast, threatening to spray and bubble and break through any spaces between the rocks. So I took a very deep breath, like I tell the twins to do whenever their own surging emotions threaten to overtake them. Theo's bag-shaking was uncool, but it was the fact that he interrupted me that really bugged. It happened to me everywhere: at work, the family dinner table, the hardware store, on the phone with telemarketers. Sometimes the dog even barked at me if I got halfway through a sentence and nobody else jumped in to take care of it.

"Well, I need the new strawberries for the kids' lunches," I replied, opening up my bag. "But I also have this weird pureed stuff," I said, holding up the pouch I'd bought at New Seasons earlier.

He looked over, his brows in a deep V. "A pouch? Is it for babies?"

I turned it around and read what the charming, irresistible she-devil of a deli worker had written on it, in black marker: "It says . . . 'Immunity Booster,' but I can't read the last part. Something . . . 'Restorative'? I don't know. Whatever. It's green and edible. I sampled some at the store."

He grunted in amusement. "Pass."

I tossed it in the trash with some other bits of paper from my pockets, then started to pack the twins' lunches. But when I pulled out the carton of organic strawberries—which had cost what I imagine a two-acre strawberry farm will run you in other states—I noticed a fuzzy gray coating on three of the biggest, reddest berries.

"What the—" *Mold?!?* I clamped down on the curse words that had assembled for duty on the tip of my tongue, then swept the whole carton into the compost bin with an expensive *thunk*. I marched back to the couch in stormy silence and sat down next to Theo, this time doing my best not to leave any space between the two of us. Sure, this was the guy who'd just shaken his chip bag at me. But it was also the guy who'd slept only three or four hours a night for seven months straight, just as I had, when Jojo and Frankie were born prematurely and needed constant care.

I'd already dammed up the hurt I'd felt earlier, and could more or less ignore the heartburn that still gurgled inside me. All I needed now was to avert my eyes from the commercial on television, which was hawking some expensive cream to women by reminding them of some body part they were supposed to get rid of. Through force of will, I banished all those things to a place in the back of my mind, because the thing I wanted front and center right then was Theo. I wanted to be as close to him as possible—to have him support nearly all my weight.

I nuzzled into him, and he shifted so that my head could nestle into the space between his neck and shoulder. *How many nights have gone by,* I wondered, *when we've said less than four sentences to each other? When was the last time we talked about something besides the kids, our broken fridge, the mortgage, or an older and ailing relative?*

When were we supposed to talk like we used to? Did Theo miss that— ache for it, even—the way I did?

He leaned against me, too, and I ran my hand across the taut, dark denim of his thigh. It was a comfy arrangement, but it unfortunately gave me a good view of the laundry basket. I liked to joke that I had a "mom lobe" in my brain—some pulsing clump of gray matter that prompted me, every waking moment, to manage our household. It signaled me to Google stuff and make calendar entries during PTA meetings, and at home it refused to ignore the dust bunnies that ventured boldly from underneath the TV stand, and the stains on the carpet that grew and multiplied at a pace rivalled only by said bunnies.

I didn't say anything to Theo, though, about any of that. I closed my eyes and sent my mind in search of better thoughts. It found plenty of them, mostly from Theo and my first years together—when we'd had a surplus of time, of jokes and good-natured barbs, and of sex.

We'd met on a warm pool deck at the University of Whisper Valley, a few weeks before the start of our sophomore year. It was one of those waning

August afternoons that's both luxuriously empty and also a little bit frenzied—the kind of day that compels you, sometimes without your realizing it, to do everything you can to wring the last bits of summer from it. Theo was a California boy, born and bred, and he'd just founded the university's first water polo team, as if that were the most natural thing to do in a mostly clammy, mostly gray place like our valley. These facts did as much to make him an object of fascination to the rest of us as did the effortless way he carried his surfer-boy good looks.

For my part, I'd made it through my first year on the swim team without finding anyone who tempted me all that much. Which is saying a lot, frankly, when you spend most of your time wearing nothing but tiny, stretchy bits of fabric, toning and strengthening your body, or on a dark charter bus en route to a rival college. But my father had just died, before I could meet him, and strange new clouds were forming in my mind that year.

But Theo? Theo wasn't just a looker—he was a talker, too. He had so much to say and ask that I wondered at first, I'm slightly embarrassed to admit, whether there might be something wrong with him. He asked me all kinds of things, even after we'd only just met: Did I personally identify with the kids from *Goonies,* and if so, which one? What did it mean that I was a history major *and* "pre-law"? Also, why did I have such a beef with companies that pre-mixed the fruit into their yogurt? Later on, after we'd been dating a while, he'd ask me on the regular why he hadn't met my mother yet. I'd met his parents a bunch of times, after all, whenever they drove or flew up from Oxnard.

Now, with his thumb and forefinger, Theo lifted my chin toward his, looking at my mouth the way I imagine a wolf looks at an especially plump rabbit. There wasn't much sun or salt left in his hair and skin anymore, but the rest of him still carried the shape and bulk of his water polo days. He'd softened a bit in recent years, which only made him more teddy-bear like, and he and his post-surfer-dad looks remained an object of fascination, now at the Hoffman and Healthy Start drop-off lanes.

I slipped my hand under his T-shirt and onto the warm expanse of his back, and he pulled me toward him by the nape of my neck, then on top of him, where he had free access to my ass and thighs and the place where my shirt escaped from my waistband. I had to bash down some mental images that crept back to mind from that stupid commercial, with its insidious suggestion that I had too much . . . I dunno, *woman* on my body? *Blech.* But I eventually succeeded, and as Theo wrapped me up in his considerable warmth, my brain slowly freed itself from its worldly concerns, and began to simply enjoy itself.

Unfortunately, however, poor Frankie chose that exact moment to let out a distressed squeal from the corner, and Theo and I both went still—all the new heat we'd generated escaping rapidly from the slim spaces between our limbs and torsos.

"*Ugghhhh,*" I whispered right next to his ear, "there goes our janky smoke alarm." Theo stayed quiet, though. Once upon a time he would've laughed at that, or offered up a conspiratorial comeback.

"*Moooooommy?*" This time it came from upstairs: Jo was awake, too. "MOOOOMMY?"

Frankie heard her call and sat bolt-upright, bursting immediately into tears. Jo's wailing escalated, too, and if you've never been stuck in a confined space with two toddlers screeching in stereo, well, congratulations! You must live in a place that frowns upon torture. Theo and I stood, resigned to this pause in our make-out session. "Which one do you want?" I asked as we re-tucked and adjusted our clothes and body parts.

"Whichever."

My "mom-lobe" did that thing it often did—a thing most moms do, I suspect—where it triangulates, calculates, and mitigates all of the factors in a crappy situation, in an attempt to make everyone in the room as happy as possible. "How about I take Frankie upstairs and put him back with Jojo?" That way, I reasoned, they could calm each other down, leaving Theo and me free to return to our smooching. He'd even have time to stash his laptop safely away, while I was up there.

I went to the corner and scooped our little guy up, his silky hair plastered to his face, all of him warm and damp against me. When I got to the bottom of the stairs, I called out softly to Theo, "My skin felt weird, too."

"Huh?"

"At the PTA meeting, when I had all that heartburn and stuff? It was like . . . like my skin was being pulled in all directions." I shrugged and started up the stairs. "Fingers crossed I'll be right back down to—"

"Actually," Theo replied, scratching his head, "don't worry about it, OK? I've got a shit-ton of emails to reply to." Then he blew me a quick kiss—the saddest possible signal, I thought, that our intimacy was over for the evening.

I turned to face the stairs, and to hide the way my eyes had begun to twitch from the onset of tears. I looked down at Frankie and wished I could cry the way he and Jojo could, loud and long and in a way that brought people running, determined to fix whatever was wrong. And I wished right then, as I often did, that Theo and I could just make out at a dingy roadside bar somewhere, like the smitten sophomores we'd once been. Or that the stars, moon, and our kids' sleep schedules would align just long enough for us to have a good, hard fuck against an inappropriate piece of furniture.

Because that was the real problem when it came to our marriage, or so it seemed to me at that time: two toddlers with erratic needs. Well, that and the stress of two jobs, one less secure than it used to be. Oh, and a teenager.

***

An hour later, I was still lying in a toddler-sized bed with one kid curled against my left side and the other snuggled up on my right, scrolling through messages in search of Ellen Stout's email address.

Making friends had gotten harder in recent years, and that had chipped my confidence in a few spots. I had three kids who were eleven years apart, first of all, which I believe is some kind of anti-Golden Ratio for the modern family: It's not very common, and not at all harmonious. Our house was a cacophonous mess, and what's more, I had a "pay the bills" job, in marketing, whereas Ellen had a serious career at a prestigious research institution. A few laps around the school and some shared observations about Hollywood might not have meant as much to her as they had to me. The only value-adds I had to offer my friends were a handful of diaper-changing hacks and a pathological need to connect with them on the regular, thanks to growing up adrift from any real family.

Eventually I found one of Ellen's messages, from mid-July, in which she declined my invitation to meet at the river to watch the Dragon Boat Races, but asked me to keep inviting her to stuff anyway. With her overfilled schedule, she'd written, she was likely to say no a lot—or not answer at all—but wanted to come to things when she could. I hit reply, and wrote:

> *hi ellen, how are things? I was hoping to talk with you after PTA tonight, but I dawdled too much and missed you.*
>
> *think you'll come to the walking bred anytime soon? it's oscar season after all, and there are a lot of important films coming out that I'm really excited to not-see. how about you? which ones are you most looking forward to missing?*

I paused and stared at my words. Were they too lighthearted? She had just been treated horribly, without recourse, by a white man in a position of authority in front of the wider—and mostly white—community. It occurred to me that a perky, frivolous email was not the response she needed from us white women in attendance.

As a kid, I'd figured most things out by trial and error. Like how to insert a tampon, minutes before the starting gun for the twelve-and-under medley relay. Like the importance of not asking the woman in front of you in the supermarket checkout line how she got that epic bruise on the back of her knee. The upside of my experiential approach to life was that I got comfortable being wrong a lot of the time, and wise to the fact that certain kinds of mess-ups might appear benign from my child-high perspective, but turn out to be harmful to someone else. Say, for example, when a battered woman's boyfriend is standing right behind her, and is massively allergic to any discussion of her body. The downside was that I accrued yet another reason to keep my mouth shut, and as a female, I hadn't been lacking for those. I started typing again:

> *im sorry mr. terrence was so awful to you. sue-beth bamford and I are trying to find out who those guys wearing all-black and the hats were. -harry*

I wanted to add: *I always knew he was a sexist prick; now I know he's a racist one, too.* But it occurred to me that I might be making too many assumptions about how Ellen had taken Mr. Terrence's behavior. Would I be recalling a situation she'd rather move on from? Maybe she'd taken it in stride, and I'd be forcing her to dwell on it some more.

Then again, maybe a single line calling the incident "awful" was woefully insufficient. Perhaps I shouldn't send a message at all; I should just talk to her in person, it seemed, about the whole bad-cop/bad-cop thing. But the next PTA meeting was a month away.

I read my draft once more, and moved the sentence about Mr. Terrence to the first paragraph. I decided to chalk up my hesitation to the general anxiety I'd built up around meeting new friends, and hit *Send* before I could second-guess—or was it seventh-guess?—my words. In the end, I knew that if it had been me at that microphone, I'd have been shaking with a combination of rage and revenge fantasies, at the least. Maybe Ellen needed someone to commiserate with. I turned off my phone and placed it on the floor.

"Mom?"

I looked up and saw Bret's silhouette in the doorway. "Yeah, honey?"

"Coach asked me to go to the Yarn Barn tomorrow, after school. To get posters and stuff for the Bellwether game."

As she spoke, Frankie gave an irritated whimper and rolled over, grabbing a fistful of my hair before settling down again. "OK. I can probably drive you," I whispered in reply, rubbing my eyes as if the right amount of pressure could push this new information into my brain—so that I wouldn't have to pick up my phone again.

"Actually, you don't have to. Coach is going to drive." As my eyes adjusted to the dark, I could see more of Bret's outline and how she was twiddling with a lock of her longish, straight hair. A few weeks earlier, when she announced she was borrowing her father's razor for "a quick trim" and then disappeared into the bathroom, I'd braced myself when the door swung open again just a few minutes later. Sure enough, I was gobsmacked by what I saw. But not because she was crying or bleeding or anything; she'd simply transformed herself, with swift ease, from the young girl whose every mole and scar I could describe in minute detail to someone who resembled the lead singer from some cooler-than-cool rock band, circa 1974. I can't say for sure if it's what she was going for, but she had instantly levelled herself up when it came to the appearance of worldliness.

"Why is Coach going to the craft store?" Assistant Coach Sullen was new to Hoffman that year. I didn't know much about him, only that Bret found him "kinda chill."

Her shrug was barely visible.

"Are the other girls going?"

"Mooooom! *Duh!*"

"*Shhhhh!*" I hissed. Bret, Theo, and I all had to operate in "stealth-mode" at night, walking and talking as quietly as possible. Once in a while, though, one of us forgot about our sleeping-toddler overlords, and accidentally said something at normal volume.

When neither twin stirred, Bret picked up right where she had left off, surly tone and all: "Of *course* the girls are going. He's taking *all* the captains. Obviously."

"Please speak to me in your regular voice, babe." All I really wanted in life, that day and every day, was for everyone to do their part in making our house a "whine-free zone." No one listened when I brought it up, though, even after I'd written "No more whining!" on a piece of notepaper, labelled it "MOM'S CHRISTMAS LIST," and taped it to the front of the refrigerator. Bret and Theo had just chuckled over it and pronounced it one of my lamer jokes.

"Is Coach a good driver?"

"Moooooom—of *course* he's a good driveeeeer."

"Regular voice, please." I lifted my pelvis and wrestled with the waistband of my pants. Why did everything fit me so differently than it used to, despite the fact that I weighed basically the same? Pregnancy had been awful, sure; but it wasn't like I had grown a third butt cheek or something.

"Why do you wear those?" Bret asked. "Those old jeans?"

My face flushed. My own daughter was calling me out on my weird attachment to my pants. They'd been part of my life since before Theo and I had received the shock of our lives on the fuzzy monitor at the OB/GYN office, and I *loved* them. Plus, I was hardwired for thrift.

"What? *These?* These are in good shape! I save us money by wearing my old stuff."

"Yoga pants are totally acceptable, you know. So are leggings. Aunt Sooby practically lives in them."

"Yeah, well. They're not my thing." I knew perfectly well how sweats and yoga pants camouflaged all the crumbs, snot, and newly reshaped body parts that plagued moms, in direct proportion to how many children they had. I just personally didn't care for them. I wore suits to work, which was a rarity in the greater-Portland area, and blazers and button-down shirts most other places. All in a range of blacks, charcoals, and obsidian tones that comforted me, thank you very much, in a world that did not offer up comforts as often as I would like.

"So is torture your 'thing'?"

"Am I not allowed to be vain, now and then? Is vanity off-limits to moms? I'll add it to the list, right after 'being overprotective,' and just before 'not protective enough.'"

"*Yes,* Mom. You're allowed to like your jeans. And you're allowed to be all . . . nonconformist and stuff."

I smiled. She was a sweet one, our Bret, underneath all the hormones that swirled around and enveloped her, like the marbling on some faraway, jewel-toned planet. "Thank you for noticing that, honey—"

"But they do fit you really weird," she blurted out. "They totally do, Mom—sorry."

I sighed. Vanity and I were old friends, it was true. But we'd recently become somewhat estranged.

"And Coach is *totally* a good driver. And I need a poster-board for my history project, too. So can I go, please? Please, please, *please?* The captains always make posters for the Bellwether game."

Captains. Funny word, that. Here was my little girl, my first baby, my thoughtful and conscientious child—now a freshman, and already an elected leader on her volleyball team. She had always been encouraging to other girls, on the playground and elsewhere. But there was something new and awesome in her embracing the mantle of "captain," and from her very first high-school match, too. Not even Mr. Terrence's ongoing presence at the periphery of her games—he was still one of the varsity coaches—could dampen the joy I felt watching her. When she brought home her official volleyball jacket for the first time and I saw the word "Tri-Captain" embroidered on the chest in gold thread, it occurred to me that she must've inherited some kind of, like, leadership gene or something from Theo's DNA. His parents had been diving coaches for forty-two years, whereas my own mother looked upon every club, committee, and association that extended her an invitation with the warmth and openness of a gargoyle. She'd never explained her bone-deep distrust for groups, but then, she barely talked to me at all.

I certainly hadn't had any gold thread on my letter-jacket in school, and unlike Bret, who practically lived in hers, I'd often "forgotten" to wear mine on the right days. Not because they were uncool; swimmers had a ton of cachet, actually, in the Social Gospel of Hoffman High. It's just that I looked at it and saw a piece of outerwear that wasn't water-resistant enough for someone who walked or biked everywhere. In *Oregon.* What I didn't see was a reflection of my commitment to anyone. So when one of my coaches pulled me aside one day and suggested I "become more of a team player," it had little effect. I chose dryness, and I chose to focus on the pool, on Sooby and the other kids we hung out with, and on getting more babysitting hours. I didn't mind that a reputation for piddly acts of rebellion began attaching itself to me like a remora. But I failed to consider that reputations—whether good or bad or neutral—are wont to mutate. When my classmates later voted me "Most Likely to Turn Hermit" at our Senior Banquet, it stuck in my craw.

"If the other girls are going, and you go straight there and come straight back, you can go," I said finally. Then I lightly, and haphazardly, pressed my palm to my lips several times, in homage to the sloppy manner in which Jojo and Frankie "blew someone a kiss." I giggled when Bret did it back to me, her splayed fingers barely making contact with her mouth.

As she scampered back to her room, grinning, I thought of something else I should tell Ellen about, and picked up my phone to send another email:

> *hi again, I forgot to mention that you're also welcome to join the book club I'm in. sometimes we get together and talk about the intriguing book none of us had time to finish. other times we just email each other from our couches, about the book club meeting none of us could get to. OH, and do you know about the Scarehouse event, at the end of the month???[Ghost emoji, pumpkin emoji] -h*

Our book club was slated to meet in just a few nights, in fact, which was very exciting for me. It was a highlight of every month, getting to sit around and chat with other adults and nosh on real food. I hadn't finished the *Oprah's Book Club* book we'd selected, but I'd gotten farther than usual. And I'd probably be able to look up some Amazon reviews at work during lunch, to see what other people had thought of it. Not exactly the rich literary experience one hoped for when joining a book club, but I'd take it.

Before locking my phone again, I skimmed my other emails. There was one from Jo and Frankie's teachers, giving Theo and me our second warning that the lunches we packed contained foods that fell "outside of Healthy Start's guidelines." There was a message about the statue, too, and how the unveiling ceremony was still on for some date in November. Normally I avoided Mr. Terrence's messages that close to bedtime; I had enough trouble falling asleep without adding another round of god-awful heartburn to the mix. But seeing his name whisked me straight back to the gym, with its stuffy air and all the moms and dads suffering through it in order to listen to the guy. I pinched the bridge of my nose and squeezed my eyes closed as it hit me—like the stench of the pig shit they keep in those enormous lagoons—just how badly I'd botched things earlier that night.

Gunsmoke Guy aside, it was absolutely fucking unacceptable for Mr. Terrence, or anyone at all, to speak that way to Ellen and I should have spoken up, for fuck's sake, raised my hand or shouted out or shot a fucking spitball at the man. Whatever it took to make that plain, basically. But I didn't. I hadn't. I'd abandoned another mom when she needed me, and yes, Ellen needed *me* specifically. Because I was the only person there who was primed to call Mr. Terrence out. Fuck—I *wanted* to let that man have it. I daydreamed about it sometimes. And what would it have cost me, personally? Some parents would think less of me, would be less inclined to invite me to things? They'd begin to think of me as not being in their camp, in a way? Abandonment issues be damned—I could weather all of that. This didn't just feel like a Mom-Fail but a Woman-Fail, and in my mind at least, a Friend-Fail, too. I'd done what I'd sworn, many years earlier, I would never do: I'd left a friend to fend for herself.

I was still contorted in self-disgust when Jojo woke up and clambered over me, planting her bony elbow in the middle of my chest and stomping on my pubic bone like a determined gymnast, on a vaulting run for Olympic gold. I withered into a fetal position from the searing pain in both my primary and secondary sexual characteristics as she trotted off calmly to the bathroom. When I could finally straighten myself out again, I picked my phone off the floor again and Googled *teenagers driving safety friends cars boundaries*. Then waited for Jojo to call me in to help her.

Because if anyone tells you a three-year-old can wipe their own butt, what they're really telling you is that they aren't to be trusted. With much of anything.

1.3   MONDAY 6:30 P.M.

We'd just pulled up to a red light when my daughter—the little one—used some colorful language to call the driver next to us a "bastard," at the very top of her lungs. I slunk low in my seat, wishing I could disappear, then nearly fainted when I saw that the man was a biker the size of our furnace.

It was the day after the PTA meeting, and after leaving work, I'd taken the twins to their "dance" class, picked Bret up from volleyball, and driven the four of us to dinner at Red Robin. Now, we were on our way to meet up with Theo at the school.

It turned out, thankfully, that the biker was a *Hamilton* fan, too; and as we waited for the light to change, he belted out the next lines of the song. Jo and Frankie squealed in delight and clapped for him, and I was sure they'd try for an encore at every intersection thereafter, with other unsuspecting drivers.

When the traffic got moving again, the four of us sang *Hamilton* at the top of our voices. I drove with the windows down whenever I could, which was pretty much all the time in that strange run of dry weather. And since, as predicted, I was the only one who stopped singing at the next intersection, I pretended to try and shush them, leading all three to hoot with laughter. They found my impotence so hilarious that big, round tears were soon tumbling down their cheeks—and mine, too. I repeated these faux protests for a couple more lights, just to prolong the wacky happiness of our evening.

Once I stopped my *shushing* routine and the kids had settled down, I glanced over at Bret. I started to ask about the history project she'd been working on, out of genuine curiosity more than parental concern. But she was smiling so broadly, and chasing absently at the hairs lashing her freckled cheeks in the wind, that it struck me as a moment worth savoring. I kept my mundane question to myself and focused instead on the road ahead, and the way the sun and sky seemed to be going through their own bedtime routine—the horizon a bed they took turns resting in, and tucking each other into.

When I couldn't tolerate the Open Mom Issues ping-ponging inside my brain any longer, I asked, "How was your shoulder today, B? That was quite a collision you and Chloe had."

She shrugged with her non-injured shoulder and drew her knees to her chest. It seemed we weren't going to talk about that.

"So, who all went to Yarn Barn today?" I asked, following up on our conversation from the night before. I reached for my necklace, as was my semiconscious habit. Bret had given me the silver chain when Frankie and Jo were born, along with a flat silver charm on which she'd etched their birth date, and her own. Each delicate line and sweeping curve comprised dozens of teeny-tiny punches, all of which she'd made herself with some special tool she'd known about, because even then, she knew a lot about making things, and she made them well. But my fingers came up empty that day; I didn't wear the necklace—my most precious of "time cards"—when I thought there was a chance I could exercise that day.

She took a few seconds to pick at the ends of her hair in silence. "Jasmine and Hannah," she replied finally.

"Hey," I went on, "what about the Homecoming dance? Did you decide about going?"

"I'm still thinking. I don't have a dress or a date or anything."

"I used to go with my friends."

She was quiet a minute. "Coach told me that we don't have time for boys, anyway. Or girls, or whoever."

"When did that come up?" I asked, keeping my voice and eyebrows level. My poker face had always been strong, but I couldn't curb the sudden turn in my gut as I processed that bit of information.

"That dress in the back of your closet is pretty cute, though," she said, ignoring my question.

"Say what, now?"

"You know—the sequined one. If I go to Homecoming, can I wear it?"

"So, wait: I can't wear my classic jeans anymore, but that spangly number from twenty-some years ago is 'pretty cute'?"

She shook her head at my apparent cluelessness. "That's the way the fashion cookie crumbles, Mom."

"They don't have cookies in fashion. Cookies don't exist there."

She laughed, and I swear to you, the warmth of it reached all the way to the marrow in my bones. Then she turned toward the back and said, "Frankie and Jo are like, so out of it right now."

I glanced in the rearview mirror. The twins' heads did look rather heavy on their shoulders, and their eyelids were closing up shop, too. But both were still mumbling along to our family's favorite lines from the musical.

When I pulled into the school parking lot, Theo was standing next to his Explorer and looking into his phone. He was going to take the kids the rest of the way home, and I would meet up with friends from my walking group, for the first time in weeks. I couldn't wait.

"Hey!" I called out the window as I pulled in, a couple spaces over.

"Hey." He pushed off the car with that cute butt of his and came over, still looking at his phone.

"How was your day?" I asked.

"Mmm?"

"How was your day?"

"Oh. Fine."

I hesitated to probe, knowing that work wasn't so much a sore subject for Theo as an ugly bruise of sorts. But since he no longer automatically told me when something important occurred in his life? Well, a-probing I had to go. "Was everything . . . good at work?"

"Yeah! Of course." He put his phone in his pocket and gave me a peck on the cheek. "I mean, as good as usual anyway."

I tried to nod in a way that encouraged him to keep talking. *Was it possible to claw an older version of someone back to the surface again?* Because I needed Chatty Theo back—so, so badly. "Yeah?" I asked dumbly.

"Most of the office was in Seattle today, so it was pretty quiet."

I decided to stop there, though I was curious why everyone would go somewhere without him. "So, Jo and Frankie are pretty sleepy. Why don't you just take them home in the van, and I'll drive the Explorer home later?" He nodded and I checked my phone for the umpteenth time. "Have you seen any of the other moms, by the way? I'm wondering if our walk was cancelled or something."

"See you back at the house." I wasn't sure if he had missed what I said, or just chose to ignore it. I had to repeat myself all day long—teenagers and toddlers weren't that different, in some respects—and I was often too worn out to keep the pattern going at night, with a grown-up.

I turned and stepped onto the walkway when I heard Theo call out, "Be safe—OK, Harry? Are the overhead lights going to come on?"

I turned back and nodded. "They're supposed to. Oh! I meant to tell you: I told the twins no screen time until they pick up all the toys in the family room. And the birthday card I got for your mom is on the table, you just need to sign it. Also—last thing—can you stop at New Seasons real quick, for something we can put in the lunches that meets school rules?"

But Theo was already reversing out of the parking spot by the time I finished, and was putting all the windows up as he went.

"Hey—babe? Did you hear me? Healthy Start said no more saltines, 'cuz they're too salty, and the strawberries were moldy, so—"

He scowled and put the car in park, then rolled his window back down, every movement telegraphing annoyance. "*What?* Harry, I can't remember all these things when you just rattle them off to me. Not like you can."

"Uh . . . ?" His answer confused me, then angered me. My heart felt like it was pounding out a war march, but instead of opening my mouth and tearing Theo a new one, I defaulted to the M.O. I'd developed in childhood: ruminating on what I might be missing, or misunderstanding, instead. In less than a second, I was giving Theo the weakest of waves, and he gave me the weakest of nods, and we went our separate ways.

I started up the walkway in a funk, not bothering to wait for the other moms. Before I'd gone twenty yards I'd come up with a litany of things I could have, and perhaps should have, said in response: *You get the school's emails. You have the same information I do, in writing. Why do I need to tell you at all?*

And most important of all: *How am I supposed to tell you things, anyway?*

I yanked up my zipper and shoved my hands in my pockets. I resumed singing *Hamilton* under my breath, and picked up the pace. But no matter how much I tried prolonging it, the ebullient mood the kids and I had enjoyed in the car was gone.

Would I feel better, I wondered, if I'd stood up to Theo right then, for his dismissive words? Would I have been a better role model, to my daughters especially, if I'd stuck up for myself even as my precious "me time"—and the October air I so loved, with its woody smells and its perfect level of chill—dwindled away?

I kicked a piece of gravel with my toe and hugged myself. What if I got home later and Theo told me he'd been passed over for some big assignment that day at work? Or that he'd had another "performance review" because his boss was some kind of sadist who got off on sticking them into everyone's calendars, willy-nilly? In either of those scenarios, I'd be relieved—deeply relieved—that I hadn't reacted in the spur of the moment.

My days were made up of zillions of these little negotiations, challenges, puzzles, and mini-debates. All day long, things dropped into my lap and demanded a custom-made solution. Typically, they were small, sometimes silly things—like that time I stood for ten minutes in one spot at Target, trying to solve the advanced calculus that is toilet paper pricing (two-ply and Mega-roll and Textured? Oh, *Christ*) because we'd gone over budget that month and I was feeling guilty. Yet sometimes, these negotiations only *seemed* piddly and forgettable, when in fact they were quite weighty. Like the morning I'd sat in traffic, trying to convince myself we were doing the right thing by keeping the twins at Healthy Start, as that was the only preschool location that made it possible for me to get to work on time after drop-off, and in spite of the fact that Frankie had just sobbed himself into a stupor, like he'd done every morning since starting there.

These things exhausted me, much more than anything I was paid to do at work and in a whole different way than competitive swimming ever had. (And I swam in the NCAA finals! Division I, baby!) Some nights, I'd lie in bed while Theo slept and wonder if I was missing a gene, or deficient in some substance that's needed in the blood, or otherwise running on empty when it came to some biological thing that enables a person to perform decently as a parent and spouse. God knows, my own mother had flat-out refused to engage in any of the endless, agonizing, and occasionally piss-ass negotiations of domestic life. (If I needed a new sweater? I got my own sweater. Eventually. With money from lifeguarding, babysitting, or selling the crappy little crafts I made.) Perhaps Mom and her twin brothers hadn't had the good fortune to get that stuff passed on to them, either; my grandmother—my mom's mom—had died a very young woman, and I knew little about her.

With my brow furrowed low, in a shape that says, "Piss off, I'm pissed off," I glanced at the time on my phone. I figured I could probably make it around the walking loop one time before I worked up so much wife-guilt that I rushed home to run the twins' baths, so that Theo wouldn't have to do it all himself. *Me time, my ass.* I bet he didn't feel guilty whenever I did bath time alone. Or ran to the grocery store. Or lay in bed with the twins for an hour, to get them to fall asleep.

My phone buzzed as I neared the part of the walkway that turned and ran along the side yard of the school. I pulled it out again and saw a message from Gwynne, the loose organizer of the Walking Bred:

> *Hi Harry, I'm soooo sorry, but I just realized the school office left you off the email asking us not to walk at the school tonight. Something about construction? Running late today?! I told her to make sure to add you to the list next time!!!*

I exhaled hard through my lips, sputtering like an old jalopy. *Seriously?* I rarely had the chance to do something for my own enjoyment, and I'd already argued with my husband in order to be there.

Fuck it. I decided to keep walking around the loop, even if it was against the rules. Annoyance is a potent fuel, and pretty soon I was motoring along the path, scrolling through emails as I went, hoping to check off some of my to-do list. I hadn't heard back from Ellen yet, nor was there any update from Sooby on her conversation with Mr. Terrence about the Gunsmoke Guy. I closed my email and picked up my pace even more.

I had just opened my banking app—to see how far along we were in saving for a new refrigerator—when my toe rammed into something, *hard*, and briefly caught on it. An enormous tree root had broken through the concrete and I'd built up so much momentum before hitting it that the rest of my body kept barreling forward, taking to the air like a baseball player diving for a wide hit. I skidded along the ground several inches and my phone went flying, too, landing somewhere in the distance with a *clatter* and a low-pitched *plop*.

And let me tell you: As the laws of nature go, gravity might be a bitch, but friction is an absolute *cunt*.

I wanted to keep lying there—flat on my face and lingering in self-pity, in the middle of the path. But the sound that had come from my phone had raised all sorts of flags in my frazzled brain: *Plop?* Why *plop?* How *plop?*

I slowly pushed my chest off the ground, then my pelvis, then my knees. I hurt in roughly a dozen places, from the elaborate inner clockwork of my knees to the swaths of skin on my palms and face that were now raw with road rash. I grimaced as I walked my hands backward, toward my feet. Once I was stable, I brushed some grit from the indentations in my cheek, then stretched my arms and shoulders a few seconds. When I finally took a step, pain shot from every joint like fireworks.

I limped forward, wincing, and noticed for the first time the rings of yellow CAUTION tape strung up ahead of me. They blocked off the walkway and encircled the shallow basin to the right of it, which surrounded the school's old, long-broken fountain.

This was the spot where Mr. Terrence and his crew were installing the new statue, hence the yellow tape, the scattered equipment, the plastic tarps. If I hadn't had my nose stuck so far into my screen—something I harped on Bret about—I might've noticed earlier that the area was one giant hazard, and the reason the Walking Bred had been cancelled.

Still, I couldn't leave without my phone. So I stepped off the path and ducked under the CAUTION tape, onto the first broad terrace of the old basin. At the end of the second terrace was another strip of CAUTION tape, and beyond that, a large plastic tarp had been draped loosely around the base of the fountain. It wasn't pinned down, and as I crouched low and squinted into the dusky light, I could see that it was covering up some still-wet concrete.

Oh, God: "Plop."

I hobbled forward and tore down the next bit of tape, then knelt down as my knees throbbed with pain. I lifted the tarp and sure enough, there was the top of my phone—barely visible in the sticky goop. It must have landed hard, and at just the right angle, because it was really *in* there, looking like it was indulging in some kind of fancy spa treatment.

"Noooooo," I whimpered, crouching on the farthest edge of the step. I stretched my arm over the wet gunk. "No, no, no, no, noooooooo!"

I couldn't quite touch the top of it with the tip of my middle finger, so I pulled my arm back and adjusted my feet. And with the toes of my shoes cantilevered over the edge, I reached out again: *"Come to Mama,"* I whispered.

Then I lost my balance and fell into the concrete, because of course I did. And even though I landed on my feet—and even though it was less than a foot deep—it was really, *really* wet. The gloppy, gritty mess crept over the top of my running shoes and against my ankles as I reached down to grab my phone before it sank into the stuff and disappeared. As soon as I made contact, however, a *ZIIIIIP!* ran up my arm and through my chest: It had shocked me, knocking me flat on my back. Needless to say, I dropped the piece of shit right back into the goop.

I sat up with a growl, and with my chest heaving, my hands clenched, and my eyes closed, I let out a savage, unhinged *yawp*. And I let it go on and on, delirious and satisfying, as if I were scraping every last bit of air from the crooks and crannies of my cavernous swimmer-lungs. I let it go on and on and then on some more, even though the sound of it was only part-roar and also kind of squealy, and even though lots of men have told me over the years—on and off the internet—that such high-pitched noises are unpleasant to them.

When I ran out of breath I opened my eyes. Then I struggled to stand up, glanced around, and thanked the Lord I was still alone.

My eyes came to a rest on the covered-up fountain, whereupon it dawned on me that it *wasn't* actually the fountain; I recalled Sooby saying that Mr. Terrence had taken that to the dump already, so the enormous, plastic-wrapped object must be our new statue, partly installed. I glanced around again, sheepish and furtive this time. I was already in deep, as it were; why not have a lookie-loo at our much-hyped statue? It was a gift for the mamas of Straussville, after all, and I was a Straussville mama!

Holding my arms akimbo, I lifted a foot from the wet concrete. There was something creepy about the difficulty of moving in that sticky, sucking stuff, and it accelerated my already-skittering heart rate. I cringed as I lunged forward again, and when a rivulet of sweat ran down my temple and hit the open scrape on my cheek, it might as well have been acid, so badly did it sting. With my crazed eyes, frizzy and disheveled hair, and the pale concrete mottling me from head to toe, I probably looked like a proper zombie.

When I finally reached the statue, I took the house key I'd zipped in my pocket and tried sawing through the nylon ropes for several minutes, getting sweatier and more frustrated by the moment. Describing this now, I'm a little embarrassed at how determined I was to see the statue; why did I want to see it so badly in that moment? I can't be sure, but I do remember whisper-swearing at Mr. Terrence as I worked at the ropes.

Eventually, I gave up sawing and started yanking on the tarp with both hands, trying to pull it out from under the taut rope. An inch or so slid out, so I adjusted my grip and tried again. Another inch came free, invigorating me to stay the course. I was desperate for a win at that point, no matter how petty or nonsensical.

When the edge of the tarp finally came out from under the ropes, I stopped and swiped my forehead with the back of my sleeve. Then I lifted the plastic high enough to make out the words on a plaque at the bottom of the statue:

To the Moms of Straussville,
Thank You

I brushed my hands together. I'd always assumed the statue would be of some notable mom from our area, most likely one from the Hoffman family tree. Given Mr. Terrence's involvement, and his obsession with what he called our "frontier heritage," it was probably some matriarch who'd crossed the Rockies by covered wagon back in the day—one who'd made it over the highest passes without eating any of her fellow pioneers. I pulled more of the plastic from under the ropes, in search of a plaque with a name on it. The process went faster now that there was slack in the ropes, and I soon had the tarp completely free. I bundled it up and set it aside, then adjusted my waistband and stood tall so I could take in the entirety of the roughly twelve-foot statue.

I started shaking pretty much immediately, as my anger metastasized into full-blown fury. It was *not* a statue of a Straussville-area mom, cannibal or otherwise. It wasn't a statue of any particular person, living or dead, and nor was it a well-known character like Ramona Quimby, immortalized with such charm in a public park in nearby Portland. No, our new statue wasn't of a human being at all.

It was a stick figure.

And not just any stick figure! This one had a purse in the crook of its arm and bob-length hair, and it was holding the hand of a *child* stick figure, standing next to it. It mimicked—albeit not exactly—what you see on those yellow School Crossing signs.

The hell?

Maybe it was selfish of me, but the cancelled afterschool programs weren't the first things to cross my mind, and neither were all the other worthwhile things we could have done with the Hoffman family's largesse, had we been given a choice in the matter. We could've replaced the elementary school's junky furnace, for example. Or opened a rainy-day fund, to provide for afterschool programs in the event someone gave us a "free" statue that turned out to be anything but. Nope, I didn't immediately "think of the children."

What did have me shaking in my new concrete shoes was that somebody had thought a giant, costly stick figure would make moms feel like valued members of the community.

I did not feel valued by this thing. I felt the opposite of valued.

My chest flared, the way it had the night before, but I took steps to calm myself: I closed my eyes and counted down from five. I inhaled through my nose and exhaled through my mouth. I tried as hard as I could to be reasonable. Maybe I was missing something.

Was the Hoffman family making a political statement with this statue? *Maybe that one granddaughter, the one who'd dropped out of Reed to pursue her passion for goat herding? Maybe she was going through an artsy phase.* Maybe she, or somebody involved in this donation, had been making a point about how our society treats moms.

Because a stick figure wouldn't be so terrible if it were a metaphor for the way we talk out both sides of our mouths when it comes to anything mom-related. The way we tear individual moms down, calling them "selfish" or "ungrateful" on Facebook, then turn around and treat the *idea* of motherhood as something lofty and perfect and deserving of greeting cards and cut flowers once a year. A piece of art that intentionally depicted mothers as generic symbols rather than real people might be interesting, and provocative. Maybe this was social commentary about the way most moms are walking, talking, miniature New York Stock Exchanges—handling an enormous amount of business every day, mostly for the sake of others, under intense pressure and scrutiny. And while our labor helps keep society humming, a lot of people don't understand how essential it is, and some people actively scorn it. Such a seriously weird contradiction—smack-dab at the heart of modern Western motherhood—would be a worthy subject for public art. Then again, odds were slim that Patrick Terrence had championed a piece of art that invited our community to ponder this.

I noticed, then, that there was a second plaque on the base, with a longer inscription:

"A MOM-UMENT"
*From the Hoffman Family
and Patrick Terrence*

This brought all wishful thinking to a halt. Because clearly, we were meant to take this crappy statue at face value.

What's more, all of the moms, myself included, would be expected to show up at the unveiling ceremony in a month's time, baked goods in hand and kids in tow. We'd listen to speeches and clap politely because someone had spent money on us, and now our kids were sacrificing their Gay-Straight Alliance and their Chess Club for us. We couldn't possibly be so ungrateful as to point out that the whole thing was actually a hideous boondoggle.

I looked it over again, one last time, trying to see in its scant lines anything that resembled my friends, or myself: I looked for Ellen's award-winning research, Dianne's tireless commitment to her art therapy studio, or the way Sooby had single-handedly gotten our marching band to the Macy's Thanksgiving Day Parade the year before. But I couldn't find a whiff, a spirit, or a trace of any of those things. How could I, when the "mom" in front of me had no meat on her bones whatsoever?

It's a scary feeling, I gotta say, the first time a whole part of your brain shuts down. It's downright chilling when the part that goes dark is the one containing all your rational thought, and the part that's gunning to take over is a great ball of rage that's been growing there without your noticing it or tending it all that much. I felt like a giant switch was being flipped inside my head, in slow motion, and I had an eerie sense that it wasn't ever going to flip back. I saw sparks and flickers at the edges of my vision, and heard a hiss or two, right before everything went black. My brain, apparently, is a lot like a decrepit old house that no one has bothered to bring up to code.

The last things I would remember from that part of the evening—for a while, at least—were the violent shaking, the blinding white light, and how very peeved I felt at having passed on my favorite fry sauce at Red Robin. Because I was about to have some serious heartburn regardless.

1.4 MONDAY, JUST BEFORE 9:00 P.M.

I woke up under water.

Everything was pitch-black, and my legs and waist were tangled up in something. It took just a few seconds for panic to set in.

But I'd been a swimmer from the time I was a baby, with sausage-link limbs and a mother for whom lakes and rivers were a cheap way to get away from whomever or whatever she needed to get away from. I'd been a lifeguard, too, and I kept to the water right up until I got pregnant with my own two kielbasa-babies, in a difficult pregnancy that had cleaved my strong swimmer-core in two and then left it that way. So even though I hadn't been in a lap pool in years, my muscles were full of water-memories: of frog kicks and rescue drills, of deep dives and cross-body carries. Pregnancy had robbed me of the stable knees and back that carried me across the finish line of a half-Ironman, but it hadn't taken the water out of me.

Now those instincts helped me figure out which way was up. They helped me kick and pull, in spite of my legs being caught in something, and in spite of my water-logged clothes. They helped me find a surface with air on the other side, which I gulped at ferociously the second I broke through.

I couldn't focus very well, and had no idea where I was. I looked up at the stars as I treaded water, then turned in circles and tried to spot something familiar. I rubbed my eyes with the backs of my knuckles and blinked hard, and when they finally adjusted to the darkness, I could just make out a familiar green line in the distance. I'd solved one of my mysteries, at least: I was in the Straussville Reservoir, surrounded by an iron fence topped with a decorative copper element turned green.

Something was still wrapped around my legs, but I knew I could probably swim with it trailing behind me. So I started for the fence, doing freestyle with my head out of the water.

If you don't already know, swimming with your head above water for an extended period is hard as *fuck*, even when you're fit. And I was not fit. It took several minutes of agony, with my lungs feeling like they were on fire and my quads, too, to reach the fence. Once there, I gripped the concrete base and took a rest, hoping to get back enough strength to haul my weak ass out of the water and then over the spiked, eight-foot fence. With my hands shaking, I reached up and grabbed one of the metal bars. Then I took another rest.

I pulled myself up just enough to heave one of my legs out of the water, and as soon as I got my toes—toes that were bare, for some reason—onto the concrete base, I rested again.

After doing the same with my other leg, I pushed hard with both feet and pulled even harder on the iron bars, and finally got myself out of the water.

I clung to the fence and let the reservoir run off me in ragged streams. Then I climbed the thing as gingerly as I could, cursing the day I was born, as I scraped my torso—which was *also* bare—on one, or perhaps three, of the spikes.

Once I was aground on the other side, every cell in my body conspired to have me splay myself out on the cracked walkway to soak up whatever warmth still lingered in the asphalt from the afternoon sun. But I willed myself to remain standing, hugging myself to still the shivers as I shook the water from each ear. I spotted what appeared to be a streetlight, beyond a stand of trees, and shuffled toward it.

When I got within a few yards of the light, I stopped and looked down at myself. My jacket, T-shirt, and sweatpants were in tatters, the seams all split, the remains of the fabric barely clinging to my hips and shoulders. The sight of myself in such a state stirred up other, much older fears.[6] Wrapped around my bare feet and ankles, too, was foot after foot of bright yellow CAUTION tape.

Things started to come back to me then. Some things, anyway: I'd been at the school for my walking group. I'd been staring into my phone while angry speed-walking. I tripped and fell. My phone did a full-twisting back-layout into some wet concrete.

But then what?

Had I driven my car into the reservoir somehow? I didn't have alcohol at dinner, and I couldn't even recall getting into my car again. Had I wandered off the school path, and toward the reservoir? Had I been hit by a car? There was only one maintenance road to the water basin and it was gated and locked, accessible only to state vehicles. What's more, I'd regained consciousness in the middle of the reservoir—much farther from shore than where a car-related accident would've left me.

The longer I stood there the harder I shivered, and I knew that getting dry and warm had to be my first priority. I wrung some water from the strips of fabric hanging off me and was relieved to discover that my shredded jacket still had one pocket intact—the small, zippered one I kept my keys in. There was no cell phone, however, ruined or otherwise.

I set out toward the school. The streets were familiar and well-lit, but that was a double-edged sword: I didn't want anyone to see me, since there was a good chance I'd already done something illegal that night, and didn't need indecency charges added to my rap sheet. These more affluent parts of

---

6   This is a vulnerable and scary state for any woman, but it also sent my brain back to my childhood. In Oregon, a lot of the kids are half-feral; muddy skirts and boots are de rigueur at certain playgrounds and it's treated like part of the local charm. "Keep Portland Weird" and all that. But as a child, I'd been poor, and poor kids don't qualify for this particular charm offensive. Neither do Black or brown kids. The looks I got from parents left deep marks on me, as if by laser, which is why I wear suits to work, despite it being too formal; it's the real reason I eschew yoga wear.

Straussville are a lot like the American towns you see on TV, in those shows where improbably clear-skinned teenagers live improbably independent lives, usually involving some paranormal phenomenon that they have to fight, or maybe embrace. The buildings, trees, sidewalks, and gazebos seemed to be arranged to be maximally photogenic—and to have excellent lines of sight. I decided I'd better jog as best I could.

When I reached the school, I made a beeline for Theo's Explorer and rummaged around the back until I found the Goodwill donation I'd put there weeks earlier. Then I got in and, with the heater blasting me from all sides, wrestled my still-damp skin into his old UWV sweatshirt and a pair of ratty cargo shorts I'd been glad to say goodbye to.

It was nine o'clock according to the clock in the dash, which was a relief; I hadn't been gone that long, and Theo wouldn't have started worrying about me, unless of course he'd been trying to reach me. I threw the car in reverse and backed out. But instead of heading toward the exit, I went the opposite way—toward the side of the school where I'd fallen and lost my phone.

I barely remembered to put the car in park when I got there, however, because the entire area was a disaster zone. It looked like one of those towns that local news stations like to zoom-in and linger on for days after it's been devastated by a terrible hurricane. Everywhere I looked, the ground was torn up. Big chunks of earth and concrete were strewn about, as were pieces of busted-up construction equipment. There was no longer any demarcation between the fountain area, the grassy playground, the walking path, and the loading dock. The statue was gone, too—its base like a forlorn stump after a forest clearing.

What the hell had happened here?

I turned the radio to a local news station and closed my eyes, gripping the wheel, trying to recall the rest of the evening after losing my phone. I remembered, then, seeing a bright white light, and wondered if perhaps it'd been lightning. I opened my eyes and surveyed the scene again, but there were no puddles on the ground, no dampness to suggest a storm had come through. And it hadn't been a *flash* of light, anyway; it had been like some-one had trained a giant spotlight in my face for several seconds.

I leaned over the wheel and looked up at the cloudless sky. I didn't believe in UFO sightings; I'd always leaned more Scully than Mulder. But absent a more rational explanation, anything seemed possible.

Suddenly, in the low murmurs of the radio announcer, I heard the word "ape-like" and reached over and turned up the volume:

> *. . . Authorities are advising residents of the Gussman neigh-borhood to be on high alert tonight after several residents reported loud noises in the wooded area around the Straussville Reservoir. Jeb Herner lives across the street from the park, and said he went onto his front porch as soon as he heard it. "That's when I saw this big animal, moving through the trees . . ."*

I smiled. Lulu the gorilla must have gotten loose from the Oregon Zoo again! Quite the escape artist, our Lulu; she'd twice made it over the wall of her enclosure, the second time carrying both her babies. As a fellow mom of twins, I felt a strong kinship with Lulu, although I wanted to suggest that she leave the kids at home next time and take the silverback from the next enclosure instead.

But then the broadcaster said:

> *. . . Zoo officials have confirmed that they'd accounted for all animals at the time of the incident . . .*

I rested my forehead on the steering wheel, noticing for the first time that my head was pounding and my eyeballs and tongue were dust-bowl dry.

OK: Lulu was in custody. So what could possibly have caused all this damage? And so soon after I'd been walking here? Local teenagers started their Devil's Night shenanigans a little early sometimes, didn't they? And since "Bigfoot" was a popular symbol of our region—a mascot, almost—one could easily find a respectable costume in most major shopping centers that time of the year. Maybe that explained things.

> *"It was really dark, so I could only see the outline of it. And this might sound crazy, but whatever it was . . . looked like it was being attacked."*
>
> *Attacked? How so?*
>
> *"Well, it looked like it had, like, a huge stick insect on its back. That part was weird."*
>
> *Mabel Plinkton also lives across from the park, and she says a low rumbling sounded to her like someone speaking. "It sounded like shouting. But in a really, really deep voice. Like, a monster's voice." Asked what the voice had said, Plinkton replied, "JUST YOU WAIT."*
>
> *And now, the weather on the nines. With rainfall at a record low, local foresting experts are worried . . .*

My hands trembling, I reversed the Explorer and stomped on the gas. As it swung around, the force of it sent Theo's Wonder Woman bobblehead—which Bret had suctioned to the dash years earlier—toppling over and tumbling under the seat. But that was the only thing I remembered from the drive home that night, because my thoughts weren't on the road.

Instead, they were hyper-focused on a surreal possibility. The few details I knew about the previous couple of hours cycled through my mind again and again: Something had torn around the schoolyard like the Tasmanian Devil; a huge unidentified creature had gone on a moonlight hike to the reservoir, yelling *Hamilton* lyrics and toting along a large stick insect for company; I had woken up in the reservoir with my clothes all torn and police tape—like the tape around the statue—entwining my legs. I also recalled how the night before, my skin had bubbled as if something was poking at it from underneath, and I'd been momentarily overcome by heartburn so intense it seemed . . . supernatural.

The longer I chased these thoughts, the more certain I became, in some forgotten and obsolete part of my gut, that I was the one who had wreaked all this havoc.

The rational part of my brain objected, of course. How could I have carried out such a thing? How could any one human, let alone a weak-ass mom of three? It was unbelievable—literally. It was ridiculous. Besides, I would remember if I'd played even a small part in this wreckage; I might not win any leadership or civic participation trophies anytime soon, but I owed more than most locals did to the Hoffman schools, and I'd fight for them if I had to.

As these thoughts thrashed around inside me, each one seeking some foothold or advantage over the others, I recalled a few occasions when I'd been utterly certain about something, only to discover later that I'd been utterly wrong. (See: Armstrong, Lance. And: Vanilli, Milli.)

As I considered all this, the chaos began to recede into the background of my consciousness, and a single idea came forward and stood apart from it all: Maybe I hadn't laid waste to the schoolyard, the old fountain, and the statue. Maybe some giant . . . creature had done it. And maybe that giant creature had come out of me.

No one was up when I got home, and I was supremely relieved not to have to explain why I was shaking and running a cold sweat under the billows of Theo's old sweatshirt. My head still throbbed, and my insides felt shriveled up and sunken-in on themselves as I clomped toward the kitchen, dazed and panicked all at once.

I went straight to the kitchen sink and stuck my head under the faucet. I was guzzling cold water when out of nowhere something banged into my knee from the side. I yanked my head out of the stream and turned toward it with a snarl—a human-ish snarl—but it was just our little terrier-mix, Critter. She squealed and scuttled under the tall rolling table we used as a kitchen island, and after I shook myself back to my senses, I crouched low and cooed to her in my best Dog-Mom voice.

"Oh, *hey!* I'm sorry, girl!" She always jumped up and threw herself against my legs when she needed something, so I stood up and opened the back door so she could go outside and pee. Then I went over and filled her food and water bowls, chuckling with forced amusement at the absurdity of my actions: I was almost certainly in "shock," if I remembered my lifeguard training correctly. Yet I'd slid easily into Mom-mode the instant an open mouth appeared, pointed in my direction.

My chuckling sputtered out soon enough, though, when I returned to the back door and found her food untouched, then spied her small snout peeking out from behind the shed near our back fence. She was a shrewd, confident little dog, and typically wolfed her food down. I picked up her bowl and after giving it a few shakes, set it near the door, which I propped open. Then I turned my attention to the cabinets where we kept our human vittles, because I wasn't just parched and dehydrated; I was also famished.

I grabbed everything edible that didn't require any cooking, then tore into the boxes and bags with abandon. I opened tins and jars, too, some with thick layers of dust on top. Using just my fingers, I stuffed all the wasabi peas, turkey jerky, strawberry jelly, nut butter, and I don't even know what else into my gaping maw, and as I did, I paced around the kitchen, breathing through my nose and only stopping when I needed to fill up my hands again. Food dribbled down my chin and onto Theo's old clothes, because once I got started, I found that I couldn't stop feeding myself. There was no one to judge me but Critter, and I already knew how (gross) and what (even grosser) that dog could throw down.

Walking back and forth, still jittery and damp, I went over what Mabel Freakin' Plinkton had said to the reporter: A creature of some kind had said, "JUST YOU WAIT." It was the exact line from *Hamilton* I'd been singing as I started my walk; I'd sung it over and over again, in fact, because I was so worked up about Theo. What's more, everything I'd seen, touched, and heard since waking up, ten feet underwater—from my torn clothes, to my wet hair, to the yellow CAUTION tape—suggested that I'd turned into something, or that something had come out of me, and that that thing was supernatural and enormous and destructive.

When my belly was finally sated, I sat on a stool and reached under our island-table to Critter, who seemed to have forgiven my earlier snarl. She was a former stray, and brazenly opportunistic when it came to food, shelter, and protection. After four years with us, she still had no firm favorite in the Lime family. She switched her allegiances as needed, her affection fluid and unreliable, and we sometimes joked about who or what she might have been in a past life to have become so perfidious: A Malfoy, or a Machiavelli perhaps? A housecat? She inched slowly toward my hands, and after some hesitation, her slimy, pink tongue went to work on the stretch between my fingertips and wrist. As she got the last of the gunky food off them, I was stunned to see no trace of the scrapes I'd gotten—or thought I'd gotten—when I tripped so spectacularly and skidded across the pavement at the school.

I pulled my hands back, and with growing hope, gently patted one side of my face then the other, over and over, finding nothing but smooth skin and some maple syrup. If my skin was unblemished, perhaps I hadn't tripped after all! "Oh, thank *God*," I sputtered, letting my forehead fall onto the tabletop as once again, my swirling fears ebbed a bit. I gripped the sides of the table and drew in a long breath, and when I exhaled, sat up and touched my cheeks again; still no scrapes! Only some ice-cream sprinkles, which fell from my forehead and onto the cruddy table. I wiped at them in a half-assed manner as Critter whined and did three of her best tricks, probably hoping I'd give her some of the jerky.

But I couldn't focus on Critter; I'd just been given reason to believe that matters weren't as freakish and terrifying as I'd imagined since waking up in the reservoir. Perfectly healthy skin on my hands and face had to mean that I hadn't fallen, and that most or all of the evening's events had been some kind of weird dream. I'd probably had nothing to do with the destruction.

(I didn't think about my cell phone. I was still in too thick a fog, and too desperate to hold onto an explanation that was rational and that didn't put me at fault. And in jail. Or Area 51.)

I stood up and swayed a couple of times, then grabbed the back of the chair for balance. I stumbled in the direction of the family room, and after a brief attempt to wrestle myself out of Theo's voluminous sweatshirt, gave up and focused all my effort on making it to the couch. From the corner of my eye, however, I noticed a slip of paper on the island, and stopped for a look:

Had a headache so I went to bed. Hope the twins' new lunches pass muster w/ the cracker police. -T

Even though exhaustion—and a now-constant, low-level sort of fear—surrounded me like a haze, I still noticed that there was no "I love you" or hearts or anything in Theo's note. That's how worried I was about our marriage. But "cracker police" probably counted as a joke, I rationalized, so I clung to that part of it, and to the crumbs of comfort it brought me.

Because a joke was evidence that Theo and I were still on the same team, and still the people we used to be; it was evidence that I was still human, that the universe hadn't suddenly turned itself inside out. I stumbled the remaining distance to the couch and let myself trust-fall, face-first, onto the worn cushions. I rolled onto my back, feeling heavier than I could ever remember feeling, just as Critter jumped on top of me and turned a few circles on my midriff before plopping down with a huff. She often communicated in gruff exhalations, including snorts and fake sneezes. Then she closed her eyes, and I did, too, craving sleep and oblivion.

Again and again, though, my idiot brain tried to reboot itself, because some sleep-hating part of me was hellbent on re-crunching all the data points I could remember from the evening. I would be on the verge of REM, and my mind's eye would throw up a scene from the destroyed fountain for further consideration. Or I'd hear the voice of the news announcer, repeating for new emphasis one of the details mentioned by a kindly Gussman resident.

Each time, I shut it down by reminding myself: *You don't have any cuts or scrapes.* That one fact allowed me to believe that I'd only dreamed those outrageous things about the schoolyard and statue—a theory further supported by my long history of working myself into a tizzy about Mr. Terrence and his unchecked influence at the school.

Eventually, my brain gave in to this good sense. The evidence was empirical, after all, my theory robust. And in accepting these, I could finally sleep. It was the first time in fourteen years that I didn't think to set a morning alarm.

1.5   TUESDAY, 8:00 A.M.

I woke up to the sound of the front door closing. Or rather, I woke up to the dog's legs tearing across my chest because *she* had heard the front door close and had no choice but to go bark at it.

I rubbed my eyes in slow circles, and when I blinked them open, realized that I'd fallen asleep on the couch. I further realized that I was wearing Theo's old sweatshirt, and that it was grimier than ever.

I sat up and blinked some more, thanks to the harsh morning light coming in through the front window. I held up a forearm to block the sun, just in time to see Theo open his car door, dressed for work. I wondered, groggily, if he had kissed me goodbye before leaving; it wasn't unheard of for one of us to sleep in an odd place—we had young kids, after all. I tried not to interpret a kiss-less goodbye as another indication that the universe between us was still expanding.

I lay back again and heard a rustling, crunching sound from somewhere underneath me. I reached around and fished a crumpled foil wrapper from between the cushions. Upon flattening it out, I recognized the familiar logo of a "lactation bar"—the same awful kind I'd reluctantly eaten back when I was nursing the twins, because even though we were paying to rent a hospital-strength breast pump,[7] I still needed whatever help I could find to make enough milk for two preemies. I sat up and swung my feet to the floor, setting my forehead in my hands.

---

7   It's true: Those things are so unwieldy, they come with their own set of wheels. That makes it easier for moms to keep pumping even when they're walking around. Yaaaayyy.

Oh, right. I remembered, then, how I'd stuffed myself the night before, with anything that seemed reasonably safe for eating. That, and not some bloody massacre, explained the pinkish-red stains all down the front of me. But why in the world had I eaten so much? Had I been drunk? My body and head certainly felt off, but not necessarily hungover. I curled my bare toes into the carpet fibers and willed my brain to wake all the way up.

I'd fallen asleep, I recalled, convinced that I'd dreamt up a series of bizarre happenings, among them a rough spill I'd taken at the school that had left me pretty dinged-up. But as I lifted my head and looked again at my unscathed palms, I felt something very unlike relief building in my gut. It felt a lot more like dread, as there was still a whole lot of weirdness that needed explaining.

The biggest question mark—the one glaring at me like a neon sign— was this: If I'd dreamt taking that faceplant on the walking loop, where did the dream end and reality begin? Because I was damn sure I hadn't imagined waking up in the reservoir. There was no other way I'd be wearing Theo's gnarly castoffs. But how the hell had I gotten in there? And why had I been so hungry afterward that I'd ingested an expired lactation bar, along with a pound or four of other stale and questionable things? I patted myself down and slid my hands into every crevice of the couch, knowing that if my cell phone wasn't within arm's reach—and it wasn't— losing it in the wet concrete was another thing I could confidently put on the "reality" side of my ledger.

What in the fucking *fuck* was going on?

When I heard the first of the kids begin straggling down our creaky stairs, my Mom-lobe mercifully kicked in. Shit needed to get done and done fast on school mornings, so I stood up and threw myself into it in all the usual ways. And for once, I was grateful for the chaos of it all. Because in the midst of our erratic tornado of mismatched socks and raised voices, dog hair and sticky Cheerios and half-done homework, I was almost distracted from the pit in my stomach. At least for a while.

"What the *heck*?" Bret called out from behind me in the kitchen, after I'd taken a seat at the old desktop we used as a family computer. It had occurred to me that I'd better dash off a quick Facebook post, warning all my contacts that I'd lost my phone.

"Did you see this, Mom?"

Shit. I hadn't cleaned up all the shredded cardboard, torn plastic, and piles of food residue I'd made during my little gorge-fest the night before. Determined not to reveal anything on my face, I double-checked my composure before swiveling around to face her.

"JO? FRANKIE?"

"Bret, it's OK," I said, raising my hand and then jerking it down again when I realized how badly it was shaking. "It wasn't the twins."

"Who else would tear into every single sugar packet, Mom?" She held up an empty plastic container. "And eat all the ice cream sprinkles? And—"

"Critter got into the trash," I blurted out. Then I swallowed hard, trying not to choke on the lie I'd just told. (Or the fact that I'd just thrown my dog—a mama herself, probably a few times over, according to the shelter where we adopted her—under the proverbial bus.)

"Ughhhh! I thought she was over that! She's going to get us ants!"

"You're welcome to clean it all up, honey, since it bothers you so much," I added as I turned back around.

"You know, I should actually go finish getting ready."

"I thought as much," I replied as I scanned my email, trying to focus my attention on anything truly urgent there. I was getting up from the chair and about to grab my bag when my eyes landed on an address in my inbox that I'd never seen before: *leahvivianmorton.* Leah Vivian Morton was my mother's name.

My mother had never emailed me. I couldn't have told you whether she had an email account or even a computer. Only that she'd moved into the home of her boyfriend within the last couple of months. I sat all the way down again and clicked it open.

The subject line was empty, and the content extremely short:

I thought you might like this.

That was followed by a link to a news story about a local person running for Congress, who apparently was garnering attention for her "new ideas" on reducing crime in Portland. Her name was familiar: Olivia Patchett-Parker was a member of the wealthy Patchett family, who collectively owned a ton of local stuff—shopping centers, or maybe meat packing plants?—and apparently she was making history as the first woman to run for the seat.

I blinked and shook my head, clearing away the mild shock that always attended contact with Mom outside the biannual phone calls I made to her, at the holidays and at Bret's birthday. Equally confusing? Ma wouldn't even join the freakin' Points Program at Fred Meyer; what chance in hell did a political party have of earning her support? I made a quick note in the calendar reminding me to start calling her on Jo and Frankie's birthday, too. Then I deleted her message without replying and wrangled the twins into their coats and shoes—two times each, because they didn't like the way I had done it the first time—and tried not to physically drag either of them, or their equally sluggish sister, through the front door.

Out in the driveway, I had just finished buckling Jo into her car seat when I noticed that our recycling bins were still at the curb, empty now. I walked over to wheel them back to the side of the house when I spotted an orange ticket stuck to the side of a bin:

FINE: $80

Underneath it, someone had handwritten:

Plastic bag violation

"Oh, come *on!*" I said aloud, stomping my foot and hitting my thigh with a slap. We'd been warned once before that it was against the rules to put our glass bottles in bags. But we Limes considered it a victory when we remembered to put the bins out on the correct day at all.

"Moooooom," Bret called from the minivan. "We're so late!!! Don't make me honk the horn."

"*Bret,*" I replied through gritted teeth, trotting toward her. "I swear, if you honk that horn a *single* time, your cell—"

Hoonk! Hoooooooonk!

I reached the window and glared at her. "BRET," I hissed, gripping the door.

"I didn't honk a single time," she replied, trying to suppress her giggles. "I honked *twice.*"

"*We . . . are not . . .*" I seethed, emphasizing every word, *"a honking . . . FAMILY."*

"Everything OK out here, Mrs. Lime?"

It is a truth universally acknowledged that if a parent raises their voice at their child, or does anything else they will later be ashamed of, a neighbor, stranger, or long lost enemy will spontaneously appear on the scene to bear witness to it.

I spun around and faced our neighbor Justin, who was standing in his driveway. I sighed and gave him a wave that came out looking more like I was shooing something away. Him, maybe.

"Yeah, Justin. We're fine. As always."

"Hi, Justin!" Bret called from behind me. He gave her a tip of his invisible hat, which bugged me only slightly less than his insistence that my kids all call him by his first name. Even when I was in crisis, the man made me salty.

"OK, Mrs. Lime. Glad to hear it," he replied, smoothing at a wisp of gray hair near his temple. Then he nodded toward the curb, and I braced myself for some comment about our bad trash-day habits. "Could I give you some help with your leaves, there? When the rain starts, they'll clog up the sewer and sta—"

"I see you've got one of your . . . what is that, Justin? A BB gun?" I interrupted, fingering the charm on the end of my necklace, which I'd grabbed from next to the computer a few minutes earlier.

He swung his long, not-real gun around, and cocked his head at it. I couldn't help flinching. Justin was always carrying one of his fake guns and it was fucking weird, not to mention unnerving.

"This?" he replied, laughing aloud as if I were the idiot on the sidewalk that morning. "This is a paintball shooter. Nothing to worry about, Mrs. Lime."

And you can thank your own white ass for that, I thought as I got into the van, *because a lot of folks would get shot for walking around with that thing in public.*

The kids finally got buckled up and we got moving, Bret settling in to finish her math homework and the twins quietly taking in all the passing cars and houses. I couldn't enjoy this rare moment of peace, however; the shaky scaffolding of doubt I'd put together the night before—my flimsy reasoning for disbelieving that I'd gone full-Taz at the school—had fallen apart and I'd tumbled right back into fear. Now, instead of wracking my brain to remember where I'd stored our Halloween decorations, or guessing what Jojo could have meant when she'd called out to Frankie earlier, from the toilet, that she had "caught one," I was stuck in a far more sinister loop, frantically sorting through the details from the night before, looking for one that might prove I wasn't a monster.

But what if I *was* a monster?

Waiting for a chance to turn out of our neighborhood and onto the arterial road, I practiced breathing normally. And as I turned to check the traffic from the right, I thought I saw Bret cock her head at me. I turned quickly back, and spotted Christy Holmes in her running clothes, jogging toward us. I had to quash the urge to take a reckless turn into traffic to avoid speaking to her. And that urge, for the record, irritated me twice over: Christy was a good friend, and I got to see her too rarely. But right now I had to get away from her as fast as I could, because I might be some kind of monster and I might have destroyed an acre or more of public property, and I didn't have a handle on it all yet. I put down my window as she approached.

"Hey," I called out, trying to impersonate my normal self. I prayed I didn't sound as maniacal as I felt. "How are you?"

"I'm excited for book club tonight! I'll make something *gratin*, and some of those little tartlets again," she said, making the shape of one with her fingers. "They were a hit last time."

"Awesome! That's so great!" I replied, forcing a smile. There was no freaking way I could go to book club that night. "Uh, I'll bring a cheap bottle of wine," I replied with a thumbs up, trying not to cringe at my corniness—and dishonesty—as I did.

"I've got a few iced teas I was going to serve," she replied as she leaned close and inspected a blemish on my driver-side door.

"Oh, OK. I won't then," I replied, chucking innocent-sounding words into the air. "We should all probably cut back, *amirite*?"

Her brows did a little jump. "Brian seems to think so," she said.

Shit. So much for innocent words. "Oh, what's been going on with your wrist?" I replied. There was still no break in the traffic, so I was forced to keep grasping for safe topics.

"What?" Her blue eyes searched my face, in what looked like a flare-up of panic of her own.

"You had a brace or something on it, at PTA? I was worried our most decorated local surgeon had busted up her best cutting hand or whatever."

"Ohhhh, *right*," she replied over a breathless laugh. "Yeah, that was just some tape. I had, like, a little tennis mishap the other day." She tugged her shirtsleeves down, well-past her wrists, and looked up at me again. "So did you hear about what happened?"

My innards curdled. "What happened where?"

"At the school."

"What school?"

She looked briefly confused, then replied, "You didn't hear about all the damage?"

When I lifted my shoulders in reply, I got my first whiff of the stink happening in my armpits. Do stress hormones make your sweat smell differently? Something, at any rate, was *off.* "I lost my phone, so I'm a bit behind on everything."

"Some vandals tore up the playground, on the elementary side," she replied. "And the loading dock, and the whole area, I guess."

"Whoa!" Bret interjected. "*What?*" I was thankful she spoke up so that I didn't have to. I wiped some sweat from my upper lip.

"The new statue is gone, too," Christy continued. In the back seat, Jo and Frankie had begun a heated argument involving their favorite cartoon characters. I turned and tried to shush them without seeming like I was shushing them.

"Wow, Chris," I finally replied, giving the twins one last stink eye. "That's just . . . *wow.*"

"Right?" she replied. "It's time to get more security, I guess."

"For sure."

She stepped closer and reached toward me with a reassuring smile. "One sec, Harry." I froze as she picked something out of my hair, near my temple. Then she pulled her hand back and shook whatever it was away, adding, "You had a little . . . something in your hair. A chip of paint or something."

"OK, that's my turn—bye-eeee!" I called out as I lifted my foot from the brake and peeled out onto the bigger road. I had no idea why there was paint in my hair, and no idea what I should—and shouldn't—tell people about whatever had happened. As we picked up speed, Bret turned on the radio and for once, I was thankful when all they could talk about was politics.

When we turned onto the school grounds, the drop-off lane was empty, which was odd.

"Did you forget another major holiday, Mom?" Bret asked as we pulled into the drive and headed toward the front of the school.

"Columbus Day isn't a holiday, Bret. It's an abomination."

"Yeah, but it's an abomination we had the day off for."

"Oh, look—there they are." A large gaggle of parents had assembled around the main door. I should've parked and gotten out and joined them,

I know; I should've tried to blend in, to express my shock and concern, to react in the blandest way possible.

But I was too panicked. I pulled up to the curb and tried to coax Bret out of the van as fast as I could: "OK, bye honey! Bye! Love you. Bye. *Go.*" But even with me tossing kneepads and other bits of her volleyball uniform at her, she took forever getting out. Thankfully, the only mom who reached us before I could leave was Sooby, who jogged around to the driver-side door. I tried to calm myself as I put the window down.

"Can you *believe* it?" she gasped as she grabbed the bottom of the window frame.

My pulse spiked again, but I squished my mouth into a disappointed line and replied,

"Craziness, just *craziness!* So what are people saying? What—I mean *who*—do they think—"

"Oh, that's right—I forgot that you lost your phone," she said breathlessly. "Well, people are posting the *craziest* theories. I mean—*wait.* Why are you so sweaty?"

"Huh?" I swiped a hand across my forehead. It was damp, all right. Right up to my hair line.

She screwed up her face and balled her fists. *"Harry?"*

I pretend-glared back at her. *"Sooby?"*

"Did you go to that new hot yoga class this morning, without me?"

I laughed, sputtering out what felt like a whale's worth of air. "No, I absolutely did not go to hot yoga." Trying to keep the conversation away from the damage at the school, I asked, "Hey, did you talk to Mr. Terrence about . . . the thing?"

"What thing?" she replied as she scrolled through something on her phone.

"That weird cop or whatever, at the PTA meeting? You know—the one who 'went all John Wayne' on Ellen?"

She glanced away, squinting. "Yeah. I mean, I met with him. But it was getting late, and I didn't want to be a nag or anything." She stuck out the tip of her tongue and crossed her eyes, as if she were being sarcastic.

I squinted back at her as it dawned on me that I'd been naive, thinking she would hold to our plan, or to anything that might cast Mr. Terrence in an unflattering light. But then, this was an unusual situation, and it required an unusual response; this couldn't be chalked up to some absent-mindedness, like the time Mr. Terrence wrote me a lukewarm recommendation for my application to the honors program at UWV, then postmarked it one day after the final deadline. This time he'd blatantly acted like an asshole, only two nights earlier, to a fellow mom. "Sooby, you are not being a *nag*," I said quietly, scratching my shoulder after tripping on a couple of my words. "You're a board member. You're supposed to speak up about that sort of thing."

"Hey, by the way," she said, circling a hand in front of her genital area. Then she nodded toward mine. "How are things going down there?"

Sooby's lewd gesture distracted me from my own distraction tactics. "Um, *whaaat?*" I gave her my best impersonation of a Rodin statue, my elbow resting on the door. "I'm probably going to be late for my staff meeting, but I kind of want to see where you're going with this."

"*Your vagina,*" she whispered, pursing her lips. "You told me it was itchy, remember? Did you try that recipe I sent you?"

"I did, thanks. Though it turns out, apple cider vinegar isn't the cure for everything."

"*No?*" She looked genuinely pained that one of her natural remedies had been found lacking. "That's odd. It works for everything else."

"Mmm. Yeast infections need drugs, apparently. Pricey ones."

"Next time, try—"

"Do *not* say 'coconut oil,'" I interrupted, holding up a finger. "So help me God, do not come at my vagina with coconut oil. Or chia seeds."

She crossed her arms. "Come on, Harry," she muttered. "I know better than to bring chia seeds to a vagina fight."

I gave her an appreciative snort, and she smirked back at me. We were cool, as always.

"Seriously though, Soob—Mr. Terrence *has* to listen to you, even when he's busy."

She took a deep breath, then lowered her voice and asked, "And how's *your* progress, Harry, getting that cute husband of yours to pull more of his weight around the house?"

I turned and faced the dash, hoping she hadn't caught the sudden flare of my nostrils. Not from anger, but from the tears that were prepared to explode onto my face, the instant she called out my homelife. You'd think that with all the practice I'd gotten as a kid, when my mom shut herself in her room with just her television for company most nights, that I'd be excellent at disguising hurt feelings. And I was, most of the time. But Sooby was one person I'd never had to fool; and Theo was a subject I'd never had to fool anyone about.

"Whoa, OK," she said finally. There was surprise in her voice, the way the words didn't come straight out of her mouth at lightning speed like usual. "OK. So, that was totally out of line on my part. I'm sorry, Hare. I should know better—"

"It's fine, Soob. That's actually not the—"

"No! No, it is not fine! Your dad was across the country with his other stupid family all that time, and you don't know what a dad is supposed to do. I get it."

"But it's not—"

"And your mom has been no use whatsoever, avoiding you like a plague all those years only to take off for Hawaii the minute you turned eighteen."

I gave her a half-smile. "Thanks, Soob," I said softly. I'd decided to go along with her insistence that my tears were related to my parents' neglect. Specifically, that my father had left Straussville at the end of a visiting pastorship without acknowledging the sudden and suspicious swelling of local sixteen-year-old Leah Morton,[8] and that she'd go on to barely clear the lowest bars of parenthood. These were old facts, but they were hard ones, and over the years Sooby had helped me grind them into fine jokes. Besides, I was

---

8   In his defense, he was apparently dealing with some preexisting conditions: fatherhood and marriage.

struggling to digest that I was possibly, or even probably, part-monster now and had little room on my plate for a side of marital woes.

"You wanna punch me in the face?" she asked. "Because you can, I totally deserve it."

I guffawed at this, and before I could put my hand over my mouth, sprayed a bit of spit and snot from my nose, causing Sooby to howl with a mixture of amusement and disgust.

Jojo spoke up then, from her perch behind the passenger seat, her voice tremulous and small and not at all what it was normally like. "Mommy? You crying?"

I sopped at my face with the cuffs of my shirt as Frankie chimed in, "Mommy? What's sad?"

I approximated as much cheer as I could, and turned toward them as their eyes darted. "No, no, guys!" I said, resisting the urge to sniffle one last time. "I'm fine! You know how Mommy's allergies are."

Sooby sighed and put her hand on the car door. "I'll talk to Mr. T about the guys at PTA. I promise."

I reached out and gave her a quick squeeze, and said goodbye. The two of us had pushed each other's buttons enough for one morning.

As I pulled away from the curb, I allowed myself a few more seconds of relief: I'd made it through our first drop-off without revealing anything incriminating, or monstrous, about myself. I waved to Dianne, who was busy getting all her kids out of her parked car, then grabbed a Burgerville receipt from the floor, and with one hand scribbled down a reminder to bring her my bag of shoes.[9] But I didn't stay in mom-mode for long; as I pulled onto the main road, and then into the turn lane for the preschool, I heard the radio announcer say the word "statue." I turned the volume up high, feeling more and more nauseated with every word:

We have breaking news: The statue reported stolen last night from the grounds of Hoffman High School has been found.

---

9   Women's feet often get bigger, by a half-size or so, after a pregnancy, and my favorite old shoes were too small for me now. Luckily Dianne's feet had increased to my old size.

Workers from the State Parks department arrived at the site of a repair project near the Straussville Reservoir early this morning, and upon opening the door to the restroom pavilion discovered the statue inside. No further information is being released by the department at this time, but sources from the scene told KSTA that the statue, which had not yet been fully installed or revealed, was found jammed inside one of the men's toilets, upside down . . .

I closed my eyes. *Please, God—please let there be no evidence. Do big apey-bear monsters even have DNA, God?*

I looked down at my hands and remembered what the twins had been yammering about earlier, when I was trying to talk to Christy.

"Hey, guys? Tell me again what happens to the wolf-guy in your cartoon, when he gets an 'owie'?"

"His owies go away," Frankie said.

"He's not a wolf-guy," Jo added.

"How fast, Frankie? How fast do the wolf-guy's owies go away?" A couple drivers laid on their horns behind us; I'd been sitting there with my turn signal on, I realized, even though no cars were coming. I waved in apology and made the turn.

"So fast!"

"He's *not* a wolf-guy," Jo said, her little face contorted with frustration in the rearview.

"SUPER FAST, MOMMY," Frankie went on, ignoring her.

Now Jo closed her eyes and *screeched*, the force of her little lungs jarring all of us to attention in the small space. Then she turned toward her brother: "STOP SAYING THAT!"

The color drained from Frankie's face, at about the same rate that Jo's became redder. And as I pulled up to the school curb, I searched my hazy brain for the right parenting strategy—the one I'd read about years before, that some expert had deemed the best and kindest way to prevent a tantrum.

But I gave up almost immediately. I was verging on hysteria; the radio news was filling my car with reminders of the chaos and damage I might have caused; and yet another driver was honking at me to finish up already. I mean, I couldn't scrape together enough brainpower and patience to be the ideal mother under the best circumstances.

Besides, my little girl was probably still upset from having seen her mommy start to cry; I was sure my allergy bit hadn't fooled her. Part of me wanted Jojo to let 'er emotions *rip* right then—to descend into complete and total freak-out mode. *Because God knows,* I thought to myself, *somebody in this family should be freaking out right now.*

It didn't happen, though. I could see her taking the deep breaths I'd taught her, the little angel, which was probably for the best.

"I know, Jojo. I believe you, honey," I said over a sigh. We made eye contact in the mirror. "I'm sorry we ignored you."

Frankie gave me a wide-eyed look and then turned toward his sister to see if my apology would pass muster.

"But, whoever this . . . *character* is, Jojo," I went on, "when they cut themselves, the cut just disappears?"

She smiled. "Yah," she replied calmly.

"Yah, Mommy," Frankie concurred, and two of them smiled at each other and resumed their jabbering.

But I couldn't join in their playfulness. New fears were taking shape in my mind: Perhaps I *had* fallen and torn up my skin. If I was going to start believing I'd changed into a big, apey-bear monster, was it such a stretch to believe the big, apey-bear monster could heal itself "super fast"?

Or was that one fantastical detail too far?

1.6   TUESDAY, 1:00 P.M.

When I got to the office, I summoned all the brain cells that hadn't been conscripted already by monster-related worries and trained them on my work. The mindlessness of certain tasks was a blessing for once, and it turned out to be a surprisingly productive day of summarizing meetings, replying to meeting invites, and replying to emails about meetings, among other things. Perhaps my Office-Lobe just wasn't in the habit of talking all that much to the rest of my brain, because for long stretches I managed to rein-in my suspicion that I'd transformed into a monster.

I was so industrious, in fact, I didn't have time until lunch to email Theo telling him my phone was gone. I even mentioned that I was thinking about going to book club, that's how normal I'd convinced myself I felt. I also made an appointment with my doctor for the following day, telling the receptionist I was having ringing in my ears, seeing flashes of light, and that my heartburn had gotten worse.

I wasn't able to banish my fears entirely, but by the time I picked up the kids and got home that evening, things had gone so normally for so long, and I'd become so adept at not thinking about the monster, that I'd sort of lulled myself into a false sense of safety. I was cheery, almost.

I was cooking chicken and trying to block out the sound of various Nick Jr. theme songs coming from the family room when Frankie marched up to me and announced, "Teacher Flavia stole my pretzels."

"She did?" I licked something off my finger, hoping it wasn't raw poultry juice. I'd never been much of a cook. "That's . . . weird. Did she think they were someone else's?"

But he was staring at the ceiling with his hands down the back of his pants, his mind having moved on to other things.

I went to the computer to check for an email from the school, only to remember I'd started a software update and that it wouldn't be useable for another half hour. "Bret, have you seen Frankie's lunchbox?" I asked, tapping my fingers on my lips.

She was in our breakfast-nook-slash-dining-room, just off the kitchen, working on a poster for her American history project. But with our dishwasher running and the TV on, it was impossible to have any kind of conversation. When she didn't respond, I called out again, a bit louder.

"Mom, it's right *here*!" she replied. Somehow, she got to be annoyed about the fact that I'd had to ask her something twice. Teenager logic, I guess.

"Can you please open it and see if there's anything in there?" I asked as I turned on the oven light. The chicken looked pretty much the same as when I'd put it in, for some reason. I felt the door; the last thing we needed was another broken appliance, and I'd been hoping the oven would hold on awhile longer. I turned the temperature up a few degrees, hoping to speed things along.

Bret hadn't answered me, again, and I suspected all the parenting books said that allowing your kid to ignore you wasn't a good move. But just then Frankie wailed from the family room, "*Mooooooom*! Jojo had an accident on the chaaaaaaiiiiir."

"NUH-UH!"

I took a deep breath. "What kind of accident?" I asked as I stirred the veggies on the range. My healthy side dish had sat for too long, and half of it was now stuck to the bottom of the pan.

"The big kind."

I turned the temperature down on the veggies and called out to Bret—again. I did feel bad about this, as she was diligently doing her homework and the assignment involved art and history, her favorite and best subjects. "Can you help the little ones, please? I know you're trying to concentrate, hon, but I've got a lot going on here."

Instead, she stood up and unzipped Frankie's lunch container, pulled something out, and marched it into the kitchen. "Here," she said as she handed it to me.

It was an envelope addressed to "the caretakers of Frankie Lime." Inside it, a note read:

Please be advised that foods included on our list of banned items will no longer be allowed in the classroom. You are receiving this note because one of our Guides had to confiscate the following food from your child's lunch today: _______________.

In the blank space, someone—Flavia, one presumes—had written "pretzel crisps (hi-sodium)." The letter concluded with:

Please remember, too, that we recommend a variety of food types be included each day to ensure our children learn the importance our community places on proper nutrition.
Your friends,
-The Healthy Start Team

"Frankie?" I called out. He'd gone back to the family room. "Were you hungry at school today? Did you have enough to eat without your pretzels?"

He didn't answer so I walked over and stood by the armchair where he and Jo were sitting, cheek by jowl, even though the entire sofa was empty. It was the kind of adorable scene I'd always pictured—fool that I am—when I imagined what life with twins would be like, before I experienced the real thing. I paused the TV and they looked up at me in unison, their little heads tilting to the same side, like puppies from the same litter.

"Frankie, I'm sorry Mommy and Daddy didn't put the right thing in your lunch today. Jojo, did this happen in your class, too?"

She nodded. "Teacher Ben gave me orange slices."

"OK," I replied over a sigh. "I'll go to Whole Foods after Daddy gets home, and stock up on stuff they'll let you eat." That meant I was officially skipping book club, which I knew was the safest choice right now. I still had to avoid conversations in general, because the vandalism at the school would be on everyone's minds. Plus, hearing people talk about it would rachet up my anxiety even further. Still, it bugged me to miss book club, and also: Why was I always the one giving up my time for the kids? Why not Theo?

"Jojo, do you have a poo in your pants, or a pee?"

"I have a toot," she said. I reached over and lifted her up, tilting her to one side then the other, both surprised and relieved that it was, in fact, just gas.

I hit play on the TV and headed for the kitchen, but stopped when my foot landed in something mushy.

"Eww! *What the*—?" I stopped and lifted up my foot. "Dog puke?"

Critter was an inveterate puker. Our vet told us soon after we adopted her that "some dogs just like to puke." So I'd bought special cleaning supplies and the five of us became intimately familiar with the contents of her stomach. In those early years, that tended to range from yellow to brown, chunky to slimy, and watery to desiccated, depending on what she'd been able to pull from the trash that day.

But this wasn't yellow or brown; this was green. And I'm not talking spinach- or olive-green. I'm talking lime-Jell-O green.

"Did Critter eat . . . lime Jell-O or something?" I asked the kids, my chest clenching as I wondered whether someone, perhaps me, had tracked something strange and slimy into the house the night before.

There were murmurs of ignorance, then a reminder that I hadn't bought them Jell-O in "forever" because I was "a meanie." I sighed, retrieved the cleaning supplies, and got on hands and knees to clean up the mess. I smelled something burning in the kitchen, and figured it was the veggies, which were already a lost cause.

"Where *is* the dog, by the way? Has anyone seen her?" I asked as I rubbed vigorously at the weird residue. It was soon clear, however, that this was one mess that was going to leave a mark.

No one answered. Again. "Bret, do you want to go to Sierra's house tonight or not?"

"Critter's over there," she replied, pointing to the sofa. The cushions were empty, but I could just make out a pair of green eyes, glowing at me from underneath it.

I went over and bent all the way to the ground, then called to her in a lovey-dovey voice. But she refused come out, no matter how much I cooed.

Was she still scared of me because I'd snarled at her? I sat on my heels. Did she sense something . . . *different* about me? I went back to the kitchen and returned with cut-up bits of hot dog, but she wouldn't budge. I pressed my cheek further into the carpet, which was less clean than I care to admit, and spotted something else under the couch: I slowly reached out, trying not to alarm Critter, and pulled out a crumpled-up paper ramekin like the one I'd been handed at New Seasons the night before. It had little teeth marks on it. *Phew!* She must have eaten some of that weird green puree from the other night. As domestic crises go, canine indigestion was far preferable to the possibility I'd left a trail of fluorescent green slime through the house.

I got up and made an appointment with the vet, then finally got around to checking the chicken. Turns out, that was the thing I'd smelled burning a few moments earlier. And between that, the pretzel-crisps incident, and the way I'd gobbled up half our grocery inventory the night before, I couldn't remember a time when I'd felt farther away from the likes of June Cleaver.

At seven-thirty, with dinner sitting cold and barely edible on the table, and Bret over at Sierra's to work on her history project, Theo still hadn't come home. If I'd been planning to go to book club, he would have made me very late. And if he didn't come home soon, I might not make it to Whole Foods before they closed, which also irked. When I dialed his work number, I got his voicemail, but he did pick up when I called his cell phone.

"Are you on your way home?" I asked, managing to keep my tone calm. We absolutely needed some groceries that night, but I really didn't want to run out to the all-night store. It was considerably farther away and at that hour, their poorly lit parking garage would be empty and creepy af.

"No, I'm headed to that dinner thing."

"What 'dinner thing'?"

"The thing I texted you about."

"Theo, I lost my cell phone—remember? From the email I sent you earlier, about book club?"

"Oh *shit*, Harry—I totally forgot. But I gotta go to this thing. Some higher-ups are in town from Seoul, and I can't get out of it. I'm sorry."

I sighed, rubbing my forehead as if it, too, had a stain I needed to remove. "How long have you known about the dinner?"

Silence.

"Theo?"

He sighed. "I don't know. Two weeks, maybe?"

"Why didn't you put it on the family calendar?"

More silence.

I closed my mouth on the sigh that ballooned in my chest, and instead sputtered, "I . . . I—"

"Actually, my battery is about to die, Harry, so—"

I didn't get a chance to ask him to stop for groceries.

***

"Then the Papa Bear said, 'Someone's been eating my . . . *French fries!*'"

Frankie cackled so hard at this that he fell back and hit his head on the bedroom wall. Which only made him laugh harder. "Noooo, Mommy, *no*! It's porridge!"

"Sure, whatever, porridge," I replied, sighing dramatically and pretending to be offended. "But it's porridge *a la French fries*."

He giggled some more and turned over, a satisfied smile on his face.

The twins and I were having our own sort of book club, which involved me recounting a simple story from memory because my hands were too busy hate-folding the laundry to hold a book, my mind too agitated to spin some new and complicated tale. Jo had fallen asleep quickly, and Critter was zonked out on the floor with her legs sticking straight-out, rigor-mortis style. But I'd poked her in the belly with my toe a couple times and she'd replied with a drawn-out grunt, so I knew she was at least breathing. Bret was still at her friend's house, and Theo was still at his mother-effing work dinner.

"And then the Mama Bear said . . ." I continued, trailing off as I folded the last pair of superhero undies and tossed them back in the basket. I wanted badly to get out of their bedroom, because I needed badly to sit by myself awhile, in the quiet downstairs, preferably with some greasy food and a glass of wine in front of me. And lo, Frankie's breathing *did* seem a bit more even to me—more natural. I couldn't be sure that his eyes were closed, however, because he had curled up against the wall.

"And then the Mama Bear said," I whispered again, gently raising myself from the edge of Jo's bed. Neither kid moved, so I tiptoed toward the door, reveling in my sweet, sweet ninja skills, then added, *"Imma just order pizza."*

"Mommy, you didn't finish!" Frankie shouted, suddenly bolt-upright. And before I could assure him that I *would* finish, he yelled again: *"Pleeeeease, Mommy?"* until both Critter and Jo were awake, too.

But at least he remembered to say "please."

Forty-five minutes later, I finally trudged downstairs, all three of my children home, quiet, and tucked away upstairs. I looked at the clock on the microwave: Ten o'clock. For school lunch the next day, I made Jo and Frankie each a whole-grain wrap with some veggies and a yogurt-based dressing, with a side of slices of dried apple I'd found earlier in the console of the minivan. I knew Jo would lick off the yogurt and ignore everything else, and Frankie would only eat the apples. It wasn't enough food for them—not food they would eat, anyway—but our last orange had black spots on it and I wouldn't dare give them blueberries again, since they'd already had diarrhea once that week.

I considered asking Theo to run out to the all-night grocery store when he got home, but quickly dismissed the idea. I knew I'd have to convince him that it was his turn to go, not mine, and that would mean dredging up exhibits A, B, and C of all the things I'd done lately, for the kids and the house and the yard and the dog and the bank account. And him. And didn't people on talk shows refer to that as "keeping score"? Certainly, everyone knows that "keeping score" in a relationship is just plain petty.

Right?

I didn't want to die on that hill. Theo and my relationship had been too epic a thing to let it die an ignoble death on the side of Mt. Chore.[10] So I went back to the cabinets for the umpteenth time and stared at the graham crackers and such. Some of the foods were on the brink of expiration. Others I'd scarfed down myself the night before, because monster-ing consumes hella calories, apparently. Everything else violated the school's lunch code, by dint of too much salt, too much sugar, too much GMO-whatever. *It's all too much bullshit, if you ask me.*

It was close to midnight when I saw Theo's headlights in the driveway.

"Hi," I said flatly when he opened the door. I'd spent the previous hours assembling and reassembling myself, so that by the time Theo got home, I'd look and sound like the same super-stoic version of Harriet that he'd married, almost fifteen years earlier. And that suddenly felt messed up to me.

"Hey," he replied as he set his things down. When he'd gotten his coat off and was heading into the family room, he added, "I'm sorry about earlier, babe."

I shrugged, my face an emotion-free zone. It was the same placid expression I'd pretty much lived in before meeting Theo—a purposefully inscrutable look that he'd dubbed "Harry face" within days of meeting me, and that he mimicked in good-natured fashion until I couldn't look at him anymore without betraying my amusement. Except now, there was no risk of me laughing. "I'm taking the dog out," I said as I clipped the leash onto Critter's halter. "We'll be a while."

---

10   I can tell you the exact moment I knew Theo was a keeper. It was our senior year, and we were sitting at some twenty-four-hour diner, off some remote highway in eastern Washington, at some godforsaken hour of night. (His water polo team was headed home following a tournament held at a small private college six hours away, and I'd hitched a ride on their bus so I could visit the school's Rare Documents Collection for my history thesis.) "Which of these do you want?" I mumbled over a yawn when our platter of chicken and waffles arrived. He glanced at each and began singing "You're the One That I Want" to the one closest him, *Ooo-ooo-ooos* and all. While his hyper-masculine teammates, his coaches, and strangers in nearby booths looked on. When he looked up at me and sang a few bars in *my* direction, the defenses I'd put up around my heart, and my feelings, fractured a bit along the edges.

"OK." He was already on the couch with his laptop open. "I've got a bunch of work emails to deal with, then I'll hit the hay. I'm beat."

"You know," I said as I turned toward him, cool as a cucumber, "you can talk to me about stuff whenever, T. There's never a good time, so just . . . please, tell me? If and when stuff comes up?"

Then I left, reminding myself to be thankful for all the help I did get from him; I knew it was more than a lot of women got.

1.7   TUESDAY, 10:00 P.M.

Fallen leaves covered our neighborhood streets, and to my surprise, their brilliant hues glistened under some of the streetlights. Folks had taken to watering their trees, trying to keep the weaker ones alive, which was bizarre. This is Oregon, after all. Here, the saying goes, you plant something one day and the next day you need a map and a chainsaw just to get out your front door. We were not accustomed to such a dry autumn.

I don't know if it was the unexpected beauty of the damp leaves underfoot, the autumnal smells, or the glittering perforation of stars overhead, but my anger and fear seemed to let up a bit. Even Critter seemed a little better, and as taken with the sensory pleasures as I was.

The soft cushion of wet leaves probably explained why I didn't hear the bigger dog coming. It wasn't wearing a collar either, so no ID tags jangled to alert me of his approach.

Critter knew, though she barely had time to whimper before the golden-colored blur reached us without slowing down even a tick. I was still standing there like an idiot when he tackled her to the ground and pinned her there, leaving her as vulnerable and frantic as an overturned pill bug, her pale throat caught in the vise of his mouth.

I came to my senses and yelped, then dropped to the ground. My first instinct was to try and pry him off of her, so I jammed an elbow under the bigger dog's throat and leaned my whole body against his, screaming "LET GO!" and "DROP IT!" It was totally ineffective.

The dog hadn't closed his mouth all the way, thank goodness; he seemed to be showing Critter "dominance"—he must have weighed eighty pounds, to her ten—or so I gathered, from the hackles standing up along his back. But regardless of whether he meant her real harm, he wasn't letting go. I was going to have to pry his jaws open.

With my fingers trembling, I wrapped my hands around his snout, one on each jaw. But the pads of my fingers slipped along his tapered canines, and at one point I accidentally pinched his gums with my fingernails. He growled and bit down harder on Critter, whereupon she squealed in pain.

"FUUUUCK!" I screamed. I was becoming frantic, and running out of ideas. *I'm so sorry, girl,* I thought, *that I blamed you for my mess at home. And I'm so, so sorry I made you go to that training bootcamp, after the man who lives next to the dog park complained about all the peeing on his azaleas.* "COME GET YOUR DOG!" I lifted my head and shouted at surrounding houses. "SOMEBODY PLEASE, COME HELP US!" I swore an oath to whatever Saints of Good Pets there might be in the universe, that if Critter and I managed to survive this, I would immediately become a much, much better dog owner.

Just then, a gurgly, wailing sort of sound came from Critter. I froze, as did the bigger dog, and we both stared at her. Her strange howling—or baying, or whatever it was—had started out low, but when her aggressor still hadn't moved off or let go, her protests grew louder, and a whole lot scarier.

Seconds later, when the big dog *still* hadn't budged in spite of her shrill warnings, the nails on all four of Critter's feet shot out to the size of small machetes.

I gasped and scrambled to my feet, my hands covering my mouth. Critter's bony little legs—which a second earlier had pawed helplessly at the air—now spun furiously at the dog, and she opened her mouth to reveal row upon row of sharp, serrated teeth. Each of them was bigger than my house key, and together they could've made a great white shark go green with envy. The big dog let go of her and scurried away, squealing as he scooted under a nearby bush.

I was still breathing wildly, dumb with shock, when I heard a lazy whistle from a nearby yard. I glanced over but didn't see anyone, and when I looked back at Critter, she was all-dog again—standing on all fours, wagging her tail, no signs of shark or wolverine to be seen.

The person who'd whistled finally appeared from around the corner, the scent of patchouli arriving before her. She ambled over to us with a glass—yes, a glass—of something milky-looking in her hand, smiling as if she didn't have a care in the world. "Jerry? Oh, there you are, my good boy!"

"This your dog?" I asked, my heart pounding as Jerry shot out from under his bush. On instinct, I jumped back and yanked Critter with me, but he was like a different dog now, fine in both body and spirit. He loped over to the woman and after standing up on his hind legs, put his paws on her shoulders.

"Who's my sweetest boy?" she asked in a raspy voice as Jerry swiped his tongue up and down her face, from her lips to her bloodshot eyes. "Who's my very best boy?"

"So, hey," I began again, trying to force out some words between heaving breaths. "I just . . . Jerry here . . . Jerry just tackled my dog."

"Did he?" she asked, laughing loudly as she scratched his ears. "He's so friendly like that."

"No, see," I said, still trying to catch my breath. I struggled to find the right words, one eye trained on Critter's teeth and paws, which thankfully still looked normal. "This wasn't, like, a friendly thing. He knocked her to the ground, and he pinned her there."

"He's just, like, really *really* friendly."

My breathing wasn't slowing down, even though I tried to inhale and exhale deliberately. I could feel my anger bubbling up and it became a real struggle to keep my voice neutral. "You don't understand—he had my dog by the throat. He growled at us, and I couldn't get him off."

"Hey," she replied, her tone spiky all of a sudden. She looked away from Jerry, who pushed off her shoulders and loped toward Critter and me again. "Chill out lady, OK? Your dog probably growled at Jerry."

Ohhhh, boy. Here we go.

"*Jerry* was off-leash," I replied through gritted teeth, pulling Critter close to me as the other dog circled us, albeit this time without any menace. "*Jerry* charged at us. And my dog's been kind of sick today. We just wanted to walk in peace."

Her grin dimmed a little. "Wait—what the fuck are you doing out here with a sick dog? He could give whatever he's got to Jerry or something."

I gaped at her as the simmering in my chest started up again. And as Jerry stood on his hind legs and put his paws on *my* shoulders, I half-yelled, "Are you kidding me? You're the one letting your dog run wild—and breaking the law, I might add—and you're gonna criticize *me* for bringing mine out to take a shit?"

She sputtered at me and waved her hand—a slovenly sovereign, too cool for my lame, law-abiding ways. "I don't know what's up your ass, lady, but you really need to get that checked out." Then she sauntered off.

This time, my transformation didn't take as long. In a matter of seconds, my whole torso went from burning hot to an intense bubbling and bloating sensation, as if I'd been poisoned. The buzzing in my ears came next, and a few seconds later, the white-hot light took over my vision.

This time, however, I didn't black out. I knew what was happening.

This time, I would be certain it wasn't a dream.

Normally, I'm a wimp when it comes to gross-out, horror-movie stuff. I even fainted once during biology class—my head greeting the linoleum with a *THONK*—when we watched a video that showed just a few seconds of brain surgery.

But the thing that happened to me on the street that night? *That* I watched. *That* I heard and felt as it happened, limb by limb, in a state that approached rapture.

Every part of me moved in a way that it shouldn't. It was fascinating to me, and it was beautiful. I watched as my tendons, ligaments, and muscles slithered like snakes under my skin. I listened to the satisfying crackle of my bones, as they grew to new lengths and poked and prodded at the skin that bubbled and stretched to accommodate them. It reminded me of my emergency C-section for Jo and Frankie, when the doctors yanked my intestines this way and that before rearranging and re-stapling my organs together again—except this didn't hurt, and I wasn't scared.

And oh, how I grew: My hands, which had slipped so easily through the loop on Critter's leash an hour earlier? Larger than the tire swing in a nearby yard. My pants and shirt? Stretched, ripped, and frayed as my enormous thighs took up all the space they needed. My upper body spread out so wide I could have easily wrapped my arms halfway around the Straussville water tower, and by the time a full minute had passed, my head and shoulders had shot up among the telephone poles lining the street.

I grew so fast, in fact, that when my head became snagged between power lines, I didn't have time to disentangle myself before they overstretched their limits. I saw the first sparks fly from the corner of my eye, then heard the low *snap! snap!* as they detached from their poles. They fell toward Jerry and without thinking, I reached out and caught them, midair.

Electricity coursed through me, and I closed my eyes and opened my mouth, in greater pain than I've ever known—not counting pregnancy or childbirth, obviously—expecting to hear the roar of a prehistoric beast come out of my gaping maw. But to my surprise, the only sound I made was . . . a whimper of sorts. I looked around until I found Critter, who appeared to be fine; she was sitting calmly under a tree, not far from me, licking her anus. I could smell burning hair, however, and another odor I couldn't quite identify, and when I whirled around I accidentally hooked my arms on some more wires, tangling myself up further. The sparks grew and multiplied as more lines broke free, from poles on either side of me.

I reached out and grabbed all those wires, too, and got zapped a whole lot more. I was starting to feel kind of impressed with myself: I was quick all of a sudden! I was *agile*! But then I realized the acrid odor I'd smelled a moment earlier was burning flesh, and that it was *my* burning flesh.

I reeled backward and into a streetlight, ramming the glass casing with my shoulder, smashing it to bits. It and the rest of the streetlights went dark, followed quickly by the windows in surrounding houses. The only things illuminating the street, then, were the cars whose alarms had gone off, their headlights blinking steadily as if they, too, were flabbergasted at the events unfolding before them.

I wasn't being electrocuted anymore, thank goodness, so I focused on wresting myself free of the wires. When I finally got them off me and glanced around, I spied Jerry's owner running away from us, near the end of the street, slipping on wet grass and stumbling over political yard signs like she was in some kind of steeplechase event, and she was one very stoned horse.

Jerry, however, was sitting on top of my foot. My enormous, bare foot—and when I looked down at him in the darkness, he waggled his whole body in response. And I have to admit that in spite of the events that led up to that point, the damn dog was starting to grow on me.

I tried calling out to his owner, but I still couldn't get any words out. *You gotta leash your dog!* I wanted to say. *He could get hit by a car! Or hurt somebody! He could be confiscated, or even euthanized!* But I couldn't push the words from my brain to my vocal cords; everything was so new to me. My size. My shape. My species.

I stood there, sputtering and whimpering and panting, screwing up my face and even drooling a bit, until I finally found one English word I could say out loud. I grabbed Critter in one hand and Jerry in the other and ran after his owner, every footfall rumbling the earth like a shot from a canon.

Luckily, the woman hadn't gone far. I found her on the porch of a small bungalow, struggling to get the door open. As I got close, she turned toward me with a look of terror, and really, who could blame her? I didn't know what I looked like at that point, and God only knew what facial expressions I was making as I struggled mightily to say my one word.

"CONFISCATE!" I said finally. It came out warbly and uncertain, a croak-like sound, yet also much louder than I'd intended. The woman didn't react, however, so I said it again, even louder: "CONFISCATE! CONFISCAAAAATE!"

I held Jerry out to her, my palm open and flat, and he wriggled like a puppy delighted by all the ruckus. I willed her to understand me: *Take your dog back! Keep him safe!* But "CONFISCAAAATE!" was the only thing that would come out.

She fainted right there on her porch.

I bent over and peered at her, and Jerry jumped up and licked my face. "YOU BETTER GET THAT CHECKED OUT, LADY," I croaked.

What the hell? I threw my arms in the air. Finally—*finally*—I managed to say a full sentence, and Jerry's owner wasn't even awake to hear it. My hands fell to my sides in frustration.

A siren wailed from some distance away, and I knew I needed to get away from there fast. So I put Jerry down and secured him next to his owner, with whatever stuff I could scrounge up in her yard. Then I grabbed Critter and bounded down the street, toward our house. I was still a ways off, though, when the treetops over the next hill lit up in flashes of blue, red, and white, and the sirens pierced my ears at a volume I hadn't known they could reach. I winced and skidded to a stop, then turned for the nearest backyard, where I could move under the shadows of our neighborhood's giant fir trees.

I said a little prayer that I would make it home without being seen, although truth be told, I wasn't nearly as afraid as I should have been. I didn't dwell on what would happen if the police captured me—to my family, to my life.

Instead, I marveled at what my body could do, as I leapt over a fence in—you guessed it—a single bound. Normally I had to be careful not to strain a muscle just vacuuming our family room. I smiled as I jumped into the next backyard, and the one after it, wobbly but uninjured, and imagined the owners calling the seismological society to report a series of small quakes.

I was so busy admiring my enhanced agility, as it happened, that I forgot all about our neighbor Justin's year-round, heated pool. I'd also gotten a bit overconfident in the yard before his, and underestimated the steepness of a slope there. So Critter and I ended up landing at Justin's not with a sure-footed *boom* but an awkward, belly-first *splash*, sending a small tsunami of water slopping against the back of his house. Grateful for the ongoing blackout, I made sure Critter was doggy-paddling behind me as I swam to the edge. When I reached up to grab the sides of the ladder, I was relieved to see my own pale, human hands. I'd changed back into Harry, thank goodness—albeit a near-naked, Dickensian version of Harry, who apparently hung out in her neighbors' pools like a creeper.

I'd just reached the gate in Justin's fence, Critter under my arm, when I heard a door open behind me. I turned and saw a figure step onto the back porch, the barrel of a gun visible in its profile. I was pretty sure Justin owned real guns in addition to his fake ones, so I said another little prayer, this time that he maintained the hinges of his gate as lovingly as he did the mud-flaps on his pickup truck. Then I ever so slowly lifted the latch, and when there was a crack big enough for me to slip through, I left.

I scuttled through the back door of our own dark house, put Critter down on the cold tile, and studied her anxiously for a moment. But she only wagged her tail and went to her water dish. I drank, too, gulping down what felt like a gallon of water, straight from the sink. Then I slopped around the kitchen, mawing my way through a three-year-old fruitcake I'd pulled from the back of the hall closet. This time, I tried to avoid gobbling up anything I might need for the kids' lunches as I paced back and forth, dripping water and stale crumbs all over the floor. Because in that moment, I had no idea how to proceed with my life.

Have you ever read a mystery novel, or watched a cop show, and wondered how you would act after committing a crime? Would you bungle the cover-up? Would you turn yourself in? I hadn't actually committed a crime, or at least I hadn't done so on purpose; but that's the best way to describe my state of mind that night. On the one hand, I felt guilty, almost ashamed, for not staying put when I first heard the sirens. I hadn't waited for police to arrive, and I had no intention of heading to the nearest station and turning myself in now that I was Harriet again.

Yet on the other hand, I felt resigned to standing there alone and confused with my new reality. Because I couldn't imagine any way to tell the authorities what had happened to me—none that wouldn't get me taken immediately to a psych ward for an involuntary hold. Hell, I didn't even want to tell Theo or the kids. I couldn't imagine revealing my monster-hood to any of them, and it saddened me to realize that was partly because my own family wasn't in the habit of listening to me, either. I was worried they'd freak out, but I was more worried that they'd be no more likely to believe me, and support me, than the strangers at the police station.

I forced myself to sit down at the kitchen table, but my knee pumped in sync with my skittering heartbeat. I tried resting my chin in my hands, then folding my arms in front of me, but I couldn't find a way to just *be*— to sit, to settle—that didn't make me feel like I might explode. My eyes fell on Frankie and Jo's comic-book-themed lunch boxes, stacked on top of each other and kind of filthy, much like their owners at the end of each day. I jumped up and took them to the sink and gave them a good scrub-down, then looked around for one last snack to pack inside. It's incredible, isn't it? The power of the Mom-lobe?

I didn't gain any comfort from these tasks. I hated packing lunches in the best of times, and I didn't like it any better now. I chucked a ziplock full of graham crackers in with each lunch and scribbled a note to their teachers:

Dear Friends, Due to a family emergency, we were unable to provide Jo and Frankie with a lunch today that fully adheres to your rules. We advise that you allow them to eat these graham crackers anyway, if only to emphasize the importance our community places on not being wasteful with food, and on the critical role a full belly plays in a child's ability to focus during the school day. We appreciate your understanding as we continue working toward a solution on this matter.[11]

---

11   Being a professional communications manager might not be glamorous, but it has its benefits.

I went upstairs and tiptoed into the little ones' room, where I pulled Frankie's blanket off the floor and draped it over him, then fished Jo's flashlight from under her sheet and stashed it in the dresser. Back in the hallway, I didn't see any light in the crack under Bret's door, so I went to Theo's and my room and got into bed next to my softly snoring husband. I seemed to vibrate all over with an enormous, full-body ache.

Lying there in the dark, exhausted and depleted, sent my brain back to my swim-team days. Even in high school, we had anywhere from two to four hours of grueling practice, every day but Sunday. Afterwards my body would feel drained, but also suffused with a sense of purpose. I always had a feeling that I was preparing myself, for something that was yet to come.

This extreme fatigue piqued another unexpected memory and I sat up abruptly, raising the bottom of my shirt so that I could see my abdomen in the dim light. And there they were: The bumpy arc of my C-section scar and the pooch of my belly, both of which had come into this world on the same day Jo and Frankie entered it. I took a deep breath as relief shuddered through me. To my surprise, I was glad they were still there. There were some marks even a super-healing monster could not, and should not, erase.

2

I'm not sure what woke me the next morning, alone in bed. I'd slept through Theo's alarm, and without a phone, I couldn't even tell the time. That alone was enough to panic me, but as soon as my mind drew up a fuzzy sketch of my current predicament, I launched myself from bed and flew to the stairs in a terror, imagining all sorts of terrible things that might await me.

But when I got to the bottom, the little ones were eating cereal at the kitchen table, Bret was combing her hair in the front hall, and Theo was standing behind the couch folding laundry. Everyone seemed to be listening to a segment playing on the local news, except for Critter, who was sitting on the rug, alternately licking her toes and then sticking them into one ear. I took in the overall scene with an enormous surge of those happy, lovey-dovey brain chemicals people talk about.

"Morning," Theo said when he saw me. "You OK?"

"Huh?" I was so taken aback by the trace of a smile on his face, so rare had that become, that I was momentarily struck dumb. I looked down at myself and patted my head, neck, and torso, half-expecting to find my hair singed or my clothes full of burn holes. But the old T-shirt and shorts I'd thrown on before collapsing in bed the night before were just tattered in the normal way—not like something you might see, say, on Lou Ferrigno in his best-known role.

"Come see this woman on the news," Theo said in a flat voice, tucking one of the twins' teensy shirts under his chin, where a scruffy beard continued to spread, seemingly unchecked. "She lives a few blocks from here, in that house with all the Tibetan prayer flags on the ground? She's on here telling reporters that she saw some kind of, like, big creature last night."

"Huh," I said again as I sunk into the couch. I prayed there were no witnesses, or at least none with a cell phone camera. I noticed Theo looking intensely at the TV, and on some new instinct, took the opportunity to grab a few of my older shirts, pants, socks, and underwear—stuff I wore mostly around the house—from one of his piles without him noticing. Then I asked, "Hey, do you want me to fold the rest, so you have time to shave?"

"You've probably seen her big ol' golden retriever around," he replied, ignoring my question. "She never puts a leash on the poor thing, and I can't tell you how many times I've seen it almost get hit by a car."

"Mmm," I replied. I slunk over to my work bag and stashed my pile of clothes inside. I had to be prepared for anything. I returned to the couch, thinking it wasn't so much a new instinct as my usual Mom-inclination, only on steroids now. I flinched at first when Theo gripped my stiff shoulders, but soon relaxed into his affectionate squeeze.

"And get this," he went on, letting go of me and returning to the clothes. "She says that when she woke up this morning, she was tied to her own front porch. *With* the dog."

"Heh," I offered limply. "Heh, heh."

"No, really—the cop confirmed it. They were both tied up, with her Tibetan prayer flags to boot."

I groaned and bowed my head. "*Ohhhhhh, that has got to be so offensive.* That's offensive, right?"

"I'm guessing it's less offensive than her leaving them in the dirt all the time. But wait, here's the best part: She's got like a bazillion of them, right? And whoever did this, her creature or whatever, wrapped her and the dog up over and over, like mummies. The police had to cut them out."

He bent forward and picked up a pair of my underwear, laughing aloud in that low, rumbling way of his. Startled, I tried to remember the last time I'd heard it: A few weeks? Months, even? I reveled in the warmth and generosity of it, how it reverberated in my own body whenever he was close. *Maybe we* are *still on the same team. Maybe we* are *still our same old selves, the same snug-fitting pair. Maybe we're not actually changing in all these ways we never expected.*

"Hey," I whispered when he leaned low to grab another wrinkled something from the basket. "You seem happier this morning. I'm glad—I've been worried about you."

"I'm just glad nobody was hurt," he replied as the news anchor came back on briefly, followed by the reporter on the scene.

I turned my neck around and craned it a bit to look up at him. What did the morning's news, about some incident the night before, have to do with the mood he'd been in for months?

I rubbed my eyes and turned forward again. But then I froze, because on the television a man passed behind the news reporter, maybe a few yards back, and he was wearing the same distinctive, cowboy-esque black hat and uniform I'd seen at PTA a couple nights earlier. He was onscreen less than a second, but I would've sworn it was the same man who'd approached Ellen in those tense few moments at the school. My heart released a single, enormous pulse as the hairs on my arms and neck and thighs shot upright like a thousand tiny soldiers reporting for duty. When the screen switched back to the anchor, who introduced the meteorologist, I grasped around me for the remote so I could rewind it a few seconds. But as I did, I saw Theo use it to click the television off from behind the couch.

I turned back to the blank screen. Had I just seen what I thought I'd seen? Should I try to find out, or let it go? It must have been a coincidence, I told myself; and even if it were the same uniform, from the same law enforcement outfit, it was probably just some jurisdiction or department I hadn't heard of.

I needed to chill the fuck out, I decided. My moment with Theo had left me with a sense of security for the first time in a while, and I was determined to avoid facing the day—and the real world—a few minutes longer. Not only on account of the monster that might await me, but also the unpredictable boss and angry traffic I'd have to contend with.

"Moooooom! You left your email open again!" Bret shouted. She was still standing in the foyer but with her volleyball now, practicing quick sets against the wall. "And why is Brandon's mom emailing you?"

"Who's Brandon?"

"Uhhhh, Brandon *Stout*? The starting goalie on the soccer team?"

"Ooh—Ellen emailed me back? Yaaaaay," I said as I got up and trotted toward the computer. I felt surprisingly lighthearted, and eager to focus on something diverting. "Yaaaaay, Ellen."

"How's your shoulder, Bret?" Theo asked. "Does it still hurt at all?"

Bret answered him with a detailed explanation of what her physical therapist had advised her, how Coach Sullen had suggested she ice it, and what she'd read on the internet about rotator cuff injuries.

"Wait, wait, *wait*. Bret, my darling? How come you answer your dad when he asks about your shoulder, but not me?" I asked as I went through the motions at the computer. "What am I, chopped liver?"

"Come *on*, Mom, get dressed. We're going to be late!" she scoffed as she resumed her sets. But I turned my attention to Ellen's email:

> *Hi Harriet,*
>
> *How are things? I'm sorry it's taken me so long to reply to you. I'm not sure if the Walking Bred is on hiatus after the incident at the school, but I was wondering if I could take you up on your offer to get together sometime. Maybe we could try to— dare I say it—catch a movie?*
>
> *-Ellen*
>
> *P.S., Who can think of the Oscars at a time like this? I haven't stopped mourning the end of summer blockbuster season. Which I totally missed, of course.*

I wrote back that I definitely wanted to try that, and that we should grab dinner, too. I offered up some evenings I might be available in the next month, hoping that by then, I would have this whole monster thing figured out.

2.2   WEDNESDAY, 9:00 A.M.

Once in my cubicle, however, I couldn't think of anything but the monster. I bit my fingernails and stirred my coffee with a wooden stick, replaying the past two evenings over and over again.

I'd undergone a full-body transmogrification—twice now—that would make even the most spectacular of butterflies bow down in deference. But I couldn't keep myself focused on the question of how and why it'd happened. I'd wonder, for example, if I had a genetic mutation but couldn't fathom why such a thing would reveal itself now and in this manner. I couldn't remember being part of any freak accidents in any laboratories involving spiders, gamma rays, or anything else. And I knew I hadn't been born on a faraway planet, where consonant-heavy "K" names were de rigueur, or on an island enshrouded in fog and secrecy and probably a lot of estrogen.

Then I'd begin to panic as I realized, time and again, that I had no real leads to go on. And since I was less stricken when I slipped back into memories of *being* the monster, I closed my eyes, put my headphones on to dampen the noise of ringing phones and printer jams, and attempted to dive back into that other . . . *being*. My hope was that somewhere in the dreamlike, cinematic madness of it all, I might see some new detail that would offer a clue as to why I was transforming into something straight out of a comic book.

Everything I called to mind from the night before had a fishbowl quality: Things looked hazy, as if I were looking out through an immense, darkened window that someone had smeared generously with Vaseline. And things felt . . . spacious in there. Like I had a lot of room suddenly, where I previously had too little.

That's all I could remember. The rest of the experience kept slipping from my grasp, the corporeal changes too all-consuming for me to remember much else. This was not a comfort.

Most striking of all was my sense that I wasn't in full control of the monster's behavior. When I (or it, or she, or we) grabbed hold of those live wires, it was on reflex. When I ran after Jerry's owner, my legs got moving before I knew it was happening. You'll recall that we Limes weren't even a "honking family," and yet whoever or whatever was inside the monster's body with me—let's call it the monster's psyche, for lack of a better term—seemed all too happy to indulge in some serious earth-shaking.

So who was my co-director on this movie, and what were they like?

There were only two things I had any certainty about. The first had come to me the night before, as I peeled myself out of wet rags for the second night in a row: It sure seemed like being dunked in water was what changed me back into Harriet. So I knew what to try if I turned into the beast again. Either that or I'd seen *Captain Underpants* a few too many times with Frankie and Jo.

The second thing I knew was that I'd been really frustrated and angry the moment before I'd changed, both times. All my life, I'd been exceptionally good at keeping my feelings under wraps. But now, anger wasn't so much slipping through my fingers as gushing from every pore. Could that be what triggered all this? If so, why didn't people who regularly went postal turn into monsters, too?

And holy *shit*, what did Critter have to do with this madness? When Jerry tackled her, she'd gone full honey badger, albeit some mutant version, and only for a few seconds. And unlike me, she'd changed back to herself without being dunked in water. Maybe the wet leaves on the ground had been enough to do the trick.

I squeezed my eyes shut and rubbed at my temples, hard.

C'mon, universe. What new kind of fuckery is this?

When I'd bitten three of my nails down to the quick, causing one of them to bleed, I got up and grabbed my bag. I told a few colleagues that I needed to buy a new cell phone and go to a doctor's appointment, and that I'd be gone for the rest of the day. On my way to the elevator, I ran into my boss.

"Everything OK, Harry?"

"Hi, Bob. Yeah, just going in for a checkup," I replied, glancing at the wall clock behind him. We had a pretty good rapport, in my opinion; I was the only one on the ten-person staff who had worked with—well, *for*—Bob since he started the company. My relative longevity had given me a bit of clout, if only at the annual holiday party, when I was pressed for embarrassing stories from the far-back of Bob's closet.

He was typing something on his phone as he stepped closer. "Hey, I was going to ask you. I just read that book about working moms and kids and stuff?"

When he looked at me for signs of recognition, I could only blink at him.

"You know—the really big one, by what's her name? Kathy something?

"You mean the one by *Kithie Carroway*, I think her name is?"

He snapped his fingers and looked up. "That's the one."

"I heard about it, but I haven't read it," I replied as I snuck another glance at the clock. I was starting to sweat.

"Is it . . . are we not supposed to read that one, now?" he asked, apparently misinterpreting my expression. He looked at his phone again as behind him, our part-time accountant, Yvette Santos, emerged from the bathroom and headed toward our suite of offices. When she saw us, she made an exaggerated show of tiptoeing and held a finger to her lips while suppressing an impish smile.

"Has she been cancelled, this Carroway woman? I haven't been on my Twitter lists in a minute."

"I . . . I don't know."

"Shoot. I already talked about it on my podcast, too."

"I wish I had time for parenting books, but I'm in the trenches right now," I replied. Then I allowed myself a modest *humph*.

Alarm set in across Bob's features, and I started to think I'd been too forthcoming about finding life as a parent anything less than blissful. He put a hand in his pants pocket and rubbed at his chin. "Harry, let's not use that word. It's insensitive."

"Uhhh," I blinked back at him. "Sorry?"

"We shouldn't be comparing our petty problems to those of the men and women who serve in our armed forces. That was one of my biggest takeaways from our Respectful Workplaces seminar a few months back."

"Oh!" He was talking about *trenches*. "Yeeeaaaah, sorry about that." I pressed my lips together as behind him, Yvette was swiping the bottom of one index finger across the top of the other in a *tsk-tsk* gesture. It was tough not to sputter violently with laughter, especially because she was in the military herself. I imagined her faux-hawk—hair buzzed close to her scalp on the sides, longish and wavy on top—probably pushed the envelope with her commanding officers in the National Guard, but I was also certain she was a devoted service member. At the office she always wore conservatively tailored suits, and her overall look struck me as a perfect encapsulation of her rigorous, no-nonsense approach to her work and more playful attitude to most everything else.

"Seriously, Harry. I know it's your 'thing' to go around making 'wise-cracks,'" Bob said, making air quotes, twice. "But our men and women in uniform put their lives on the line for us."

"Yes, I know," I replied as Yvette slipped inside the office. She and I didn't cross paths every day; my role in communications didn't deal directly with her side of things at Mullins Creative. Plus, she worked half the week for a collection of other small firms in the area. I wished I saw more of her; she'd just given me the best thirty seconds of my workday by far.

I squinted at Bob, hoping it came across as the polite squint I intended. *Members of the military do put their lives on the line for us. Just not, for the past century or so, in trenches.*

He reached out and squeezed my arm. "At any rate, let's all try to bring our cultural sensitivity to the off-site."

"Wait—what?" I called out to his back as he opened the door to our suite.

"Our annual off-site meeting!" he replied without turning around. "It's next week, and we're going to spend a big part of the day ideating on how we can be a more inclusive place. So that's good timing, sounds like."

He walked off and I hightailed it to the elevators, where I took some of my anxiety out on the down button, punching it several times with a knuckle. On top of everything else, had I just been deemed insensitive by my boss?

***

On the drive to Best Buy, more monster-obsessing: Like, why couldn't I speak very well when I turned into her? A witness did say I'd been yelling *Just you wait* as I marched through the woods with the statue in tow. With Jerry's owner, I couldn't say what I meant until there was no one around who could hear me. Which was aggravating.

Why had I only been able to squeeze out a single word—"confiscate"— when the woman was conscious? And why had the monster chosen that word? Then I remembered: It was from the passive-aggressive note I'd gotten from Frankie's teacher earlier in the day. Confiscating my kid's pretzels had been a dick move; it made me feel like a bad mom, and demanded that I make yet another run to the grocery store.

I turned into the Best Buy lot and searched the rows for an open space. And I wondered, too, what the monster would say the next time she came out—and whether or not I could influence it. If I said something to myself when I was regular ol' Harry, and repeated it over and over, would that be the thing the beast said next time?

What did I *want* her to say, anyway?

I turned down another row of parking, imagining which phrases she might come out with. I'd practically moaned the word "CAAAAAAAAAAKE" earlier in the drive, after spotting a woman carrying a three-tiered, butter-cream masterpiece from a bakery near the office. And when I saw a guy leave his shopping cart at the edge of the parking lot as I pulled in, I'd growled, "PUT THAT BACK, YOU MONSTER."

I laughed aloud at the thought of the monster saying those things, but the humor drained from me entirely when it occurred to me that the words I actually needed to practice—over and over and over—were "PLEASE DON'T SHOOT."

I finally found an open spot, but couldn't take it; the owner of one of those customized "Sprinter" vans—a favorite among hipster, upper-class dads in our area—had parked diagonally in the adjacent space, and across the line. No vehicle could fit there, except maybe a Vespa. I muttered every foul curse word I knew and invented three or four more for good measure. Then I drove to the Target parking lot, parked, and even though I was still in my work shoes—which had a wide, two-and-a-half-inch heel—jogged the distance back to Best Buy.

I was able to corner a polite, twenty-something associate with a fledgling mustache after only a short wait. He confirmed I was due for an "upgrade," and thus a hefty discount on a phone, then helped me pick one out. He had just finished taking my information—and I was congratulating myself for checking this off my to-do list—when we came to a problem: Our family's cellular account had an overdue balance of $188.82.

My whole face burned. Theo and I each paid half of our household bills, and the phones were his responsibility. I tried to maintain control of my breathing as I wrangled with the man, trying to find a way to leave there with a phone in my hand. If I paid the balance right then, I asked, could I get the phone? No, the payment wouldn't be recorded immediately. What if I paid full price, and skipped the "upgrade" discount? Sure, if I didn't mind spending more—like, several hundred dollars more.

So, no—I would not be leaving with a phone.

My sense of accomplishment fizzling away, I closed my eyes for a few seconds, trying to stave off the frustration, embarrassment, and guilt—yes, guilt—trying to light me up like so much tinder. Because how many messages had I missed, since losing my phone? How far behind was I, on the workings of school committees and changes to sports schedules? I was sweating through my blouse under the arms, and was probably beet-red, as I apologized to the guy for "wasting his time." When he suggested I order a "refurbished" phone from their website—because it would be less expensive—I thanked him twice more and complimented his mustache.

And then I felt utterly stupid. And idiotic. And silly. Because I was embarrassed and apologetic for something that wasn't my fault. And because I'd have to spend another day—at minimum—without a cellular tether to my family and job, I was allowing mom-guilt to be the cherry on top of that shit-sundae. Which was infuriating.

So I straightened myself up to my full height and set my mouth in a firm line. I made eye contact with the associate and leaned all the way over the checkout counter. The man's eyes widened and without breaking eye contact, I snatched his entire stack of Best Buy bags with one hand and a fistful of cheap black pens with the other, accidentally knocking over their little cup and sending it clattering to the floor. When all had gone quiet again, I gave the man a taut nod, placed about 25% of the bags back—so he'd have something for the rest of his shift—and marched out of the store like a mad woman.

Back at the car, I flung the side door open with a *bang* and chucked the Best Buy bags into the way-back, making a mental note to recycle them later. Then I started rooting through the clothes I'd taken from the laundry that morning. I needed to be at my doctor's office in a matter of minutes, but with that bitter brew of guilt, frustration, and embarrassment roiling inside me, I worried it might slop over the edge at any second and I'd find myself full-monster again.

This time, I wanted to be prepared for it. I wanted to have clothes to put on, the next time I found myself near-naked, post-monstering, and that meant stashing some necessities in a few places around the neighborhood and near the schools. Besides, my doctor was less than a mile away, inside the Willamette Medical Center. I started throwing together provisions as fast as I could.

Putting together outfits was easy; most of my clothes were dark and featureless, so no one in my family would notice if I came back wearing something different than what I left in. And even if, God forbid, someone found a shred of fabric on some tree branch in the monster's wake, there was no one I could think of—not even Sooby—who would recognize it and think, *Oh, definitely. That's SO Harry.*

It occurred to me that I could use the Best Buy bags I'd pilfered to keep my outfits in, so I retrieved a few from the back as my thoughts continued to whirl. (Had Theo's mom, Grace, from whom he'd inherited his chatty ways, begun to worry when I didn't respond to her litany of texts as quickly as usual? Had she called our local police to inquire if they'd found her daughter-in-law "dead in a ditch" somewhere?) I threw a bottle of water and some energy bars into each bag, too, snagging them from the earthquake kit we kept in the van, per City of Straussville guidelines. As I divvied up the emergency cash I kept in the glove compartment and added it to the bags, I got especially worked up about my phone situation, and in particular the damn unpaid bill. Plus, I was pissed at how utterly dependent I'd become—all of us had become—on these slim bars of glass and silicon and who knew what else.

When I'd assembled four monster-care bags, I folded them down and wedged them under the twins' huge and very dirty double-stroller, in the back of the van. Then I scrambled into the driver's seat and took off for the medical center, trying my damnedest not to speed.

2.3 WEDNESDAY, 1:00 P.M.

It was already five minutes past my appointment time when I pulled into the parking garage. The man in the booth opened his glass window and for some reason, looked at my van and me as if he were appalled.

"Uh, yeah. I know you want everybody to use that new parking app," I said in a rush, holding out a ten-dollar bill. "But can I pay you in cash, please? Real quick?"

"Ma'am," he said, swinging his elbow over the side of the booth. His expression changed from horror to something more like condescension as he took off his wool beanie and scratched at his wiry, salt-and-pepper hair. "You gotta—"

"I lost my phone, OK? And, yeah, I know there's a big dent in the door, and bird-poop everywhere. I'm way overdue for a wash." Six minutes late now, and counting. I leaned toward him. "Just *please*, sir. Take this and keep the change. Consider it a tip."

His face melted into a smirk as he replied, "Lady, I'm just tryna tell you that your door is wide open. Maybe that's how you lost your phone."

"What?" I whipped around, and saw that he was right. For fuck's sake—I'd driven, what, a mile?—like that? I liked driving with a lot of wind in my hair but still; even I should have noticed the whole side of my vehicle was open to the elements.

"You should prolly close it, before that fancy stroller falls out. Or a kid. Consider *that* a tip," he replied as he snatched the bill from my hand. He was still cackling as I drove down the first ramp into the garage.

The first available spot was on the bottommost level, and by then I was nine minutes late. I sped up the three flights of stairs, two at a time, and down a few corridors while the strap of my bag hopped up and down on my shoulder and my lungs burned, beads of sweat rolling every which way under my blouse. I was still panting when I reached the Family Health suite and got in line to speak to the receptionist, whose desk was also behind a sliding-glass window. When it was my turn, I rattled off a quick hello, my name, and my date of birth.

He stared into his monitor and tapped something out on his keyboard. "It's hospital policy to wait ten minutes after a scheduled start time," he replied in a muffled voice.

"OK?" I said, still out of breath. Thanks to the sprint I'd taken to get there, splinters of pain were shooting up both of my shins, and my lungs continued to smolder.

"OK, so it's fifteen minutes after your scheduled time," he said, snapping his chewing gum and glancing at the wall clock. "Almost."

"OK?" I glanced at the clock, too. It was fourteen minutes past my appointment time, and I was too out of breath to even begin explaining myself.

"Ma'am, per hospital policy, we already gave your appointment to the next patient."

The edges of my vision began to turn white. *Wow, Harry. WOW. How many fails can you have in a single afternoon?* I refocused my eyes, onto my disheveled reflection in the reception window. I thought I looked taller than usual—taller, even, than the poster of a giraffe taped up to the column behind me, where nurses measured the kids who came through.

I was ready to panic—*was I becoming the monster?*—when I bent my head down and remembered the chunky heels I was wearing. Then I had a good laugh at myself: I was *not* turning into the monster, for God's sake. With my chin still on my chest, my hands resting on the ledge of the reception window, my chuckle swelled into a full-throated laugh. I was running low on blood sugar, I realized; without meaning to, I'd skipped both breakfast and lunch. I hadn't eaten since the ancient fruitcake.

"Would you like to reschedule?" the receptionist asked, his tone laced with irritation. "What did you come in for today?"

"I'm having . . . strange episodes."

"Can you be more specific?"

"I see flashes of light. My chest burns. I feel like . . ." My voice trailed off, and I wondered if I tossed out the word *homicidal*, he'd give me back my appointment. What the hell was I going to do if I couldn't see my doctor? "I lose control of myself, OK? Just for a bit."

"You're welcome to take a seat, ma'am. Maybe one of our doctors will have a cancellation."

"Uh," I took a wobbly step backward, then another. I tilted my head back ever so slightly and took in the smell of hamburgers that had started wafting through the room. I suddenly realized how urgently I needed to eat one.

"Ma'am? Do you want to see if an appointment opens up?"

"Uh . . ." Man, those hospital burgers smelled delicious. I don't think I'd never jonesed for protein quite so badly before.

I should have listened to the receptionist, I know; the rational thing to do was wait for the next available appointment. But instead, I leaned over, slipped off my shoes, and left.

I shuffled along the linoleum in my tights, toward the main lobby of the hospital, because that's where the smell of the burgers and other foods was coming from. I eventually found an elevator I could take five floors down to get there, and squeezed in with about ten other people by folding myself down like an umbrella.[12]

The foot traffic in the lobby was even more dense. I looked around the tall and impressive space—with its woody, Northwest décor—and was surprised when the fine hairs pricked up along my neck, arms, and back again, the way they had in front of the news that morning. I stopped and spun around in place. This time, the pimpling that ran across my skin like armor spanned a much bigger area, and the seemingly electrical sensation that came with it was nearly triple the intensity. I scanned the drawn faces in the crowd for one shaded by the brim of a black hat; I searched between mylar balloons for an all-black uniform.

Then a sound kicked on inside my ears—a humming of sorts. When it intensified into a squally buzz that grew painful, too, I dropped my shoes and pressed my palms against the sides of my head as my field of vision

---

12   I was rank, I knew, smelling of the same tangy, earthen odor I'd first noticed when I chatted with Christy the day before.

began to shift and expand, as if I were a human telescope. Suddenly I could make out the finest veins in the granite of a far-off wall, and felt certain I must be hallucinating.

Next I was bombarded on all sides by sounds, smells, and other sensations I couldn't begin to sort through. I felt like I was spinning, first in one direction then the other, whipped back and forth and around again in a way that made me feel not just dizzy but extremely heavy—like that carnival ride that plasters you against the metal sides of its cage before spitting you out again, staggering. My army of fine hairs remained standing, having grown in number, height, and utter certainty that some unknown danger lurked nearby.

I needed to leave that place at once, I knew. I spun around one last time and took a step in the opposite direction without checking if the path was clear, and collided chest to chest—or chest to head, rather—with a petite, white-haired woman in a lab coat.

"OOOF!"

"Oh, my."

My bag went flying, her bag went flying, and we each grabbed a hold of the other to keep from falling. The surprise impact dampened the sensory onslaught I was experiencing, but I still felt panicked and very weird.

"Ma'am, I am so sorry!" I began, still planning to run out of there before my monster emerged. The woman was looking down, adjusting her oversized glasses. "Holy shit!" I cried when she finally looked up at me. *Dr. Morris?*

"Yes, Harry," she replied, as calmly as if we'd just brushed elbows. She had been my gynecologist from the time I was sixteen, through Bret's delivery, and up until I got pregnant with Frankie and Jo. Seeing her caused my hackles to lower, slowly, and the voices and odors receded to the back of my mind, where they kept up a low-grade hum. "And if you want a hug, you can just ask for one. Same goes for tackles."

"Did you see a guy in a black uniform around here?" I asked, wild-eyed.

"No, I'm afraid I was looking at the floor. Deep in thought, per—"

"Wearing a black hat?" I said, motioning around my head. "Like a Stetson?"

She searched my features. "I'm sorry, but I was preoccupied, Harry. Is everything OK?"

"Uh . . ." I said, letting go of her arms. "I mean, yeah. I'm fine." The crowd had thinned out a bit, so we didn't have to stand in such close quarters. I retrieved her bag, then mine, and when I handed hers over, her colorful acrylic bangles made a familiar, pleasant *clacking* sound, like misfit windchimes. You might think that memories associated with someone who shoves a cold speculum into your vagina would be deeply unpleasant, but Dr. Morris had had a way of making those uncomfortable moments a skosh more tolerable.

"I haven't seen you in ages. How long's it been? Five, six years?" she asked.

"Uh," I stammered again. *Shouldn't I be getting out of here?* "Yeah. Something like that. Five, almost? It's more efficient to do my pap smears at my semiannual physicals, so I haven't had an actual gynecology appointment since Jo and Frankie were born. And they turn four, pretty soon."[13]

"Are you headed to an appointment?"

"No," I replied as I shook myself out. My heart rate felt normal now, and it no longer seemed like I might transform.

"Then what has you loitering in the busiest part of the hospital, if I may ask as an old friend?" she asked in a lower voice. I opened my eyes and saw that she was looking at me quizzically.

"It's a long story, and I really should get back to work," I replied. I looked around for a wall clock, but no sooner had I found one than I closed my eyes and pinched the bridge of my nose, trying to put a lid on the emotions that had surged up in me again. "I was *supposed* to have an appointment with my doctor, but I was late, so they gave it to someone else. And I lost my cell phone the other day, so I had to stop at the store—"

---

13   Upon learning I was pregnant with twins, Theo's insurance insisted I begin seeing a specialist called a perinatologist, in place of an OB/GYN. I needed more oversight compared to when I was pregnant with Bret, according to the medical establishment, because twins and other multiples are a "high-risk" condition.

"Honey?" she said, setting a hand on my wrist.

"But then I couldn't get it—a new phone, I mean—because we haven't paid our cell phone bill in over a month, but I didn't know that—"

"Honey."

"Which is a whole other issue, of course, and then because I'm a total idiot, I drove here with the side door of the van wiiiiide open—"

"HONEY. Honey, honey, *honey!*" She grabbed my other wrist, too. "It's OK. I'm sure you have your reasons. No need to explain yourself. Can you walk with me, for a bit? I have this wonderful new office, and I'm so tickled about it."

I nodded, and she asked, "Where are your shoes?" like it was totally normal that I wasn't wearing any. I saw them a few steps behind me, retrieved them, and put them on. Dr. Morris hooked her arm through mine and I let her lead me along, back into and through the grand lobby, down a couple of stairwells, and through a complex set of turns to a part of the hospital I'd never been in before. As we walked, she chatted lightly about a range of things, and I was glad for the chance to simply listen to her. I looked her way at one point and my mouth fell partly open; her presence was so warm and familiar, it made me want to admit everything to her. *Everything*—monster and all—on the spot. But I clapped my trap shut again, right-quick; I hadn't planned on telling my regular doctor all the gory details of my monster problem, and had yet to weigh the pros and cons of confessing it to anyone.

We'd been underground several minutes when we reached a noticeably grungier section of the hospital, where the paint peeled from the walls and the ceiling tiles drooped precariously.

Dr. Morris clapped me on the back, startling me with her strength; she was a long-time tennis champion, I knew, and I reckoned she still played. "Try not to look so horrified, Harry. There's a lot of stuff under construction down here, and I'm still moving in."

She pulled out her keys as she stopped in front of a nondescript gray door. I was about to joke that I should've been dropping breadcrumbs along the way when I saw a small stickie note at eye level, where someone had dashed out *Sarah R. Morris* in fading blue ink. My hand came up to the tiny pink square, as if of its own accord. Not many passersby, I reckoned as my palm came to rest on it, would know how much weight it held, at least in Dr. Morris's eyes: "Sarah" had been the name of her only child—her daughter, who had been stillborn. "No, it's . . ." I stumbled on my words, determined not to offend. "It's . . . I'm sure it's great."

She unlocked the door and motioned for me to enter. "You know, I still tell people about my unflappable friend Harry, the incredible swimmer. Always so stoic, always ready with a wry comment! But you're going to make me a liar, if you keep wearing all your feelings on your face like that."

We entered and she flicked on the lights to reveal a modest, fluorescent-lit room, windowless and nearly filled to the edges with what I assumed were pieces of equipment and furniture, all of them still shrink- and bubble-wrapped.

"A couple months ago, I convinced the hospital to lease me this space. I'm finally starting up a research project I've always dreamt about," she said as we went through a second door and into a private office. She hung her lab coat on a hook.

"The hospital didn't want to give it to you?" I asked as I collapsed into an upholstered chair, its generous cushions hugging me in all the right ways. There was nothing sterile or clinical here—only a warm and inviting space with a solitary window well, all of it comfortably crowded with framed images, book-laden shelves, assorted memorabilia, and a scattering of unruly plants.

"You might say they were reluctant to give it to me, yes," she replied as she sat in the desk chair and faced me, lacing her fingers together. "I suspect they think I'm past my prime. Way past. But then I received a very large research grant, and money can weasel its way through most anything."

"What it's for?"

"Oh. *Well,*" she began, sitting straighter and taller, as if to honor the significance of her words. "We're going to study a whole range of topics.

Topics that researchers and medical doctors have done too little to investigate in the past. Have you ever heard of fetal microchimerism, for example?"

"Say what, now?" I pursed my lips together, "I mean, I've never even . . . what is it called, again?"

She waved both hands in front of her. "Let's not get into that right now. Let's just say there are things that are unique to the female anatomy—types of cells, for example, biological processes—that are still mysteries, even to us scientists."

"That's me—the final frontier," I said with a laugh. I reached out and turned a small figurine on her desk so that it faced me. It was some kind of animal I hadn't seen before. "Why haven't people studied those things as much?"

"Well, historically, men made the big decisions in scientific research. Who gets public funding and such," she said as she turned to her computer screen and clicked around for a bit. "There are more of us—women I mean—in research these days. But we're all competing for slices of the same pie, and it's a shrinking pie."

I nodded and sat back, having forgotten about the figurine on her desk and what it depicted.

"Those of us who study things that are only found in women are playing catch-up," she added, a rare grace note of dejection in her voice. "Still, it's very exciting to have the opportunity. It's a big deal, and to folks outside of Portland, too. I'm already getting calls for tours, press interviews." Her pride was evident in the great, pink blooms on both her cheeks.

"That's great, Dr. Morris. Congratulations."

"But we're here to talk about you, Harry. Is there anything I can do for you today? Should I open you up? Your medical chart, I mean?" She turned back to her screen and a few clicks later, chin in hand, began scanning what I assume was my medical history.

I breathed in and watched the buttons of my shirt rise, and concentrated on lowering them down again as smoothly as I could. I could see myself confessing everything to Dr. Morris, I realized.

"Remember those supplements I took, back in the day?" I began. "Do those things have any weird side effects?" I asked.

"Honey, you took prenatal vitamins," Dr. Morris replied, pursing her lips. "It makes some people constipated, but not much else. Why?"

"Well, I've been having these . . . I've been having these weird episodes. My chest burns—not like heartburn, but all-over burn—and then I see flashes of white light."

Dr. Morris poked around in my chart while she asked me the usual questions: Had I been having headaches? (Yes, though I suspected dehydration was the cause.) Increased my alcohol consumption? (LOL, no—wine is expensive.) Had I taken any drugs or changed my diet? (No and no. I still subsisted on leftovers, taken cold and surreptitiously from the twins' dinner plates.)

"I see that your thyroid, iron, and other levels were just fine at your last physical," she said, still squeezing her chin in one hand.

"Yay me," I droned, gently turning over a pad of sticky notes on her desk.

"When was your last period? Any chance you could be pregnant?"

An enormous sob came barreling up out of me.

"What is it, Harry? What's wrong?" she asked.

My forehead crashed into my hands as I sucked in another lungful of air, this time with an ugly gasp.

"You aren't quite yourself today, are you?" Her tone surprised me with its softness, as if she wasn't taken aback by my sudden eruption.

"Oh, God, Dr. Morris. If I were pregnant right now, on top of everything else . . ." I let my words peter out to nothing; I didn't want to think about the various terrible ways that sentence might end. Instead I just shook my head, still cupped in my hands.

"So—you are *not* pregnant, then," Dr. Morris continued. "What else can you tell me, Harry?"

I held my breath as I sat up again, doing my best to command any additional sobs to go back down whence they came. When I finally let the air out, in a long and shuddering sigh, I wiped my nose with the back of my hand the way Frankie or Jo would, and saw that Dr. Morris had placed a full-sized Moonstruck milk-chocolate bar on the edge of her desk. I offered her a weak smile, then tore it open and wolfed it all down in a few unladylike bites.

"When I had the first . . . episode," I began with a shaky voice, "which was just the other day, I blacked out—"

"Blacked out?" she interrupted. Her brows furrowed. "What were you doing when that happened?"

"Uh, is this conversation . . . confidential?"

"Yes, dear."

"I was—"

"I'm only obliged to tell the authorities when a patient poses a major public threat."

"Uh, OK." Well, *fuck*. If anything counts as a major public threat, it's a big ape-y bear monster. *SHIT.*

"Please go on."

Shit, shit, shit, FUUUUUUUCK. I couldn't tell Dr. Morris my whole story after all. If I did, she'd have to turn me in to the cops or whoever. My arms and legs started going numb. I wanted to cry, but instead I eked out a small smile and said, "That's pretty much it, I guess."

"That's everything?" she asked, her disbelief plain. She sat up straight and shifted her tone again, as if realizing she'd scared me with her mention of the authorities. "There must be some other symptoms, or details, you can give me. What else has been going on in your life?"

What else could I tell her, if not about the monster? There I was, sitting across from an excellent doctor who knew me well and whom I'd always cared for, and for once in my parental life, I didn't have anywhere else to be right away. I was mildly numb through my whole body by then, a low-level vibration of sorts that matched the sensory input still droning steadily in the back of my mind.

My life had been far from perfect even before the monster showed up, so I figured there had to be ways to take up Dr. Morris's offer of help, without risking arrest. I tried to quell all thoughts of the monster, and instead asked myself: *What, in the simplest terms, do I need right now?*

"Here's the thing, Doc," I blurted out suddenly. "I've been a little bit broken for years."

She nodded, her expression fixed on mine. "And now, you feel like you're falling apart?"

I nodded. "When I had Bret, I felt . . . shaken up. Like a soda bottle. But when I got pregnant with Frankie and Jo, it was like somebody threw me out a window. A really high one."[14]

We were quiet a moment. Then Dr. Morris said, "Remember a while back, when we talked about depression?"

"Yeah. You asked me if I was still able to enjoy the sorts of things I used to enjoy."

"Right. And I asked about any anger you might be feeling."

Startled, I stared at Dr. Morris a few seconds, unblinking. Did she know something? But she was looking down, presumably at the fanciful shapes she was tracing on the desktop with her finger. "Not everyone thinks about anger, when they're wondering if they or someone they love might be depressed. But these things manifest in all sorts of ways," she went on. She stopped her invisible doodling. "Anyway—I digress. Back then, you told me your childhood had given you a lot to talk about with a therapist, but that you didn't have time to see one, and didn't think you were clinically depressed. What about now?"

I gave her an especially tall shrug, and ignored her mention of anger. "Do I still enjoy things? I wouldn't know! I don't do most of the stuff I used

---

14   Whenever somebody asks me how my pregnancies went, I ask them to imagine having an autocrat in their gut. After declaring the place "dry" on day one, they start an ambitious building program. They build all kinds of things, to cement their legacy. The locals aren't crazy about all this new density, and they begin to resist. It's too late, though, because this politician is using their power of eminent domain to take control of major organs, even moving them around for their own ends. Before they can finally be forced from office, they've inflicted major structural damage on your once-spectacular abdominal wall, which you proclaim a historic landmark and remove from daily use.

to, because I don't have time. Gardening, going to book club. Triathlons." I snorted out that last one. "I couldn't do a lot of that stuff even if I had the time, my body is so broken."

She inclined her head at me. "Harry, you're still quite young."

"Really? You think? When I was pregnant with the twins, and Theo's insurance made me see that perinatologist instead of you, he kept referring to me as 'geriatric.' I even saw the word on my medical chart one time, and I was only thirty-five."[15]

She gave me another sympathetic tilt of the head. "I know, honey. The obstetrics profession could do a better job with its terminology. And so many other things, really."

I blinked back tears, shook by Dr. Morris's display of sympathy, and by the benefit of the doubt she offered me. "Either that, or woman-years are basically like dog-years. Like, we get seven years older for every one year a man gets? Is that how it works?"

She laughed, absently rearranging some of the items on her desk. "I know we're guilty of infantilizing the women we care for. We tell you what you need, what you must do. And at the same time, we treat you like you're . . ." She looked at the ceiling, trying to find the right words there. "Like you're nearly decrepit. As if women are immature and yet on the verge of expiring, all at the same time."

"Yeah. Kind of like avocados."

"See? There's the old Harry I remember."

"I dunno, Dr. Morris. Avocados are great and all, but I feel like . . ." I stopped, then waved my hands around with my eyes closed, looking for the right words. "My brain is so clogged up with mom-shit, all the time, that I think of myself more like . . . I think moms are more like *toilets*."

Dr. Morris gave a sad little laugh. "Please don't say that, Harriet. You are *not* a toilet."

---

15   The "geriatric" thing didn't bother me nearly as much as having to go through this different, scarier, and—according to our insurance company—more "dangerous" pregnancy without Dr. Morris by my side. I didn't complain at the time. I was too shocked. I just nodded and followed instructions.

"You're right," I replied. "We're more like septic tanks."

We were chuckling at all this, but saying how crappy (har!) I felt, out loud and without censoring myself, was both liberating and distressing. As I pushed at my unshed tears with a balled-up tissue, and our amusement ebbed away, my chest flared in the ominous way that had become familiar to me by then.

Holy shit. I gripped the armrests and tried to tamp the monster back down, before she could show herself. The humming started up again in my ears. *What the hell? Now I don't have to be mad—or at least not explosively mad—to turn into a monster?* Dr. Morris was looking at me quizzically.

"Um. Yeah, we're like septic tanks. Moms are buried." Speaking was suddenly a bit of a struggle. Parts of my hands and arms felt like they might explode, so I squeezed the armrests even harder.

"Harriet?" she asked, her voice tighter than before. "Is there anything else going on you'd like to tell me about?"

"Second of all," I went on, ignoring her question. I had to, if I had any hope of remaining calm—and remaining Harriet. I wondered, briefly, if there was a therapy pool somewhere nearby, in the event I needed to dunk myself. Also, was my earlier numbness related to transforming? "Second of all, moms are taken for granted. We take care of thousands of crappy little tasks our spouses and kids barely think about."

"That's usually the case," she replied. She got up and walked around her desk, looking for something. "Harry, how are things with Theo?"

That I *definitely* didn't want to answer. My eyes were still closed, but I thought I sensed her next to me, so I cracked one open. She was standing right there, peering down at me. "And here's the kicker, Doc," I went on as she pulled a spray bottle from behind some vines on one of her shelves. "If we moms suddenly stopped functioning, our whole community would go to shit."

"Yes, Harry. Although let's remember—we could say those things about a lot of groups," she replied, spraying the waxy leaves of a nearby plant. Some of the mist hit my face, and I squinted both eyes again. "Immigrants. People of color. Those who are transgender."

"I agree," I replied, relaxing a little. "A lot of people get dumped on. They need our attention, too."

"The elderly."

"Asylum seekers."

"The infirm."

"We could go on for a while."

"Do you need a cup of water, dear? You look like you could use some water."

She took a cup down from a cabinet and went out to her main room again, then came back with it filled to the brim with water. Before she could hand it to me, however, she stumbled; I swung my knees to the side, having seen it coming, so only a small amount spilled onto my lap. Still, my features went all knotty, as I'd been hit with a peculiar revelation: Dr. Morris had been winning her age bracket in tennis tournaments for decades. She did not drop balls; this was well-known. I assume it meant she didn't often drop cups of water, either.

My heart rate accelerated a bit. Was it possible she'd spritzed and spilled on me intentionally, because she somehow knew about my condition? Or was I losing my whole damn mind?

"I have to go to a meeting now, Harry," she said, glancing at her clock, her features pinched. Was she having uncomfortable thoughts, too, behind her somber expression? Dear God, was she devising a way to turn me in? My heart rate went up even further. "But this is obviously something we need to keep exploring. I have to insist on putting you in my schedule for a real appointment, at the next opening. And until then, you must do your very best to—*look at me, dear*—to minimize the things that are upsetting you."

"Upsetting me how?"

"The things that are causing you stress. Things that . . . elevate your emotions."

I threw her a quick side-eye, despite being on edge at the thought of her turning me over to the authorities. "Doc, if I knew how to get rid of stress, I would have done it a long time ago. Also, I'd be rich."

"You're not listening to me, Harriet." She reached up and put her hands on my shoulders. "You're going to come back and see me, very soon. And in the meantime, *don't* indulge your anger."

"I never said I was angry. Plus, all the parenting books say it's unhealthy to bottle up emotions—"

"I'm not asking you to bottle it up for the rest of your life, Harry. I just want you to avoid, for now, anything that triggers big emotions for you, OK? *All* big emotions: anger, frustration. Even guilt and embarrassment."

I nodded. I was quite calm by then, actually; all of the monster-related symptoms I'd been fighting moments earlier were gone. I wasn't sure if that was because of the water, or if my own efforts to calm myself had fended off the transformation.

"You can *do* this, Harry."

I sighed. "Fine. I'll get rid of upsetting things. I'll call the kids' school and tell them to stop sending me snippy notes in their lunch boxes—doctor's orders. And I guess I'll have to put my broken refrigerator on the curb. Because there's no talking to it, I've tried."

"I hope you're taking me seriously."

I cocked my head at her, a current of something different running through me. "Of course I do, Dr. Morris!" The words came out almost in a whisper, as if her suggestion had shamed me. "Jeez, if there's one thing you can count on me for, it's to hear you, and believe you."

She smiled and went to lift her lab coat from its hook. I put my purse on my shoulder, and we turned for the door to the corridor.

"You know what that makes me realize, Doc?" I continued. "There is one thing that separates moms from all those other groups we were talking about—the ones getting shit on in life."

"What's that, dear?"

"Everyone claims to love moms, right? We get a lot of lip service, from all sides of the political spectrum. We're up there with baseball and apple pie."

"Indeed. Put on a pedestal, as they say. And?"

"And yet nobody listens to us when we say we need something."

She nodded. "Moms and veterans, I suppose."

"Like, when I tell people about my difficulties during my pregnancy with the twins, and they say, 'Oh, it couldn't have been that bad.' As if I'm remembering nine months of my own life wrong. It's like telling somebody you have a toothache, and their response is, 'That can't be right. I don't have teeth but if I did, I'd be better at having them than you are.'"

"Like I was saying earlier, we infantilize you."

"But people *believe* infants when they have toothaches. We give them teething rings and whatnot. And ice. There's a whole industry for it."

"Well, infants have a way of screeching about it."

Back in the lobby, I promised her I'd check diligently for her email with an appointment time. We said our goodbyes over multiple hugs. As I took the shortcut to the garage she'd told me about, I felt better—more optimistic, and safer, in a way—than when I'd come in.

But as I got into the van and took my place in the long line of cars waiting to exit into the waning late-afternoon light, that optimism began to wriggle from my grasp. Like clockwork, my brain defaulted to its usual behind-the-wheel ritual: *What should I worry about first?* The obvious answer was the possibility that Dr. Morris knew I was the monster. Still, I sifted my fingers through my hair and tried to focus on remembering—and by "remembering," I mean "stressing about"—the kids' upcoming appointments, classes, clubs, and so on. I was responsible, after all, not only for the havoc the monster might cause, but also for any that occurred in my household if I forgot to pick up someone's medicine or whatever.

Still, daily chores were no match for the terror I felt when I imagined being found out as the monster's alter ego—and then ripped away from everyone and everything I loved. Or for my dozens of questions. For example: Why I hadn't I gone full beast-mode in Dr. Morris's office? Was I gaining some control over the monster, or at least the emotions that set her loose? I pulled up a car-length, then waited some more. As my attention jumped from topic to topic, in the 24-7 mosh pit my brain had become, a maroon Subaru entered the garage and pulled up next to me. The window went down, and when I saw that it was Ellen Stout, I sat upright and waved.

"Hello, there!" she called out, her trademark smile flooding me with a surge of happy emotions. It was our first in-person encounter since the PTA meeting, and while she had every right to call me out for failing to support her that night, it didn't surprise me when she greeted me as if the incident hadn't happened. I made a mental note to find another time to address it with her, to ramp up my efforts to figure out who those men-in-black were, and what Mr. Terrence had to do with them.

"Hey, Dr. Stout! How's it going? What are you doing here?" I asked before remembering she was entering a medical center and that was an intrusive question. I closed my eyes and added, "I mean—not that it's any of my business, I'm just . . . it's just good to see you. Sorry—I didn't mean to be rude."

She laughed. "That's OK, Harry. I'm headed to a meeting, actually. No biggie. And please call me Ellen."

I nodded, then slumped my face into the hand propped up on the door. "I just realized, all the conversations I've had with my friends lately have been just like this one—out the window of my car, with the engine still running. That's so sad."

"I have those, too. Trey and Brandon call them my drive-thru friendships." She looked down, and gave one of her little huffs of laughter again. "I told them they'd be a lot more satisfying if they came with fries."

I laughed aloud, but Ellen's face turned serious. "Oh, wait," she continued, waving a hand as if to erase something she'd thrown into the air. "I didn't mean that talking to you isn't satisfying, Harry."

"It's totally OK," I replied, still smiling. "It's funny!"

"Yelch," she said with a look of disgust, presumably directed at herself. "I shouldn't have said that."

"Are you kidding? I wish I'd thought of it myself." I glanced ahead. The car in front of me hadn't budged, but there was no one in front of Ellen. "I should let you go," I said.

"I should probably keep moving. But I'll chat with you over email."

I gave her a wave and a pressed smile, and she pulled off. Drive-thru conversations were unsatisfying, yes; still, I felt a noticeable lift after our brief exchange.

The garage finally burped me out, and as I pulled onto the road, I thought about how Dr. Morris had been so adamant that I keep my "big emotions" in check until we could meet again. She'd seemed very concerned about my mental state. Did that prove she knew I was the monster? Or just that she was a good doctor, and a good human?

2.4   WEDNESDAY 8:30 P.M.

The second email from *leahvivianmorton* arrived later that day. I was sitting at the family computer, tackling my to-do list while Theo washed the pots and pans from dinner. This time, Mom's message contained a link to a news story about "rogue waves" along the Oregon coast, and that's it. There was no signature and no comment; not even an errant keystroke graced all of that leftover blank space. I deleted the message, just like the first, and got back to my list.

That might seem cold-blooded, I know. But I think we've established that my attention span around that time was like a fruit pie that had already been sliced among too many takers—mangled beyond recognition. Besides, Mom had never made it a secret that she didn't want me to see her as an example or an authority figure, and I'd accepted that a long time ago. It was unusual that she was suddenly initiating contact, sure, but these random communiques piqued neither my interest nor my emotion all that much.

I took a sip of my cherished, semiweekly glass of Trader Joe's pinot noir[16] and looked up some movie times that I could send to Ellen for our get-together. When I didn't find any theaters around Straussville with showings that worked for me, I gave up and replied to a message from the volleyball coaches instead, asking them how many parents had signed up to chaperone a weekend tournament in Seattle that was coming up. Then I giggled my way through Sooby's third ALL-CAPS email of the day. In this one, she lovingly informed me she'd signed me up as a chaperone for the Homecoming dance. She ended with:

And FFS, Harry. Get a new phone!!!!!

I replied:

I'm working on it. Any more from Mr. Terrence re: his behavior, and those goons, at PTA?

I started to move on to my next thing, but a fresh reply from Sooby appeared in my inbox within seconds:

PHONE, HARRY. PHONE. If you're not text-able by the end of the week, I'm gonna sign you up for all ten PTA subcommittees [smiley-emoji, winking-emoji]. OH, and Mr. T didn't have anything to do with those "goons." He doesn't know anyone who wears a uniform like that. Drew a blank when I asked him.

---

16   See how I noted the cheap-ass brand of wine I was drinking? And that it was only one glass, and that I was grateful for it? Women feel the need to state things like this all the time, because we're used to having to preempt the inevitable criticisms that come at us when we admit to doing something for our own enjoyment: *Maybe if you didn't drink, you wino, you'd be able to afford that new fridge by now.* And so on. Because it only takes one instance of being wrong about something for a lot of men to completely dismiss everything else we say.

Her automatic faith in Mr. Terrence bothered me. I knew for certain I'd seen him and the guy in black exchange nods. I took a few minutes and considered how to reply, but it was a complicated thing to tackle in writing. I eventually sent the following:

> *Are you going to the boys' soccer game tomorrow afternoon? It's part of Homecoming, and I'm going to suggest to Ellen that we meet there since her son Brandon will be playing. Talk more there?*

I wanted to end it with some kind of jokey threat of my own, but Sooby was a hard person to threaten, or embarrass. I had scrapbooks full of photographs documenting every middle-school slumber party we'd been to. But she'd put many of them on social media herself, along with ample documentation of Satchel's home waterbirth.

Again, her response came quickly:

> *Aren't you the one who says we ought to take people at their word, Harry? It's a nothing-burger, dude. We need to move on and focus on fixing the schoolyard!!!!!*

I grabbed the receiver for our house phone and dialed her cell number. It went to voicemail, so I hung up and jotted off another reply:

> *I eat nothing-burgers for breakfast, Soob. [smiley-emoji, winking-emoji, devil-emoji]. And even if he doesn't know the guy in the uniform, talking to Ellen that way was totally out of line.*

Immediately after sending it, I closed my email. I wasn't looking forward to her response. There were a couple of matters Sooby and I studiously avoided talking about over the years. We loved each other like hell—there was no doubt about that. But even between besties, once you bury an unresolved issue, any new arguments take place on less-than-solid terrain.

I glanced over at Theo's back. He was still scrubbing dishpans over the sink, quiet and pensive. The happiness that had bubbled up in him that morning over the antics of our neighbor seemed to be all tapped out. I didn't begrudge him his feelings; like I'd told Dr. Morris, all the parenting books emphasized how important it was to acknowledge that stuff. But when were he and I supposed to discuss the gazillion little things we needed to discuss—the unpaid phone bill, for starters? I decided to wait a bit longer to speak up, and instead opened the refrigerator door and sorted through all the condiments, pulling out ones that had expired. Which was a lot. As usual, we had an obscene collection of pickles, because Theo always came home with pickles when he went to the store, no matter how many we already had.

"Hey," I said, breaking our long silence. "One day, we should throw a big anniversary party for ourselves in the backyard. Get all your relatives to come up for it."

Water continued to gush from the faucet as he scoured a frying pan like it was a car seat with some kind of unexplained blood stain.

"Everyone who gets married should recite new vows at some point. Don't you think? 'Cause after you've been with somebody a while you can get, like, really specific."

Still nothing. So I kept babbling, sorting jars, and enjoying my Two-Buck Chuck.

"*I, Harriet, still take thee, Theo, as well as all your dills and gherkins, your spears and butter chips . . .*"

"Brian's leaving Christy," he suddenly blurted out.

I choked on my wine. "*What?*" I hoped I'd misheard him.

"Brian told me he's getting separated," he said a bit louder, over the rushing water.

I waited to see if he would turn off the faucet so we could hear each other. When he didn't, I went over and stood next to him.

"What did he say?" I collapsed a little against the counter and my free hand shot up to my forehead. "What *happened?*"

Theo shrugged and scrubbed some more, then let out a hefty sigh. "Apparently, they've been having some issues for a while."

Brian and Theo had lived together during our senior year of college, having met in the athlete's locker room, where Brian was waiting for physical therapy for a lacrosse injury. They'd stayed in touch after graduation, mainly so they'd have a workout buddy every now and then. He'd met and married Christy several years later. She and I'd gotten to know each other through book club and PTA and whatnot, and they were among our closest couples-friends. This was sad news for both of us, and tears welled up behind my eyes. "Can you turn off the water and come sit with me, so we can talk about this?"

We sat on the couch, a cushion apart, both of us rubbing our faces in different ways. "Wow. I'm just thinking how long it's been since we hung out with them."

Theo let out a quick, humorless laugh. "Yeah, I can't even remember the last time. Not without all the kids, anyway."

"Did the two of you hang out recently? When did he tell you?"

"He texted me that he wanted to talk, so I called." He went silent for several seconds, then added, "A few days ago."

I stoppered the disappointment that welled in my throat. *Shouldn't he have told me right away?* Then again, I hadn't told him that I sometimes turned into a big apey-bear monster. Sooooo—even steven, I guess?

"What else did he tell you?"

"You can't tell anyone this part," he said, reaching out and squeezing my thigh. He held onto it and I practically moaned, it felt so good.

"I won't."

"He said he's been taking medicine for depression, and that Christy takes something, too. I didn't ask for details. But apparently, he left a couple pills sitting out one day, and Zach got them."

I slapped both hands over my mouth. Zach was their young son. "*When? What happened?*" I asked after letting my hands fall to my lap.

"A while ago, I guess. They took him to the ER, and they did the whole stomach-pump thing. Nothing terrible came of it, but I guess Christy freaked out—"

"Wait, wait—hang on. What do you mean, 'freaked out'? Like, what specific actions were taken?"

"You know Christy. She's always been a bit . . . overbearing."

I bit my tongue—again. That is not how I would describe Christy. She'd seemed agitated when I saw her during her run, but 'overbearing'? Christy Holmes? Never. "Just to confirm—this is *not* the Bryan and Kristi from 'TnT,' that twins and triplets support group? The ones always sending those emails marked 'urgent,' practically demanding that we join them and pay their enormous dues?"

He gave me an incredulous look.

I threw up my hands. "Well, I don't know! The Christy Holmes I know holds herself to a really high standard, yeah. She's got a lot on her plate, and she gets it all done and done well. But I've never thought of her as 'overbearing'." What did he even mean by that?

"You don't think she's used to people giving her what she wants? That she expects people to 'fall in line,' as Brian put it?"

"What? *No!*" I replied, shaking my head to further emphasize how enormous a "no" this "no" was. "What are people giving her? Like, her way in an argument? Or are you talking about her awards, and magazine covers? Either way, that's just not true, Theo. Christy works really, really hard. She puts in the time and effort and then some."

I suspected the subtext of Theo's question was that Christy owed some portion of her success to the fact that she was beautiful, and that the people who doled out awards and honors in medicine and so many other fields were often straight men who saw women for their physical attributes above all else.

"All I know is, Brian says she hasn't been able to get past the pill thing."

"Meaning, she doesn't trust him with the kids anymore?"

"She insists they do everything her way, he says. And she's pissed off, twenty-four seven."

Hmm. Interesting. Recalling Dr. Morris's comments about depression and anger, I said, "Well—hear me out. Maybe since she's been struggling with depression, too, maybe it's not Brian she's really angry at. Maybe she's just . . . angry in general. And it gets projected onto Brian."

He shrugged and took his hand off my thigh, leaving me unmoored. I might have even whimpered. "You'd have to ask her therapist, I guess."

We both stared into the empty fireplace, blackened with decades of soot. I tried not to let my brain turn the mundane sight into a symbol of what we were talking about, but failed. The windows on either side of the hearth were open a few inches, and the breeze fluttered our old, too-short curtains. "Is there any chance they'll just separate for a bit?"

"I don't know. It didn't sound like it."

"Whose idea was it?"

"His, I think. Oh—by the way, the preschool wrote us another note. What did you put in the twins' lunches today?"

"Graham crackers," I replied, then slapped my forehead. "*Shit!* That reminds me. I forgot to stop at the store. *Again.* Fuuuuuuuuuuuuuck!"

"Just get something delivered!"

"It's too late to get something delivered, T. Plus, with the fees and a decent tip, it costs ten extra bucks, minimum. And I *hate* throwing money at stupid stuff like this."

He laughed weakly. "You know what? Screw 'em. Who cares if they don't like the stuff we put in their lunches? It's good enough for us."

"Yeah, but it confuses Frankie and Jo when their teacher takes their food."

He scoffed and shook his head. "Remind me again why we send them to that place? One month of tuition costs as much as a semester at UWV, at least in our day."

"They're going to start charging us, too, for whatever non-GMO, gluten-free stuff they start giving the kids when our lunches don't pass muster." I put my face in my hands. "Uggghhh. This stuff is really killing me, Theo."

I heard a peripheral chuckle. I waited for him to massage my shoulder, or crack a joke about what punishment awaited us if we accidentally sent a kid to school with a piece of single-use plastic in their lunch.[17]

---

17   A public caning, probaby.

When Theo didn't reply, I looked up. "What is it?" I asked. "What's funny?"

"Nothing." After a pause he added, "It's hard on me, too, you know."

"I agree, babe. I didn't say otherwise."

"But I don't think you appreciate, Harry," he said sitting up a little, the couch groaning in complaint as he pushed up the sleeves of his button-down shirt, "just how much I have to deal with."

"OK," I replied, determined to listen. *At least he's talking!* "Tell me, then."

"I worry all the time that I'm not making enough money, or that I'll get laid off."

"I know you do, babe. And that's a lot of pressure," I said softly, rubbing his back in sweeping circles. "Plus, you manage people at work, and—"

"And if I couldn't find another job, then we'd *really* struggle with money. And I don't think I could go through it again, Harry. I can't go through what we went through when the twins were born."

I nodded again, recalling what a rough time we'd had. We were lucky that I could take leave from work, but only a fraction of it was paid. Money became scarce and we accrued considerable debt. I put my arms around Theo and squeezed hard. "We'd figure something out, babe. We'd have to tighten our belts again, but at least we wouldn't be totally isolated like we were back then."

His eyes stretched tall. *"Yeah."*

On top of the financial strain, Theo and I had become near-recluses in our own home[18] as we cared for two underweight preemies[19] almost

---

18   We hung heavy drapes in every room, because anyone in our situation, I guaran-Goddamn-tee you, does everything possible to help their babies—one colicky and one with acid reflux, among other ailments—sleep even the tiniest bit better and longer.

19   They needed to be fed every three hours for a few months, then every four hours for a couple months, and so on. They stumped multiple lactation experts with their refusal to "latch," so I latched myself to a hospital-grade breast pump we rented for $75/month, causing the skin on my hands to crack and peel open because its many parts needed washing so frequently. I also bought breastmilk from another mom, and added a bit of powdered formula to that. All day every day, for months, we focused on them gaining enough weight to stay alive.

entirely on our own[20] for the better part of a year.[21] Not sleeping more than three or four hours at a time, for months on end? Not leaving your home or spending time with friends? Living every day with the sound of babies crying incessantly? Sleep deprivation plus confinement and isolation plus relentless, loud, jarring aural input in a small, enclosed space: These are some of the same tactics that, when taken to extremes, are used to torture people.[22]

I don't mention this because I think Theo and I are special,[23] but because I know we're not. Lots of babies are born prematurely, and it shouldn't be a newsflash that providing twenty-four-hour care to someone who can't care for themselves is hard work, and highly stressful, and isolating.

Like all kiddos, ours grew out of their diapers, and things got easier. But as with all parents, some of that shit stayed with us, and with our marriage. I got stretch marks from pregnancy and a long, raised scar from my C-section, but neither Theo nor I had any visible marks from the postnatal strain we'd endured. It changed us, though. All that pressure has to go someplace; my scientific aspirations may have fizzled out in high school, but I'm pretty sure that's a law of nature or something.

"I would just . . . I dunno," he began again. "If I lost my job it'd make me . . . I don't know, feel ashamed, I guess."

---

20   If you're sitting there thinking, "Why didn't they get their older kid to help?"—Bret was at volleyball camp for the first six weeks. Plus, at eleven, she didn't have any babysitting skills yet, and certainly not with preemies. Also, my mother-in-law would've been brilliant, but Theo's dad was going through intensive chemo at the time. We were too . . . I dunno what—shy? Ashamed? Proud? American?—to ask for help from anyone else.

21   Theo used up his paternity leave while the twins were still in the NICU, so his days were spent at work. After eleven months away from my own office, I went back because I was at risk of losing my position—and because we couldn't keep living on 50 percent of the income we'd earned before.

22   Does it make you uncomfortable that I'm comparing pregnancy, labor, and taking care of infants with torture? People sometimes think I'm being hyperbolic when I tell them how hard pregnancy was for me. "They're just *babies*," they say. "People have been having babies for millennia." But you know what else women have been doing for millennia? Dying. Dying from having babies.

23   I feel like I have to explain every last detail to you, lest you read this stuff and deem me overdramatic. It's so freaking exhausting, staying above criticism.

"No one would shame you, babe. Our friends would rally around you, and stand by you till you got back on your feet."

I should have stopped talking at that point and just hugged him in silence. But for some reason I added, "I wish I could say the same for moms."

He leaned back, breaking our embrace. "What the hell, Harry? I have stuff to worry about, and so do you. Period."

I pulled my arms into my lap, feeling like a misbehaving child. Why couldn't I let him have his feelings? Why couldn't I just *shut the hell up*? We were quiet maybe ten seconds. Then I continued to not shut the hell up.

"Do you remember the time when I spoke up at that one PTA meeting, when Bret was in middle school? I went up to the mic for the first time, and said that the drop-off lane had gotten dangerous on account of the construction on the front sidewalk. Remember that? It's literally the only time I've ever spoken there."

"Yeah. And?"

"And the next day, the editorial board of the *Straussville Ledger* published a piece complaining about the 'mommy brigade'—which isn't a real thing, by the way, I've Googled it several times—and how this nonexistent 'mommy brigade' was threatening to derail important infrastructure projects, with their 'overblown' and 'personal' concerns, quote, unquote?"

"People are always going to be assholes, Harry. But it's not the Olympics. There's no medal for shittiest situation."

I harrumphed, and for the first time, thought I could feel the monster rustling inside me somehow. But I forged on: "Tell that to Dianne. She let her oldest daughter walk the new baby to CVS for bread, because her fiancée Kendra can't drive and Dianne was at work. Somebody called the police on them, so she's got a record now. I feel like she deserves a medal of some kind, at the very least."

He pressed his fingertips into his temples, which in my two decades of knowing him had always been a sign that he was done talking.

"I wonder if she has a mugshot," I mused. "It's probably great. She's so photogenic."

"I can't talk anymore right now."

"*Theo!*" I was irritated by then, my heart pumping harder. He and I had avoided subjects like this for a very long time, because neither of us wanted to spend what little time and energy we had left at the end of the day arguing about stuff that seemed intractable and unsolvable.

Also, these things often made me feel ungrateful as *fuck.* Mind you, I knew that all the household stuff I did was weighty, in both a physical and mental sense. But whenever I thought about broaching the topic of our unequal burdens with Theo, certain musty voices from my childhood began clearing their throats and lobbying for me to keep my trap shut. The *Little House on the Prairie* books I'd borrowed from the library, for example. Also, *Sunrise on the Willamette,* the gossipy news and talk show I'd watched every morning before school like it was my religion. Turns out that the stolid pioneers of yesteryear and our region's most vivacious talk show hosts agreed on at least one thing: *Women who don't bear their burdens quietly ain't right!* Where men have a Y chromosome, we have extra loads of laundry + perennial dish-duty + incessant carpool-driving + more missed work when the kids are sick. *Our domesticity is innate,* they told me. To try and change it would be preposterous! And also, petty!

Still, on that night with Theo, my damn lips just wouldn't stop flapping. "Theo, a minute ago I acknowledged how stressful it is for you to be the bigger breadwinner in the family. Can you acknowledge, please, that parenting stresses me out in different ways? And that some of those ways . . ." I searched for the right words. Why do things as fundamental as parenting and marriage turn out to be so fucking complicated to talk about? "Can you please just believe me, when I tell you my problems have serious consequences, too? Painful ones?"

"I need to be done talking right now," he said again, still rubbing his temples.

This is when I knew that the monster wanted to come out. The longer Theo refused to hear me—refused to believe me, really—the more insistent she became under my skin.

I let my head fall back and gave our ceiling a glare it didn't deserve. But a split-second later, I yanked it up again. "That's another thing: Moms can't complain. Not about the crap we have to deal with. We can't whine—even though everyone else sure as hell does—or claim that anything is skewed harder on us. We're just supposed to take it. 'Like a man,' I suppose. Which is ironic."

I got up and headed for the door, but after I opened it I turned around again, still boiling mad. "What if it had been Christy who left her pills where Zach could grab them? Hmm? Do you think those ER doctors would've cut her a break? Or do you think they'd have gotten on the phone with her licensing board, before you could say *double standard*?" Then I stepped outside and shut the door gingerly behind me, because even when I was pissed to the high-heavens, I still remembered not to make too much noise lest I disturb my precious children from their precious-ass rest.

I marched to my car and grabbed three of the Best Buy bags I'd packed earlier. I'd managed to avoid turning into the monster that afternoon—and again on the couch with Theo—but I knew I had to be fully prepared for the possibility.

Standing and shaking at the foot of our driveway, my monster-care bags in hand, I considered how I might calm all the fury coursing through my veins. Where is all that stuff supposed to go, after a heated conversation? I didn't feel like I could wander too far from home and my responsibilities, so a brisk walk around the neighborhood would have to do the trick.

I made my way down one street, then another, under a moonless sky. I didn't need the extra light, however; I was noticing I could see more things more clearly than before this whole monster thing started. All of my senses had . . . improved, I guess. I could feel, under my feet, the rush of cars on the freeway a half mile off; I could hear the running of a sink from a home with the kitchen window cracked open. These were part of the relentless hum that seemed to be settling, gradually, into my psyche.

It was still a puzzle, however, why some sensations evoked a big response in me and others didn't. A sound could startle me, like the screech of a housecat defending its territory a few blocks off. But nothing on that walk raised the hairs on my body—my bristles, my hackles—the way something had in the hospital, twice, and on the TV news earlier in the day. I didn't know if those instances had anything to do with the guys in the black uniforms and the Stetsons, but my gut told me they did.

I was nearing the edge of our neighborhood when a flutter of something made its way up my back, and an unfamiliar voice spoke up from that same part of my brain—that primal lobe that had cracked itself open, the night at the statue. (Mind you, I am making a metaphor here; I'd had a crazy couple of days, but I wasn't literally hearing voices.) It said:

You don't have to keep her inside, Harriet.

I stopped walking.

"The *hell* is wrong with you?" I whispered aloud to myself, my breath visible in the chilly air. Just hours earlier, I'd been relieved by signs that I was learning to control the monster and since then, I'd been less fearful that I'd accidentally cause chaos, destroy things, or—God forbid—hurt somebody. And now I was thinking of turning her loose? On *purpose*?

I started walking again, toward an intersection where I could turn back in the direction of our house. But then I felt the flutter again. It didn't seem to be in my spine; it was traveling through me in a way I couldn't pinpoint, as if I'd grown some new part of my nervous system the past few days, or maybe tapped into one I hadn't been aware of having. "Get control of yourself, Harriet," I mumbled.

You could practice controlling her, Harriet.

I broke into a run. Toward home. I figured if I could make it back to our house, back to the familiar sights and comforts of my life, I would return to my goddammed senses. I'd see and smell and hug everything I valued—my husband, kids, and dog—and everything else that could be taken away from me the moment I got myself into monster-type trouble. I just needed to get home again, right away. Besides, jogging was probably a lot more effective than walking when it came to squeezing all that adrenaline out of my system. "Jesus! This is not a game!" I grumbled under my breath. And just in case any more rogue voices with terrible ideas decided to chime in before I got home, I started singing to myself, the same tune I'd sung to Frankie and Jo earlier that night, while tucking them in:

Home, home on the range
Where the deer and the antelope play . . .

You should let her *out to play, Harriet.*
I skidded to a stop. "OK. FINE. *FUCK!*"

I had to face it: Part of me desperately wanted to be huge and strong and toothy again. Part of me liked being scary, hairy, and dangerous to know. My glut of adrenaline was fueling that urge, I was sure, but I also couldn't deny anymore how very *done* I was with the way I'd been feeling all these years, in my usual role as human-Harriet.

And what was this "way I'd been feeling," for as long as I'd been a mom? Actually, since adolescence, or maybe since I first understood that I was a girl? I couldn't quite name it yet, and I'd obviously failed to explain it to Theo just now. It was a muddy feeling; a quicksand-type feeling. It did not allow me to feel huge and strong.

I remembered how Dr. Morris had stopped me from explaining why I was standing in a shoeless stupor in the hospital lobby, miles away from the stuff on my to-do list. *It's OK,* she'd said. *I believe you. Walk with me. And if you want, tell me more.* How comforting that had been! How uncommon.

My thoughts turned, then, to a slew of other incidents that were not at all uncommon, and not at all comforting: When the owner of the dog that attacked Critter told me I was the problem, not her. When Brian—and Theo!—blamed Christy's "overbearing" nature for their marital problems, though I knew that was a distortion at best. When Mr. Terrence convinced adults and kids alike, for the umpteenth time, that his way was the right way, even though it meant cancelling programs so that we could install the shitty statue his rich buddy had commissioned.

And then there was the fact that I'd become invisible to Theo, or perhaps akin to an annoying roommate he tolerated but took little notice of. Most of the time, when I believed something unfair had happened to me out in the world, I brushed it off and didn't mention it. When I did tell Theo something that didn't sit right with me, he believed me but also sometimes downplayed the incidents: *I bet he didn't mean it that way, he just phrased it badly.* Or, *Some things are not worth getting upset over.* He didn't realize that most of the things he put into that bucket—then set aside, and forgot about—were things that didn't affect him, or at least not very much.

So, yeah. All of that. I was so fucking *done* with all of that. Of being told I was wrong about something when I knew I was right. Of being told I was ungrateful for something I hadn't asked for. Of being told I was fighting unwinnable battles—*small-minded* battles. These were the stubborn headwinds I'd grown accustomed to. They pushed against the words I screamed into them (if only in my head), and roared back their response: *You're mistaken. Your story isn't relevant. You're too sensitive. You're actually lucky. You don't see things clearly. You're naïve. You're irrational. You're hysterical.*

Here's what I knew for certain at that point: My monster was strong. She was power incarnate, and in choosing to keep her bottled up inside, I was choosing weakness. And who in their right mind chooses weakness?

I spun on my heels, away from home, and jogged toward the center of town instead. That night, calming my fears would require more than a strenuous walk. Full-on running wasn't an option—my knees and back couldn't take it, not since I'd carried those bowling balls around in my gut, one or two at a time, for seven and nine months respectively, before expelling them in rough fashion.

But monstering? This, I was realizing, was a new option for me. This was *cardio.* This was *self-care.*

Besides, as a woman, I'm reminded all the time that it's my job to protect myself, wherever I go. And if protection is a reason some people carry guns,

I should be able to bring my monster around. *You want to bear sidearms? I want to bear arms that could crush something with a single blow.*

I could already see the top of Straussville's electrical substation, over the trees.

2.5   WEDNESDAY, 9:30 P.M.

Seriously, the HELL is wrong with you, Harriet?!

I stared at the chain-link fence separating me—Harriet, in human form—from the substation. I'd speed-walked the mile or so there without any want for my jacket. Now, though, after several minutes standing outside the fence, my body wasn't the only thing that had gone cold.

"Sure, Harriet. *Sure,*" I hissed. "You figured out what makes the monster come out. Great job. And you can kinda, sorta keep her inside. *Brav-the-hell-o.*"

I'd gone there intending to create another power outage. I hadn't figured out the details. I just knew that the only reason the monster had remained unseen the night before was because all the lights had gone out. If I wanted to go rampaging around town again, I'd have to make it extra-dark.

I hugged myself, partly to still my shivers and partly because I was ashamed. Power outages put people in danger! A lot of people! Creating one would require an act of vandalism, and I wouldn't be able to look Bret in the eye if I tore up any infrastructure, not after I ratted her out in third-grade as the kid guilty of finding Georgia O'Keefe–type shapes in the cracks of the bathroom stalls then labia-ling them with anatomically correct terms.

I loosened my grip on my Best Buy bag, unrolling the top and then rolling it back up again. I'd stashed the other two under a bush by the high school and at the preschool on the way over. Those two pitstops had reminded me that I was a *mother*, for fuck's sake. I couldn't go raging around town, like a teenager after a big football game! Or like a white dude in an oversized pickup truck, for any reason whatsoever.[24] I needed to demonstrate good citizenship! I had responsibilities that wouldn't be taken care of in the event I got locked up in jail. Or Animal Control.

I left the substation, head hanging, and trudged the rest of the way to Main Street. It felt strange walking around that part of town without Theo. He and I had loved to do that, and not just in Straussville's cute little central district. Whenever we'd had the chance to travel, we walked as many of the town or city streets as we had time for, hand in hand, trying out whatever café or diner struck our fancy, croissant by croissant.

Make no mistake: I was still pissed at the man. But remembering those walks softened that a bit. Perhaps it sounds too simple, or too good to be true, but the walking, talking, wandering approach we'd been prone to, once upon a time, had gone a long way toward keeping us happy. What's more, it was damn cheap and easily done, as hobbies go. When Bret was born during an especially cold winter, however, our walks became less frequent. And then with the difficult second pregnancy, followed by two babies at once, followed by two toddlers with less impulse control than Jerry the dog? Somewhere in there, Theo and I all but abandoned our favorite pastime.

I reached the stretch of Main Street that most people referred to as "downtown." It's only six blocks long, but it's a charmer: An old-style pharmacy and soda fountain joint shared the stretch with a newer wine and cheese store, a gun store, a bank, and a smattering of bars and restaurants. At seven o'clock on a weeknight, many of the establishments were closed.

But some kind of festivity was happening a couple blocks to my left, where a small but dense crowd had gathered on the sidewalk under the strands of white lights someone had strung up between the buildings and a pair of

---

24   Stereotypes suck, don't they? I know. I'll stop slapping you with this one as soon as the world stops referring to double-strollers—a genuine goddamn necessity for any person with more than one baby and/or toddler—as a universal symbol for overprivileged and clueless moms. I won't hold my breath, though.

food trucks in the parking lane. I decided to walk that way, toward the laughter and eager conversation. When I got closer, I saw that the storefront was a campaign office for Olivia Patchett-Parker—the same congressional candidate my mom had emailed me an article about. Before I could turn away, I accidentally made eye contact with a glad-hander in a navy sports coat.

"Hello, there!" he called out. He waved me over with one hand, and held a red Solo cup in the other.

"Hi," I said as my feet turned his way. My manners were on autopilot, yes, but I was also a teensy bit curious about this politician my mom had emailed me about. "What's happening here?"

"Hi, good evening!" he replied, holding out a hand for me to shake. "We're phonebanking for Olivia Patchett-Parker. Do you know her? Here— would you like a beer?" He held out his cup, then turned one leg toward the food trucks behind us. "Don't worry, I haven't had any yet. I'll go grab another one."

"OK, thanks."

He squeezed past some people to the front of the line, where a staffer in a white polo shirt dispensed another beer from the row of kegs in front of the trucks. He walked back to me, his trim haircut firmly in place. "I'm Joe," he said as we touched cups. "I'm Olivia's volunteer coordinator for the Portland area. *Cheers.*"

I told him my name was Jane.

"So, Jane—do you live in our district?"

"I do."

"Then you should come volunteer with us!"

Joe seemed like a genuinely, if somewhat desperately, friendly person, but I couldn't help recoiling at his tone, at the cant of his grin. Or maybe it was the monster who didn't care for him. It was as if my new monster-senses were picking up something my new monster-lobe didn't like, but wasn't able to translate into human yet.

He waved his beer around and said, "We have a good time, as you can probably see."

I glanced at the nearest of the two food trucks, where servers were handing burritos down from the large window on the side. From the other, oversized churros were being passed into outstretched hands. Both trucks said *Patchett-Parker for Congress* on the side.

"Seriously, though," Joe went on when I still hadn't answered. "You should really think about volunteering, Jane. You seem like you'd be good at it."

I glanced down at my nondescript jeans, T-shirt, and cardigan, which had looked almost chic on the hanger at the Rack, but had turned me into a sad sack of juice and bone as soon as I put them on. Haggard middle-class moms, I gathered, were a demographic that Olivia Patchett-Parker was keen to appeal to.

I threw back the last of my beer—which turned out to be a tasty, and rather strong, double IPA—in a few unladylike chugs.

"I don't have any time," I replied, thinking again of the leisurely walks and hand-holding Theo and I had given up. "Maybe if you offered childcare," I said, giving him a jokey wink and pretending to elbow his ribs, "I could get away and phonebank once a week or so."

He only smiled, so I added, "Actually, the high cost of childcare is probably my biggest problem right now. Is that something Olivia Patchett-Parker would do something about, if she got to Washington?" I asked as I grabbed another Solo cup from a passing server.

"You mean *when* she gets to Washington."

"Right, sure." I took a substantial swig from my new beer. I was getting less presentable by the moment. "Seriously, though, Joe: Childcare. Too expensive. Too difficult for parents to jury-rig together. *Go.*"

"Well, Olivia's first priority does concern children, in fact. And she intends to propose a nationwide ban on abortion after the point when a doctor can detect a heartbeat."

I cocked my head at him. "I was asking—"

"It's an issue that's really near and dear to Olivia's heart."

"I understand. I was hoping you could tell me—"

"BILL!" he yelled out suddenly, causing me to flinch and duck. Joe kept calling out and waving over my shoulder. "BILL! HEY THERE, MY

MAN! YOU GOOD? YEAH? OK, WE'LL TALK. OK. GOOD TO SEE YA, BUDDY." Then he brought his eyes back to mine and said, "So, yeah, Olivia would fight passionately for the right to life . . ."

If this conversation had occurred even a few weeks earlier, I might have just wandered off, or if I was feeling bold, replied, *Joe, hey. My question was about childcare. Can we get back to that?*

But taking things in stride hadn't been working for me. Remaining polite in the face of other people's rudeness had gotten me exactly nowhere. Also, I was a bit drunk.

So I made my eyes go crazy-wide at Joe. Then I finished my beer, tossed the cup in a nearby bin, and brought my hands to my cheeks, as if he'd just told me I'd won the political equivalent of the lottery. "Oh my *gosh*, Joe!" I exclaimed, clapping my hands together and smiling as wide as I could, at least while my jaw was hanging open. "Would she *really*? Is that *true*?"

At first, Joe seemed pleased with my enthusiasm. "Uh, yes. Yes, ma'am—the issues of the unborn child are really close to Olivia's heart."

"Joe! *Joe!* That is just wonderful. That solves everything!" I exclaimed, shaking my head as if I were dumbstruck by my incredible good luck. I reached out and clasped one of his hands with both of mine and pumped it up and down.

He was still smiling, though he seemed a little nervous.

"Which reminds me, Joe, do you know what's near and dear to *my* heart?" I asked.

From his hairline all the way down to his collarbone, he started to turn pink.

"Do you know? What's near to my heart?" I asked again. With one hand, I kept a firm grasp on his, while covering my heart with the other. [25]

---

25   My body was considerably weak in most places, but not in my hands and wrists; I'd developed the grip of a champion rock climber, thanks to alternately pushing a heavy stroller and holding Frankie and Jo's hands. As toddlers, they never came across a rusty nail or used condom in the gutter that didn't require their immediate, up-close investigation. And the little punks still ate everything from cottage cheese to buttered noodles with their fingers, leaving all twenty of them about as easy to hang onto as so many baby eels.

He wiped at his forehead with his free hand. "No."

I lowered my hand and pointed to a spot on my midsection. "My uterus," I chirped. "And my ovaries—just here and *here*."

There was a sudden lift of Joe's chin, a nearly imperceptible twitch of his nearly imperceptible lips. He tried to pull his hand from mine but I wouldn't let go.

"Wait, I better double-check that's really an ovary," I continued, pushing three of my fingers into my shirt and then deep into my abdomen. "I can usually find one," I said, pushing around, "because they get sore on certain days. *Ahhhh, yes,* that's the stuff. Right there."

He turned from pink to greenish-white as a look of disgust took over his face. *"Excuse me,"* he whispered through his teeth, *"but I have serious work to do here. And you need to leave."*

I lowered my own voice and pulled him toward me by the wrist. "Wanna feel?" I replied. He tried to yank his hand away, but I had quite a grip, even in Harriet-form. When the tips of his fingers came right up to my abdomen, I added, "If you're lucky, you can feel it releasing an egg. I can, sometimes."

"SECURITY!"

Smiling broadly, I finally let his hand slip through mine. I could tell in my peripheral vision—which had gotten significantly wider, compared to my pre-monstering days—that people were staring at us.

I turned and marched triumphantly through the crowd, which parted for me—I enjoyed that—as I headed toward the opening between the food trucks. "Sooooo near to my heart," I said in a sing-song voice, to no one in particular. "*Connected* to my heart, actually."

"Hey!" a voice called out. "Hey, Frankie's mom! Is that you?"

I turned and saw Flavia, one of Frankie's teachers—the one who'd recently taken his pretzels. She was standing with two other women, each of them holding a paper plate and the sugary-brownish remains of a super-sized churro.

At the sight of her enjoying such an unhealthy food, my hackles went up for real.

"You're Frankie's mom, right?" she asked.

"Uhhhh, no. Sorry." I grumbled, turning away and stepping outside a cone of light from an overhead streetlamp. *No,* I thought. *I am Harriet.*

I walked briskly toward the end of downtown, where the cross streets became smaller and darker, and the pedestrians fewer. I struggled to regulate my breathing as I considered where to go in that part of town where I could remain out of sight. I had a monster inside of me, after all, and was less and less certain she needed to hide away there all the time.

I reached an especially quiet street and turned down it, and after a few blocks reached a bigger road. I followed that for several minutes and was pleased with myself when I got to the entrance of the Madeline R. Hoffman Memorial Golf Course and still hadn't turned into the monster. *Pretty solid proof,* I thought, *that I've got some control over this thing.* As I redoubled my speed, the first notes of "Eye of the Tiger" were already sounding in my mind.

***

When I reached the rough at the first hole, I broke into a sprint and started to let her loose. Within seconds, my sneakers were gone. The bottoms of my feet grew leathery pads—some the size of dinner plates, some as big as manhole covers. My enormous toenails (claws?) sank into the hard-packed fairway and churned up loose dirt behind me, like a combine digging into sponge cake. These beast-feet were made to connect with bare ground—to stabilize and propel, to overtake prey and escape predators.

Once my shirt, pants, bra, and underwear tore apart and fell away from me, nothing impeded the cool night air from scouring my every surface, from deadheading every nerve ending. It welcomed each new cell to life and I tingled all over, ashamed of nothing. I looked up and laughed, gruff and mucousy, even as I realized that driving with all the windows down would no longer have the same power for me.

I slowed down and came to a stop when I reached the cover of trees. I reached over one shoulder but couldn't get to a stubborn itch in the middle of my back, so I plopped on the ground and went at it with the claws on one foot, à la Critter and other dogs and cats everywhere. *Ahhhhhhhh. That's the stuff!* It was so satisfying I could have cried. I stood back up and brushed the needles from the fur on my butt.

Drawing the resinous air into my lungs, I put my hands on my hips, turned around, and considered what to try first. Mr. Rocky Balboa had done a lot of cross-training, I recalled, and I wasn't going to call it quits after one invigorating sprint. I looked up into the thick canopy and squatted slightly, curled my toes into the cool cushion of dirt and needles, then pushed gingerly against the ground. I sailed upward, using only a fraction of the power I'd had coiled up in my massive quads and glutes. With my heart thudding in excitement and fear, I reached the height of the first major branch on a nearby grand fir before descending in a straight line and landing with a mostly muffled *thud*. Right away I crouched low again—my knees at an acute angle this time—and pushed off once more. This time I went a few branches higher, and as I descended in another clean line, my mind flicked through memories of the excruciating pain I'd felt whenever I sat down or stood up after my C-section.[26]

"Hoooooo!" I called out once I was earthbound again, unable to contain my glee. *"Hoo-hoo-hoo!"* I cried again before realizing how stupid it was to make so much noise. I clapped both hands over my mouth and ran circles around a nearby tree instead.

For my next jump, I wanted to launch myself still higher—but also to cover some distance. Aiming for a decent-sized clearing a few dozen yards into the grove, I positioned and repositioned my feet, squatted low again, and pushed off the earth as images of the Hulk played on a loop in my mind.

But this jump wasn't as controlled as anything Hulk's animators ever cooked up; I accidentally put some torque into the thing, and began turning and rolling in what felt like four different dimensions. My muscles seized

---

26   For *weeks* after that surgery, even when Theo had a spare hand to help me on or off the toilet, I paid for every trip to the bathroom with searing pain across my abdomen. It was like I had an old zipper there, and it was failing: Failing to hold together my skin and muscles. I wore a wide, tight band around my waist to stave off the sensation that my guts were about to fall out.

with fear, knowing that unless I righted myself quickly, I could meet the business end of a splintered trunk on the way down.

I windmilled my arms and kicked wildly, and after considerable flailing—and with the benefit of some new monster sense of which way was up and which down—I managed to slow my roll a bit and land, inelegantly, on bent knees and wrists. I breathed deeply with relief and decided to try something tamer.

I walked up to a western red cedar and gave its trunk a light hug. Long, hard points emerged from all my fingertips—to match the ones on my toes—then pierced the thick bark of that centuries-old tree like butter. Pleasurable chills ran from these extremities to deep inside my core, and pretty soon I was scurrying easily up and down the thing, carrying my weight without the slightest strain. I was fast. And it was *fun*.

As I practiced climbing—scurrying up a fat trunk, backtracking a bit, and reversing course again—I realized that while the monster was by no means heedless, she took greater risks than Harry ever did. She was more free-spirited, more freewheeling. I also discovered some sounds the monster could make: I could coo, grunt, hoot, whistle, and even giggle in merriment. I could blurt out "UH-OH" when absolutely necessary.

After a few minutes of trunk-work, I began to feel certain pangs related to my normal life. I thought it must be getting late. As I climbed the last stretch of another red cedar, to the highest point that would bear my weight, I knew I needed to get home. But I sat there a few seconds anyway, then a few minutes more. I wasn't quite ready to leave.

Because unfurled in front of me was the bulk of Straussville, its far border formed by a meandering stretch of the Whisper River that was perfect for tubing on in summer. I could see the graceful spires of the old bridge, and the industrial district on the far shore. When I turned and looked behind me, I could see the flickering lights of Portland.

And within the bark and other fibers of my fragrant tree, among the leaves and branches and up in that rarefied air, a multiverse of birds, rodents, and bugs went about their nightly business. They seemed unbothered by my presence, chirping and screeching as if I were just another animal in their biome. Maybe they knew that this creature—which I took to be supernatural, or at least entirely new to our planet—had always been inside one of those too-soft, too-bald, too-pokey mammals wandering around beneath them. Maybe the squirrels had been waiting for my monster to show herself.

It occurred to me then that I didn't know what I looked like. I raked my claws through my thick, thick fur, watching the dense strands fan out and fall back in place with an iridescence that might've been from the hair itself, or from the skin underneath it, I couldn't tell. Fur covered pretty much all of me, fanning over my shoulders like the iron pauldrons on a medieval knight. I felt around on my skull, realizing I had longish "hair" not unlike my regular human style, which made me happy; I'd had this haircut forever, and I loved it. When I got to my forehead, I felt some disappointment upon finding I had only the slightest bumps there. (I mean, if you're not going to have full-on horns, why have anything there at all? Also, what's a hornless monster to do when she feels stabby?) I dragged the pads of my fingertips across the fuzzy planes of my face. When I got around to drawing a finger along an eyetooth, I was surprised to find it extended a couple inches longer than I'd expected. I stuffed both hands into my mouth and found I had lots of alarmingly sized and shaped teeth, all throughout my jaw, not unlike a hyena. How odd! And fascinating! I took brief stock of the rest of me, down to the leathery bottoms of my feet, tickling myself accidentally, which made me giggle.

That's the other thing I realized that night: I didn't have to stay mad once I'd changed into the monster. The monster could feel delighted, amused, tired, bored, terrified, and presumably a lot of other things, and still be a monster. So far, the only thing that turned me back into Harriet was getting soaked with water. I made several mental notes to keep a close watch on the weather forecast.

My remarkable sense of smell no longer overwhelmed me. It was as if my nose had a million new connections to my brain—and perhaps a new lobe to process them all, I couldn't say—and all of these worked nonstop, sorting through the myriad odors passing through them. I could tell, to the yard, the distance to my favorite restaurant, Gary's on the Whisper.

As I breathed in the prickly, floral scent of the life all around me, I felt sad all of a sudden. Because human-Harriet would never get to enjoy these things—not in the way the monster could, anyway. Human-Harriet could never be alone in those majestic trees at night and frankly, she found it diffi-cult to relax by herself at any time of day, in any place.

Then my power-nose detected a familiar food truck. My memory lurched back to the party outside the campaign office, and all the frustration I'd felt there. I could smell that the truck had been parked within spitting distance of the twins' preschool . . . where one of my monster-care bags happened to be stashed . . . with fresh clothes inside . . . that I happened to need right then.

***

The street lights and buildings were all dark when I reached the churro truck. I'd tried jumping a few times on the way, to see if I'd gotten any better at it. But I was only marginally less shaky at those big leaps than I'd been at the golf course, so I mostly tiptoed, sticking to the shadows. It turned out that I had whiskers, too, which were remarkably helpful for detecting the prox-imity and movement of things.

I picked the truck up easily, like a laundry basket, and turned toward the preschool with a huge grin on my face.

It wasn't until I got to Healthy Start that I had some misgivings about my plan. It involved trespassing, and trespassing was illegal. This was an unlikely detail to spark my conscience, perhaps, given that I'd just stolen a motor vehi-cle. Still, as I approached the school's play yard I decided to stay outside of it, and stand flush against the eight-foot fence instead. From there, I opened the truck's rear doors, lifted it over my head, turned it nose-up, and shook the thing.

Foil-wrapped churros tumbled from the back by the dozen, each making a surprising number of *thunks* and *plunks*, as I'd inadvertently dumped them on top of the school's jungle gym. At least the sounds covered up my giggling, in case anyone could hear. Then I dutifully scooted away from the climbing structure so that the plastic utensils falling out next would make quieter landfall—on some gravel or bark dust, perhaps.

But that was not to be. All the shaking I'd done had freed a number of large pots and sheet-pans from inside the truck's cabinets, and these, too, fell to the ground—and on top of each other—with all the obnoxious *CLANGS* and *CLATTERINGS* you'd expect. I started to pull the truck toward me again, thinking the racket over, but no: In a surprise finale, five or six enormous plastic buckets *ka-THUNKED* down on both sides of the fence, their lids popping off in explosions of sugar and cinnamon that left me coated in the stuff—and full-on hysterical with laughter.

When nothing more would come out of the vehicle—even when I held it over my gaping maw and tapped on the end, like a ketchup bottle—I turned it around and placed it in a legal parking spot.

I grabbed a handful of churros from the jungle gym and sat down on the sidewalk, but it was hard to get the tinfoil off with my enormous fingers, and the churros were so small—not enough reward for all that work. Instead I licked some of the crystallized sugar and cinnamon from my hands (paws?) and then up both forearms. Indulging my feline side, if you will. Then I got up and peeked over the fence to survey my new, monster-made landscape. I felt satisfied, sated even, in ways I couldn't recall feeling before, and it wasn't from the little taste of sweetness I'd just had. Perhaps monster-Harriet wasn't exactly more reckless than human-Harriet, like I'd thought; maybe her priorities were just in a different order. She certainly had "BIG FUN" much higher up on her list.

I had stood up and was brushing some of the sugar from my hands, about to head home, when I heard a voice from behind me. "I hope you plan to reimburse the owners of this vehicle, for their products and equipment, Mrs. Lime."

And I knew right away who it was—this person who knew who *I* was.

I tried to arrange my features into an expression that suggested I was confused. *Peacefully* confused. I couldn't predict the words that might come out of my mouth, so I needed to play it safe. To play it dumb.[27] I really hoped he didn't have a gun.

So I blinked, let my mouth hang open, turned toward him, and leaned forward until my knuckles touched the ground. He did have a gun in his hand, pointed not exactly at me, but not exactly away. *Would a little drool be too much?*

"I know who you are," Justin said. He was wearing actual pants, although still in his flip-flops. He moved a toothpick from one side of his mouth to the other, and I kind of wanted to reprimand him for driving around with a choking hazard between his lips. He probably thought it looked cool.

"I don't believe for one second that you don't know who you are, Harriet Lime. You're way too smart for that."

Who would have guessed that my weird, gun-toting neighbor knew how to flatter a big apey-bear woman? Seriously, though, it felt nice being recognized as more than a snot-rag in ill-fitting pants for once.

But more urgently, my weird, gun-toting neighbor knew I was a big apey-bear woman! This was very bad, right? *Harriet, you should be freaking out more about this,* I thought, and I shook my head to clear it out a bit.

"Ah-ha! *See?* That's exactly what my neighbor Harriet does," he practically crowed, lowering his gun all the way.

"MUH?" I grunted at him.

"That's what she does—I've seen it a million times. Like, when she's trying to make herself think something, but it's not what she really thinks."

Oh, *geez.* Weird Justin was observant, too! And philosophical! How was it possible he knew me so well, when the only words I'd ever said to him were trite platitudes, muttered across two driveways and a strip of grass? And now, "MUH."

But again, what the hell was I doing just standing there, letting my mind wander? Where was the flash flood of fear and worry that should have engulfed me by then? Didn't monster-Harriet care that she might get

---

27   All women learn this at some point. If you meet one who denies it, please know they simply haven't gotten there yet. Eventually, we all have to act like we don't know something we actually know. In some cases, our lives literally depend on how convincing we are.

me—us—into serious trouble? Didn't she agonize, like human-Harriet did, over the possibility she might never see Frankie, Jo, Bret, or Theo again, except maybe from the business-side of some thick plexiglass?

Could plexiglass even contain this monster?

I eventually recovered enough sense to recognize that I needed to leave. But if I just ran home, Justin could potentially arrive there around the same time, since he was driving. He might even follow me, depending on the route I took.

Think, smart lady monster. Where can you go to change back into Harriet, where you won't have a neighbor on your tail?

Wait—do I have a tail? I turned around in circles, trying to look at my butt. How had I failed to realize, back at the golf course, that I had a beautiful prehensile tail I could've been swinging around from? I smacked myself on the forehead.

"I'm going to head out now," Justin called out, turning toward his truck and opening the door. "I'll see you tomorrow before school, like usual. Unless—" he added, putting a flip-flop on the step of his cab, "unless you need something, Mrs. Lime. Do you need anything?"

After a momentary struggle between my compulsion to thank him[28] and my tactic of pretending I was dumb, I finally replied, "MUH." Apparently, monster-Harriet was even more flippant than regular Harriet.

He got back into his truck with a smirk on his face and that silly toothpick still dangling from it. Then he made a three-point turn and was off. As soon as his truck turned out of sight, I retrieved the Best Buy bag I'd left around the side of the building. With my huge hands, I couldn't open the water bottle I'd stashed, so I squeezed it until it exploded, and learned the valuable lesson that a 20-ounce Aquafina is not enough water to take the monster out of me. I used the hose in the preschool yard to really douse myself—again, tricky when you have ginormous hands.

28　I was just a kid when I learned that when a man offers me something, regardless of whether he is sincere and kind, or menacing and self-serving, it's best—and often safest—to express my gratitude. Even if he's a person with authority, like a librarian, and even if he switches *between* helpful and creepy. Say your thanks, stoic little Harriet. Say it quickly and *go*.

Back in Harriet-form, I put on my dry clothes, counted the cash I'd put in the bag, and left it on the dash of the food truck. I felt guilty; $30 wasn't enough to cover the stuff I'd wasted. On the other hand, it would've pained me to leave much more than that in what was essentially a donation to the *Patchett Parker for Congress* campaign.

I speed-walked home. I approached our house from the side opposite to where Justin lived, and for the last stretch crept slowly through the very back of my neighbors' yards. I thought this the best way to avoid triggering any motion-sensitive lights but unfortunately, just as I'd reached the last lot before ours, I set off a whole choir's worth of barking, yapping, baying dogs. Our neighbor Ed came onto his back patio wearing a robe and some old sneakers. I crouched low and tiptoed another half-dozen yards, until I reached my own back fence and slunk over it.

"Oh! Mrs. Lime, it's just you!" Ed called out, scratching his terry-covered belly with one hand, his bald head with the other. It seemed he hadn't seen me until I was in my own yard. "I thought you were that animal that's on the loose. You better be careful out here, young lady. A bunch more people saw it tonight, you know. It's been all over the channel five news."

It took every shred of willpower I had not to respond to him with a polite "MUH!"

"Thank you," I said instead, giving him a wave. "I sure will, Ed."

2.6   THURSDAY, APPROXIMATELY 11:00 P.M.

I went inside, slaked my monstrous thirst, tended to tomorrow's lunchboxes, checked my email, and stuffed my face with leftover bits of pizza crust—cold and stale from a box on the counter—while Critter loitered, curious, at my ankles. Every so often she *schnuffed* at me and I *phuffed* back at her and frankly, I welcomed the conversation. "Are we building rapport? Is that what we're doing here?" I asked as I put away a bag of frozen peas and the remaining frozen pizzas, which someone had left out for who knows how long. "You're telling me I'm your favorite, aren't you?" I asked after one of her wetter sputters. I decided to ignore the growing pile of dirty dishes in the sink and trudged upstairs to my dark bedroom. After peeling off my shirt, pants, and socks, I let myself fall back onto the bed.

Theo was in the bathroom, and by the time he came out, I'd steeled myself for whatever conversation we might have, and however angry and accusatory it might become.

After climbing into bed and stretching out on his stomach, he cast an arm over me and when it landed across my abdomen I flinched a bit. I also whispered *"Sorry"* for some reason, my voice ragged with mucous and sounding every bit as confused and conflicted as I felt.

Theo heaved a long sigh, and with a single flex of his arm, scooched my body toward his. Then he turned his head and faced me, just inches away, inundating me with warm breath. The familiar scent joined and mingled with the sweet-and-salty notes of his skin and sweat, which had already invaded my system the second I opened our front door.

"That must've been soooooome walk," he whispered.

All my nervous energy came sputtering out of me in a rush of uncontrolled laughter. It then switched abruptly to a sob, then back to laughter again, at the mercy of some weird new coding that my human brain didn't have the proper security clearance for. I brought the back of my wrist up to my eyes, a reflexive gesture that announced half-heartedly to the darkness: *When they come for me, I would like it on record that I* know *I've become unhinged.*

I turned and peeked at Theo from underneath my wrist and was startled to discover that his eyes were wide-open and darting. Not because he could see me—his pupils were still dilated from the bright light of the bathroom—but because I'd been coming to bed for months by that point, only to find his eyes (and arms) long-closed. I watched, now, as one lower eyelid spasmed every few seconds as if on repeat. When he brought a knuckle up to rub at it, I had a foggy half-memory of seeing the same thing on some recent day, though I hadn't wondered if he might have a chronic problem. When he gave my limp torso another big tug that brought me smack up against him, I turned to look at the ceiling again as another stream of emotions came shuddering out of me—another erratic mash-up of ha-ha-has and half-sobs that left me feeling like a broken spigot: useless, wasteful, gushing.

"What's wrong? You OK?"

"Yeah," I managed. "Just . . . overwhelmed."

I eventually managed to stop my weltering, or at least the noise of it. It would take a good while longer to successfully dam up all my bodily fluids, and even then I was anything but calm.

"Are we OK, Theo?" I asked, my voice still viscous and uneven.

"'Course." His eyes had stopped searching me, and now he closed and opened them with purpose, like a beacon.

"How are you sure?"

"Because we're Harry and Theo. We've always been Harry and Theo, I think, because I can't remember a time when we weren't."

We were silent for several seconds as I contemplated his meaning.

"I can't be *me* without you," he whispered. "Talk tomorrow?"

I nodded, which he either saw or felt before closing his eyes. He was asleep within seconds.

Clearly, I no longer knew how to feel or act. Way too many things—emotions, unknowns regarding the monster, the everyday barrage of responsibilities—were competing for my attention. I'd been furious at Theo, then craved being the monster. I'd been ashamed at that longing, then nostalgic for a dreamy stroll with the same husband I wasn't through hating-on for the evening. I got angry again (and a little passive-aggressive, to be honest) at the campaign office. I'd been joyous and hyperalert at the golf course. And now, I felt enormously relieved—relieved that Theo and I hadn't fought more when I got home; that we had emerged from our earlier fight, both in forgiving moods; that his ongoing exhaustion prevented him from demanding immediate answers about where I'd gone and why I'd been out so long.

Relief turned out to be the most enduring sensation of the night. Relief, I was learning, was something you could experience without real peace. Because I was no longer wondering if Theo and I had changed in fundamental ways over the years, and whether this had begun pushing us apart; now I *knew I* had changed, and I couldn't deny it anymore. Worse, I'd begun to like this new model of myself and was beginning to fear that I'd have to choose one day, between the cozy but suffocating domesticity I had there with my husband and kids, and the unlimited, raw potential of my monster.

I lay there and fixated for some time on how Theo knew, or claimed to know, that our relationship was OK: because we were, and had always been, "Harry and Theo" in his view. As if we were a fixed pair. As if we were not self-contained beings who could and would thrive if someone took a bolt-cutter to our precious, longstanding "and." I didn't have any epiphanies on the matter, unsurprisingly, before exhaustion began making its rounds in me, pulling down blinds and turning switches in my brain, powering-down limp body parts, one by one.

That night was the first time I dreamt about my next-door neighbor— Justin, not Ed. I *always* dreamt about Ed, because he bore an unfortunate resemblance to my seventh-grade social studies teacher. That man had scarred me for life by making me stand in front of the class after a pop quiz and read aloud some of the answers I'd gotten wrong.[29]

In tonight's dream, everybody in town was a monster except me. But they were all afraid of me, possibly because I was still the oddball in this flip-flopped scenario. I don't remember there being any narrative to the dream, but at some point, Justin started shooting at me in my driveway, with a gun that was not only real but also really, *really* fast. I saw all the blood on the Grand Caravan and thought I was a goner.

---

29   We're all just one letter away from turning "public" into "pubic," OK? I make one typo and *boom*, I'm a pervert.

But I didn't die. I just kept going, wounds and all, because I was apparently immortal—but also a hemophiliac? It was strange.

I woke up and trudged to the bathroom, and was in the midst of an unusually long shower when Theo opened the door without knocking. "Have you heard any of the news this morning?" he asked, all brows and down-turned lips.

"No," I replied from the warmer side of the sliding glass door.

"Do you know there were several more sightings of that . . . big . . . *whatever*? A bear I guess, last night? Where were you for so long?"

I ran my hands through my hair, rinsing out the conditioner. I'd been comforted by his affection the night before, and I was comforted by his concern that morning. Maybe that explained my sauciness. "I thought they said it was 'ape-like.'"

"People are saying all kinds of things, Harry! It's green, it's red, it's purple, it's camo-colored."

"Better not feed it after midnight."

"Harry, be serious. The police are saying there might be more than one."

"Eh," I flopped a hand at that. Indeed, I was abnormally calm compared to the prior few days. Maybe the monster's comparably *laissez-faire* approach to life was rubbing off on me? "That's just people looking for attention."

He leaned on the door frame and ran a hand through his hair. From where I stood, he appeared to be shrouded in steam, adding to the impression that he was fuming. "Babe—you don't seem too concerned by this, but I am. You gotta get a new phone. Why don't you let me order you one online, since getting to the store is such a pain?"

I'm happy to say I didn't even remember the overdue phone bill in that moment. I nodded, and drew a heart in the condensation on the glass door. "That'd be awesome, T. Thanks."

"And please don't go on any more walks until they catch this thing, OK?"

He started to leave, but I called out, "Hey! One more thing?"

He came back in and closed the door behind him, and I opened the glass door and motioned him toward me. He frowned but stepped forward anyway, and I reached out and took his hand. "I'm sorry I worried you," I said. Then I tugged him toward me for a kiss. He wasn't expecting it, and his bigger body lurched toward mine.

His frown faltered a bit, if only on one end. I leaned away from the stream of water to meet him halfway, and was pleased when his frown wavered ever so slightly more. But just then, the door to the hallway flung open and a blur of a child rushed by us. I held onto Theo and watched as Jo situated herself on the toilet. Neither of us moved at first—it wasn't unusual for these potty-runs to be false alarms—but when she started singing, and pulled out her biggest Richard Scarry book, there was no choice but to call a rain delay on whatever it was we'd been doing. Or pee delay. Shower delay? Whatever.[30]

I told all three kids they could stay up an extra half hour that night if they got out of the house and strapped into the minivan, with all their school accoutrements, in the next three minutes. Everyone was doing their part hurrying things along when the doorbell rang, something I couldn't recall happening so early in the morning before. When no one went to the door, it rang again.

Theo got to it first, and when I reached the foyer and stopped behind him, I saw that it was Justin. He saw me before I could duck out of sight. "Hello, Mrs. Lime," he said with a wave.

"Hi. We're running really late today," I said over Theo's shoulder. "I'm sorry, but—"

"He just wanted to see if we recognized this," Theo interrupted, turning around with his palm out, cradling a small pile of silver.

---

30   By this point, you might be feeling put off by all this potty talk. Everyone who has small children, and actively cares for them, talks about pee and poop a lot. So anyone reading this is going to have to get used to the poop. And if you can't, stop reading this, OK? Because you won't be able to handle it when I get to talking about the viscosity of cervical mucous, the relative clotting tendencies of menstrual blood, and the possible meaning of its color variations, from near-black to pink. Just kidding—I'm not going to talk about those things. But seriously, get over any problems you have with poop, right now.

"I found it in my yard," Justin said in that peculiar way he sometimes had, like he was trying to cosplay as Bruce Willis. "Thought maybe one of the kids dropped it or something."

I peered into Theo's hand. It was mangled and broken into several pieces, but I knew immediately, thanks to my super-senses, that it was my necklace—the one Bret had given me, with the specially designed charm. I looked up at Justin, my eyes teary, and he looked back at me for what felt like several seconds. I sensed Critter approach me from behind and sit down a few feet away.

"You recognize it?" Theo asked, looking back inside the house, as if impatient.

I closed my eyes. *Damn it.*

I considered saying that I didn't; that way, I wouldn't be tacitly admitting I'd been in Justin's yard a couple nights before. I wouldn't be admitting I was the monster.

But then I'd be throwing away one of my most prized possessions. One of Bret's earliest creations—or what remained of it, anyway—from the age when she was first evincing signs of her talents.

Critter did a few loops around our ankles, only to sit down again in the spot she'd just left. "You have the weirdest dog, you know that?" Justin said, gazing at her with what appeared to be real interest. "She was so affectionate to me the day I moved in. Now it's like I don't exist."

"Everyone thinks their pet is the weirdest," I said in a rush. *But yes, you happen to be correct.*

Theo grunted. "The first couple months we had her, she was so used to starving on the street that she'd gorge herself on our trash every night. We had to put a bear-proof latch on the bin."

"Really?" Justin asked. He crouched down and held out a palm, cooing, "Poor baby girl! You must've made yourself sick doing that." The dog pulled her head back as far as it would go and curled her lip back, which gave the impression she was disgusted with Justin when really, she was getting ready to scratch herself under the collar with a back leg.

"You'd be desperate, too," I added, now with a touch of irritation in my voice, "if you were constantly on the verge of having to feed another litter of babies . . ." My voice slowed to a stop as I realized that Justin's approach had not triggered any of my monster-senses—not just now, and not the night before either. Even more strange, Critter hadn't bothered to bark at his approach.

"Tell you what," Justin said, standing up and returning us to the topic of the necklace. "I'll hold onto this. If you hear anything, or find out it belongs to someone you know, just let me know."

I nodded. He was sparing me from having to answer his unanswerable question, and I was relieved for it.

"That was weird," I said to Theo once he'd closed the door. But he was already back to his morning routine. It wasn't like him to be indifferent about sentimental items, and it stung a bit when he didn't show much interest in Justin's find. The sting intensified as it became clear that the warmth we'd shared in the bathroom and in bed the night before had vanished.

Something else occurred to me then, and I looked down at my ring finger. *Christ.* My wedding band had broken off, too? God only knew where that had happened, leaving a potential clue that I was the monster. Although apparently, I didn't need to worry about my husband noticing it was gone, which seemed like less of a silver lining than a leaden one.

I closed my trembling fingers into a fist and squinted, hard, as if I could squeeze all the pain and worry from my features. What was I doing, wearing every goddamned emotion on my face? That's why I'd avoided book club and other parents over previous days. But I knew I couldn't keep it up— especially not at home.

"KIDS! *NOW!* LET'S GO!" I yelled up the stairs. Then I picked up my keys and turned to the door.

2.7   THURSDAY, 1:00 P.M.

All morning long, my colleagues speculated about the monster. The monster they called "him." Unable to escape it, I'd put in some earbuds and played classical music, emailed Christy asking when she might have some time to catch up, then tried to get down to work while maintaining a mental countdown to our afternoon staff meeting. Bob would be in attendance, and I figured everyone would tone down the creature-talk.

They didn't. Half an hour into the meeting, Gil from graphic design blurted out, "OH MY GOD, SOMEONE GOT A PICTURE."

Everyone else pulled out their phone to search for it, while I just tried to keep my panic at bay. I still didn't know if the monster's face resembled my own, and whether a decent photo might out me as the person underneath all the fur. I didn't want to find out while sitting among the nine people with whom I grudgingly spent most of my waking hours.

I glanced at the double doors of the conference room, and the ones beyond those that led to the lobby. I considered faking an emergency and excusing myself, then speed-walking in the direction of the bathroom off the elevator bay. Once out of sight, I could pass the bathroom and go down the emergency stairwell, then straight out of the building. A nearby Applebee's had a few TVs in its bar, and they might be showing some breaking news about the photo.

But Gil pulled it up while I was still in my chair. *"Ughh,"* he groaned. "It's totally grainy!"

I leaned toward Yvette, who flinched when she discovered someone peering over her shoulder, staring at her phone. She laid a hand on my arm in a smiling apology, then adjusted herself so that I could see her screen, too. I gave her a weak smile in return.

The photo was not a good one, thanks to gods and goddesses everywhere. It was a fuzzy black-and-white image of a very tall creature in midstride, pulled from a traffic camera near the golf course. It wasn't nearly clear enough to make out any details with the naked eye.

I released a tiny huff of relief without meaning to, and unfortunately Bob heard it.

"What's funny, Harriet?" he asked, scrolling on his phone, every bit as engrossed as the rest of us.

My jitters ratcheted up in intensity, and I prayed my vocal cords wouldn't show it as I muttered, "Nothing. It just . . . it just looks like somebody's playing around." I slouched down in my seat.

"Yes, I think so, too," Gina added. She was our office manager and receptionist, and didn't speak up often in those meetings. She wore colorful, asymmetrical clothes and her hair in a salt-and-pepper pageboy, all of which paired nicely with the declining amount of fucks she had to offer the world. "Somebody's trying to recreate that famous Bigfoot picture. Quote, unquote."

There were murmurs around the table, some nodding heads. "But who is that tall? Look—his head is higher than the traffic light," Gil replied.

"Why are you assuming it's a 'he'?" Yvette asked.

Our seven white male colleagues chuckled awkwardly.

I leaned over her arm again. "Looks pretty androgynous to me."

"I mean if anything, it looks like it has smallish breasts," Yvette went on. I tried not to turn red as she added, "Not that that means anything."

"OK, OK," Bob spoke up. "Yvette, please—remember from our Respectful Workplaces seminar, how we agreed not to talk about the body?" Bob sure seemed hellbent on getting his money's worth from that seminar.

We'd already finished our official agenda for the meeting, but no one got up to leave; everyone (but me) was absorbed in zooming into the photo and scanning around, as well as their smartphones could, and several of the guys indulged in more speculation about the monster. Maybe it was because the body parts they discussed weren't primary or secondary sexual characteristics, but regardless, Bob didn't put his usual kibosh on their talk.

"It's kinda ripped, yo! Those are some big guns under that hair."
"I thought it'd be much hairier, actually."

"Is it me, or does it look mad? Why is it mad?"

"Yeah, I'd feel a lot better if it were smiling."

I was more than ready when Bob formally ended the meeting. I wanted to get out of there without spraining a muscle from all the eye-rolling I was having to suppress.

As we filed out the door, with Yvette in front of me, I touched her lightly on the shoulder and asked, "Hey, everything OK?"

She whipped around, on edge in a way that was out of character.

"What's that?" she asked, adjusting and readjusting the collar of her blouse.

"I asked if you were doing OK because I made you flinch earlier, and again just now—sorry about that."

"Not at all, friend," she replied, back to her usual, breezy manner. "I'm good. I'm totally good."

2.8   THURSDAY, 3:00 P.M.

"Thanks for meeting me here, instead of going out to dinner," Ellen said as we chose a spot on the metal bleachers and unfolded the wool blanket she'd brought. We'd decided to meet at Brandon's soccer game after school, because we hadn't been able to find any other time we were both available, absent postponing it till the New Year. Her features, usually so open, pinched a bit as she added, "I miss too many of Brandon's games. And Trey's."

"This pretzel and cocoa are all saying dinner to me," I replied as I sat down.

"And I guess we'll never earn our Mom-Martyr badges if we take ourselves out to eat now and then."

"Right?" I said through a bite of my pretzel. "Who do we think we are?"

The crowd was unusually big for an afterschool event, and on a weekday no less. But it was the soccer team's official Homecoming game, and the other sports had ended practice early so everyone could come out and show their support. With the year's first big dance coming up, all of the glances and grins and nervous laughter seemed to pass from teenager to teenager at a higher voltage than normal. The whole lot of us seemed more restless than usual, though I suspected it might be a misfire from some new monster-sense I didn't yet have a hold on.

I spotted a line of familiar jackets on the lowest bleacher. The word HOFFMAN arched over the image of a volleyball on the back of each, and I sensed Bret among them before I saw her.

My hackles had been up since I'd first parked my car, and now I knew why: Farther down, Mr. Terrence stood at the base of the steps, holding court among a half-dozen parents and Coach Sullen, who headed up Bret's JV team.

"You know, I'm sorry about the PTA meeting the other night," I said to Ellen after a few minutes. It'd been four days since the incident, and I still wasn't sure how to talk about it. "I should have done something when Mr. Terrence spoke to you like that. And I wish more people had seen how that guy in the uniform came up to you, at the microphone." *And I wish Sooby hadn't swallowed it when Mr. Terrence said he had nothing to do with it.*

She finished chewing and replied, "I think plenty of parents heard Mr. Terrence talk to me differently than the other moms. I wish more of them treated that as a problem."

I nodded. "Yeah. That was . . . disturbing."

"But not surprising." She gave her brows a quick lift and took another bite.

"He cuts people off all the time. I guess back when he was a super-popular teacher, he got used to everyone shutting up and believing whatever he said, kids and parents both."

She cocked her head at me. "But does he sic cops on people, all the time?"

I stared back at her. I'd brought up his history of crappy behavior because I wanted her to feel better about the way he'd behaved toward her, by suggesting she wasn't alone. But we both knew what differentiated her from the moms who'd gone up to the microphone before her. "No. I think he sicced that cop guy on you because you're Black, and you stood up to him."

"Indeed."

Brandon had his first major save, and Ellen started to stand up and let out a little squeal. But she seemed to catch herself, staying put and clapping politely instead.

"I read in a book somewhere, when the boys first started playing sports," she said, "that parents shouldn't make a loud fuss on the sidelines because your kids might get overly concerned with pleasing you. But sometimes, I just want to jump up and down and scream, you know?"

"What does Brandon think about it?"

Just then, Brandon made another, even more spectacular save—diving in the air and to one side, tipping the ball away on some kind of penalty kick. And again, you'd have thought the seat of Ellen's pants had snagged on the bleacher: She did a little bounce and a yelp, then allowed herself the tiniest fist pump.

"He says his head is so in the game, he doesn't even notice stuff happening off the field." She shrugged. We both glanced around at the people on each side of us, who were mostly white, and had known each other, by and large, for a great many years.

"It kind of seems like you want to cheer for him," I said.

She squinched up her face and answered ruefully, as if confessing something. "I do. I actually did a brief stint as a cheerleader, back in the day. It's not in my nature to suppress my enthusiasm." Then she pulled a bundle of fabric from a large canvas tote between her feet.

"I'll cheer with you, if you want," I whispered conspiratorially, wiggling my butt around and repositioning my feet a few times. "Do you remember any old cheers?"

That got a laugh, but she didn't look up from what appeared to be a sewing project. "No, my tenure was pretty brief."

"How come?"

Her whole upper body rose and fell as she considered her words. "Well, I had peppiness to spare," she began with a nervous laugh, her eyes not leaving her needle. "And I'd been a gymnast, so the acrobatic part was fine. I just . . . I just don't do well in front of crowds. I don't do well with . . . performing," she finished, giving her head several small but vigorous shakes.

There was another shot on the Hoffman goal, and when Brandon scooped it up easily, I stood up and whooped and clapped—while Ellen stayed put and laughed at me.

"Ellen, *c'mon!*" I said, motioning for her to join me. "It's *go*-time!" I did the wave a couple times, too, by myself, staring at her with my eyes bugged out. I only stopped when we both cracked up and a bunch of people, including most of the volleyball team, turned and looked at us. A few folks had their brows in a snit—not that I cared—but most seemed amused. I even caught Bret smirking at me. And eventually, Ellen did stand up and clap, but only because it was half-time.

"You know what's crappy?" I asked after we'd sat back down.

"How much time do you have?"

I grunted in agreement. "It's crappy that you had legitimate beefs with the way Mr. Terrence was handling the meeting the other day, and the way he wanted to pay for cost overruns on the statue. But rather than working on those things, we're analyzing his reactions to you, and a cop's, for f—" I looked around. I didn't know Ellen's policy on foul language.

"For fuck's sake?" she said in her most chipper tone.

"But you got his attention, at least. You called him out, and you did it in a way I haven't seen at PTA before."

She shook her head slowly, as if to reject the compliment.

"What?"

"Sometimes I'm glad when I find something to say that makes somebody's ears prick up, ears that need pricking. Other times, I wish I could summon the ability to—I dunno—be a bit more politic. Like I said—speaking like that, in front of a room? Not my thing."

"Well, I thought what you said that night was pretty awesome. I've been realizing lately just how batty I've driven myself all these years, trying to figure out the magical combination of words, or the correct tone of voice, or the right level of civility that would make people listen to me. Like, really *hear* me."

Ellen nodded. "I think that's true for a lot of women. This idea that there's a particular way to make your point that will finally get through to people like Mr. Terrence, and they'll say, *'Oh, right! I can't believe I didn't see that before!'*" Her impression of the man was spot-on.

When the ball stayed at the other end of the field awhile, far from Brandon, I asked Ellen about her research at Hind Labs. She sat up a little straighter and while her eyes stayed on her sewing, her whole face brightened. "We're getting ready to begin a study that looks at the cells that make up the human placenta, which is a subject relatively few researchers have taken up before," she said. "It's still basic research, but I hope that with more of us focusing on these things, the findings will eventually help more women, Black and brown women especially, survive labor, delivery, and the whole postpartum period. To thrive, even."

"That reminds me," I began, recalling what Dr. Morris had said to me about her upcoming research. "Do you know Dr. Miriam Morr—"

"OH, I LOVE DR. M!" Ellen exclaimed, turning toward me along with several of the people around us. "Oh my God, she's one of the reasons I decided to take the position at Hind. She reached out to me when I was still in Seattle, and asked me to be on her new board. What a lovely human she is."

"The loveliest," I replied, smiling with her. "*Dr. M*, I like that. Makes her sound like a superhero. And that whole 'fetal microchimerism' thing she's going to study? Like, *whoa*. It sounds fake, actually," I added, recalling how she'd explained that women often have cells from their former fetuses inside them for a long time after they're no longer pregnant.

Ellen gave me one of her giggles. "It does sound fake, doesn't it? Kind of makes you wonder if the ancient Greeks were right about any of their other beasties and monsters."

My whole body flared with alarm, so it was lucky that Ellen was glancing at her lap at that moment. "Say what, now?"

"Oh, I'm a mythology geek," she replied, taking a sip of her cocoa. "The Chimera was a monster in Greek myth. It had body parts from different animals, usually a goat, lion, and serpent."

"Huh." I hadn't heard that word divorced from its *micro-* and *-ism*.

"These days, we call something a *chimera* when it's a mash-up of two or more distinct things. Things we tend to think shouldn't be mashed together."

"Huh," I said again, looking out at the field without really seeing it. "I wonder how many moms know they've got the DNA of their own little beasties roaming around inside them."

"I know, isn't it wild? There are other kinds of microchimerism, too." She gave me a rundown of several other types, including one in which a twin retains some of the DNA from their former womb-mate.

"Whoa," I said, my arms limp and my hands hanging by the sides of my legs. "That's totally wild. I never thought about that." The whole topic was kind of thrilling, and I was about to say as much when Ellen offered a self-effacing grin and slouched for a second, adding, "That was quite a ramble, wasn't it?"

"What? No! It's fascinating."

"I know I tend to go on and on about it."

"Seriously, Ellen, I was wondering if it'd be too weird to tell you that you were giving me chills."

"But—I'm also trying to avoid apologizing for silly things, and to worry less about how much airtime I take up in a conversation. And then I get all confessional like this, all of which, I realize, might be shooting myself in the foot as far as making friends here goes," she said without looking my way.

"Call it 'confessional' if you want, but I like it when people are . . . open, I guess? I wish more people would say what they mean. Not fewer."

"Oh, GOD—me, too!" she cried, looking straight at me, enthusiasm coming off her in waves. "And it's better here than in Seattle. I could hardly believe it when I moved here and discovered that Portlanders actually want an answer when they ask, 'How's your day so far, ma'am?'" she said in the voice of a goofy teenage boy.

"Yeah, people here get offended when perfect strangers *don't* tell them how their day was."

"It's so refreshing," she went on, shaking her head slowly as she returned to her sewing. "And I'm totally serious—it's so much less work, not having to figure out if every question is a real inquiry or a pleasantry. *So much less.*"

She looked up, tilting her head to see past me. When I turned around, I saw Sooby for the first time that afternoon, standing at the railing with her mother, Regina Bamford.

They were probably hoping to catch Satchel's eye; Sooby's daughter was easy to spot on the sideline, thanks to her long strawberry-blonde hair and trademark gold and purple ribbons, the Hoffman school colors. On football nights, she could be found among the varsity cheerleaders; but at soccer games, she was there in her capacity as team manager. I'd known Satch since she was an infant, and had seen through the years how she'd begun showing signs of the same compulsions—or perhaps I should call them talents—to organize and systematize, categorize and mobilize, that I knew so well in her mother.

When she finally glanced toward the stands, her arms crossed and her brows all-business, Soob and her mom waved and resumed their way along the bleachers, eventually making their way up to Ellen and me.

I stood and hugged Regina, then gestured toward Ellen. "Mrs. Bamford, this is Ellen Stout, another mom—oh crap, sorry, Ellen. This is *Dr.* Ellen Stout. She directs the reproductive sciences department at Hind Labs. Ellen, this is Regina Bamford, the saint who organized a meal train for Theo and me after our twins were born, making sure that we had homecooked dinners delivered to our house for a solid month."

They shook hands, and I continued, "And Ellen, you already know Sooby, right? Shit, sorry, I mean Sue-Beth."

They both nodded, and we all laughed at my incompetent introductions as Ellen and I cleared our bags from the bench in front of us.

"Harry thinks she has special nicknaming privileges, because she's known me since the fifth grade," Soob said as she sat by Ellen's knee. Mrs. Bamford sat beside mine and rested her arm across them.

"Actually, it was fourth grade, remember? We were both in Girl Scouts," I replied.

"You were not a Girl Scout!" Sooby scoffed, looking as if she'd gotten an unexpected mouthful of lemon. She was one of those women who got away with using a sour tone on occasion, because people either knew it was playful or were too intimidated to test it.

"All right, all right. Let's say we've known each other since the Orthodontic Age, and be done with it," I said, putting my palm up. "So, Ellen, has Soob already got you on five of her committees? Or eight, or twelve?"

"Not yet," Soob replied, before Ellen could answer. "But now is as good a time as any to ingratiate myself. How's the game so far?"

While she peppered Ellen with questions, I leaned forward and put my hand on Mrs. Bamford's shoulder. "I haven't seen you since Judge's funeral. It was a lovely ceremony." Sooby's dad, a prominent judge, had died the previous summer from a heart attack. As a kid, I'd hung quietly around their house most summer afternoons, after Mrs. Bamford brought Sooby and me home from the pool, where they'd paid to add me to their membership and for me to join the swim team there. Her dad sometimes brushed what few hairs he had left on his head so they stood on end while he held court on the back patio, grilling burgers and singing some Italian aria—poorly—just to make Soob and me giggle. I knew his death had left a huge hole in their lives. "You must really miss him," I added.

She smiled and put her hand on top of mine, giving it a squeeze and holding it there. She was immaculately dressed, just as she'd been back when she'd stood on the sidelines for Sooby's field hockey games, or sat in the bleachers with Judge for football. She stood out, then and now, with her crisp seams and thick curls that never went loose. I still didn't understand how she got those crewneck, cable-knit sweaters over her head without stretching any of the stitching or squishing her hairdo, but I liked to picture some elves or small forest creatures sewing it onto her, à la Cinderella.

My hackles began to vibrate, so I sat up again. Mr. Terrence and his wife Marjorie were standing at the bottom of the bleachers, directly in front of us.

"So you moved down from Seattle," I heard Sooby say to Ellen. "Did you grow up there? No, wait—let me guess!" I turned toward them, mainly to check on Ellen. Being stuck in conversation with Soob was something you had to really want; sometimes even I found talking with her to be a mental and emotional workout. Ellen, however, was smiling from ear to ear, otherwise still absorbed in her sewing.

"I'm getting, like, a vibe of . . . midwestern . . . *positivity* from you. But also, there's a twang of some kind? Did you move around a lot as a kid?"

Ellen quietly made a few stitches, and when no one spoke for several seconds, she looked up at Sooby and feigned confusion. "Oh, do you want me to actually answer that one?"

I laughed.

"Yes, please," Sooby replied, unfazed.

"Not a lot, no," Ellen replied.

It seemed they were having fun, and when Sooby guessed correctly on her first try that Ellen had grown up mostly in Oklahoma, we were all impressed. Still, I tried to offer Ellen an out. "Soob, don't you want a tofu-dog from the concession stand, now that you got them to stock those for you?"

"Don't worry about me, Harry," Ellen replied, giving my shoulder a gentle shove with her elbow. "Like I said, people who are straightforward are my kind of people."

Soob shot me a victorious look and continued her interrogation. "Also, do you prefer to be addressed as *Dr.* Stout?"

Ellen looked at the sky and let her sewing fall into her lap. "It's hard, you know? Because I want to say that I prefer using that title only at work. In any professional setting, really, like conferences and such. But it does go a long way when I put 'PhD' in my email signature, I've noticed."

"So how should I introduce you?" Sooby asked again.

"You sure you don't want to take notes or something?" Ellen teased.

"Nah," she replied, tapping her temple. "Steel trap."

"It depends on the person I'm meeting, I guess. Actually, do you know what? Screw it. Go ahead and introduce me as 'doctor,' Sue-Beth. I'll take it from there."

"And *you*," Sooby said, lowering her tone and also her sunglasses, so that she could glare at me like a schoolmarm. "New phone yet? Or no?"

I wanted to talk with Sooby about the PTA thing, and not my phone, which only reminded me of the monster. But as I cleared my throat, everything felt shaky suddenly, from my vocal cords on up to my lips. I could challenge Sooby on almost anything, it seemed. Just not the eight-hundred-pound gorilla that was Mr. Terrence. I dodged both subjects.

"Oh, wait—guess who I got my first email from?" I replied. "Two, actually."

She pushed her glasses back into place and shrugged. "I dunno."

"I want you to guess."

"Ooo, ooo—can we do it twenty questions–style?" Ellen asked.

"Sure," I replied.

Ellen launched into a strategic list of questions: Was it a person? Did any of them know this person? Did *I* know them? Were they famous? Was I the only recipient of said emails?

Sooby, who was annoyed when I didn't answer her about my phone, was nonetheless pulled in. "I've got a question. Do you like this person?"

I paused. "Whew. That's a tough one."

"It's your mom."

"Bingo," I replied over a forced laugh. From the corner of my eye, I saw Ellen look up from her sewing, her hands still. I'd never mentioned anything about my childhood to her.

"Whoa," Sooby replied. "That's . . . that's *weird*. What were they about?"

"She sent me two articles, one about rogue waves and the other about Olivia Patchett-Parker—"

"Whoa—seriously?" Now Sooby was piqued. She had disliked Patchett-Parker for as long as I could remember, but I'd never been able to figure out why. I knew it started well before the latter was elected to the state senate, and I knew that Judge and Mrs. Bamford's social circle intersected with the Patchett-Parker family's, and the Hoffmans'. But I'd never gotten close enough to the center of that Venn diagram to determine the origin of Soob's beef.

"So hey, also," I said quickly, before I could lose my nerve. "I wanna hear exactly what Mr. Terrence said, when you asked him about the meeting. Did he say he didn't *see* the Gunsmoke Guy, or that he didn't *know* him?"

She let her head tilt back as she rolled her eyes. "*Ugh*, you couldn't trust Mr. Terrence if your life depended on it, could you?" Then she cupped her hands around her mouth and turned toward the bottom of the stands. "Mr. T! Mrs. T!" she called out. When they looked up, she gave them a big wave and motioned for them to come up.

"Soob! Let's not . . ." I groaned. It was dawning on me—too late—that Ellen hadn't looked up from her sewing in several minutes, and maybe I shouldn't have brought this topic up with her and Soob together, and definitely not with Soob's mother and a crowd of others within earshot.

Mr. Terrence gave Sooby a look I recognized from my school days—his *Patient Dad of Demanding Child* look—something he handed out during his better moods. The throngs of people who came up to him at school events seemed to puff him up in self-importance, as if he were shoring up power over our realm rather than supporting a couple dozen kids on their big day. I supposed I'd have to suck it up and be one of them if I was going to get any answers from him on the PTA issue, but now really did not seem like the right moment.

I glanced at Ellen, who made firm eye contact and said, "I don't feel a need to talk about that now."

"Soob!" I hissed, poking her hard on the top of her shoulder, right in the recess of her clavicle. "Don't involve Ellen in whatever we talk about, OK?"

"*Ow!* What the—why?" she asked, grabbing her shoulder and glaring back at me with confusion and irritation jumbled together on her face. "You just—"

I walked my tone back a bit, and even put my hand on her shoulder and gave it a conciliatory rub. "Sorry. Look, Ellen doesn't want to talk about it right now," I replied, trying to force some airiness into my voice. When I looked up again, Mr. Terrence had started up the bleachers to us.

"You gals can talk to him about the men in the black hats," Ellen added, "but I'll just stick to my sewing. Thanks."

"OK, OK. I get it," Sooby replied. She'd accepted my quick shoulder massage but her expression held on to a trace of alarm. "That hurt, by the way. Have you been growing out your nails?"

Mr. Terrence exchanged hellos with Sooby and her mom first, and I wasn't surprised when he knew Mrs. Bamford already, by name; their family had always been involved in the schools, and Judge Bamford had been a well-known figure.

"Hi, I'm Patrick Terrence," he said, extending his hand to me as if we were strangers. I could practically feel Ellen's surprise, from a tiny shift in her body language, but it wasn't the first time his memory had misfired where I was concerned. When I showed up to the office at the high school a few months prior, to register Bret for freshman year, he happened to walk by as I came out. He gave me that *Howdy, Ma'am* nod-and-smile thing he gives to every woman he doesn't know, followed by a sharp double take in which his features seemed to shrivel in on themselves. It happened fast—he didn't even break stride—but there was no mistaking he'd recognized me. It might have been from physics class, or because I'd once been the annoying girl in his Science Club. Heck, I was also best buds with Sooby, his best disciple. It was a curious switcheroo; he couldn't be bothered to make note of me on the front end of our passing interaction, but was clearly disquieted afterward.

I took his hand. "Hi, we actually—"

Before I could finish, Sooby jumped in. "Her daughter Bret is one of your setters, on the JV team." Now my metaphorical hackles were up, along with my anatomical ones. Sooby's habit of telling my stories for me was starting to bug me, even though her spin on my life was generally positive. "She's also the mom who wanted to know about the guy in the black uniform and the hat, at our last meeting."

I wanted to pick her up and toss her into the juniper hedge behind the bleachers. Not only for dominating the conversation but for forgetting—or just plain skipping—an introduction between Ellen and Mr. Terrence.

"Is that right?" he replied, pulling up on his waistband, which struck me as a "tell" of sorts, as he'd also done it when he was hopping mad at the PTA meeting. "I don't keep track of everyone at those meetings. I'm sorry I can't help you."

A jarring *crack-crack-crack* came from Ellen just then, and I looked over to find her cracking her knuckles—hunched forward slightly, still looking intently at her sewing. Mr. Terrence and Sooby looked her way, too.

"It's just that," I began, rubbing my palms up and down the denim on my thighs, "the guy I'm talking about really stood out. He was menacing, kind of. There was a second guy, dressed like him, in the lobby, and I saw another at the medical center the other day."

I sensed Ellen stop sewing.

"I've been doing this for decades, ma'am. And I'm not the youngest of men—I can't recall specific comments from all my hundreds of events over the years. I wish I could." He laid a hand to his chest, in that preferred gesture of lying liars everywhere. My eyes moved from his hand to the button he wore over his heart: *Terrence for County Commissioner.* Ever since he'd announced his candidacy a few months earlier, I'd been sort of hoping he'd get elected, because then he might leave his PTA post. But now my stomach sank at the thought that he could soon be inflicting his authoritarian ways on much of the Portland metropolitan region.

Again, Ellen folded one hand over the other with a startling *puh-puh-puh-POP*, and this time I nearly laughed aloud. To me, knuckle-cracking is what mafia guys do—the "muscle" who intimidates the shop owner who owes the don some clams or whatever. Yet here was this petite, cheerful

person, producing this startling sound every time Mr. Terrence said something inane. I wasn't sure what it said about Ellen's state of mind, but the
habit was a wordless protest of sorts, and it was glorious to see it distract
this overbearing man and derail his train of thought.

He pushed his glasses up his nose, which I thought of as his *Don't Push
Me, Kid* gesture, then turned back to me. "How come I haven't seen you at
any of our volleyball family potlucks?" he asked, changing the topic like a
seasoned politician.

"I—"

"Harry's not much of a joiner," Sooby said, interrupting me.

Now I wanted to toss Soob into the *other* juniper hedge—the one that
ran along the front of the school—because that one I knew to be infested
with spiders. Was I that bad of a storyteller or something? Was my breath
terrible? Why in the world did she take over whenever the topic of conversation was, like, my character?

"Ah," Mr. Terrence replied, adjusting the brim of his cap, the one with
Hoffman Pioneers embroidered across the front in gold thread. "Only child?"

Sooby nodded and gestured back at me with a thumb. *"Swimmer."*

He smiled and touched his nose with a forefinger, as if crediting Soob
for having gotten the correct answer. They sounded like doctors discuss-
ing a diseased patient, and continued to flat-out ignore Ellen, so *wow*, how
had Soob and I been best friends all this time without me realizing she was
essentially a different person when Mr. Terrence was around? A jerk-person?

"Oh, you two! If Harriet's a bit of a lone wolf, she deserves to be. She's
had to go it alone in life," Mrs. Bamford chimed in. She looped an arm
around my waist and gave me not so much a hug as a brief squeeze between
her palms. "I admire that. Judge always admired that in her, too."

I knew she meant to compliment me, but to my ears, her words trans-
lated as: *"Wow, Harriet. Great job with all that struggling!"* I flashed back to
adolescence, to one of the zillion times I'd gone over to their house for dinner.
I'd been putting my jangly keychain into my bookbag when Mrs. Bamford
called out to me from their kitchen. She was standing there in her clean, dark

socks, her posture like a ballerina's. "Harry, is that you? Or some friendly janitor?" She and the Judge had laughed, so I did, too, because apparently, being a janitor was funny.

"Yeah. I'm quite the rugged individual," I replied, my thoughts muddled. Mrs. B gently moved a thick curl from her forehead and waved to someone across the bleachers.

"Love it," Mr. Terrence replied. "Love that pioneering spirit." His expression had changed at the mention of Judge, and now his eyes kept returning to me, which was unsettling.

I whipped back to Soob. "Is that why you didn't come over, after Jo and Frankie were born?" I asked, my soft tone at odds with my laser-like stare. "You thought that might be too much 'joining' for me?"

She widened her eyes briefly, then looked away, blurting out, "Mr. Terrence, you know Dr. Ellen Stout, of course." Now that she wanted to change the topic, she'd remembered to introduce Ellen.

Mr. Terrence raised one of his boots and rested it on the bench between Ellen and me, and I grimaced as he leaned toward her. Firstly, because holy *hell*, who does that? Back off, close-talker! And secondly, because I knew how much the man reeked of cigarettes.

"Ma'am, I want to tell you, personally, that I was not myself the other night. My wife's got me on these patches, you see, tryin' to make me quit," he replied in a soft voice, flexing at the elbow and pointing at his bicep. We were to understand, I guess, that underneath the nylon of his windbreaker was a nicotine patch responsible for him behaving like a total dick. "And things can get a bit . . . *gladiatorial* there, in the big gym," he added with a wry grimace, as if PTA meetings were some kind of epic clash rather than the bureaucratic proceedings we all knew them to be.

"Oh," Ellen said politely, glancing quickly at his arm before looking back at her sewing.

"Come see me during my office hours sometime, and we can talk. Get to know one another." He backed away from her personal space and stepped back down to the lower bench. Then he turned and appeared to take a new interest in the game, nodding his head absently. When a Hoffman player scored a goal and we all clapped, Mr. Terrence took the opportunity to excuse himself. He said in a low tone, "I've got to go speak with some of the men on my statue crew. We've got lots more work there now, but we'll get it done. And that reminds me, ladies, if you haven't already done so, go ahead sign up for a clean up shift. We can't all be armchair critics."

He looked directly at me during that last part, and I tried not to let my consternation show. *So which is it, my dude? Do you admire lone wolves? Or find them to be rude armchair-dwellers?*

"Sue-Beth, I want to go speak with Beau Hoffman," Mrs. Bamford said. "Harry dear, can you give me a hand?" I gave her both my hands to push on as she raised herself to a standing position. Ellen stood with her, then handed over her coat before seeing she got a firm hold on Sooby's arm for the walk down the bleachers. "My knees aren't what they used to be, ladies."

Sooby didn't make eye contact, or even turn toward us when she said goodbye. This was such a departure from her usual effusive ways that I began to think I wasn't the only one who'd been left off-kilter by our conversation. Perhaps the scent of sweat I'd picked up from her wasn't from any physical exertion, but rather an emotional disturbance that mirrored my own. Her mom gave us a quick wave, and they were off.

I waited until they were all out of earshot before turning to Ellen. But she spoke up first: "Well, *that* was some bullshit."

"Right?" I whispered. "I love how he turned things around, and made it sound like his bad behavior at PTA was your fault. And also his wife's fault, for wanting him to be healthier."

She gave an exaggerated, playful sigh. She'd already picked up her sewing again, which I'd gathered by that point was a Halloween costume of some kind. "And what kind of mom are *you*, missing all those potluck dinners?"

"A . . . busy one?"

"And did you catch that eyeroll?"

"No."

"Oh."

"Wait—what did I miss?"

"Oh, I don't want to make you feel bad—"

"I'd really rather know, I promise."

She sighed. "When he tilted his head in your direction. It was subtle. But he rolled his eyes, too."

"Hmm. OK, thanks. Not surprising given the things he and Sooby said out loud."

"There was a lot to unpack in that convo," she added, shaking her head. But when she hunched over and focused intently on her sewing, I took it as a sign she didn't want to take up that particular chore just then.

I tried to enjoy the rest of the game, but couldn't keep from rehashing the earlier conversation. Even though the air was still dry as bone, it seemed to hang around me like a wet, woolly shawl and I felt dizzy, my whole body disquieted and on high alert, right down to the finest hairs. *Is this my new normal?* I wondered. *Is the thrum in my ears ever going to stop? Or will it be like this only when there are bad guys around?*

When the game ended, Ellen and I took our place in the slow stream of people leaving the stadium. "Sue-Beth is a hoot," she said as we inched along. "A bit worshipful of Mr. Terrence, but a hoot."

I gave her an exaggerated squint. "She didn't introduce you to him."

"I noticed that, yes," she replied matter-of-factly. Then, after a pause, "Her mom is so . . . elegant. Regal, almost."

"Are you saying nice things about them for my sake?"

"No. It's just one of my survival skills," she replied. "I learned a long time ago that I can't afford to hold a grudge when someone is impolite. For a lot of reasons."

We were quiet a couple of minutes. My feet kicked up some dust and gravel as I shuffled along, my shoulders hunched too far forward, as if something stronger than simple gravity was pulling me toward the earth.

"I think I've always given myself a break," I said finally. The sun was in our eyes then, and I appreciated not having to make eye contact with anyone as I went on. "As far as pushing Sooby goes. It's easy to obsess about all the trifling, petty stuff Mr. Terrence does to this day, and forget the crazy things he did when I was in high school." When she looked at me questioningly, I gave her a quick recap of the glass-smashing incident. "It's like I filed that away as ancient history, and told myself, 'Well, this is Sooby's thing.' It's her thing to have some kind of blind loyalty to this angry, insecure old man."

Ellen was looking at me, waiting for me to go on.

"But," I continued after a time, "at PTA the other night, we got to see that his menacing side never went away. His willingness to threaten never went away. But we let him enjoy a kind of second honeymoon when he became PTA president."

"Those are what I like to call 'quiet things,'" Ellen replied. "Stuff that's not illegal, and not against any bylaw. But that has a bad effect on someone. Or lots of someones."

I told her about missing the van headed to that Science Club event after being just a few minutes late, and about the lukewarm recommendation letter he'd written for me and then mailed after the deadline for the UWV honors program. "Thank God Judge Bamford was my other reference. I'm pretty sure he made a phone call for me, too."

Ellen gasped. "You were a budding scientist in high school? OK, OK—now I really do hate the man. Was he targeting you for some reason?"

"I don't know, but you'd think he'd have a stronger memory of me if he was," I replied. "I do think he likes things the way he likes them. In the case of Science Club, he likes a row of blue blazers, crisp white shirts, square jaws, and trim haircuts—every meet."

Ellen snorted. "I get it now."

"I was always a little too . . . " I trailed off. "Wavy? Earthy, maybe?"

"You don't need to tell me about that, Harry. I could write a book on what it's like to feel too-this or too-that."

"I can only imagine," I said.

"Let's face it," Ellen said, "the man is popular. People don't want to fight with their friends. Or their idols, as the case may be."

We approached a gate that led into the parking lot. "I figure most people dislike the thought of fighting—like, *really* fighting—with their friends. But . . ."

She looked over at me when I paused. "But some of us . . . hate it more than others," she finished for me.

I looked back at her as tears formed suddenly in my eyes. "Next time," she went on, "maybe you can tell me more about your mom and stuff."

I nodded, and after stepping out of the way of the people behind us, put up my arms and asked, "Can I hug you?"

"Actually—no, Harry. I'm so sorry, but I'm not much of a hugger."

"Oh, OK. No problem. I mean, that's why I asked."

She smiled at me in the way I was beginning to think of as her default state—genuine, but with a spark of bemusement—then put out her hand and squeezed mine tight. I still felt too vulnerable to remember to ask her why she felt that way about fighting with friends, too.

We'd learned that we'd both be chaperoning the Homecoming dance, and decided that would have to serve as our next "get-together" since both our calendars were more or less full in the coming weeks.

Once she'd gone, I waited at the edge of the parking lot to catch Bret on her way back to the locker rooms. She was with Satchel when I spotted her, and I called them over. "Hey, babe—you still getting a ride home with Sierra's mom?"

"Yep," she replied, her thumbs tucked behind the straps of her backpack. "She's dropping us off at our house, and Satch is gonna hang out, too."

"I brought some pumpkins we can carve! And I haven't seen Jo and Frankie since last spring break—can you believe that?"

"Right—when your poor parents were so sick with the flu. How could I forget?" I'd helped out by driving Satchel to a hair appointment that week. The stylist swooned at her gorgeous locks, telling us the color was the "holy grail" of his profession, and that she must swear, hand to God, that she'd never, *ever* dye it. I love Satch like my own blood, and normally I'd be pleased for her to get a compliment, but the stylist's dogged insistence left me a little dyspeptic. Was it the rosy-wheat color itself that he loved, or the fact that it was . . . virginal, somehow? I'd cleared my throat and asked when we'd be finished, and he took the hint. On the way home, I'd joked that I thought he might tip *her* in the end.

"Oh—and did you hear I got my learner's permit, Aunt Harry?" Satchel asked now, beaming.

"I did not—congratulations." I gave them each a quick squeeze and they turned to go.

"Bret, please tell your dad that Ellen and I cancelled our dinner, but I'm going to knock out some errands instead. Thanks, you two! Have fun! But if Frankie and Jo tell you they know how to use knives, don't believe them, OK? Mommy does *not* let them use knives, no matter what they tell their teachers. OK—byyyyeee!" We blew each other a half-dozen slapdash kisses, in the twins' preferred version of the gesture.

I got in my car and impatiently made my way to the highway, with no intention of doing any errands whatsoever.

2.9   THURSDAY 5:30 P.M.

I drove for a half hour, stopping at five different gas stations and two convenience stores before finally finding a place—a Walgreens—with a working pay phone.[31] I had no idea how much it cost to make a call, it'd been so long since I'd used one, and previous users had done their best, the bastards, to scratch out the instructions. Still, I heard a dial tone when I picked up the receiver, so I hung up and went inside to get some quarters.

I speed-walked through the place, grabbing a couple of newspapers, a Gatorade, a pack of Twizzlers, a road atlas of Oregon and southwest

---

31   I still knew the locations of most convenience stores and quickie-marts in town, as I'd relied on them as a kid for the occasional breakfast or other meal. They had long hours and bright lights in their parking lots.

Washington, and some beef jerky. But when I turned down a random aisle on my way to the cashier, I spotted one of those plexiglass cupboards—the kind with a sliding door and lock—and my beast-mom pulse threw a raging shit-fit. I bobbled my snacks as I clamped a hand onto my chest. But I knew right away why it'd happened.

A few months after the twins were born, and I was sapped of all energy, mental acuity, and hope, I'd moped my way to a grocery store late one night in search of the specific type of baby formula that Theo and I added to bottles of my breast milk. We'd always ordered it online, so I didn't know until that night that our local market kept the stuff locked up. I burst into tears at the sight.

A man in a Trail Blazers jersey and skinny black jeans stopped and offered to buy me a can. I explained that I was able to afford it, thank you, and he moved on. But I stayed awhile, cross-legged and a bit catatonic on the floor, at a loss for why baby formula—of all the tens of thousands of foodstuffs for sale in American supermarkets—needed to be locked up. Formula only has one use—to feed a newborn baby. And newborns have, at most, one other option for getting any nourishment. So why were companies treating it the way they do razors, laptops, and cigarettes? I eventually got up and found a stock employee, who then found a manager, who went and retrieved a key from some other manager. By the time he came back and opened the sliding door for me, and stood next to me while I took a few cans from the cupboard, I wanted to start throwing shit, or lighting shit on fire, or lighting shit on fire and then throwing it.

"Excuse me," I'd blurted out, interrupting the man while he hummed to the Muzak. "Is it store policy to make every shopper feel like a criminal? Or is this just the way you treat new parents?"[32] He pursed his lips and escorted me to the register, where he glared at me while I paid. I passed a rotating greeting card display on my way to the exit and I

---

32   I didn't learn—or didn't notice, I suppose—until a few years later that some things that are made for and marketed to people of color, such as hair care products, are also frequently locked up as a matter of policy.

literally gagged; when I got home, I told Theo I never wanted another Mother's Day card for as long as I lived. I understand how supply and demand works, but what does it say about our country that I can saunter into almost any store, in almost any town, and find an obscene variety of potato chips at any hour; but when I needed to get my hands on the only consumer product that an infant can safely consume, I had to wait fifteen minutes for it to be unlocked and then consent to being escorted to the cashier and watched while I paid for it?[33]

After breaking my twenty—the only cash I had left after stocking all my monster-care bags—I went back outside and set my snacks and one of my newspapers at the base of the pay phone, atop the broken concrete with its dingy polka dots of old gum. I tucked the other paper under my arm as I picked up the receiver and put in my quarters. I fished in my pocket for the scrap of paper I'd torn from the back of my day planner, where I'd written Mom's home number in case of emergency.

Dread was the only emotion I'd ever felt when initiating a call with my mother, and it squicked me out that night, to be sure. But that old discomfort was negligible against the newer sensations gripping me at every moment— sensations I could only interpret as my first monster-withdrawal symptoms. Since leaving the high school, I'd felt as if multiple giant insects were crawling across my skin, and yet no amount of scratching offered me relief from their imaginary trespass. I was distracted, too, as I lifted the old receiver and put my coins in the slot, by the ever-present fear that someone—perhaps my next-door neighbor—could and would out me as the grainy giantess in the traffic photo.

I dialed the number and while it rang, leafed through the newspaper in search of articles about the monster. There were a couple of items, but very little information I hadn't heard already. Calls to police suggested that more than one resident had gotten a clear glimpse of me near the

---

33   I assumed that some parents must be stealing the formula, given how crazy-expensive it is. But when I Googled it later, I learned that some enterprising crooks had figured out how to lift and hoard the stuff, then sell to mom-and-pop shops in far-flung places, where it was scarce.

golf course, while others claimed to have spotted me in neighborhoods far away from anywhere I'd been. I also noticed that reporters all referred to the monster as "it," while the people they quoted said "he" in every case, just like my coworkers.[34]

I let the paper fall to my thighs with a scoff. Their getting my biological sex wrong made me want to write a letter to the editor, or maybe turn up outside the newsroom window one day and show them the underside of this here ship, if you know what I'm saying.

When no one picked up, I tried Mom's cell. I'd barely folded the paper back down when I heard someone answer.

"Hello?" she said. There was a rustling, like someone was moving the receiver through a swatch of fabric. Her voice sounded older than it should have.

"Hi, Mom. Mom?"

"Yes?"

"Mom, it's Harry. Calling from . . . calling from outside."

"Oh." She paused, and a loud foghorn-type sound went off in the background. "Hi, Harriet."

"How . . . " I looked at the sky and released the breath I'd been holding. "How are you?"

"Fine. I'm fine." She'd always spoken very slowly, pausing between words and even some syllables, as if she thought they needed extra cushioning around them, in preparation for some future blow. It was a habit that made my toes curl, because even though I didn't speak with her all that often, when I did, I was always in a hurry to get it over with.

"I got your two emails," I said, shrugging even though there was no one to see it.

When she didn't reply, I went on. "I didn't write back. But I just wanted you to know that I lost my phone, so it's been hard to reach me." I felt like I

---

34   It just occurred to me that the papers might be referring to the monster as "him" because if they implied it might be a "her," half their audience would stop reading about it. Did you know that most men don't *tampons cheese dog-poop bags* read stories where the protagonist is a woman? Not many *sugar flour tweezers* people know that.

was ten years old again, screwing the tip of my sneaker into the pavement. I even pulled my hair over one shoulder the way Bret did, and was surprised to recall how I'd once had the same habit.

"Uh-huh."

"And hard for me to get back to people."

"Mm-hmm."

"Why did you bring me to the lake, to swim?" I blurted out suddenly.

There was another long pause, but this one I could forgive. *What the hell am I doing? Did I really drive around for a half hour for this?* When Mom finally spoke again, it was in a tone with a bit more definition to it. "What's that?"

"You used to bring me to Cabott Pond when I was super-little, right? Like, a baby? I was just wondering why you did that . . ." My voice trailed off because the last part of the sentence was the biggest and I had to struggle to get it out. "And also, why you stopped."

"We stopped, yeah. You'd already—"

"Got it," I replied, not meaning to interrupt. I'd mistakenly thought she was done speaking. "Oh—what was that? Sorry, go ahead, Mom." I suddenly really wanted to know the rest of the sentence.

It took her several more seconds—with another of those super-sized honking noises in the background—but she eventually replied, "It's fine."

"No, Mom—tell me. What were you going to say?"

"Nothing."

I sighed. Pulling the words out of her felt like pulling my own teeth.

"Well, I just wanted to thank you for your email, and let you know that even though it's hard to get a hold of me right now . . ." My words trailed off. I didn't know what I wanted to say. I was rambling. "I'm just saying you should still try. To reach me, I mean."

There were a couple more deep whooshing sounds. "OK, thanks."

"How is your arthritis, and everything?" I asked, trying to keep things as simple as possible. I didn't ask: *So why 'rogue waves'?* Or: *Are you in some kind of shipping lane?*

"Uh, you know—I don't know. Fine, I guess."

"OK. I should let you go."

"Thanks."

"OK, bye now," I said, frowning as I pulled the receiver away from my ear.

I was so eager to end the call that I barely caught her last words before our connection was severed: "I just didn't want you to drown, Harriet. Like Mama did."

So that's how I found out, at age thirty-eight, that my grandmother had died by drowning.

Under normal circumstances, that information would have hit me like a lightning strike. I might have called my mom back and attempted to wrench out of her the reason she'd waited so long to tell me that a nana I'd never known had died a horrible death. Or maybe I'd have rushed home to be comfortably numbed by the endless urgency of my household routine. But there was no "normal" in my life anymore.

***

I really should have gone home. I should've gone home and planned out what to say to my boss at our upcoming off-site meeting. I should've done whatever it took to get a new cell phone. I should've made a point to talk to— and possibly fool around with—my husband. And even though I would've preferred to pry off all my toenails and hand-feed them to a barracuda, I really should've spent some time figuring out how my goddamn neighbor had uncovered my goddamn secret. But I couldn't bring myself to do any of those things.

This is what I did instead: I took out my new road atlas and spread it on the hood of the Caravan, where I could study the locations of all the wooded areas in the region. I looked at parks and forests within reasonable driving distance, so I'd make it back home before it got too late. I tried to recall whether those places were sufficiently dark, heavily forested, and devoid of people. In the end, I determined that a state forest in the town of Winslow, to our southeast, fit my needs best.

I drove out there, parked in front of a half-abandoned strip mall, and got out of the van. I barely glanced at the pawn shop, nail salon, and empty storefronts as I was too busy beaming and bouncing on my heels—this even though my nostrils burned from some toxic odor I'd probably only detected thanks to my powerful new monster-senses.

I was fizzing with impatience to become her again. I seemed to have developed an adrenaline-lust, and now that I had a second to consider things, my rational brain threw up a few concerns on the matter. Like, what if there were limits to her healing ability? What if I learned the answer to that after making a wrong move, and busting myself up?

I made a half-assed attempt at a mindful breathing exercise, hoping to calm my body; I tried to lengthen my spine, to stand tall. *You can spend time as the monster,* I said under my breath, *just don't push yourself to new speeds and heights every damn time.* These mantras did nothing to relieve the fierce itch I had going, however, or to slow the expansion of the cavity inside me that wanted filling. So I let myself loose.

I sprinted through the parking lot, past the strip mall, and across their back alley, ignoring the splintering pain in my knees, knowing it would soon be over. From there, I entered a defunct industrial lot that was scattered with the rusted-out hulks of old lifts, like the man-made buttes of some dystopian planet. I was so pumped as I closed the last hundred yards to the forest that I let the beast out to fly a little early, before reaching the cover of trees.

The transformation happened quickly; I hardly noticed it anymore. The night went from dusky and quiet to thundering and atremble in an instant. But after jumping over some train tracks—which I thought were the last barrier between me and the forest—I landed in a clogged drainage ditch instead, where a permanent and rather nasty puddle turned me immediately human again.

I let out a raging "MOTHER-*FUHHHHHHHH!*" and crossed my arms over my nearly bare chest as I scurried up the steep side of the basin. Heading back the way I'd come, I was relieved that I'd learned this lesson—the "watch out for catchment basins, dummy" lesson—in an abandoned area.

Back at the van, I mopped myself off with an old towel. Then I tried again, this time keeping the monster inside until I got all the way to the forest, where I crept into the dense thicket like a mite crawling into a burr. I closed my eyes and within seconds, felt the top of my monster-head meet the resistance of the clumped and tangled canopy. I reached up and pushed the branches gently away and opened my eyes again. When they'd adjusted to the darkness, I ducked low and moved toward the tiny clearing I could make out with my excellent new vision.

Once there, I sat on the ground and reached up again in order to brush my head free of the—I froze. *What in the WHAT, now? I have HORNS?? REAL horns? Where the eff did they come from???* It was true: Unlike the previous night, when I'd had only disappointing nubs, I now had two honest-to-goddess horns, pointy points and all. *Jesus be a wildebeest,* I thought as my adrenaline surged. Now, I had reason to suspect I hadn't been late in discovering I had a tail; rather, I hadn't *had* a tail the first time or two a monster came bursting out of me. I swiveled at the waist to look at my butt, and was relieved to find I still had the thing because *shit*, what if I could also *lose* a feature? I was stuck between competing exhilarations, and a few fears, too; what if this huge new part of myself never stopped morphing?

I looked up into the giant fir trees that twisted up and away from me, like a grove of spiral staircases serving some tucked-away world of elves and gnomes and such, and I knew what I wanted to do in this place: I wanted to suss out the monster's abilities. *My* abilities. I wanted to test myself in these trees.

I began modestly, jumping just a few yards in the air and grabbing a branch that looked sturdy at first glance, but immediately snapped like a toothpick and dropped me on my ass in the pine needles. Notably free of embarrassment, I stood up and sidestepped to a different tree and a different branch and tried again. When that one creaked loudly under my weight, I moved on again, then again. I eventually found a branch that could hold me, then another, and I gradually figured out what to look for—what to listen, smell, and feel for—in the age, size, and species of the trees.

I grabbed one of the monster-rated branches with both hands and swung forwards and backwards on it, joyously, then did the same with only one arm. After that, I swung all the way around with a *hoo-hoo-hoo!* as my stomach lurched toward my pelvis and my fingers nearly lost purchase on the bark. The knotty, ridged stuff rubbed against my palms, sending feedback to my monster-brain without abrading my thick skin.

The first time I flung myself out of a tree—which is a phrase I never expected to write—I didn't cover much distance. I wobbled and stumbled the landing and had to plant a hand on the ground to keep from falling. I tried again and again until I conquered it, each time starting off a bit farther from the ground.

After that, I couldn't resist trying to backflip. I'd done hundreds of reverse-tucks as a kid, off docks and diving boards from Straussville to the UWV campus and back. But now it was pitch-dark, and I was high above hard ground. If I was going to fall backwards, I reasoned, I needed to catch a good branch with a good grip and most important of all, it needed to be instinctual. I prayed to my primate ancestors that it would be.

I leaned backward until my butt lost contact with the branch, then arched my back and curled upward. When I was nearly upright again, I reached out and found a branch—right where I needed it to be. I grasped it easily with both hands, then let my body swing forward and let go again. I let myself fall again and again like this, flipping and swinging and hooting as I descended in a kind of ecstasy, all the way to the forest floor.

Thoroughly satisfied with my progress, I engaged in a little self-care: I rolled in the groundcover, stretched a few minutes, then rubbed my back up-and-down, back-and-forth, against a tree. It felt almost orgasmically good.

I felt an urge to get moving again, so I jumped up the nearest red cedar and tree-travelled toward another side of the forest. I climbed to the uppermost reaches of a grand fir in a spot bordered by a six-lane highway, dotted on the opposite side with commercial development. I sniffed the air of the human world beyond, marveling at the way my ears swiveled to and fro of their own accord, catching sounds from every direction and parsing the incoming data: airplane engines, buzzing highway lights, the whistles of faraway trains. When I picked up a ship's horn sounding from the far-off Willamette River, a fragmentary memory from my call with my mom floated to the forefront of my mind, only to dissolve the very instant a pair of mating insects flitted close by and my whiskers twitched involuntarily, warning them off.

I realized, then, that I wanted more than to be strong and powerful. That was so *yesterday*. Now I yearned for people to see me, hear me, and smell me being strong and powerful.

And I know, I know—*I know*—as a responsible mom, I should've done everything possible to keep the monster out of sight. The more people who saw her, and the clearer those sightings became, the sooner someone besides Justin would connect her to Harriet Lime—human, wife, mother of three, marketing professional.

But my frustration had been cranked up to new levels by last night's fight with Theo. And by the fact that whenever I told somebody I was struggling, their response was typically more pushback. By Sooby and Mr. Terrence downplaying that there had been a menacing, unidentified officer at PTA, and treating Ellen differently from everyone else. By Sooby and Mrs. Bamford describing me as some kind of shining example of self-reliance, which was alien to me. I yearned to bare my teeth, flex my muscles—to make myself as big as possible.

I also wanted to fix all the broken shit that had been annoying me. I know that's not what most beings with superpowers do in movies and comic books. But none of those characters—nor you—are working mothers of three. Every day, all around me, annoying shit drove me cuckoo-bird. Annoying shit inconvenienced me, made me late, and sometimes reminded me that life was unfair—like the extra hoops parents had to jump through to buy baby formula. Most of the time, I couldn't do anything about these things because I was trapped inside a puny, hairless human, one with a droopy bladder no less, that was at constant risk of collapsing—and this is true—into her vagina.[35]

I'd taken a huge risk yesterday at the golf course, after all, and the world hadn't ended. If tonight the monster wanted to roll and revel in her monsterness, like a dog in some foul carcass in the woods, who was I to tell her no? Harriet was—I was—part monster now, and I can only assume nature intended monsters to live differently.

There was, however, one big difference between last night's monster-escapade and tonight's: I'd been human-Harriet when I decided it was safe to go tooling around the golf course. This time, it was monster-logic that found it acceptable to be seen.

Monster-Harriet was fully aware, mind you, that once she was seen there'd be no going back. She apparently didn't care if she became notorious like Bigfoot and Nessie, or if people hunted her as some new species of big game, or even—*yikes*—if the police or military came looking. Monster-Harriet found our invisibility worth risking.

Meanwhile, human-Harriet had a nest to protect and bird-mouths to feed. She had mated for life and was still, for the most part, glad for it. I didn't understand yet how these two brains coexisted inside of me. But it was important they come to some kind of power-sharing arrangement, quick, if my family was to stand a chance at making it through all this. Because the monster had the capacity to destroy us all.

I watched the highway for about a minute, and was surprised when only six vehicles went by. I didn't hear any sirens, or sense any obvious dangers.

The first thing on the monster's agenda, also known as *Harriet's List of Grievances, Petty and Otherwise,* was across the highway from my perch in the grand fir, and a couple hundred yards to my right. It was the all-night grocery store with the too-dark parking garage, which was mostly empty at night. The market had been a lifesaver when the twins were infants, but I'd tried to avoid patronizing the place after a woman was assaulted in the garage

---

35   And again, if this squicks you out, or if you can't tell me what a pessary is and what it has to do with pregnancy, kindly refrain from butting into my medical care.

one summer—not only because I was fearful, but because the owners had done nothing to improve the security there and it bugged me.

When the highway was clear of cars for nearly a mile in both directions, I emerged from the trees and strode quickly and carefully, trying not to make any tremors. I reached the parking garage with my heart pumping fast and peered into the second floor. It was as dark and grim as ever.

I turned and glanced around, relieved when I didn't see anyone. Now that I was actually out in plain sight, my plan felt different. It felt . . . irresponsible. I could easily be spotted from the cars passing on the highway, from the garage, from nearby storefronts and parking lots. But no one had stopped or even slowed down as yet.

I reached up to grab one of the tall, spindly streetlights next to me, the kind with the cobra-shaped head. I bent it toward the garage and twisted it, illuminating the top floor. I did the same with another light, for the next floor down, and again for the ground floor. Puffed-up with satisfaction at the speediness and good results of my labors, I considered my mental list again.

From behind me, I heard the tinny beep of a car horn and then a truck's lower-pitched *blaaat*. In the split-second it took to whip my head around, everything I'd done as the monster flashed before my mind's eye and my heartrate skyrocketed. But the sounds turned out to have nothing to do with me—the truck had cut off the other driver, leading to their testy exchange, and both vehicles moved along. Still, the stress of believing myself seen and therefore caught—and, *oh my God*, probably imprisoned or worse—had shaken me enough to bring some human-sense nearer to the top of my mind. What if someone saw me when they were driving fast? I shivered, imagining the kind of collision I could cause.

I was being really fucking stupid.

I stood tall and looked over the garage, scanning for areas where I might engage more safely in my petty monstering. I wanted one more chance to do something I couldn't normally do before I had to head home. I spotted a newer shopping center with smaller and pricier stores.

It was situated well off the highway, so there were no fast-moving cars nearby and no tall streetlights—only human-scaled ones. I tiptoed toward it, behind the parking garage and grocery, careful to stay in the shadows. I stopped at the edge of the lot, where only my toes and the bottom part of my legs were illuminated. Then, holding onto the end of my tail— which was longer than it had been the day before, if I wasn't mistaken—I wrapped it once around me, holding it close to my body so it wouldn't accidentally smack the façade of the building or take down any of the trees in the fledgling landscape. I skooched sideways down one of the driving lanes until I reached a white pickup truck that was taking up two parking spaces.

I picked it up carefully, pinching it between my thumb and fingers as easily as if it were a chess piece, marveling at how toylike it looked in my hand. I was definitely much bigger now than when I'd tripped the light fantastic into Justin's pool. I was about to set the truck down again when it made a *chirp-chirp* sound and its lights flashed once. *Holy shit, the owner is coming!* Gasping like a schoolgirl, I bobbled the truck a few seconds before I recovered my hold and set it down, undamaged, inside the lines of a single space. Straight as a fucking pin.

I grunted softly before scuttling back to the darkness. When I stopped and turned around, I saw a youngish, gray-haired man with a paper bag in each hand, staring in my direction, wide-eyed. *Ohhhh—this is bad. He saw me.* I wondered, too, if my eyes reflected some of the light back at him, thereby making me visible to him still. *Stupid, stupid monster!* I squeezed them shut for a few seconds but ultimately cracked one open, lest I die of curiosity, and saw the man glance over at the truck, and then back toward me, then back at the truck. Then he slowly walked over to it and put a hand on the door. I took a gentle step backwards, then another. I saw him look my way one last time before I turned and shuffled, gorilla-style, back toward the park, indulging myself in a few *hoo-hoo-hoos!* as I went. I swung through the forest, jumped into the catchment basin on purpose, then ran through the old industrial site, human and naked and confident that there was one less person out there who would park like an asshole the next time he craved tacos or tofu. And I'd done it all without getting my photo taken—as far as I knew—and I didn't regret any of it one bit.

When I got home, I ignored the towers of dirty dishes in the sink and the growing pile of unopened mail on the counter, too. I stared instead at the goop piled atop our pitted old cutting board: Bret, Satchel, and Sierra had carved pumpkins all right, and hadn't finished the cleanup. But! Pumpkin guts are healthier than much of the other stuff I'd crammed into my face post-monstering, so I pulled a fork from the drawer and dove into the stuff. *Not bad*, I thought after my first scoop. I grabbed some cinnamon from the cabinet above my head and was wiping the edges of my mouth with a sleeve when I heard Bret's voice from behind me.

"I take it you didn't find a dress."

I whipped around. "What's that, hon?" I asked before jerking the fork behind my back.

"You went shopping for something to wear to Homecoming, right? I figured that's what you meant by 'errands.'"

"Oh," I replied, recalling how Sooby had volunteered me to chaperone that event. "Yeaaaah," I said over a groan, trying to put some real aggrievement into it. "No luck, I'm afraid."

"Then you should wear your old sequined one."

"*Noooooope*. No way, honey. That one is all yours that night."

"Then we should go shopping again," she said as she backed toward the doorway. "Together."

I didn't own anything, I had to admit, that was suitable for the semi-formal dance. "I'd really like that," I replied. She smiled and left the room.

I turned back to my pumpkin innards and thought about how far I'd come as a parent. I'd reached the point where I could go on a pleasant outing with my oldest child in the evening, whereas a couple years earlier I went almost nowhere, and had a near-breakdown over some locked-up baby formula when I did get to leave the house.

It hit me suddenly that *that* was the moment I'd started to become a monster inside: The formula incident was the first time I'd gone over the edge. It was the fulcrum between that old version of me and the monster version.

Younger-Harriet didn't sit on the floor and cry. Anywhere. Ever. But I'd been so raw that night, from the deprivations of the prior months. It was then and there, under the buzz of the fluorescent lights, that I began to understand that parenthood didn't *need* to be so difficult for so many of us. So divorce-causing. So breakdown-inducing.

I hadn't noticed it back then, the continental drift beginning inside of me. But now I could see it: That was the moment my anger had begun to get some light, and some oxygen.

2.10   SUNDAY, 3:00 P.M.

"*Really?* We're going to Nordstrom?"

"Yeah," I replied as I pulled out of the school parking lot a few days later.

Bret shifted in her seat, and I could feel the surge in her excitement. "Sierra and I went there with her mom, to get a cotillion dress a couple years ago. They were sooo nice to us. They treat you like . . . like a rich person or something."

I contemplated this for a few seconds. "Well, I'm not a rich person, so I'm just hoping to find something on the sale rack. Then I'm going to meet Christy at their café, because we've had a hell of a time trying to get together and she mentioned she'd be running by the mall today. Hey, can you text Dad for me, and see how things are with the babies?"

The two of us had gone to the middle school around lunchtime, to take part in a tutoring program we'd begun volunteering for. So by that point, Theo had been home alone with the twins for several hours.

A moment later she let me know his response. "He says, 'No prob, we're fine. In the garage.'"

"Tell him no table saw for the babies. Not unless they eat all their veggies at dinner."

Bret fired off the text and was quiet for several seconds.

"Did he answer yet?" I said, embarrassed at how thirsty I was for my own husband's reply.

"He says, 'Have a great time. And please tell Mom to buy herself something she actually likes.'"

I thought for several seconds, as my body temperature rose a few tenths of a degree. It had been a long time since I'd been excited at the prospect of clothes. It had been almost as long since Theo had given me any indication he paid attention to such things. Lack of jokes aside, I took his reply as a net positive.

Once we'd picked out three dresses that seemed like good candidates, I situated myself in the store's clean, spacious dressing room while we waited for the sales associate to bring me the correct size. I looked myself over in the full-length, three-panel mirror while Bret stood outside of my plush cocoon, sipping from a chocolate milkshake and occasionally telling me about something that had happened that week.

I smelled the associate's light, musky perfume before she reached us, while she was still too far away for human noses to detect it. And not to brag, but I also heard her leather-soled ballerina flats on the wall-to-wall carpet. "OK, ladies, here we are!" she called out when she got close.

I was still dressed, so I opened the door and she whooshed in—I swear, it was like she brought her own wind with her—with a bulging armful of garments. "That seems like more than three."

"I found several others I thought you might like, and brought them for you to try. Your decision," she said before floating back to the sales floor. "My name is Aria; if you need anything at all, please let me know."

"I can't try all those on," I said as Bret set her shake on the floor and began sorting through what appeared to be about twelve or fifteen items. "I don't have it in me."

I started looking through them, too, from the opposite end of the rack. "Mother of the bride, mother of the bride, grandmother of the bride . . ." I droned as I pushed each garment over. "*Funeral* of the bride . . ." I added as I paused over one especially depressing number.

"I get it, I get it," Bret replied. "Here—start with the three you picked, and I'll just—"

I pulled my tank top over my head, and the static electricity lifted my hair toward the ceiling tiles. "You'll just what?"

"Nothing."

I stopped undressing and looked back at her. *"What?"*

"I like these other two she brought. But you can skip these other ones, so I'll just take them out—"

"*Breeeeeet.* Step away from the mauve taffeta, please."

When she stepped to the side, I saw what she'd wanted to whisk away: The sales associate had included a half-dozen pieces of "shapewear" in her haul.[36]

I laughed, and examined one of the elastic, high-waisted bottoms. Then I shrugged. "A lot of people wear these. Women *and* men," I said, turning my attention back to dresses I'd picked myself.

"I mean, I just thought it was a little rude," Bret replied as she closed the door, this time staying inside the dressing room while I changed.

"You mean the fact that she looked me up and down and identified some stuff that she wanted to, like, vacuum-seal before seeing me in one of these getups?"

She gave me a sympathetic grunt.

"Stores like this remind me of the recipe websites I go to, looking for some easy, fast, potato-based meal that won't break the bank and that Jojo and Frankie might actually eat. You know the ones—they bombard you with tons and tons of ads? For food and appliances or whatever?"

---

36 Shapewear is the modern term for girdle-type things.

"I know! It's *crazy*!" Bret replied as I pulled on a dress. "They have to have a special button for all the people who need help finding the actual recipe. You know—*on the recipe page*."

"Right. Those sites know their audience is mostly moms, and mostly moms who are trying to manage a household budget."

"OK."

I glanced at myself in the mirror. "And I am . . . so bone-tired, Bret, of people trying to tell me what I need."

She turned her head sideways, but kept looking my way. "What do you mean?"

"Because I have tried and tried and fucking *tried* to tell people what I need and what I want. And no one listens to me." I pulled dress #1 over my head a little too violently and reminded Bret about the time I spoke up about the construction at the middle school and in return received a smack-down in the form of a newspaper editorial the next day.

 She reached to her shoulder for her hair. "And?"

"And yet here we are, shopping, and like clockwork, somebody rushes up and tries to predict what I need," I said, trying to force one of the straps of dress #2 up and over one of my wide swimmer-shoulders.

"Aria's just doing her job," Bret replied, still holding her hair in front of her shoulder, and standing on one foot.

I didn't want to try on the third dress, I'd decided, so I was getting back into my own clothes when I replied, "I know. I just don't care to be treated like some kind of . . . some Queen of Domesticity, with a bunch of foot soldiers running around me, trying to figure out what products I might bene-fit from. I'd gladly abdicate that throne, in exchange for the world to just freakin' believe me when *I* say what I want and need. On important stuff."

She squinted at me, and we were quiet for a few minutes as we left the dressing room and I paid for the dress I'd decided to buy. Then we continued through the Special Occasion department, believing it would eventually lead us to the café. When we found ourselves in Hosiery and Lingerie, however, we slowed our pace and glanced at some finery.

"Mmmm," Bret said as she let a gauzy camisole slide through her fingers. We started walking again.

After a couple of minutes, Bret paused and picked up a box from a display. I stopped, too, and watched as she made a confused face and set it down again. "Where are we, anyway?" she asked, frustration edging into her voice. "How did we end up in Maternity?"

I turned, looking in all directions. "I dunno. I wasn't paying attention." We retraced some of our steps. "Hang on," I said, stopping again. "I think we're back in the . . . yep, we're back in the fancy underwear, Bret. How did we—we just got *out* of fancy underwear!"

We both started giggling. "I know," Bret replied through a fit of laughter. "Seems like we should've noticed it the second we crossed back here from the nipple relief cream."

"Seriously," I replied with faux indignation. The giggles were coming on strong as I added, "And why are they sending people back into lingerie when they've just been dealing with chafed nipples?"

"C'mon," Bret said, grabbing my arm and tugging it. "Here, I'll help you through Maternity. Again."

"No : . . . please stop . . . it hurts my . . . something," I sputtered as we trotted off, our arms all entangled.

***

"I didn't even know Nordstrom had a café," I said a few minutes later as we settled into a booth. Bret was sitting next to me, waiting to say hello to Christy before heading down to browse at the bookstore.

A few seconds later, the doctor herself slid quietly into the seat across from us, her face open and bright. She wore a white sweater of some fine-looking material, and her hair was styled and in place. I smiled back at her as Bret said, "Hi, Dr. Holmes!"

Christy was a bit of a celebrity in our world. She'd been on the cover of *Healthy Oregon* a few years earlier, and was regularly ranked among the state's top doctors by an impressive array of publications and organizations.

"You OK, Harry?"

I shook my head back to attention, and realized I'd been staring at her chest. "Oh, sorry—that was weird. I was just admiring your laundry skills," I stammered. "Or your skill in avoiding all the usual mom-dribbles."

Bret groaned, and I felt her lift from the bench. "That's my cue to head to Barnes & Noble." She gave Christy a little wave and took off.

"I'll spill some coffee on it before we go. Just for you, Harry."

"Thanks. I appreciate that. Or wine."

I watched Bret until she was no longer in sight, and when I turned back, Christy said, "I'll just have coffee and some soup, I think. I'm trying to cut back."

"Oh? OK," I said, trying not to signal any particular reaction to her declining a glass of wine. I'd thought I was getting better at disguising my emotions, especially ones like surprise, worry, fear, confusion. But clearly, I still had some improving to do.

"I'm not pregnant or anything," she added. She nodded and glanced around, and though her posture was still excellent and her eyes still clear, I sensed something jump inside her, though I wasn't sure what. In spite of her relentlessly Instagram-worthy presentation, there had been something skittish about her the last few times I'd seen her—something that didn't show up on magazine covers or social media posts.

"I mean, it'd be fine if you were."

"Pregnant?

"Having a glass of wine. While pregnant or not pregnant or whatever."

"Oh." She made a motion of tucking some hair behind her ear again, though none of it had slipped out. Then she did it on the other side to another imaginary lock as she stared—a little too wide-eyed—at the menu.

She wasn't herself. I wanted to be there for her, but I wasn't sure if I should tell her Theo had told me about her impending separation from Brian. "So, how are you doing?"

I was still getting used to having a monster's sixth sense—and seventh and eighth senses, apparently—because I noticed for the first time her slightly oily scalp and the overpowering aroma of dry shampoo; a few pulls in her otherwise immaculate sweater; and the small bald spot in one of her brows, where she'd attempted to cover a scar with powder. I could tell, too, that she was exhausted down to her bones.

The server arrived to take our order. I blurted out "chardonnay" and "whatever one is cheapest" and tried not to be too grabby at Christy's menu or to shove them too forcefully into the server's hands.

"Things are OK," she replied as she looked at me with a few shallow nods. "For the most part."

Again, I could feel the sudden acceleration of her heartbeat. So being a monster had turned me into, among other things, a fleshy lie detector. I wasn't sure I wanted this perk. Was being a monster going to prevent me from talking to friends, forever? I didn't need any more obstacles to that.

"How are *you*?" she asked, with more evenness than I'd have thought possible given the change in her vital signs.

"I'm . . . I've been kind of *bonkers* lately, to be honest."

She laughed and took a sip of her water. "Oh? Good 'bonkers' or bad 'bonkers'?"

I paused. "For one thing, I'm hung up on what happened at the PTA meeting the other night," I replied finally.

"Yes! You mean what happened to that new mom, the one who's a director at Hind?"

"Ellen Stout, yes."

"What the hell was *that*?" she replied, her face flushed with real emotion. "On my way home afterward, I started going over all the stories you've told me from when Mr. T was a teacher."

"Hoffman was even whiter then than it is now. So it's only recently that he's gotten a chance to really showcase his racism."

She shook her head. "I'm glad you saw that, too. You're the first person who's mentioned it, though. You were right about the cult of personality around him."

Like Ellen, Christy hadn't gone to school at Hoffman, and had moved to Straussville as an adult. But I'd bitched to her enough over the years that she was reasonably versed in all things Mr. Terrence, and I was relieved to hear she'd had a similar reaction to the events that night.

"So you saw the guy in the back, too, with the cowboy hat?"

"In all black? Yes," she replied, squinting and taking another sip of water. "Who was he?"

"I haven't been able to find out. Yet. Mr. Terrence plays dumb about it, and Sooby didn't know."

She thought awhile, looking out the panoramic window of the café, which faced a large and mostly empty parking lot. "I've known men like Mr. Terrence, though. Since forever."

"Oh?" I replied.

"Men who, on a daily basis, behave in a way that's almost cute. And funny, I guess. So you put your guard down, thinking you're simpatico. Then one day, it's like, BOOM. There was a powder keg inside them all along, you just couldn't see it."

I nodded emphatically.

"And the eruption," she went on, "and the meanness of it—is so out of keeping with what you felt about the guy before, you look for an explanation for why it was an aberration. Or worse, why it was your fault and not his."

"Are you speaking from experience on this, friend?"

As she reached for her water, her eyes went big, and her head gave a quick tilt. "Oh, *yeah*." It was one of those flickers she gave off every now and again, like she was temporarily switching to another version of herself. She was normally forthright and self-possessed, but on certain rare occasions, her posture would slacken and her eyes would refocus, in an expression that was there and gone again in seconds. I'd gathered through what few bits and pieces she'd shared over the years that she hadn't had the easiest childhood, but was loath to talk about it with me because, as she'd once put it, "At least I had grown-ups around."

I told her about the annual Science Fair Mr. Terrence had hosted each spring when he was a teacher, which had always drawn a huge crowd and where one event—called the "Senior Launch"—was the *pièce de résistance.*

"So, the seniors were allowed on the roof of the school, and given three chances to launch water balloons into the parking lot. There was a white ribbon for the student whose balloon went the farthest, a red one for the kid whose balloon landed closest to the distance they'd calculated ahead of time, and a blue ribbon for anyone who hit a special target Mr. Terrence set up. He'd never given out the blue one before, though."

"Not at all? He probably gets off thinking he bested his own students."

"No one had ever hit the special target. Not until I did, anyway."

Christy clapped her hands together. "That's amazing, Harry! I love it. But why are you frowning?"

"Because he never gave me the blue ribbon. He disqualified me."

"On what grounds?"

"Well, he'd screwed me over in the past, so I wanted to make sure that if I hit the target there'd be no questioning the thing was wet, dammit. And that he couldn't claim it was wet from someone else's balloon. So I put a few drops of red food coloring in mine."

Her eyes narrowed. "What was the special target?"

"A 1990 Ford Mustang GT convertible. Mr. Terrence's."

"Oh man, Harry. With the top down?"

"Geez, Christy! No. I'm not an animal," I replied. *At least not back then!* "The roof was up. But it was an off-white roof."

"Ooooooh boy. And now it's a pink roof, I gather? And he disqualified you because of it?"

I nodded, and some residue of regret I had from that long-ago incident seeped into my voice as I answered, "Technically, he disqualified me because I'd put something besides water in my balloon, which was against the rules." I shrugged, suddenly self-conscious about how much I was showing I still cared. "But he gets away with ignoring rules all the time."

I tried to reach casually for my water, and in a late attempt to appear less obsessed with Mr. Terrence, changed the subject. "Hey, do you know a doctor named Miriam Morris?" I asked.

"Of course!" she said, tossing me a friendly scowl. "Are you kidding? Dr. M is like . . . well, not quite a rock star, I guess, but maybe a . . . cult favorite? Can a person be a cult favorite?"

"A person can be *anything*," I said, raising my brows. "Trust me."

She shook her head and her smile went weary all of a sudden. "She's having a hell of a time getting her new lab up and running, though. It's maddening."

"What do you mean? How the hospital dragged its ass about renting her a space?"

"Almost a year, yeah. I heard she's had trouble hiring vendors and contractors, too. And then there was the accident the other day."

"What accident?" I asked. I must have blanched, too, because Christy cocked her head at me.

"I overheard some colleagues talking about a flood in the sub-basement, and when I asked about it, they said it was in some new lab. Turns out it was Dr. M's."

"Holy *shit*, Chris. I just saw her, and everything seemed to be shaping up for her, finally."

"Some expensive equipment got ruined. Water damage. People are speculating there was shoddy work," she said as she shook her head and pulled out her day-planner, then made a note. "I should've gone down there to see her by now."

"That's . . . that's *so* weird."

She shrugged. "It's pretty derelict down there, actually. It's a shame."

"Insurance will cover it."

"Yes, but that kind of ultra-specialized equipment isn't sitting on a shelf somewhere. It's custom-made, and extremely expensive. There's probably only one or two manufacturers."

She reached into her purse and pulled out a small canvas pouch. Inside it was a medicine bottle from which she poured a couple of tiny pills into her palm. "Can I tell you something?"

"Of course."

"The baby got his hands on some . . . some prescription medicine at our house, and ate it," she said. She gave a quick scoff, one I was sure she was directing at herself. It was the sound that many women—too many of us—make when we're about to say something bad about ourselves.

Her eyes went glassy. "I should've seen the bottle where it didn't belong. I should have noticed it wasn't closed properly—"

"OH, honey. No—no, no, no," I replied, reaching out and grabbing one of her hands. "Things happen. Accidents happen. Kids get into things."

"My baby had his stomach pumped a few months ago, and all I can think about is, are my toenails neat and polished, and stealing five minutes to style my hair, and getting exactly the right Chanel lip color. I'm really fucking self-absorbed, Harry. How did I get this way?"

I leaned forward and grabbed her other hand. "Please, look at me. You are *not* vain. You are wonderful."

She didn't look convinced. "I read somewhere that husbands who visit prostitutes are turned on by how well-groomed they are," she said in a rush.

I ran a fingertip along one of my scruffy brows. "Is that true?"

She shrugged. "Like, supposedly that's what they're looking for. Why they go to them."

"The impeccable grooming?"

She shrugged again.

"And a lot wives can't meet those standards, even when they want to," I finished, contemplating this. "Moms especially. *Jeez.*"

She pulled her hands away as the server brought her coffee and some kind of red wine for me, even though I'd ordered white. I started to pull it toward me, intending to let the slip go.

"Sir, excuse me," Christy said, lifting the glass and handing it back to the young man. "My friend ordered the Underwood Pinot Gris." There was no questioning in her voice, no apology. The waiter hurried off.

"Oh God, that was my 'work voice,' wasn't it?" she said once he'd gone. "My 'bitch voice.' It seems to follow me home from the hospital more and more these days."

I waved my hands in the air, all raggedy-like, as if to disperse the rank nonsense she'd just released into it. "See, I was going to call that being an amazing friend. You were just being assertive, and you were perfectly civil. By the way, you're an amazing mom, too."

"Thanks for saying that."

"And even if you were an average mom, like the rest of us, I'd still be here singing your praises."

"You and Sue-Beth are out there trying to figure out what happened at that meeting, Ellen Stout is standing up to Mr. Terrence, and poor Dr. M's flooded out of her lab. Yet here I am, absorbed in my own . . . shit." She looked straight into my eyes as she added, "What can I do? How can I help?"

I didn't reply with suggestions. I thought she might need to laugh, so I entertained her by recounting the Spanx incident from earlier, and by relating a few of the funny things the twins had said recently. We both laughed so hard during my "Mommy, you said the fuck word" story that we were still grinning a quarter hour later, when we met Bret at the door to the parking lot and said our goodbyes.

I was lost in a tornado of thoughts—good, bad, and monster-y—when I pulled out of the mall parking lot. We were about to get on the highway toward home when I spied Bret slump in her seat from the corner of my eye. "Honey?" I asked. "You OK?"

"We're out of Advil."

"Yeah, I know. You took the last two on the ride here, remember? What's going on?"

"Nothing. Just the usual. Shoulder stuff."

"I didn't realize it was that bad."

She shrugged. Then, *"Ow."*

"Let's ice it when you get home."

"Can we stop at a CVS or something? Coach said it's OK to take, like, four or six at a time."

"Four or six what?"

"Of Advil."

"What?" I braked way too hard at the red light just ahead of us, and could practically feel her roll eyes at me.

"Moooom. It's ibuprofen, not heroin."

"That's not my concern. Well, it's not my first concern." I was gripping the steering wheel a little too hard, and I felt the tension all the way up my arms. "My concern is that your coach shouldn't be telling you how much of a painkiller you can take. And he definitely shouldn't be doing it when it goes against what the instructions say, or what a doctor says. *Christ.*"

"Mom, can we just drive home, please? He's not a bad person, OK?"

"I've been meaning to talk to you about Coach Sullen, actually. He has a . . . different approach to his players than any of your past coaches. Or any of your teachers, for that matter. He seems to have some issues with boundaries. And that bothers . . . your father and me," I said, though I didn't have any idea if Theo even knew about Coach Sullen's extensive reach into our daughter's life.

When she didn't reply, I waited as long as I could bear it, which I estimate to be about ten seconds, before continuing. "Bret, did you hear me?"

Still nothing. I stole a glance at her, then checked the speedometer to ensure I wasn't absently exerting as much pressure on the gas as I was on the steering wheel. I contorted my face and swirled my head around atop my neck, the way I did when I wanted to tamp down some heartburn, although the thing I was trying to keep a lid on right now wasn't stomach acid. "Bret, when you went to the craft store, did those other girls really go with you and Coach Sullen?" I asked, even though by then, her body language and smell and subtle sounds had already given up the answer. "And don't lie to me."

"I shouldn't have to tell you everything!"

I shook my head, hard, in an effort not to raise my voice. *Deep breaths, Harry. Deep breaths, Monster.* "Honey, you're only fourt—"

"Dad doesn't."

Rage swelled in me like some kind of celestial storm we don't yet have here, and I wanted to scream at Bret that my marriage was none of her goddamn business and furthermore, had nothing to do with my expectations for her behavior. But for the first time, I felt the monster's presence—right there with me—unequivocally. She wasn't knocking anymore; her second, singular perspective had taken up full-time residence in my mind. Concerned she might show herself, too—and in front of my daughter, on the freaking highway, no less—I choked back my initial, turbulent reaction.

Besides, as I drove—and seethed, and tried not to seethe—I considered the possibility that Bret was right. Theo certainly could be keeping something, or *some things*, from me. Recognizing this showed me how muddled I was in that moment, and reminded me that what happens between two parents is very much the business of kids.[37]

I felt the monster flex under my skin. She wasn't a fully distinct being, I was gathering; she was more like a second version of myself that had manifested in my psyche and was hanging out there with the old, human-me. And she was riveted, I could tell, by the emotional wrestling match I had going on. Because even though I was relieved that I'd been able to stop myself from transforming, my stomach still churned with the fear that my monster-ness was going to destroy my family. That was a constant. Plus, I had all this *wrath* to deal with now. Like any woman who wants to be liked, included, and successful—not to mention safe, unhurt, and alive—I'd kept my anger locked in a closet all my life. Now, the thing had nearly chewed the door off and I was grappling with the fact that I . . . didn't hate it? That my fury, with all its flagrant female-ness, wasn't as ugly as I'd been led to believe?

---

37   You know what else is the business of kids? Whether or not mommy is part monster.

The monster had no such conflict. For her, anger was the proper, even righteous, response to the situation in the car that night. If she felt fear at all, I couldn't sense it.

It was nearly dark when I pulled into our driveway a little too fast and parked a little too abruptly. I grabbed my bag and pushed open the door in a single fluid motion, then heard the sound of a continuous spray of water coming from Justin's front yard. I knew it wasn't a sprinkler. I knew he was standing outside the triangle of light coming from his front porch because I could smell him, and his exact location. I shut the car door behind me forcefully, and Bret slammed hers with an even bigger bang.

"Bret?" I called out from across the car. "I'm taking away your phone for a week, and in the meantime, we'll work out some rules for—"

"Mom, are you *serious*? Look, I'm sorry I lied, but—"

"*Bret.*" I said her name like a declaration of some kind of domestic war I'd never been in before. "Phone. Now." I held out my hand and started toward her.

"*Moooo-om!*" she part-yelled, part-whined as she backed away a couple steps. "Coach is *not* some kind of monster!"

"Oh, really?" I scoffed, letting out a humorless, almost menacing laugh. "Bret Lime, you don't know anything about the world. You don't know how much terrible shit men do. Even men we trust."

I couldn't believe the monster-rage I felt at my own daughter in this moment. I closed my eyes for a few seconds, trying to calm myself. I wasn't worried the monster would emerge anymore, but I was suddenly a little bit scared of my own fury.

"You don't get it, do you?" I went on, scorn giving my words a grotesque new timbre. "You don't see how people can destroy you without leaving a mark."

"UGHHHH!" She threw her phone into the yard in my general direction before storming toward the house. My cheeks were already overheated, along with much of the rest of me, as I turned and walked over to where it had landed, muttering, *"You'd be surprised, who is and who isn't a monster."*

"Everything OK, Mrs. Lime?" Justin called out to me.

Oh, you've gotta be fucking kidding me. He is seriously going to involve himself right now? I felt the monster readying herself, but I didn't need her just then. I wasn't prepared to hit the toggle switch that existed between the two of us, and she seemed to understand that, and settled back a bit.

"Just peachy, Mr. Justin!" I replied as I flung my purse onto my shoulder and picked up the phone. Then I gave him a sloppy salute as Bret slammed the door to our house shut. "Juuuuuust peachy."

"Can I water your lawn for you, while I'm out here?" His voice had the earnestness of a TV dad from decades yore. At that moment, anyway. He took a step in my direction.

"Nope."

"You sure?" Another step closer.

"Seriously. Not a good time, Justin. Stop right there. Please."

"Ya know," he went on, "it's OK to accept a little help sometimes."

All of the indignation inside of me—all that malignant star-stuff that had been drawn to me, then into me, my whole life—imploded in my gut at long last, like a black hole. Monster-Harriet was spoiling for a fight again, too. I looked over my shoulder at him. "I'm sorry?"

"I don't know why you're so opposed to it."

I turned and took a slow step forward, my posture bent in mock submission. "What—what is it you think I'm opposed to, again? 'Help'?"

He chuckled and came a half-step closer, to a spot where his porch light sliced him in two, from top to bottom. "I said you should ask for help more, yeah. Or take it when it's offered. That's all—"

"You think that's what my problem is?"

His *aw, shucks* mode seemed to switch off then, and I watched his silhouette straighten, and grow taller. Such a cipher, this dude. "I didn't say you have a problem, Harriet. Just that every—"

In three rapid strides I was up in his face, my voice fierce. "You're telling me you've been sitting over here all this time, in your house or your yard or your gun safe or wherever, thinking, 'Wow, all Harriet's troubles would just go—*poof!*—if she'd only accept what I'm offering her?'" Inside of me, the monster was nodding emphatically. I could picture her expression. It said, *Sing it, sister.*

"No, I—"

"Because here's the thing, Justin: Life's been beating the ever-loving shit out of me lately. I'm over here putting all my energy into blocking whatever gut-punch is coming my way next, and you're gonna complain that I won't let you remove a couple splinters from my toe?"

He inched forward then, which brought his whole face into the light. His expression was inscrutable to me but I could tell his adrenaline was up, and his heartbeat, though I didn't sense he was frightened of me. "I just thought I'd be doing something nice for you, by taking something off your list."

"That's odd. *Hmmm.* I don't remember you asking to see my to-do list, Justin. And I don't remember you asking to clean up projectile vomit, or change a dirty Pull-Up, either. What I do remember is you offering to do some things that make my front yard and house look better, all of which happen to make *your* house and yard look better. Why do you suppose that is?"

"*Jesus*, Harriet. So I own a lot of tools for home and yard projects, OK? That's—"

"Have you offered to pick up any of the dog shit in my backyard?" Monster-Harriet giggled then.

He looked genuinely confused at this. "What?"

"Have you offered to pick up any dog shit? In my backyard?"

His nostrils moved, and I wondered if he was trying to sniff for alcohol on my breath. I was really raving, I suppose. "No."

"Well, why not? Do you need some kind of super-specialized tool for that? One that's on back order?"

"I just . . . look, Harriet. You've seen me out here before, doing things on my own property. So explain to me, please, why offering to do some of those things for you, while I'm already out here, makes me a bad person?"

"Oh, cut the *shit*, man. You jumped on my case when I didn't accept your help, and I'm just trying to explain to you why I didn't."

"Why then, Harriet?"

"Because everything you're offering me has a big ol' asterisk next it. *'Must not be inconvenient, unpleasant, costly, or difficult. Is not guaranteed to be something you especially need or want right now.'*"

"I don't think that way, Harriet. And frankly, I find the suggestion insulting."

I snorted. "Look. *Justin.* I'm an expert on needing help, OK? I've needed help my whole life. And I know what it costs a person when they accept it."

"What are you talking about, 'costs'? I'm offering you a damn favor!"

"When you accept somebody else's time and effort, for nothing in return, that makes you a bit . . . *suspect.* Your neighbors wonder if you're a taker, a freeloader, maybe even some kind of scammer."

He was quiet for several seconds. "What happened to you, Harriet? Was it something when you were a kid?"

I snorted again. "What happened to *me*?" I snorted several more times, each one uglier and more satisfying than the one before. "What happened to this *country*, man? That's the question you should be asking. Because you know what's really messed up, neighbor? We act like people who need help are less American than the rest of us. Because real Americans, we all know, are independent down to their bones! Americans are all, *'Rah-rah-rah, I don't need no stinking people!'* The irony is, George Washington and all those guys? They didn't think that way. They pretty much believed the opposite, and they're the ones who started this place, for fuck's sake."

I spun around and started marching toward our front door. Halfway there I called back to him, "So don't mind me, Justin. I'll just be over here stumbling through the day. Like always." My last glimpse was of him standing there, stock-still, dribbly hose in hand, utterly nonplussed.

I went inside, threw my bag down, and sent an email to the high school principal asking for a meeting, attended by Coaches Terrence and Sullen, too, at the soonest possible time.

I checked on the twins—asleep in their beds—and cracked our bedroom door for a quick glimpse of Theo. As I took in the regular rise and fall of his torso, it occurred to me that I'd never sensed a sudden physiological change in him—a spike in heart rate or blood pressure, say—like the ones I felt in Mr. Terrence and Christy when they'd said things that weren't true. *So what had Bret been talking about?*

The floorboards groaned underneath me as I stepped gently to the bed and leaned over to kiss the side of Theo's face, right where the ridge of bone joined with the soft coverture of his cheek. And I lingered awhile, indulging in the tangy smell of him.

It had often seemed, when Theo and I talked downstairs in the wee hours and the kids were in dreamland above us, that disagreeing and hashing things out was our struggle alone. Or that not bothering to disagree and hash things out was our struggle alone. That's how I wanted it to be—that our adult difficulties wouldn't affect the kids. But in reality, whatever it is that ebbs and flows between one parent and another is the current our kids learn to raft on, before venturing into their own relationships with partners, bosses, friends, and offspring.

I returned to the hallway and saw the crack of light at the bottom of Bret's door. I tiptoed downstairs, then paced around trying to keep a lid on my surging, visceral, skin-prickling urge to turn into the monster. When I crept to the top of the stairs again, I heard Bret's white-noise playing—she listened to the same rumbling ocean sounds the twins did at bedtime—and saw that her light was out. Then I split.

2.11 SUNDAY, GOING ON MIDNIGHT

I sailed high into the air, my entire hometown underfoot.

I hadn't practiced sky-high leaps since the night at the golf course, where I'd bungled every attempt. Now I found their wobbly recklessness to be exactly what I needed: the lack of precise control, the chance I might slice myself in two on a slim antenna I didn't see coming. That night, only imminent physical danger and adrenaline could overwhelm my fears of inappropriate coaches, of spouses who may or may not be withholding things, of my own capacity for shitty parenting.

But my confidence grew with each steady landing, and with each clean line I made through the dark. Eventually the fear gave way to giddiness and I felt like Ferdinand the bull, leaping and bounding about, reveling at the uncanny yet wholly natural way my body listened and responded and did what I asked it to. I somersaulted at the peak of one jump, and on another I spun like a corkscrew. It was so exhilarating that I did it again and again and again, on the way up and the way down, too.

During one twirl, watching my tail curl around my torso, it occurred to me that I *really* needed to find out what I looked like. I'd been stupid, putting it off so long. Did I resemble human-Harriet to a degree that made this kind of semipublic monstering a terrible risk? Also, had my monster-body evolved yet again? I needed to get a good look at myself, and the only monster-sized mirror I could think of was in the city.

I bounded north along the Willamette River. It was the longer route to Portland, but I kept to the beachy areas, sandbars, and shallow islands of that waterway because I'd never forgive myself if I accidentally Hulk-smashed a neighborhood school or community garden. Besides, most of these sandy points were substantial at that time, thanks to the ongoing drought; it was easy to avoid any splashdowns that could turn me into Harriet again— bare-assed, out in the open, and far from home.

As I went, my monster-brain sorted and catalogued the myriad stim-ulations that my ears, eyes, and nose fed into it. I caught hints of the lilies at Portland Nursery, lots of wood-burning fireplaces, six different roasts of fair-trade coffee, and occasionally dog poop. Labs, pugs, and mutts mostly. It was a trip.

When I reached the Flaherty Brothers Sand and Gravel plant, which was squeezed onto one of the few larger islands south of downtown Portland, I hopped onto a large silo, iconic in its corn-yellow paint and single, royal-blue stripe. Clinging to the side of it, I took a moment to admire the city's skyline, spiked with glassy towers, then made a series of smaller hops from silo to cellular tower to riverfront park, where I accidentally frightened a homeless couple. From there, I bounced to the edge of the old railroad bridge, then dropped into the park on the opposite, downtown side of the river before springing up again, this time to a tower on the Steel Bridge. From there, I made my biggest leap yet—way, *waaaaay* up, to the rooftop of a building that some people refer to as "Big Pink," on account of its alternating bands of reflective pink glass and equally pink granite. It's the second-tallest thing in Portland.[38]

I skidded to a stop and was briefly alarmed when the building swayed beneath me. Then I remembered that structures in these parts were designed to move during earthquakes, and regained my bearings. I walked coolly to the edge of the roof, knelt down, and began to lean over.

Then I paused. Because I wasn't sure I was truly ready. Though I absolutely, one hundred percent needed to know how likely it was that someone would recognize me in the event they saw the monster, I realized I was also concerned about whether or not the monster was . . . unattractive.

I pulled back from the ledge and shook myself out like a dog, then gave myself a little growl—that gurgly, breathy noise that seemed to be one of the monster's hallmarks. It was almost cute.

Oh, man. Forget ugly—what if I was fucking *cute*? Shit. It hadn't occurred to me that I might *not* be scary; that I was more Sully than Predator. Jerry's owner had run from me, I recalled. But she'd been high. When other, more sober people saw me, would they squee rather than run? I sat back on my butt and let myself have a little pout as it dawned on me that I didn't want to be a monster if I couldn't shock, scare, or intimidate anyone. As Harriet, I already found it nearly impossible to get people to hear me, to respond with anything besides dismissal or disbelief.

---

38   It's true: Portland's second-biggest structure is conspicuously pink. As if we needed another reminder of where our culture ranks things it considers feminine.

Sooooo . . . I want to be scary-looking. Does that require being ugly? Can't I be attractive, but with authority? I'd been given a one-in-a-trillion opportunity—in the form of tremendous size, power, and a yet-untested ability to heal myself—but here I was, wrangling with the same old shit human females have had to deal with forever.

I was about to lean over the edge again when the bouquet of smells that continuously lit up my brain brought something new to my attention—something that raised my hackles. I shut my eyes, inhaled deeply, and got my first clear note of smoke.

I sprung off the building on instinct, back to my tower on the Steel Bridge. I hugged the metal and turned my head all around, sniffing fast. The northeast smelled smokier than other directions. Something out that way—past the Moda Center, a half-dozen neighborhoods from Irvington to Cully, and the airport—was the source of the smell. I recalled our newscasters' dire warnings about our strangely dry conditions, how they were just right for forest fires. I knew then that the low clouds I thought I'd seen on the horizon moments earlier were, in fact, billows of smoke and ash.

I cracked several panels of glass when I landed on one of the spires of the Convention Center, but I was trying to move as fast as I could in the direction of the smoke. I leapt to the industrial area near the confluence of the Willamette and Columbia then turned inland, traveling east along the Oregon side of the latter river. Each jump was farther and faster and less cautious than the one before it; and at the same time, the ash in the air became thicker and hotter and my visibility far worse. On one jump—out of the parking lot of a massive truck stop—I lost sight of the ground. So I decided to stick to the interstate: It had a wide right-of-way for much of its run, and I figured I'd be able to keep track of it even in dense smoke, and find room on its shoulders and feeder roads for my sloppy landfalls. Plus, the smoke kept me hidden from drivers and others on the ground.

When the ground began to roll up and down underneath me and the forest along the highway thickened like winter fur, I knew I was coming up on the Columbia River Gorge. Any other day, I'd be thrilled to be the monster in this spectacular place: I would've bounded between steep rock faces, hopped from butte to butte and from one spectacular waterfall to another. I'd have messed with any Bigfoot enthusiasts I came across, visited the lookout where Theo and I got married, and drawn every glorious, pungent forest smell deep into my lungs and bloodstream.

But by that time, the only thing I was breathing in—or hacking, sputtering, and wheezing through—was grit and ash. Now, as soon as I left the ground I could no longer see it. Worse, the highway had become a winding mountain road with no edges to speak of. I followed it loosely, in and out of any clearings I managed to spot in the woods.

When I found myself in a field of some kind after one of my better landings, I decided to jump as high as I could, in hopes that I'd rise above the smoke and be able to figure out where I was. I squatted low and launched myself with all my might, and sure enough, I reached clearer, colder air. But as I sucked in giant lungfuls of the stuff, I realized I couldn't make out anything underneath me and worse, I'd pushed off so hard that I'd lost control over my body's position in the air. I'd gotten the "twisties," as gymnasts call it, just as I began plummeting earthward, tumbling one way and the other like a gyroscope.

Pulsing with adrenaline, I tried to give in to the uncertainty of the situation, and not the terror of it. It didn't matter how far away the ground was, I told myself; it didn't matter what the surface was like there because there was nothing I could do about it. Besides—I could heal myself!

The ground didn't come when I expected it. I kept falling and falling and I was beginning to feel proud of how high I must have jumped when my back slammed into some boulders on the riverbank. The impact broke my spine in multiple places, and both my legs and arms.

Pain overwhelmed me, blacking out my vision. I lay as still as possible, but even breathing hurt. Pretty soon I started whimpering, which brought ash into my lungs, and then I coughed—which cranked up my agony still further. Gritting my teeth and squeezing my eyes shut, I willed the healing process to begin before I lost the battle against full-on crying. I thought tears might amount to enough moisture to change me back to Harriet. Whereupon I'd probably be broken for good.

A dense mental fog descended over me like a weighted blanket. I prayed I would pass out, but macabre questions kept creeping to mind: *What if I'd discovered the limit to my healing ability? If I die with my body still twisted and draped across these rocks, will my corpse be the monster's or Harriet's? Which animals would eat my body? Would I still be alive when they started?* What I did know was that I couldn't stand pain of this magnitude much longer. I began to shake, which hurt like a *mother*, and finally the tears swelled. I seethed through clenched teeth as full-on panic set in.

The haziness of my thoughts made them seem less substantial, less dire. And every attempt I made to process my situation—to find a solution to it—vanished like a wisp. I was searching for something to grab hold of, and my mind wandered back to my so-called "normal" life. But when I conjured images of my house, my office, and my town, no one there knew me anymore—everyone I knew and loved walked by me like a stranger. It was almost like my mind was asking me, "You *sure* you want to return to that life?"

Because it's true: In that life—in human-Harriet's life—I felt alone so much of the time. And really, who feels alone when they have a family around? And a whole community? Isn't that totally messed-up? I began to entertain the idea that I didn't care if I healed or not. Also, wildfires happen all the time, and the places affected always recover. Why should I sweat it?

I dashed my head to one side, trying to banish these thoughts, but that only hurt like hell. I was out of it, yeah, but not so much that I couldn't recognize the peculiar mindset I was in. These were the same insidious voices that had followed me since childhood, quietly chanting in the background of every challenge I took on: *This is the way of things*, they had told me year after year. *Give up, Harriet.*

Fuck that noise, I told them. In my head.

Give over to the pain, Harriet, the voices said.

You're a pain.

Little Harriet never had the chance to give up. Do it for her.

The tears came hard then, and I sputtered a few times in spite my efforts to keep still. As I lay there crying, I felt some new, tickling sensation, like something had alighted somewhere on my skin; my body was too badly mangled to tell exactly where. I opened my eyes and through the ash and tears saw a blurry little form, a foot away. Maybe a bird or a frog, or a woodland gnome. Who knows. But whatever it was, it burrowed into my fur in a space between some crushed half-limb and my torso. There was a similar sensation on another part of me and soon some other small creature snuggled up against me. Another followed suit, then another and another, and eventually I risked a deep breath, coughing and spitting again, in order to take inventory: squirrel, baby marmot; squirrel, squirrel, and, holy cow . . . a *pika*? Yep. Lastly, a family of ring-necked snakes. But I wasn't freaked out; I was just glad to not be alone.

Then, with a sharp *crack* that gave all of us a start, my left humerus snapped back into its socket. I tried staying still, but my body writhed of its own accord and I screamed—something the monster had never done before—as one by one my broken bones reassembled their innumerable bits of wreckage and fused back together with a kind of reverse splintering, all the while making a sound like something straight out of hell's back-gates. My vertebrae stacked and realigned, and I felt my nerves and sinews and other soft parts grow and spread like vines along all the proper pathways.

The pain began to diminish. I took a few extra seconds to lie there. When I lifted my head a little, I caught a glimpse of orange through the smoke. My new friends scurried and slithered away as I pushed myself to stand, and brushed myself off.

I leapt in the direction of the flames, without a thought to the terrain because after that last fall, what were a few ankle fractures? And since I seemed to get bigger, or stronger, or *something*-er each time I turned into the monster, I was expecting to be stronger after rebuilding myself. I headed straight for the red flames, sniffing all around me, fearfully, for the scent of burning human flesh.

I jumped as high as I could again, above the smoke, in order to determine the reach of the fire. When I still hadn't detected any humans, I decided to try something I remembered from Girl Scouts: If you dig a trench through the vegetation and the earth underneath it, you can rob the fire of fuel and slow its spread.

How wide a trench, though? How far from the flames? I had no idea. I found a spot where the trees were a bit sparse, about a hundred feet from the edge of the fire, and shoved my hands into the dirt and needles, pulling it all toward me like a plow. *(So suck it, Soob: I did do a brief stint as a Girl Scout, thank you very much.)*

After ten or so minutes, with sparks singeing my skin and smoke pumping in and out of my lungs, I finished corralling the fire. I stepped back from it and scanned the flames again. They were at least as high as they'd been when I started. I didn't know if the trench would work.

Where were the firefighters? I hadn't heard sirens since before I fell, and I heard no helicopters now. I didn't know what else to do at that point. Water was the thing that put out fires, and unfortunately it was also the thing that put out *me*. Still, I couldn't stop now.

I clutched my head and stared at the flames. *What had we done at Girl Scout camp, once we'd packed up to leave?* I didn't remember using water to douse the campfire. *Oh right! We'd used sand.*

My brain flashed back to my brief stop at Flaherty Brothers, and I turned and headed that way. I moved fast, trying to find landing spots without any people. *(Harry no smash!)* I didn't have time to care about making the occasional monster-sized pothole, or smash-landing on a trio of eighteen-wheeler cabs *(OK, Harry sometimes smash!)* at a truck dealership.

When I got back to the plant, I went to the nearest silo, squatted low, and opened a little hatch near the top to make sure it was full of sand, not gravel. I wrapped my arms around the thing and pulled upward, but it didn't budge. I pulled harder. With some cracking and rumbling, the container finally started to give, and I smiled: I was doing it. I checked my stance and tried again, redoubling my efforts and straining my quads and hams and glutes and everywhere else human-Harriet had once been so strong. I engaged my monster-core. I rocked back and forth, the way I'd taught Frankie and Jo to do when they wanted to disengage their interlocking blocks. Still, I couldn't quite dislodge it. Even if I could, there was no way I could carry it all the way to the fire in time. I needed a hack.

I stood up and spun around, searching for something to use as a crowbar. I rooted through a large pile of construction scrap before spying a neat stack of steel pylons near the edge of the yard. I grabbed one and ran back to the silo, where I stuck one end under the base and then pressed on the other with all the power I had. The metal footings that connected the immense cylinder to its concrete base screeched in protest but gradually—thankfully, fortunately—the thing came free of the ground. I grunted with happiness, which grew as it became clear that the bottom of it was still intact—the sand sealed inside. I bent the pilon in half and used it to prop the silo up at an angle, then crouched low and stepped underneath it, with my back to it.

And *oof*—no sooner had the pilon fallen away and I had the silo's full weight on me than I lost my balance and staggered in one direction and the other. I tried to steady myself but the damn thing seemed intent on getting back to solid ground.

It seemed that after all I'd been through that night, I was too weak to leap back to the fire. I could barely hold the silo, and every minute I did inflamed my muscles still further. I briefly considered trying to get a ride on one of the giant ships docked in an upstream industrial port, but that would be way too slow.

I scanned the downtown area frantically. My eyes landed on a line of industrial utility wires, their blinky red lights barely visible through the smoke and ash infiltrating the city. The wires and their enormous support towers extended for miles in both directions. I dredged my brain for recollections from physics class. And while it pains me greatly to say it, I had Mr. Terrence to thank for the solution I came up with.

I didn't really expect my plan to work. I mean, if utility wires have been so wonderfully elastic all this time, why hasn't anyone used them as a slingshot before?

I set the silo down again and jumped up the nearest ridge, where I grabbed hold of several power lines, halfway between two towers. Then I hurried back down the slope, stretching the wires, lifting them carefully over houses and trees, trying not to snap them so I wouldn't get fried. When I got back to the plant, I pulled the cables over a pylon in the riverbed, then bent the top of it into a hook of sorts, to hold the wires in place while I positioned the silo.

It was a crazy idea. A billion variables would impact the trajectory of this giant thing, and I was about to yeet it over three freaking towns. But I was fairly confident that if I overshot it, the silo would land in a broad swath of the Columbia River and no one would be hurt. If I undershot, it would land in a forested part of the gorge in the path of the fire. An explosion of sand there might at least slow the spread and give the firefighters more time.

If I *really* whiffed it, I could end up killing people. But it was my only idea, and my last chance to put out this fire. I told myself I could do it.

I also concluded I had to slingshot myself along with the silo, so I could try to steer it. Again: *certifiable!*

I got the silo in place and straddled it with my feet on the ground, praying I wouldn't electrocute myself into oblivion before I'd even released the wires. With one hand, I grabbed the flimsy ladder attached to the side, and reached behind me with the other until I found the top of the pylon. I closed my eyes, took a deep breath, and said a little something to somebody that my absurd plan would work—or at least not kill anyone. Then I double-checked my position and bent the pylon back to vertical. The wires slipped over the top and immediately propelled me and my huge sand missile high into the air, to the northeast.

I have to admit that, despite the gravity (ha!) of my mission, the flight was exhilarating— not only for the feeling of the wind in my fur as I reached the pinnacle of my trip, but also because I knew in my gut that I had nailed it.

Descending through the thickest, blackest plumes of smoke, I released my grip on the tiny ladder and allowed the silo to fall the rest of the way by itself. It hit the ground and exploded, spewing its contents up and out with such force that the stuff came back at me, probably reaching a height beyond that of the smoke. I squeezed my mouth, nose, and eyes shut tight as I plummeted through clouds of ash and now dust and dirt, too, until I landed in a hillock of sand, which only hurt my tush a little.

I stood up, coughing, then slipped and slid on my butt down to a spot where the sand was more level. I immediately felt the scorching heat underneath me, and knew that give or take a few feet of sand, I was at ground level. I heard the first siren heading my way. I couldn't see more than a foot or two through air so toxic it made me gag.

Walking in all that fine sand was slow going. I was looking for the bright orange of the flames, because I still wasn't ready to believe my plan had worked. What does it say, that with evidence literally in the air in front me—nearly choking me—I kept looking for proof that I'd failed?

I didn't find any. The sand had snuffed out most of the fire. *I* had snuffed out the fire, apart from a pair of spots where the ground rose up unexpectedly, and in the trunks of a few charred, half-broken trees. There was a small risk these smoldering bits would gain traction again, but the firefighters could handle them easily. They would have water, after all.

They'd be there any minute, but I wandered up and down the slopes a few times, calf-deep in sand, sniffing the terrible air for signs of life. I didn't detect any humans, but I knew there were animals, and that they were caught, singed, choking, buried. Cursing myself for not thinking to bring some canvas from Flahertys to cover my face with, I crooked my elbow over it while I dug with the other arm, whenever I thought some creature could be saved. I dug up several that did not make it, but squeed with hope each time I found something still hanging on to life. First, a few rabbits and one extremely angry squirrel. I cradled them to my chest and moved on, eventually finding not one but *two* litters of fox kits and a half dozen injured birds, most of the latter needing to be plucked from the crooks of trees. They were in bad shape. I wasn't sure any would make it, with the exception of the squirrel, who seemed hellbent on something that I'm pretty sure did not involve death. After getting myself turned around and lost twice, I finally found a trailhead to the adjacent state park, a stone's throw from a parking lot where emergency vehicles would probably turn up any minute.

I knelt on one knee and had just begun to unload my animal friends when I was sharply rebuked by an outcry of peeps, chirps, and growls. I stopped moving, wondering if I'd squeezed them a bit hard, and cooed at them a few times to reassure them of my good intentions. They went quiet again, their tired eyes succumbing to both the grit in the air and the weight of so much trauma, their tiny, beleaguered heads sinking into my fur.

I plopped down on my butt with a grimace, allowing my armful of miniature bosses to nestle in for a few more minutes and rest against my heartbeat. As the wailing of the sirens reached the nearby parking lot, I was still cooing to them, in between coughs.

Look here, folks. The humans will find you here, and help you. I gotta go.

I unfurled my arms once more and gently scooted them to the ground. I wished them well under my breath and trudged down the riverbank, not a moment too soon: A crew of firefighters had arrived at the end of the trail where I'd just been sitting. They turned on their hose as I made my first leap, back down the gorge, toward Portland.

On the second jump, exhaustion hit me like a . . . like a fucking silo full of sand. I kept thinking about the success of my slingshot, and the survival of those animals, and used these bits of good news as buoys when all I wanted to do was give in to the fatigue. I turned south and headed along the Willamette, back to Straussville. My jumps weren't surefooted, and they weren't nearly as high as they'd been earlier. But I was glad to make it back to the park—where I'd previously left one of my prep bags—before the sun started to come up.

Once there, I turned back into Harriet by way of the water pump in the kids' play area, then struggled to get each of my legs into my pants. I had so little of anything left—energy, brainpower, will. I considered curling up in a ball under a picnic table and sleeping there the rest of the night. Or maybe two or three whole days.

But my family would be worried sick if I didn't come home. So I trudged through the trees to the nearest road, and weighed the pros and cons of hitchhiking. I decided I didn't have the bandwidth to deal with a driver with bad intentions, so I walked. Very slowly, with my eyes half-closed, all the way back to my house, where I stumbled inside and collapsed on the couch, without checking on Critter and without eating any of the congealed mac and cheese that had been forgotten and left out on the kitchen counter and in the sink, in three different bowls. I didn't even eat the stale goldfish crackers at the bottom of Jojo's backpack, which was right under the couch, within easy reach.

3

3.1 MONDAY, AROUND 7:00 A.M.

When I woke up a mere hour later, my body hadn't recovered to the degree it had after my previous monster-pades. I guess breaking the better part of my bony skeleton, not to mention inhaling a metric fuck-ton of carcinogens, takes longer to heal from than a few patches of singed fur.

Sounds were muffled, the light of dawn seemed far away, and moving was not an option. I detected, barely at first, the sounds of Theo and the kids waking up. But when those noises travelled downstairs, bringing with them the smells of toothpaste and soap and such, I still didn't move. I thought I heard Bret say the word "migraine" at one point—which wasn't too far off the reality—and miraculously no one, neither adult nor teenager nor preschooler nor dog, came over to poke or prod me. They made and ate their own breakfasts while slowly, my senses came back to me. At some point, I heard Theo muttering, sounding already short of breath, that he needed to run. It was the one day of the week when he picked the twins up from school, and always felt compelled to squeeze more than usual into his time at the office. When I heard him ask if I was OK to drive the kids to school, I tried to nod. I was still wondering if he'd been able to detect it when I heard the front door click shut behind him.

When I was finally able to sit up, I thought I might be sick. My head thumped and both my vision and hearing seemed to have made some kind of U-turn, because sounds and lights no longer seemed dampened; now they were way too intense. When Bret, Frankie, and Jo came through the family room, I preemptively forbade any television, music, or other outside noise for the remainder of the morning, despite no one asking for such things.

I came close to calling in sick to work, which in addition to being more or less true, would have had the benefit of getting me out of the off-site meeting that was to take place that day. But taking a sick day would mean one fewer vacation day, so I pried my ass from the sofa cushions and got my mind in gear. Two semi-clean items of clothing, one glance in the hall-way mirror, and zero showers later—the "bedhead" look is always in style, right?—we all got out the door at more or less the same time as usual. And I didn't even care if Justin was outside waiting for us; it felt like a triumph to be moving in some semblance of a human routine.

Once in the driveway, Bret followed me to the driver-side door and handed me the twins' lunch bags. "Dad made these," she said as she squinted over my shoulder, into the glaring sun. "I reminded him."

I was startled when she reached out again, and I looked down to see that she was handing me her oversized, mirrored sunglasses—a prized and *très chic* possession she'd treated herself to on her last birthday. I put them on and leaned over to get a look at myself in the side-view mirror. I'd expected them to feel outrageously wrong for my face and sure enough, they were too big, too cool, too ridiculous. Which is to say, they were pretty fucking wonderful.

I stood and faced her again, but only to mumble my thanks. I was too depleted of energy, both mental and physical, to jump back into the serious issues we'd fought over the night before. I was in no condition for a rematch, and besides, Bret's defenses—and chin—were still decidedly up. I did, however, briefly but seriously consider offering to let her drive us the few miles to school. Because chances were good that even at the tender age of fourteen, she'd have done a better job of it that morning.

I got into the driver's seat and hesitated several seconds, trying to remember what I was supposed to do. Frankie and Jo filled the void by peppering me with Halloween questions.

"Are witches real?"

"Errr . . . yes."

"They *are?* But not mummies, right?"

"Mummies are also real. Sorry."

They gasped and exchanged looks of morbid delight before resuming their own private conversation.

I reached over my shoulder for the seatbelt, and wondered why I didn't have a pit of despair opening up inside my gut, the way I did when I woke up after first turning monster. I felt like I'd done some good by putting out the fire, but even so—in the course of the same night, I'd had a huge fight with Bret, cussed out my heavily armed neighbor, busted up a bunch of property, and nearly died. A couple times. *Why so unserious, Harriet?*

"Mommy?" Frankie asked.

"Hmmm?"

"You made a weird noise," Bret said. "You like, groaned or something." She imitated me, sounding like a cut-rate Halloween decoration with a dying battery.

"I'm going in to see the principal today," I said by way of reply. I turned the ignition and shifted into reverse. "Come hell or high water. And I want both coaches to be in on that conversation, too."

She didn't respond.

"You and I will talk later."

"Mommy?" Frankie again.

"What is it?"

"You did the noise again," Bret explained.

Jojo chimed in from the back seat. "So are ghosts real?"

"Err," I replied, still preoccupied with my own thoughts as I pulled onto the road. I had forgotten to eat anything, and that was a big part of my current problem. "I don't know, honey. Maybe."

"Maybe?" Bret interjected. "Never thought I'd hear that from you."

"Yeah, well," I said as we peeled out of the neighborhood. *Just wait until one of them asks about monsters.*

I was more awake by then, thanks to the feeling of the wind on my bare neck and forearms. And with Bret next to me, I couldn't keep from reliving our fight, examining and regretting the details of it all. I mean, I had *fucking laughed at her.* My firstborn. My one-time baby who'd had, I'd swear on my life, the most adorable fingers and toes of any baby, ever—all of them long and kind of bulbous on the ends, as if she were destined to grow up and be a concert pianist, or maybe a tree-frog. I fucking laughed at my latter-day preschooler. I laughed at my talented, sweet tween—my thoughtful, conscientious teenager. It all seemed like proof that human anger—and mom-anger in particular—was every bit as ugly as I'd once thought.

*****

After dropping the kids at school, I headed to our biannual off-site meeting, at a family restaurant in the same office park as our own building. The idea for it, according to Bob, was that we'd all get out of our "marketing heads" for a bit and talk about elements of our working lives that were harder than they needed to be. Office culture, work-life balance—stuff we could tackle together, as a company. It was a nice idea, but we tended to cycle through the same list of problems, time after time.

The restaurant had decent food, but the atmosphere wasn't conducive to staying awake. Gina had reserved a small, cozy room with dark paneling, dark wood floors, and dark drapes. The heat was on full-blast. She and the staff had arranged the tables in a square and set up a few easels. After serving myself heaping portions of the bacon, eggs, and fresh-baked biscuits from the buffet at the side of the room, I chose a chair opposite the wall of windows, in the hope that some slim ray of light would make it into the room and ping my brain in the event I started to nod off.

"Good morning," Yvette whispered as she dropped her bag on the table and took off her long, tailored coat, its hood lined with faux fur. "Someone's hungry this morning," she added as she eyed my plate.

"Morning," I replied, moving the crap I'd splayed all over the table when I got there. She set down her bag and to-go coffee mug. Gina nabbed the chair around the corner from her.

"Thanks for doing all this, Gina," Yvette said.

"Yes, thank you, Gina. Looks great, as always," I added.

"Thanks, ladies."

"All right, folks, now that everyone has their breakfast in front of them, I'd like to launch into the agenda items we have right away," said Gil. Bob made an effort to spread around various opportunities to "lead" like this. These opportunities tended to occur on initiatives and activities that didn't impact our bottom line, but whatever.

After nearly clearing my plate in a matter of minutes, I sat low in my chair, my butt near the edge of the seat, my head barely clearing the seat-back. I probably looked to my coworkers—and my boss—like a teenager who didn't want to endure yet another family gathering. But I didn't feel surly, actually. I felt like one of those beanbags you toss at the "cornhole" board in the backyard, a flimsy lump of threadbare material and mystery filler, half-sagging off the plywood. Not even my thoughts seemed able to get anywhere that morning.

"Harry?" I heard Gil say. "Your turn."

Fuck. What were we talking about? I pushed my feet into the floor so I was a bit more erect and turned to Yvette, wordlessly seeking some hint from her about what everyone had just been talking about.

Her eyebrows arched high into her hairline, her whole face itching to release a smile. "Well, Harry, I know you have thoughts about childcare, right? Maybe you should talk about that, now that we're in the open portion of the meeting?" she suggested.

"OH! Yes. We need childcare," I said, feeling relieved. I reached out and scribbled THANK YOU on my note pad, then spun it around to Yvette.

"Who's the 'we' in this scenario?" Bob asked from the other side of our square setup. He sat with his elbows on the table and his fingers on either end of his pencil.

"Uh. All of us," I replied, pointing my index finger toward the ceiling and swirling it around. "As a company, we need access to lower-cost, convenient childcare, as a matter of course. I know there are dads here as well as moms."

No one spoke up right away, and when Gil still hadn't written "childcare" on the big notepad on his easel, Gina spoke up: "Can you write that one down, Gil, please? Thanks so much."

But Gil didn't move; he just looked at Bob, then replied, "I don't see how that's something we can tackle as a small company. Bob?" He didn't even uncap his marker.

I scanned the list he'd made thus far: *composting; indoor/sheltered bike room, with lock; have an annual overnight retreat; subsidized lift passes to Mt. Hood and other resorts.*

"Harriet, do you have something for our list that, as a company, we can tackle? Ideally in a year's time?"

"Uh, yeah, as a matter of fact. I just thought of something," I said, as I picked up the last, enormous forkful of biscuits and gravy from my plate.

"OK," Gil said, finally uncapping his marker. "Hit me with it."

I stuffed the food into my face, then held up a finger to signal that I required a few additional seconds.

"What do you want to add, Harry? Or should we come back to you?" This was from Bob.

I forced some of the food down, then said, "No, no—I'm ready. I want to add . . ." I stopped and licked the sides of my teeth, clearing off gobs of biscuit dough. Then I gulped down all of the orange juice in my goblet and sat back. "Childcare."

"OK, Yvette, you're up," Bob said, trying to cover his irritation with a chipper tone. "What've you got?"

"Excuse me, one second. Shouldn't Gil at least write that down?" Gina asked. Again. "I mean, so that we have an accurate record. I have it in my minutes here, so."

"I agree," Yvette said.

A server appeared next to me to refill my glass, and when he offered to bring over the breakfast casserole for me to have seconds, I eagerly agreed.

"Yvette. Your turn," Bob repeated.

"OK, thanks. I say . . . hmm. I say that this year, I want to add . . . childcare."

"All right, ladies. I'm starting to feel a bit ambushed here," Bob said, sitting back and turning his palms to the room.

"Don't say ambushed, Bob," I said, wiping the edges of my mouth with a cloth napkin.

"I beg your pardon?"

"You can't say that kind of thing, remember? It's disrespectful to our men and women in uniform." I looked at Yvette. "Right?"

"Right," she said, her hands folded politely in front of her. I don't think she gave a rat's ass about anyone using words like ambush or trenches, but she did like to troll Bob about his efforts to be "woke."

"Ladies, I get it. I really do, Harriet. You have my utmost appreciation as a mom of young ones. But this tack you've taken isn't in the spirit of these gatherings." He always called me Harriet when he was pissed. "I'm losing patience here."

"Losing patience? Or losing respect?" Gina asked, her voice clarion and direct.

All the other heads in the room swiveled toward her and stared; Gina didn't speak up on the substance of our work, or on anything that might be unpleasant to Bob's extra-sensitive ears. "After all, you always say you want us to speak freely at these meetings. So we ought to say what we actually need, don't you think?"

"Do you have anything to add to the list, Gina? Or not?"

I rocked a bit in my chair, and noticed a few coworkers squirm, too. His tone sure could be rude for a guy who claimed to be so sensitive to other people's sensitivities.

"I was going to say . . . eldercare. But now that you've straightened us out, I'll go with family care, because that includes help for Yvette's ninety-five-year-old *abuela* as well as Harriet's babies. And yours, too, Bob."

I glanced around at other people's reactions, and my eye fell on Gil's list. "Childcare" was still nowhere to be found, but something else had been added, in capital letters and red ink:

TAKE WOMEN'S NEEDS SERIOUSLY.

I gasped in delight, and the rest of the group followed my gaze to the chart.

"Gil? What the hell?" Bob asked, his hands suddenly on his armrests, as if preparing himself to launch from his chair and tackle our unruly list to the ground.

"I didn't write that! I don't even have a red marker!" he replied, gesturing and turning pink. There were grumblings and whispers around the room, and someone pointed out that there was a red marker on the metal ledge of the easel.

Holy shit, I thought, sitting up straight. *Did I do that? Fuck—do I have telekinesis? Or super-speed? Invisibility?* I accepted thirds and fourths from several platters, all brought round to me by the servers, all three of whom seemed to be tending only to me.

Bob called an end to the brainstorming portion of the meeting. He declared the options on the list were enough to keep our team busy, then rushed us through updates on the items we'd discussed at our previous off-site meeting.

"We've had several balls in the air, as you know," he said before running down the projects someone on the team had either started or completed. He looked pointedly at me as he finished his spiel with, "Lastly, we made some changes to the old storage space, and it now serves as a nursing or pumping room, when required."

"Wait, we did?" Gina asked.

I stopped scraping the bottom of my oatmeal bowl and focused hard on a raisin there, trying to move it with my mind. It didn't work. I was probably delirious.

"Yes, Gina," Bob said, condescension nearly beating the irritation out of his tone. "Yes, we did."

"But all our photocopier and office supplies are in there," she added. "Stuff for the coffee maker and so on."

"Well, since we don't currently have anyone who is, you know, nursing, we made it into a nursing-slash-storage space," Bob replied.

"It doesn't smell good in there either," Gina mumbled in a private aside to Yvette and me.

"I think something died in there," Yvette whispered back. *"Inside the wall."*

"Bob," I chimed in, "the next time we interview some great candidate for a job opening, and give her a tour of the place, she'll see that that's where she'll be spending a lot of her time, if and when she finds herself breastfeeding. That might not land us the best talent."

Bob's eyes were closed, as he slowly shook his head. "Harriet. We're not going to dedicate a whole room—"

"It's a closet, actually," I added, just as Bret's phone started to buzz in my pocket. I took it out and saw that I'd already missed the call. I also recognized the number as the principal's.

"A whole closet then," Bob conceded, his voice breathy and eyes wide, his hands in the air, like he'd been asked to debate a squirrel and was sick of it. "I won't cordon off a whole closet for an activity that literally no one here engages in."

The conversation went on without me as I plugged a finger into one ear and listened to the new voice message in the other. It was from Kent, the office manager at the high school, and he suggested I come by before lunch, and that Ms. Moretti would squeeze me in between her other meetings. The coaches were also on campus, he said, which wasn't typically the case during the school day and he'd already called them both to schedule a sit-down.

"All we're saying," Gina said, "is that an actual nursing closet—without the paper clips and the stench of . . . of rotting rodent corpse—would signal to potential employees that we really want women to work here, with the same level of comfort as everyone else. You guys don't understand what we go through, and then pushback on us if we try to explain—"

"We aren't pushing back," Gil jumped in. "We're asking questions, and . . . pointing out . . . obstacles. Practical obstacles." Bob nodded vigorously.

"So 'devil's advocate,' huh?" I asked, closing Bret's phone. The thought of heading over to a meeting with that shitty volleyball coach, and also Coach Sullen, had trammeled all the playfulness out of me. I started to get up and collect my things. "You're playing devil's advocate on a serious matter that has no effect on you?"

"We are a business with a bottom line, Harriet."

"We're also a business with the word 'creative' in the name, Bob," Yvette said. "It says so on the website. It's also on the old stationery, but you might not know that since you don't need to go into the storage closet—sorry, nursing-slash-storage room—ever."

"You've made your point, ladies. We can move on," Bob replied.

"We always do," I added as I grabbed my coat. Then I opened my purse and tossed a few biscuits inside. "Move on, that is. I can only hope that one day, we'll be the kind of team that helps one another. Because what kind of soldier—sorry, Bob—but *what kind of soldier* keeps going when someone in their platoon falls behind? Now please excuse me, as my breasts and I have been called to an urgent meeting over at the high school."

"Just stop it with the body parts—"

"YOU SAID 'BALLS'!" I yelled back as I flung open the double doors that led to the wider restaurant. I got a few strange looks from some patrons as I put Bret's crazy-cool sunglasses on again and behind me, heard the rustling of Gina's notepad.

"She's right, Bob," she said, flipping a page or two. "I have it right here. Want me to read it back?"

I left the restaurant feeling fuller than when I'd entered, and not only from stuffing my face. At first, I couldn't identify the sensation.

Then I realized it was pride. Pride in us ladies. The tendency that Gina, Yvette, and I had for clustering together at meetings wasn't only for chatting purposes. It wasn't always a conscious thing, but I think as the only women, we sat together for comfort, and for familiarity. I'd never passed either woman a menstrual product under the table, for example, but it occurred to me that morning that we stayed in each other's orbit because there was something valuable in maintaining the *possibility* for tampon-passing and more. A menstrual product under the table is nice and all, but we needed to join hands over it, too.

A thought popped into my mind and I turned around and jogged back into the meeting, trying not to draw too much attention to myself. While Bob droned on about SEO-something-something, I crouched low between Yvette and Gina.

"If he gives you any problems," I whispered, nodding sideways, "tell him you know where the naked lady photos are on his hard drive." I tapped my temple.

Yvette giggled softly and Gina sighed. I tiptoed back out, reminding myself that if Bob didn't want anyone to know about such things, he shouldn't have asked me to advance his PowerPoint presentations, deal with his computer when his applications froze, and fill out his freakin' timecard, among other dumb shit he was perfectly capable of doing himself. I headed toward my car, slipping into my coat—or Yvette's coat, as it turned out, since I'd accidentally taken her far chicer one. I'd have to return it later; I was already running late to my meeting at the school.

3.2 MONDAY, JUST BEFORE LUNCH

I sat down on the long wooden bench in the reception area of the high school's main office. It was an old pew someone had repurposed for school use, long before I arrived as a freshman. Little else had changed since then, apart from the turnover in staff. The sun still set the far side of the room aglow, by way of two enormous windows behind the counter, adding yet another ecclesial aspect to the otherwise institutional space.

"The principal will be with you any minute," Kent said, looking up briefly from his monitor.

A door on the side wall opened and Principal Moretti came out. She reminded me of Julia Child, not only because she was extremely tall and favored clothes with silhouettes from the forties and fifties, but also because she spoke in a shouty but affable way that made me want to learn something big and complicated that I didn't have time for. She was known for her ready laughter, and for refusing to suffer fools.

"Mrs. Lime? Come in, please."

I stood and greeted her, and saw her take in my unkempt hair, the flamboyant sunglasses I'd pushed on top of my head, and Yvette's fur-trimmed coat in a single up-down scan. Normally I'd have been self-conscious about it, but again, there was no normal left in my life. "Would you call me Harriet? Or Harry. That's also fine."

She held the door for me as I went in, though she didn't reciprocate my invitation.

"So, what did you want to see me about?" she asked as she sat down. It wasn't a spacious office, and the abundance of metal, fluorescence, and cinder block did little to comfort the eyes or the rear-end. But several plants crowded around her on the floor, and framed a bright square window on the side wall.

"Shouldn't we wait for Mr. Terrence and Coach Sullen to join us?"

"Well, while we wait," she replied, turning her delicate, bracelet-style watch around in a half-circle, "why don't you tell me your concerns?"

I told her about the incidents with Coach Sullen, in the order I'd been made aware of them. "The first thing that raised a flag was when Coach Sullen invited my daughter, Bret, a freshman on the JV team—where he is the primary coach—to go to a craft store with him. She told me some other teammates were going, although I found out last night that the other girls either didn't show up or weren't actually invited. I was never a part of that conversation except for when Bret asked me if she could go."

The principal had uncapped a pen and was taking notes. "Go on."

"In that same conversation," I said, looking at the patterns in the linoleum, trying to be as objective and factual as possible. I didn't want to seem paranoid or overbearing. "Bret also mentioned that Sullen told her she didn't have time for dating or relationships." When I looked up, I saw she had paused in her writing and was looking straight at me. "Please continue."

"Then last night, Bret said she needed to stop at a store for some ibuprofen, and when I expressed my surprise that we'd run out of it already, she told me that Coach had told her it was OK to take three or four times the dose indicated on the bottle. And that's what she'd been doing."

Mrs. Moretti sat back in her stiff-backed chair. Then she picked up the phone and said, "Kent, do you have ETAs on Coach Terrence and Coach Sullen?" There was a pause, in which I couldn't hear Kent's reply, then she added, "He's not?" There was another long pause. "OK, here's what I want you to do. Get in touch with him right away, and tell him I need to see him. Today. I'll deal with the other one."

She pressed the receiver and leaned toward her laminated list of phone extensions. "Coach Sullen is no longer here, apparently. He's at his day job." I felt my blood pressure rise as she pressed a few numbers and looked back at me, her lips briefly pursing.

"Yes, hello, Eunice. Yes, it's me," she said, surprising me with a tone that was almost school-girlish. "Mm-hmm. Oh, I'm fine thank you. Mm-hmm. Yes, well, just one quick thing before I let you go: I was expecting Mr. Terrence in my office right now, for a meeting. Is he on his way or . . . ?" Her voice trailed off and she twisted a piece of her hair. I didn't know who Eunice was, but she had some clout over the principal, apparently.

There was a longer pause. "Oh, OK. I see," Mrs. Moretti replied, her eyelids flicking upward suddenly, so she could look right into my own eyes. Something about that expression—and the stilted pleasantries with which she finished her call to Eunice—put my hackles on alert. She hung up the phone.

"Who's Eunice?" I asked.

"Mr. Terrence's assistant," she replied, the warmth and brassiness still missing from her demeanor. She started moving and straightening some of the folders that cluttered her desk.

"Like, at his campaign office?"

"No."

"Mr. Terrence has an assistant at the school?"

"Not officially. But yes—unofficially."

"He isn't even on faculty anymore!"

"Mrs. Lime, we can reschedule. Alternatively, you can approach the coaches at your daughter's next game, and speak with them directly about their behavior toward your daughter."

I couldn't make sense of the change in her. I could feel the monster turn wary inside me. "Mrs. Moretti, did you hear something from the other end of that phone call that you're not telling me?"

She rose and went briskly to the door, but before opening it, she turned back, and in a much lower volume replied, "Mrs. Lime, I can tell you're on a mission here, and I admire that. I really do. But I'm the principal of a public school with nearly sixteen hundred students and no acting vice principal. We've had to cut ten percent of our teaching staff in the past two years, while our student body increased by fifteen."

"Just tell me, please, why Mr. Terrence wasn't here today?"

"Consider, Mrs. Lime, approaching this issue from the other direction. You could set stricter boundaries for your daughter."

Indignation hit me like a punch in the face.

"I know, Mrs. Lime," she continued as she whisked the door open and then stood next to it like a footman. I noticed for the first time how tired she looked. "But it's an all-day, everyday gig, this parenting business. It's what we all signed up for."

"I don't need anyone to tell me that," I scoffed as I put my bag on my shoulder and stood up. I went over and stood eye to eye with her—or eye to chin, as it were—and added, "I do need someone to tell me, though, what kind of boundary I can put up that will protect my kids from people who think boundaries don't apply to them?" The monster was nodding vigorously. Though she wasn't focused on the principal; she was already tracking Mr. Terrence.

"I strongly suggest, Mrs. Lime, that you back away from the conclusions you seem to be drawing."

It was almost noon when I left the office and set out down the hallway, stalking my prey. I rounded the corner to a hallway that led to the gymnasium, muttering out loud to myself. Unhelpful, angry things. I'd gone another ten yards or so when my pulse surged and a split second later, a door opened on the left, and out stepped Mr. Terrence. The monster reared inside me.

"Hello there, can I help you find something?"

I knew I ought to use those extra seconds to breathe deep, to improve the chances that my words would come out in a civilized fashion. But I didn't. He didn't seem nervous to see me, but my gut told me he was so accustomed to bending and breaking the truth that he was among the minority of folks who could beat a lie detector, whether machine or monster.

"Just you."

"Oh?" he replied with a forced chuckle. His faux modesty was excruciating. He had a key ring the size of a small Christmas wreath, and struggled to find the one he needed. "Is there something I can do for you in three minutes or less? I'm on my way out, as you can see."

"You didn't show up at our meeting a half hour ago. The one Principal Moretti set up for us."

He squinted at the ceiling. "Meeting, meeting . . . I thought my calendar was—oh, is this the one about Sully?"

I blinked at him. "Coach Sullen was a no-show today, too. Unfortunately."

"I guess there was a mix-up, my dear," he said in that breathy way of his, the one I'd seen him use to mime fraternity with people for whom he had no real concern. He finally succeeded in locking the door, and turned toward me. "On top of all the Homecoming rah-rah going on, it's also moving-day for Marjorie and me. So things have been busier than ever."

"Moving sucks," I replied. I was stock-still, monster-me simmering inside.

He took a small step toward me, as if to emphasize our new bond. "I gotta tell ya, it's the hardest thing I've ever done!"

"Moving?"

He offered me another of his insincere yuks. "Hardest thing in my whole life."

"Let me cut to the chase, sir, while I have you here."

He looked at the clock on the wall and folded his arms across his chest. "You've got two minutes, now."

"Understood," I replied brusquely. Then I repeated the behaviors I'd found concerning from Coach Sullen.

"Well, I haven't heard you mention a fire or anything yet," he said, glancing less than furtively at his watch. He was putting less grease into the conversation now.

The monster moved under my skin then. Part of me—a big part—wanted to let her out. She was right here, ferocious and at the ready. But we both knew she couldn't come out right then. "I beg your pardon?"

"Ma'am, I've tried to be patient here, but we play our biggest game of the year tomorrow. And this is exactly what I expected—something you could have easily brought up with me at a later time."

"No, it's not. It's urgent. One of your coaches has crossed multiple boundaries with a fourteen-year-old, and it needs to stop. Immediately." Bret's cell phone went off again in my pocket. I let it go to voicemail.

He put his hat on and his hands in his pockets, then shifted to face a nearby exterior door. "Right. I'll ask Eunice to invite the health teacher to practice next week, so she can talk to the girls about this sort of thing."

"Will the health teacher also be talking to Coach Sullen? Will she impose some rules on him, and enforce the consequences if he breaks any?"

He surprised me when he reached over and rested his hand on my forearm. "Hey, Mom. Mama *bear*. I sense that you disapprove of me for some reason. That you disapprove of a lot of things. So if you're that worried about my big bad coaching staff, you're welcome to remove your daughter from their evil clutches."

There it was, the accusation that I was paranoid. The cell phone vibration started up again, but I still didn't pick up. "So that's how you're going to play this, Pat? You're gonna act like anything short of—what, murder?—is OK behavior from your coaching staff?" I could tell he hated hearing his name shortened to Pat.

"Well, I could do more, I suppose. I'm more than happy at this point to keep your daughter out of the game entirely. That will make her safer, by your logic?"

"Oh-ho-*hooo!* Is that a threat?"

"Push me further, and I might be willing to take her off the team entirely. Would that make you happy?"

He started for the door but in two swift steps I was in front of him again, blocking him from the exit, blooming with a fury I'd never known. "One last thing, Pat. Two things, actually."

"What's that?" he asked, in a tone that was anything but curious.

"One, I'm gonna suggest you be more careful about who you threaten around here."

His pupils constricted as he brought that nasty mustache within a few inches of my face.

"Because my mom and I moved nine times before I hit puberty, Pat. And not one of those moves was the hardest thing I've ever done. Not even close."

This surprised and discomfited him; I could smell it. The guy had held a portion of my young fate in his hands all those years ago—as my teacher, reference, and faculty advisor—and he'd been careless with it. I gotta admit, seeing him wriggle under my thumb now brought me deep pleasure.

"And two, I'm gonna need you to suspend Coach Sullen, effective immediately, until we can all show up at a meeting with Principal Moretti and sort this out."

He lifted his chin in defiance.

"Because you know what else wouldn't be very hard for me, Pat?"

I lowered my voice to a whisper and smiled a big hyena smile—and said, *"Snapping you in half. Like a fucking twig."* Inside, the monster mimed a mic-drop.

I turned and left him standing there, slack-jawed and more than a little bit scared. I walked at top speed toward the double doors that led outside and shoved their metal bars without slowing down. I didn't turn around when I heard the *CRR-LACK* sounds they made, either, though I knew they normally closed with a muffled *ka-thunk*. I didn't need to look back to know that I'd ripped one of the doors off its hinges and shattered the glass windows in both. I'd done it on purpose.

I'm bummed to report that, after daydreaming about it for years, putting Mr. Terrence on notice in this manner had left me feeling like anything *but* the magnanimous heroine I'd long imagined. Because I wasn't sure precisely why I'd done it. Had I stood up to him now only because the stench of his crap had wafted into my own household? Or because my half-monster brain couldn't help itself? The purity of my rage at the beginning of our encounter was gone. My thoughts had gone turbid; I was still breathing hard in anger, but already experiencing some doubt. Maybe even regret.

There were precious few things I had any certainty about at that point, but one of them was this: My monster was no Ms. Hyde. She wasn't especially selfish, and she'd been careful not to hurt anybody. She'd helped those animals. She sometimes felt joy. It had never occurred to her—or to me, human-Harriet—that our situation presented an opportunity to do a bunch of bad shit and then blame it all on the essential, half-evil nature of humankind.

But at other times, she rattled my bones with her rage. I'd been concentrating so hard on regulating *when* I transformed into the monster that I'd failed to consider what effect this was having on me on the inside. I certainly felt the allure of losing all control; who's to say that I—human-Harriet—wouldn't eventually give in to it? It was clear that the contrast between myself and the monster was rapidly diminishing. It was impossible to say how long my inner switch—the "toggle" I used to keep her inside when I needed to be Harriet—would remain in service.

When I pulled Bret's sunglasses down over my eyes, I remembered her phone vibrating. I took it out and saw the alerts for two new voice messages, the first from a caller she had stored in her contacts: *J&F*. My pulse glitched, and I fumbled through the correct sequence of buttons in my rush to play the clipped message from an administrator at Healthy Start.

Hi Bret. This is Belinda from Healthy Start. It's now fifteen minutes past the last pick-up window for the day, and no one has shown up to collect Josephine and Frankie Lime. We've called everyone else on their list of approved caregivers but haven't reached anyone. Please call us back at this number immediately. Thank you.

I threw open the door to the van as a new wave of guilt and anger flooded my system. My temperature surged to somewhere between sweaty mess and totally fucking enraged, at the mental image of my three-year-olds sitting in the school office, confused and perhaps scared because Daddy hadn't come for them. I got so worked up, so quickly, that I was almost out of the parking lot before I remembered the second voice message. I shifted into park and went back to Bret's phone. This one was from a California area code, and which turned out to be the workplace of my mother-in-law—Grace—asking Bret to call her back immediately, as she'd just been contacted by Willamette Medical Center, and informed that Bret's dad had been in a car accident, and that no one had been able to track down Bret's mom.

3.3 MONDAY, AROUND 1:00 P.M.

I don't remember the drive to the hospital. I read somewhere that traumatic events can make a person feel like they've jumped forward in time, without warning and with no memory of the missing chunk of their life. That's how I found myself standing at the triage desk in the ER; I only figured out what happened before that—more or less—from what others told me later.

First, I learned that I'd gone back inside the school and yanked Bret from the gym with no explanation. I marched us back to the parking lot where we ran into Dianne, who by some miracle was not only on campus with her big van full of car seats, but didn't have any of her kids with her, either. She offered to take Bret to get Jo and Frankie, and bring all three home with her for a while. When I didn't accept—and appeared to be "in some kind of fugue state," she'd tell me later—she followed us to the preschool anyway. She waited while Bret and I ran in and scooped up the twins and came running out with Teacher Flavia—who'd been staying late with them— close on our tails, shouting something about an increase in late fees. Bret got outside before me and began strapping Frankie into one of Dianne's car seats, and after that, I relented and handed Jojo to Dianne. Both twins were surprised but calm. I gave all four of them a kiss and hightailed it out of there. And because I would also receive a few hefty traffic fines in the mail in the following weeks, I also know that en route to the hospital, I ran (at least) two red lights, and passed some poor motorist on the interstate by way of the left-hand shoulder.

My memory kicked back in as I stared over the head of the woman running the desk in the waiting room. She looked for information about Theo in her computer, and when I shifted my gaze to a bulletin board and then to some vending machines, I spotted a familiar form in an adjacent corridor.

"Dr. M!" I called out, my voice warbly from disuse. I strode over to her.

"What's going on, honey? Are you OK?"

"Theo." My eyes strained from the weight of so many unshed tears.

"Oh my, honey. What can you tell me? What can I do?"

I couldn't put two sensible words together, however, so after a quick squeeze of my arm, Dr. M went to the intake desk herself. After a minute or two, she came back holding a box of hospital tissues.

"We can go back now."

I looked at her. "I—I don't even know—"

She took my hand—the way a child or a new sweetheart might do—and led me gently along. I was snuffling and on edge when we stopped by a half-open curtain, beyond which I could see three more people in white coats, with their backs to us.

"Excuse me," Dr. M said in a commanding tone. They turned, and in the spaces that opened up between them I caught glimpses of a familiar head of unruly black hair. He saw me, too.

"Harry! There you are! That's my wife, you guys. That's Harry."

The doctors moved aside and I went up to his bedside, dumbstruck less by the enormous cast on his leg than by the way he was talking and behaving. I grabbed onto the upper part of his arm, where there were no intravenous tubes. I put my other hand on his temple, his brow, his jaw.

"Hey, baby," he said, a fuzzy smile on his face. "Come 'ere!" He lifted his other arm to hug me but a nurse hurried to stop him so he wouldn't pull the tubes out.

If I hadn't already been wrecked by fear and worry that afternoon, the happy openness with which Theo greeted me could have bowled me over all on its own. In my confused state, I wondered if the accident had shaken him in such a way that the Old Theo had somehow risen back to the top? And if so, what had happened to Newer Theo, the man whose wordless detachment had stonewalled and frustrated me, almost to my breaking point? Dr. M joined me at his bedside.

"Hi, darling," she said to Theo. The affection in her voice was so genuine I nearly lost it. "I haven't seen you in so very long. But you're as handsome as ever."

"Shit! Dr. Morris? Oh my God! Come here and give me a big hug, please." He was raising his arm again.

"I will give you a handshake for now, dear, so as not to upset any of your lines," she offered. "But you can have a raincheck on the hug, of course. How are you feeling, Theo? Is the medicine managing your pain?"

"Totally," he replied with a wide sweep of his arm, as if to suggest he was completely free of discomfort.

Then I understood: He'd been given pain medication, and as a side effect, it had unblocked his exuberant friendliness. The drugs hadn't suddenly turned him back into Old Theo, I knew; they'd produced a temporary, but startling, facsimile.

"All right then, that's good," Dr. M replied. "But I'm going to keep an eye on you anyway, if you don't mind. That way I can keep Harry up to speed, too."

"Oh, yeah! Of course, doc. If we had the choice, you'd be our doctor for everything. Right, babe?"

I nearly fainted. *We?*

"They need us to clear the bedside I'm afraid," Dr. M added, "but Theo, we'll be outside until you can be discharged. All right, my dear?"

"All-righty, then. See ya soon. You, too, babe. *MWAH. MMMMMMWAH.*" He blew kisses to both of us.

Back in the waiting area, I followed Dr. M to a bench against the far wall. She sat on one end, and I laid down so that my head landed right on her lap.

"This OK?" I asked.

"Sure, sure," she replied in a soft voice. She stroked my hair. "Theo's going to be OK, honey. It'll take some time, and some work, but he'll be OK."

I nodded, exhausted and confused.

"May I suggest," she began, pausing to scratch at an itch on her forehead that I suspected wasn't really there, "not only as a doctor, but as someone who knew Theo from the time before he became a dad . . ."

"Yeah?"

"Theo is depressed, Harry."

"How do you . . . has he been . . . ?" I turned my face toward hers.

"Severely depressed, as far as I can tell. I was thinking, since he'll need to come back here several times for his leg, it could be a good time for him to see someone about his emotional health, too."

I stared into the fluorescent light above us as I tried to process this. "What makes you think he's depressed?"

"A lot of things."

I turned to face the room again and slid my hands, pressed together as if in prayer, between my face and Dr. M's lap. She resumed stroking my hair, and I changed the subject to buy myself some time to digest what she'd just said. "I recently found out that my grandmother drowned, way back when."

"I know, honey. It was tragic on so many levels."

My head swiveled around again. "You knew? How did you know?" By then, I was becoming irritated, but at a vague target—or targets—I couldn't yet see clearly. For years, I'd been in the dark about critical things pertaining to my own husband and grandmother. That Dr. M knew these things when I didn't pointed to some deficiency in me, though I know it was irrational to direct any anger whatsoever at a trained professional for sharing her insights.

She exhaled. "I know for a few reasons, I guess. But mainly because your grandmother was a minor celebrity in town. She had been our "Miss Straussville" not long before, and it was in all the papers." She let out a gentle huff before adding, "Town was a lot smaller back then. And grittier."

"That's why Mom taught me to swim. She didn't want me to drown, too."

"Really? But that doesn't . . ." She went quiet.

"What?"

"Oh, it's nothing, dear. Nothing we need to get into just now."

"I just want to understand, really. It's not like I ever met her or anything."

When Dr. M finally replied, she spoke slowly. "I think your grandmother did know how to swim, Harry. In fact, I'd bet dollars to donuts that she loved the water, just like you."

"But . . ." I sat up, unable to process that information at normal speed. Something would not compute.

"Harriet, your grandmother did die by drowning. But she drowned *herself.*"

I was still dumbstruck.

"It was suicide—"

"I know the word for it!" I snapped, cutting her off. My face burned with shame, and the sensation spread over the rest of me as I struggled to put a cap on whatever it was that had burst out of me—and at someone as undeserving as Dr. M.

I saw her nod from the corner of my eye. "I'd like to help you find someone to talk to about all of this, Harry."

"Lately I feel like . . . like *all* my people are drowning, Doc. All the time." I stared at the linoleum floor a few seconds longer, my hands on my knees.

"I should probably get going," she replied, shifting her glasses.

"I heard there was an accident at your lab," I blurted out, trying to think of something nice to say, to end our conversation on a better note.

"Yes," she said, standing up. "About that, actually. Would you do me a favor, Harry, and come to a thing I'm having tonight? I want to tell you about the situation at the lab."

"Dr. M . . ." I shook my head at the floor, wishing she would leave me alone. I couldn't take any more of her kindness. Not when I felt so very unworthy of it. "With Theo being out of commission . . . and . . ." I said as I finally looked at her, wondering what she'd meant by *situation*.

"Tell you what." She pulled a pen and a scrap of paper from her breast pocket and scribbled out an address. "Come if you can. We'd love to see you."

"Is it like, a social thing?" I stuffed the paper in the front pocket of my jeans, and wondered briefly who "we" was.

She put her hands in her pockets. "Sort of. Among other things."

"OK. I'll try." I let her give my hand a final squeeze, but I still couldn't look at her.

"I expect you haven't heard all the details of Theo's accident yet. But there were no other cars involved, thank goodness. Theo veered off the road, across the other lane of traffic, and hit a tree."

She didn't need to say the rest. I knew, in spite of the fact that my brain and body were operating on fumes. It all seemed so obvious to me now, and once Dr. M patted me awkwardly on the shoulder and excused herself, I wanted to scream. At myself.

Because *of course* Theo had fallen asleep at the wheel. And of course he was unwell. I'd watched him transform over the past few years from the guy I'd known and loved for two decades into a near-stranger—one who trudged through each day with the alertness of a three-toed sloth. But somehow, I hadn't seen what was actually going on. I hadn't realized it was only a matter of time before catastrophe hit. *Jesus fucking Christ, Harriet. You've been out on the town, moving cars and shit. What other trouble is lurking at home?*

A few hours passed before the hospital released Theo. On the drive home, he sat in the middle row of the van so that he could lean against the far side and rest his leg across the seats. He also talked my whole ear off. He wondered if it's possible to do a single *shenanigan*, for example, or if those must always be done in multiples. And he was baffled—baffled!—by the fact that there isn't any green in the sunset. Or at least, none that he'd ever seen. I had no idea why these things were on his mind, and we'd nearly reached our neighborhood when he remembered to mention that Christy had come to see him at the hospital, not long before Dr. M and I showed up.

"She did?" I asked, glancing in the rearview mirror. "That was nice of her."

"Right? I told her that. It was so good to see her. She grilled all the docs about everything. When I'd have my first surgery, yada yada yada. I told her she was my first choice to do the cutting, but she said she'd have to follow along and be an advocate instead. She's so nice. She's like, tough, though."

"She is." I thought about the way Theo had described Christy just days earlier, as pushy and even manipulative. *Tough but nice* was much more in line with how the Theo of yesteryear had looked at the world: He always chose the shinier side of the coin.

I turned onto our block and was taken aback by the sight of about three times as many cars than were usually parked there. I was even more surprised when I turned into our driveway and Bret came out the front door, deep in conversation with Satchel, who was holding what looked like a garment bag. They were followed by Sooby and her husband, Philip.

I put the window down. "Hey, what's up?" Theo put his down, too, and waved.

"How's the invalid?" Philip asked. He and Satchel approached the van and when Theo pressed the button to open the sliding door, they helped him out of his seatbelt and onto his crutches, and made room for Bret to give him a gentle hug. Sooby loitered behind them, her arms crossed.

"We came to drop off Bret's backpack, and a few other things she left in the gym," Satchel told me, cheerful as ever.

"Th—thanks, Satch." I turned off the ignition and tried to figure out what was going on at our house. "We really tore out of the place. It's kind of a blur."

"Oh, and Aunt Harry? Can I borrow this dress?" she asked, holding up a hanger that had been covered with a plastic trash bag. She lifted up the bottom and I caught the sparkle of iridescent sequins.

My heart sank. "Oh, I thought—"

"Bret said it was OK, she's not going to wear it anymore."

"Uh, sure. Sure thing," I replied. I tried to catch Bret's eye but she kept her back to me.

Satchel and her dad gathered Theo's stuff from the car, and I went around to oversee their effort to walk him to the front door. Bret followed them inside but Sooby stood apart from all of this activity, which was unusual, and didn't rope anyone into a conversation of any kind, which was almost unheard of.

"We brought some dinner, too," she called out finally. "And groceries."

"Thanks," I replied flatly, then turned away as I grimaced at myself. Any other time, I'd have said, *Thanks, Sooby*. But when the affectionate nickname hadn't felt right, I'd swallowed it down. The silence that lingered in its place wasn't any more pleasant, though.

"That's Dianne's van, isn't it?" I said once I'd faced her again. "I texted her just as we were about to leave the hospital—and she's here already?"

She swiped the toe of a sneaker in an arc in front of her, back and forth. "They came earlier. She figured the babies would be more comfortable in their own house, so."

I nodded.

When Philip and Satch came back, I hugged them both. "We're sorry to have to run, but tonight's the fundraiser for the bridge," Philip said.

"Of course—no problem! Thanks for coming by; this was amazing." But when I turned to hug Sooby, too, she was already opening the door to the car.

When I stepped inside the house, I found Dianne's two oldest kids moving briskly around our first floor, completing some chore or other. The place smelled strongly of citrus and other oils, so I knew Dianne was also around, as she concocted that aromatic blend herself and hoarded it, for use whenever she stress-cleaned. What struck me most, though, was the absence of clutter. The detritus of our daily lives—the socks and elastic hairbands and half-opened mail—had been so omnipresent in our home and for so long that without it, the floors, shelves, and tabletops were hardly recognizable. It was like a craftsperson had taken a carving knife to each room, and exposed for us a fresh, fragrant underlayer of the place.

When I saw Dianne's wife, Kendra, I found my senses and hurried over to her. "Did you guys clean my house?" I asked after giving her a hug and a kiss on the cheek.

"It's nice to see you, too!" she joked, before confirming that they had. I turned and saw Dianne come down the stairs holding the handle of a mop, her face flushed with exertion. "We set up a place on the couch for Theo, and I wrote down the name of a home-care person who I think is really great, in case you need someone. It's on the fridge," Kendra continued.

Just then Jo came barreling around the corner, shrieking with joy. On her heels came Frankie, also shrieking, and then Ellen, who was smiling from ear to ear. I had no idea who was chasing whom.

"Are you guys trying to make me pass out?" I asked Kendra and Dianne, wide-eyed, when the racers disappeared around the corner again.

"You're so funny, Harry," Dianne replied as she came out of the laundry room and took the sweatshirt Kendra held out for her. She slipped it over her head, then came over and gave me a long hug. "We need to leave, and pick up the other kids from dance," she explained. "But you should call us, Harry. About anything. Oh—and thanks again for the shoes, I've been wearing the hell out of them."

They went in to say goodbye to Theo, and I turned to find Ellen and the twins on a break from their chase, enjoying a cold juice together in front of the fridge. Bret peeked sheepishly around the corner. "Dr. Stout fixed the fridge," she announced. "And folded the laundry. And did the dishes."

"Us, too, Mama," Jo chimed in.

I turned my wonderment back to Ellen. "Is this accurate?"

"I *think* I fixed the fridge. Let me show you where the hose in the back is, that had some ice buildup and . . ."

Ellen did finish telling me what she'd done to fix the thing, but I didn't absorb it. My brain was operating at 33 percent capacity, or so I estimated, and technical words were having an especially rough time getting inside. I'd already been crammed full of tricky new verbiage by Theo's doctors that afternoon.

"There I go—rambling again," I heard Ellen say with a self-effacing laugh. I started to disagree with her, when Frankie jumped in and began telling her about one of his drawings. She pretended to be enraptured by him, so I went to the family room to check on Theo. I found that Dianne and Kendra's kiddos had already gotten all two-hundred-plus pounds of my husband situated comfortably on the couch. They'd outfitted the area with TV remote, a kid-proof Tupperware container (to keep his medicine in, they explained), a bottle of water, and other practical accoutrements. And because they were related to Dianne—for whom creativity is a way of life, even in crisis—they finished up by handing Theo a reusable grocery bag full of secondhand art and craft supplies. I was thanking them profusely, and seeing them out the door, when Ellen came up next to me.

"Fuuuuck *me*," I droned. My eyes felt stuck, wide-open, like the amazement had finally been too much and a couple more fuses had broken. "I can't believe how much you all did for us."

Ellen gave one of her spontaneous giggles. "Harry. Your expectations might be a teensy bit low."

"I . . . I don't know what to say."

"You don't have to say anything. But a simple thank you is fine."

"But this is extraordinary," I replied, turning toward her. "I know how busy you all are."

We watched the kids and Theo for several seconds before she spoke again. "It is extraordinary, I suppose, in the sense that it's unusual for us to do this sort of thing for each other. To be able to do these sorts of things, even when we want to."

I gave her a dejected half-smile.

"We live too far apart," she went on, her voice oddly flat. "We have too many practices, rehearsals, tutors, and doctor's appointments to get to. Usually on behalf of someone else."

"I know! We can't make it to our book club, because we need to answer leftover work emails," I added. "Plus, the *Women's Club of This*, and the *Ladies' Auxiliary of That* don't exist anymore, so we can't meet at those either."

"And these days, whenever some new technology blows up, supposedly to make things easier for us, I can't help cringing. Like, 'Oh? You made an app that will make and serve a healthy dinner for five? Great! That's a couple more hours Gregory's boss will expect him to deal with any issues that crop up in that time.'"

I looked back at the family room, where Critter and the twins were inspecting Daddy's crutches with great interest. I felt my shoulder blades fall back, and the muscles in my jaw loosen, for the first time in I don't know how long. "I'm glad I'm not the only mom who feels stuck. Inside a closed loop, from car to home to workplace and back, ad nauseum."

"Oh, there are *legions* of us," Ellen replied.

I returned her smile, but I shook my head, too. "All I want is to sit back and listen to one of my friends, or several friends and friends-of-friends. I just want to listen to you all chat away about something. Anything. As long as it's something you're really interested in. It's not enough to brush elbows with other women at our kids' games and stuff."

"Come to that thing tonight that Dr. M told you about, OK?" Ellen replied as she picked up her coat and purse from the back of a kitchen chair.

"You're involved in that? I don't even know what it is."

"I'll be there." She pulled out her keys and after she waved goodbye to Theo, Bret, and the little ones—whose lips trembled at the departure of their new friend—I walked her to the front door. "It's a meeting, kind of. Maybe not unlike one of those old auxiliaries you mentioned, but I wouldn't know. My mom wasn't accepted by any of those groups."

Since she wasn't a fan of hugs, I mimed one for her; I hugged myself tight across the chest and spun side-to-side a few times, the way I'd always done for the kids when they needed a second or third goodbye from me, from across a room or a field or a window on the school bus. "Thank you so much, Ellen."

"Thanks for letting me play with your babies," she called from the front yard. "Oh—and if you find one of your bras in the dishwasher, or a fork in the hamper, please know I had nothing to do with that."

I let the kids spend another half hour fussing over Theo. I stayed in the kitchen, thankful for the chance to be semi-alone for a short while to collect my thoughts. Eventually I called out to Bret—she still wouldn't make eye contact with me—and told her I could put the twins to bed by myself. It was an odd choice, given my extreme fatigue. For Jojo and Frankie, going to bed was never a simple act; it was an operatic cycle.[39] Yet diving into conversation with Bret about her coach would have demanded even more energy, and besides, she seemed as wiped out as I was. It had been several days since I'd put the little ones to bed anyway, so I was suffering from a deficiency

---

39   There was the ritualistic sipping of water. All boo-boos, past and present, had to be kissed like so many gold rings. Blankets must be fluffed just so . . .

of vitamins J&F. And in spite of their protests and caterwauling, and their genius for collective bargaining, my moments with them felt particularly sweet that night.

Back downstairs, I sat down next to Theo, who was looking through his bag of secondhand craft materials. I leaned against him and rested my head on his shoulder, much like I'd done after returning from PTA, only eight days earlier. It felt like eight lifetimes.

"I'm so glad you're OK, Theo," I said softly.

"Me, too." He kissed the top of my head and his face hovered there, over my crown, for several seconds. I couldn't remember the last time he'd initiated something like that, or the last time we'd shared that much surface area for that long.

I sat upright with a jerk when I caught a strong whiff of Justin. It was pungent, in fact, in part because it was coming from inside our own foyer. I was about to jump up when he appeared, hands in pockets, at the entrance to the family room.

"Your door was half-open," he said with a shrug. I must not have latched it when I'd said goodbye to Ellen.

"Hi, Justin," I said, lowering myself back again, slowly. I'd never seen him look sheepish before.

"My man!" Theo said, waving a wooden embroidery hoop at Justin. Someone's partially completed project was still inside it. "How's it going? Why haven't I seen you around here, neighbor?"

I almost mouthed to Justin, *He's on drugs.* But I wanted this slightly weird, nondepressed version of Theo to feel comfortable flying its freak flag here, in hopes it might stick around.

"I saw a lot of activity over here, earlier, and heard about your accident. I wanted to see if there was anything, you know, that you all needed."

"That's so nice, man," Theo said as he returned to inspecting the embroidery at close range. "What do you think, babe? What's on your list?"

I looked at him like he had suddenly—I dunno—turned into a giant monster or something. The dramatic changes in Theo's demeanor were almost too much to absorb. I trained my incredulity back on Justin. "Is it upside-down day? What timeline are we in right now?"

He raised a palm to the top of his almost-bald pate, which seemed to have been overcooked by least five decades. As he ran his hand around in circles, I noticed that in addition to his threadbare denim and flip-flops, he wore a shirt that was more or less a proper Oxford, except that it'd been made with a very busy and very loud print.

"Nice shirt, Justin," I said a bit snidely. I realized, then, that I wanted an apology from him. For having the gall to stand in front of me the night before and pick apart my story. After everything I'd seen and done the previous few days, I couldn't let people do that to me anymore. I couldn't allow anybody else to tell me who I was, or what I needed.

I felt Theo look up again. "*What*? Don't listen to Harry, man. She doesn't appreciate how it's, like, business in the collar, party in the fabric. Right, my dude?"

I marveled. *My husband is making jokes again.*

"I wouldn't want to surprise somebody on their own couch in my usual attire," Justin replied, referring to his habit of going around semi-naked.

"Don't worry," I said, not meeting his eye. "It's not like we own any guns."

"Maybe not. But I'd never bet against you, Harriet, in a fair fight."

I didn't reply to that. I didn't know what to make of it; I wasn't used to feeling anything except irritation toward the man.

"How about this?" I answered finally. "You come over tomorrow evening, and we'll figure out the details from there. I can't think straight at the moment, but I know we'll need a lot of help."

He gave us a slight bow, hands in his pockets again, and turned to leave.

"Wait, wait, wait—we don't know anything about you, really."

"What do you want to know?" he asked as he turned back.

"If you're gonna be in our house, hanging out, you should at least give us your elevator pitch. Er, résumé." I couldn't shake the feeling that I shouldn't fully trust the guy.

He looked at the table, then the floor. "Uh, let's see. You already know I'm from LA. And that I was in the Marines," he began. "When I left, a guy I'd been in with asked if I had any interest in the Bureau, so I went with it."

"You're FBI?"

"No, no, no. Used to be."

"Agent?"

He nodded. "And I ended up here for the same reasons a lot of Californians do: It's cheaper." He smiled as he spoke, absently passing his fingers over the stubble on his jaw while his glance shifted about the room. Then he added, sounding oddly amused, "Also, it's much more chill. So much more chill than LA could ever be."

"Uh, OK," I said, bringing my hand to my face and squinting hard. I'd just remembered that I had never told Theo about Coach Sullen's behavior toward Bret. *Fuck!* I'd sure been overlooking a lot of stuff lately. And forgetting stuff. And ignoring stuff—partly in favor of my own wants and interests. *Is this what it's like to be a dad?* I wiped my face down with one hand, grinning slightly. "I guess."

"You 'guess' what?"

"Oh, sorry. I meant sure—I'll see you tomorrow. Thanks." When he'd gone, I turned back to Theo and discovered that in those short minutes, he'd fallen asleep. I didn't wake him up; I felt like a bad spouse and parent, having forgotten to tell him about Bret and her coach before then, but the guy needed to rest. As I pulled one of Dianne's blankets over him, I felt certain that the Ghost of Theo Past would be much faded, if not gone entirely, when he woke up. And I knew I would miss him.

3.4   MONDAY, 8:30 P.M.

I eventually gave up trying to sleep. My achy muscles begged me to stay in bed, but my Mom Lobe had kicked on again, and was pelting me with more questions, emotions, and worries than I could tolerate. So I pulled on my jeans, made coffee, and dashed off a semi-legible note for Bret and Theo—who was still asleep on the sofa—about an unspecified errand.

Out in the driveway, my heart tore a bit when I caught a glimpse of Theo's Explorer, which had been towed and left in Justin's driveway, for some reason. The collision had compacted the front-right corner so much that the steering column was now one of the foremost parts of the vehicle. We were beyond lucky to have Theo ending his day with us, snoring peacefully in the family room.

I fished inside my pocket for the paper Dr. M had given me. It read:[40]

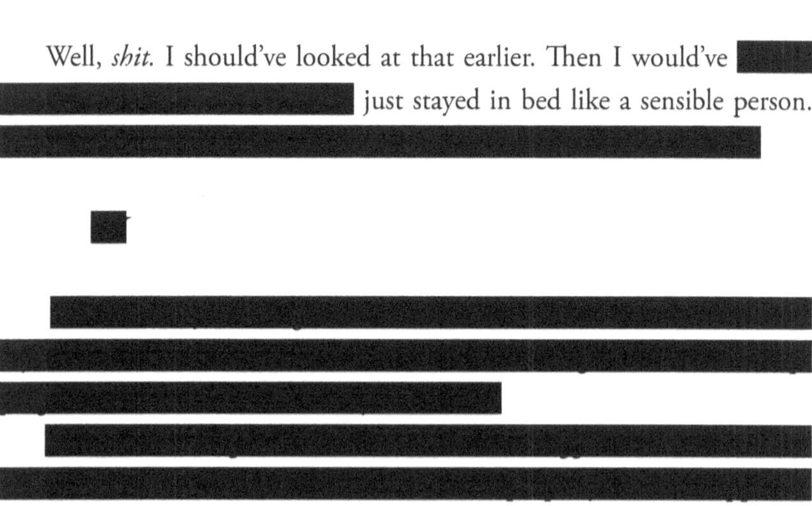

Well, *shit.* I should've looked at that earlier. Then I would've just stayed in bed like a sensible person.

---

40   Oops! I just realized you can't know this part. Instead of deleting it, though, I thought I'd give you a chance to feel what it's like to have key information withheld from you. (Kinda shitty, right? You're welcome.)

I pulled up to the place and turned off the engine and sat there a few minutes, cradling Bret's cell phone in my lap, rotating it in one hand, over and over. I scrolled through her contacts and when I got to my mom, my chest shuddered. I'd grown accustomed to feelings of unease and uncertainty whenever I dialed her number, long before that. So I wasn't expecting to be wracked by a new and unsettling feeling that I couldn't quite name.

The phone rang and rang and rang. No one picked up, and no message system kicked in, so I hung up. "What happened to you?" I said aloud, leaning against the door. *And what happened to* your *mama?*

I'd always viewed my mom like some kind of benign, feckless monster. She wandered the periphery of my life, not contributing much and not asking for much. Sooby and I had disparaged her for sport, when we even remembered she was around. But Dr. M's revelation about my grandmother's suicide had reminded me how little I actually knew of my mom's early life. As a kid, I'd been preoccupied with getting by, and was already a parent myself when I discovered Mom had been seventeen when she had me—and therefore sixteen when my father got her pregnant. I hadn't become sentimental about her all of a sudden, but I was starting to recognize the hypocrisy in the fact that I'd given Justin a hard time for making assumptions about me, when I'd never asked my mom about her younger years. Not since I was a little kid, anyway, when I didn't get an answer.

I'd said to Bret: *You'd be surprised, who is and who isn't a monster.* We had both used that word—monster—and the connection we made between it and Coach Sullen had left a foul taste in my mouth. I'd embraced that label for myself, freely and gleefully, without grappling with what I was laying claim to. We call someone a *monster* when they've done something terrible, or when they fail to behave in ways considered innately, and necessarily, human. Kind of like how my mom had lacked basic caretaking instincts when I was a child, showing no interest in my life and very little concern for my well-being. Had that been monstrous?

But what kind of monster was I? Was I destined for terribleness, or inhumanity, or was there some other choice? Could a monster's real nature be "TBD"? Would I be one who wielded her powers like a threat, as a tool for keeping people like Mr. Terrence, or even Bret, in check? I shuddered again.

I slipped the phone in my pocket and got out of the van, ████████ ████████████████████████. Next to the ████████████████ was a ███████ ████ door, and when I pulled the handle, it swung open.

Two strands of weak industrial lighting—the kind with a cage around each bulb—ran the length of a short corridor before turning to the left. The whir of a generator almost drowned out a pair of voices, but my hearing was really good now. I followed the lights to another set of doors, ██. A pair of battery-powered lanterns outlined the silhouettes of two people sitting in folding metal chairs: Dr. M and Ellen. They both stood, and the latter smiled weakly, as I made my way toward them, feet dragging as I attempted to take the place in.

"This is some eerie shit, ladies," I said, ▮▮▮▮▮▮▮▮▮▮▮▮▮▮▮▮▮▮ ▮▮▮▮▮▮▮▮▮▮▮. I picked up the pace until I reached their cocoon of light, where the only other objects were an old metal desk and a few additional chairs, still folded flat.

"I know we have a lot of explaining to do, Harry. But first—how is Theo?" Dr. M asked as she waved me over and opened one of the chairs.

"Not bad, considering. Everything each of you did, and that Sooby's and Dianne's families did? It made me think we're going to be OK. Even my neighbor came by, and said he would help us out." My eyes bugged out as I relayed that last bit, and I shook my head and sat down. I managed to eke out a few lines about Bret and her coach before my curiosity got the better of my patience. "Would you guys please tell me why you're here, now? Why I'm here?"

Ellen and Dr. M exchanged glances and adjusted themselves in their seats. "How about I start, Ellen, since I know where the story begins, and you jump in whenever you like?"

"Works for me."

"As you know, Harry, I was thrilled to receive a big research grant not long ago. I always said that if I ever got the funding, I'd name the project after my daughter. You can imagine my elation when I filed the first paperwork to establish the Sarah R. Morris Center."

"And remember how we talked at Brandon's soccer game, about my research at Hind, and how not many scientists have pursued those topics?" Ellen asked. "When I saw in a journal that Dr. M had gotten this money,

I reached out to her. I wanted us to support and share information with each other."

"And Ellen kindly agreed to serve as an advisor," Dr. M went on, bowing her head and gesturing to Ellen like a knight's squire. "She accepted my invitation to be on the board, once that's up and running."

"Oh my goodness—are you kidding? I was thrilled you asked me!" Ellen replied, holding a hand to her chest.

"You two are adorable," I interjected.

"But Ellen, your involvement has made it possible to get up and running after months and months of setbacks. I have no doubt that adding your name to the project was the piece that convinced the medical center to lease me some space," she added, determined not to be out-gushed. "Anyway, when I got to the lab the other morning, I found the place half underwater. There was a break in one of the pipes."

"So, quick question," I said. "Who's been doing the physical work of setting up the lab?"

"According to my lease, the hospital's maintenance staff can't work on anything I add to the space. But I had a postcard in my mail some weeks ago, advertising maintenance services for small businesses. And since laboratories were among the specialties they listed, it seemed like a good fit for us. I called and hired them to do the build-out."

"Did your security cameras capture anything when the flood happened?" I asked.

"Well, no," Dr. M went on. "I ordered cameras from the company that runs security for all the other labs at Willamette Med, but the shipment hasn't come in."

"We know that one of the pipes has an enormous break in it," Ellen added, "but we weren't able to do any real investigating in the days immediately following the incident."

"Why not?"

"The maintenance company I called, from the postcard? No longer answering calls," Dr. M said.

"That's weird," I said, shifting in my seat.

She told me the name of the outfit. "But don't bother Googling them, Harry. Their site's gone, too."

I felt the flare of the monster in my chest.

"That's when Dr. M called the police," Ellen said. "But they told her that burst pipes aren't in their purview, quote, unquote."

"No help at all," Dr. M concurred.

"But you . . . suspect *sabotage*?" I closed my eyes and sat on my hands, as if that posture was better for absorbing the impact of such a bombshell. "Can you tell me more about the work you were planning to do in the lab? In layman—er, layperson—terms? It's related to pregnancy, I know; is it controversial?" My mind flicked back to the campaign event I'd stopped by, with the fateful churro truck and where volunteer Joe had touted Olivia Patchett-Parkeras being a real zealot for zygotes.

"Well," Dr. M began, "I mentioned to you, Harry, that the mission for our lab is to improve how we treat women, medically speaking. To expand the tiny body of knowledge on things like female organs, hormones, chromosomes, and so on. So my proposal was for the SRM Center to expand in a couple years' time, to study a range of topics. But I intended to start with fetal microchimerism," Dr. M replied.

I felt the monster's interest pique at these words, and alarm flashed across my face—too fast for me to quash it. I was sure the other women saw it.

"You remember what I said about microchimerism, Harry, at Brandon's game?"

"Yes," I replied, trying to act like I wasn't about to crap myself. "It's when one organism contains cells from another organism. Inside it." I focused on keeping my breaths regular and slow.

"You saw the figurine that I keep on my desk, Harry, when you visited my office," said Dr. M. "I saw you pick it up and examine it. That's what a Chimera might have looked like, in the minds of the ancient Greeks. Part goat, part lion, part serpent."

Again, the monster stirred at the mention of the strange hybrid creature. And I was starting to panic. *Is a big apey-bear monster a chimera of sorts?*

"I'm using a simplified image of it in our logo for the lab."

"Doesn't sound especially controversial, does it?" Ellen asked. I started to nod, but then she and Dr. M glanced at one another, and I felt an uptick in intensity in each of them, but also a rising uncertainty, like *they* were nervous to tell *me* something. Which actually calmed me a bit.

"Well, one of the weird things about microchimerism is that once in a blue moon, the record from a court proceeding will note that a person's DNA results looked completely different, depending on when and how the sample was taken."

"Whoaaaaa!"

"Yeah," Ellen replied. "But it gets even more bizarre: In some cases, one set of test results turns out to match some other DNA, taken from some other individual."

"Damn! That's . . . that's insane."

"It's also, as you're probably gathering, of significant interest to people who want to do things without being detected."

"Ooohhh," I said, sounding more and more like Theo had earlier. "Criminal things."

They both nodded. "Yes, that for sure," Dr. M added. "But don't count out law enforcement. Even the military."

"Fuuuuuuuuuck!" I said, crossing my arms and legs and resting my chin in my hand. "But if somebody—or many somebodies—want to get their hands on your research for their own ends, why destroy your lab? Why not wait until your work was out there for stealing?"

"It's all still a mystery," Dr. M replied, her features heavier than I'd ever seen them. "Perhaps it's the work's connection to pregnancy that someone doesn't like. Who knows? Maybe someone thinks we're promoting abortion somehow."

"After the maintenance company disappeared," Ellen added, taking a quick look at her watch, "Dr. M and I were pretty freaked out. So while the hospital paid to get all the water out, we wracked our brains to figure out whom we could trust, to help us figure everything out."

"Well, I'm thankful you knew you could trust me," I said with a tremble, as guilt and fear coiled around my vocal cords. Harboring a gargantuan secret from one's friends has that effect, apparently. "What can I do?"

"Before we go any further, Harry, I need to explain how I knew that Theo . . . how I knew what Theo was experiencing, even before his accident. Do you remember what I told you?"

"You told me, very kindly, that he's depressed. And I was an asshole to you."

She smiled. "Apology accepted, Harry. Now, I knew that about him because you're not the only one around who's recently acquired some new . . . abilities."

My heart started hammering. I stood up and walked in a tight circle around my chair, holding the sides of my head. "What are you talking about?" I stammered.

"Don't worry, Harry. You're not in any trouble. Not with us, anyway. In fact, the reason we know you're that . . . creature that's been going around, putting out wildfires, is because I have a special power of my own. So does Ellen, but we'll get to that in a minute."

I sat down and stared at the ground. The panic I'd felt at first still thrummed inside me, but now it was dampened by the relief that fell over me: They knew my big, bad secret, and they were OK with it. No words would come.

"I'd been having weird episodes for some months," she continued. "I'd be with a pregnant woman in an exam room, and I'd black out—kind of like you said, Harry—but this was a very brief blackout. My brain would be doing its usual thing, and then suddenly, I'd look at my patient and the rest of the room would fade away, and the interior of her seemed to become visible. It was like I could see into her, suddenly."

"What in the ever-loving hell, Doc?"

"I know. My immediate thought was that the hospital administrators were right: It might be time for me to retire. That I was losing my mind. But then it happened again, with my next patient. And in between, everything was normal. I went to lunch at the café. I did a pap smear. I answered emails. Pfft!" she said, waving her hand, like the incident had been no big deal.

"But the more time I spent recalling these blackouts, or whatever we want to call them, more details became clear. I could bring the image of the patient clearly back to my mind after all, and I saw things about each woman's health."

"What do you mean, like what?" I asked.

"I saw, for example, in the image of one such patient, that she had endometriosis. In another, I saw she had a small tumor in her brain. When I pressed her at her next appointment for other symptoms she might have forgotten to mention, she said she'd had a dull headache in a spot where she'd never had one before."

"Dr. M can see into people, and see what pathologies are occurring in their bodies," Ellen explained.

"Damn, Doc! That's awesome. Literally. I'm in awe."

"Yes, but I can only diagnose what I see if it's something that we already understand, scientifically. For example, Harry, I can see that you have heartburn. Because I learned about that in medical school and I've diagnosed it a million times. I know what to look for. Can I give Harry an example from you, Ellen? Would that be OK?"

"Uh, sure. How does my thyroid look to you?" she asked, lifting her chin to show more of her neck. She touched it lightly with her fingertips. "Is it sluggish, or is it overexcited? Hypo or hyper?

"Hyper. Definitely."

"Bingo," she replied. "Take a pill for it, every morning. Trying to slow its roll."

"And when you came to see me, Harry," Dr. M continued, "I was just flummoxed, because I couldn't read you at all. I couldn't read you because every part of you, every cell, was calling attention to itself."

"I don't understand."

"I don't want to alarm you, dear, but another way of looking at it is that every cell in your body has some kind of pathology happening."

I squeezed my eyes shut. That did not sound good.

"That doesn't mean you're sick, though."

I shook my head. "I can't seem to get used to being shocked out of my gourd every day," I said passively, which got a laugh from both women.

"And so, in your case, Ellen, one of your abilities is that you're more or less immune to extreme temperatures? Do I have that right?"

She nodded gravely. "I realized, also a couple months ago, that I didn't burn my hand when I tried to lift a hot pan from a live burner on our stove. It didn't even hurt. Later, when I went to pull something out of the freezer, I noticed it wasn't cold and I thought the damn thing had broken. Then I remembered the incident on the stove, and started doing some experiments."

"For instance, taking an ice-cold bath, using every ice cube in the house," Dr. M added.

"I was able to sit in it for a really long time, Harry. In fact, I only got out when I got bored," Ellen explained.

I turned to Dr. M. "When you look . . . *into* Ellen, can you see something that explains those abilities?"

"I see remaining placenta cells in her, like I do in most moms. That much isn't unusual. You have them, Harry, and so do I," she explained. "But in Ellen, I can see that some of those have altered, somehow; they aren't like the others."

"We have a few theories about this, but they are, I have to admit, a bit . . . wild," Ellen added. "The placenta is unlike anything else in the human body, and it does amazing things. It's an entirely new organ our bodies make from scratch, and it's enormous! It acts as a 'smart' barrier, letting certain things pass through while keeping other things out."

"And that's just to start with," Dr. M added. "There's much, much more to it."

"Lately, I've been sensing that I can resist extreme pressure, too. Especially after Gregory accidentally ran over my foot in the driveway the other day."

She slumped as she added, "Which is annoying, actually. As a Black woman, I really don't want to be giving anyone the impression that we don't feel pain." We nodded, looking at her. Ellen had to contend with so many things that I never even had to think about, on the daily.

"Oh—did I tell you, Ellen," Dr. M said, "that I think I lit a candle without a match yesterday? On my mantle?"

"What do you mean, you 'think'?" I asked, my head swiveling from one woman to the other.

Ellen's jaw dropped. "*Really?* What could that mean?" she replied as she commenced cracking her knuckles.

Dr. M's laughter became loud and irregular, as if she couldn't control it. "I don't know, but it's kind of exciting!"

"I've never heard you laugh quite like that before, Doc," I said.

She took several seconds to compose herself. "You're right, Harry. I should take spontaneous combustibility much more seriously." But she only kept her face straight for another couple seconds before bursting out laughing again. "I'm sorry, ladies, it's just too funny."

"Do you think your abilities change from day to day, then?" I asked. "Or do they grow? Or both? Because I've been wondering if, you know, I'm a bit different each time I . . . transform."

"It's hard to say," Ellen joked. "Am I gradually discovering the different ways I can freak out my husband and kids? Or am I gaining *new* ways, from time to time?"

Dr. M sighed. "If only we had an advanced laboratory, where we could study stuff like this."

"I gotta know, Doc. When we were in your office and you sprayed me with water, did you know that water is the one thing that seems to keep me in Harriet-form?"

"No, honey. I just wanted to distract you and maybe cool you off a little."

"Is there anything else we know about the fake maintenance company? Did you talk to, or meet anyone from there?" I asked.

"I was so busy I didn't give them much attention, I'm afraid," Dr. M replied. "I did ask if they were insured, and they said they'd send proof of coverage but never did. What little communication I had with them was by phone, unfortunately, and they were only here once, to assemble a hood and to do a minor bit of wiring. I spend the day glued to my computer, and Ellen was over at Hind. That was a few days before the incident."

"I hate to say it, ladies. But it's late," Ellen said after another look at her watch. "I have to get home soon."

"But wait—we can't go yet! I still don't know why we have these powers, or whatever they are. Why isn't it happening to other people? Oh shit—*is* all of this happening to other people? Jesus . . ."

"I'm sorry to leave you with a million questions, Harry," Ellen replied. "We don't have many answers. But I *can* tell you that we suspect the strange things Dr. M sees happening inside of us are related to our strange new . . . abilities."

I must have looked like I was going to combust, because Dr. M came over and put her hands on my shoulders. "One more thing we can tell you is that *yes*—there are at least a few other women who we know have experienced some inexplicable things of late. But for now, Harry, we should all probably get home. It won't be a bad thing for you to get some rest before we need you on this."

I watched as they each picked up a lantern, and Ellen went over to a column and unplugged the lights. "What are you going to need from me?" I asked as the place went darker. I wondered if assisting in this mystery would require the monster to make herself public, and didn't know what to make of it when the idea left me feeling hopeful.

"We've got Gregory digging up whatever he can about the maintenance company, from their online presence," Ellen said. She held her breath and cracked a few knuckles as she added dryly, "So my husband is trying his hand at hacking, in other words."

"And we've got someone going back into the lab to look at the pipes for us, and gather up some of my personal things."

"OK? So where does that leave me?" I pictured myself swinging from the Aerial Tram in Southwest Portland, swatting away drones or bullets or something.

"For now," Dr. M replied, "there are two things."

"OK. Hit me."

"First, you must refrain from turning into . . . that creature."

I managed to rein in the disgruntlement I felt at this request, though my face bucked hard at the request. Not turn into the monster? At all, not matter what? She squirmed inside me as if constricted suddenly, in too tight a space. "Uhh, OK?"

"We don't know who's trying to sabotage us, and what else they might do. So for the time being, we should all avoid drawing attention to ourselves."

"But for how long?" *It's not that big a deal,* I told myself. *Deep breaths. You didn't need the monster to be a good person, a good wife, a good mom before all this happened.* Still, it chafed. I mean, what if I needed to back up my threat to Mr. Terrence?

"I can't say," Dr. M replied. "And secondly, Harry, we need you to meet with us again this Saturday evening, when we'll have results from our pipe detective, and maybe from Gregory, too."

"Oh, wow," I said, a new, stranger resistance blooming inside me. "Do we need to meet again so soon? I'm not sure what things will be like at home, until I see how Theo does . . ."

"But your neighbor offered to help out, right?" Dr. M replied.

"And—AND—that's Halloween," I said, feeling stricken without understanding why. I was now protesting having to miss out on a holiday I was ambivalent about, at best. "I know two little monkeys who will be very unhappy if I don't escort them around, begging for candy."

They looked at each other, as if they, too, were befuddled by my blanket intransigence. "We could meet somewhere near Scarehouse that night, instead of here," Ellen offered.

"Good idea," Dr. M replied.

"How about we meet the following week, when—"

"Harry," Dr. M said firmly, "this is urgent. We need to push forward for all our sakes."

"But that's not—"

"And if I may be blunt for a second, this right here is why some people believe you don't like to join things."

"OK, OK. You're right," I blurted out, feeling stung. "And Sooby was right, too: I'm not a joiner."

"That's not what I said—"

"I don't do my part."

"Let me finish, Harriet Lime!" Dr. M said, her tone commanding but warm. "I know that growing up, you had a lot of good reasons to be wary of people—of their desire for you to conform to their ways, of the big, grand ideas they wanted you to accept. You lived in a state of constant threat. Threat of hunger, threat of abandonment, and a bunch of other things."

I looked back at her as a powerful calmness descended over me.

"These days, though, please know that as your friends, we're here for you. And we'll always be here for you. Even when you don't agree with us. Even when you don't want to comply."

"You're pushing me on my own pushback, here," I replied, eking out some sarcasm when nothing else would come to me. A new peace travelled through me at a clip, out to every limb and extremity as if giving notice to the pervasive uncertainty that had curdled inside me for so long. Was that all I'd needed these many years? For someone to promise me I would always be a part of their pack?

"Fine. I'll be there," I whispered, too overcome to say more.

"Good," replied Dr. M. "Then you'll get to meet all the others. As it happens, you know quite a few of them. Dianne Chu—"

"Wait—*what?*"

"And Christy Holmes."

"I—*huh?* For real? Holy *shit.*"

"And you know at least one of the other women, but I think she'd rather tell you herself."

I shook my head as we emerged from ██████, my body on autopilot. "Dang," I muttered. "That's all I got right now. *Dang.*"

3.5 TUESDAY, 9:00 A.M.

Walking into the office the next day, I could barely grunt *hello* and *good morning* to my coworkers. I was completely preoccupied with the revelations Ellen and Dr. M had tossed at me the previous night. I took each new bit of info—about myself, my friends, and the people who might be out to harm them—and held it in my mind's eye like a relic and examined it, over and over. It was a lot.

But the stuff they *hadn't* told me was equally arresting. Like, what special new abilities did Dianne and Christy have? I wondered if their powers, and Ellen's and Dr. M.'s, too, gave them what mine gave me—a chance to break free of the restraints our society puts on women. When I was the monster, I didn't even notice all the messages telling me to cross my ankles, to smile, to lose weight, to gain weight, to shave, to stop doing that with my hair, to smile more, to hold in my farts, to get pregnant, to not get pregnant, to lean in, to lean out, to feed my baby differently, to birth my babies differently, to have more kids but also to have fewer kids, to use my organs and orifices in the way others would prefer, and so on. I hoped the same was true for my friends.

When I reached the short pass-through that led to the coat closet, I came upon Gina, holding a cordless drill. She appeared deep in thought, too, and around her on the floor was a hodgepodge of screws, brackets, and particle board.

"Hey. What's all this?" I asked as I put Yvette's fabulous coat on a wooden hanger.

"Hey, Harry. These are our new shelves. I figured we could fit all our office supplies here in this . . . space," she said as she waved her hand around, "if I installed a few of these and got some bins to sort things out."

"Nice! That's brilliant, G!" I grabbed a sticky note and after jotting a quick apology to Yvette, affixed the thing to the hanger holding the borrowed coat. "IKEA?"

She nodded as she adjusted the bit of her drill.

From the corner of my eye, I saw Bob walk briskly across the other end of the pass-through. "I think he's happy with it," Gina went on. "But he's awful grumpy this morning."

I laughed, as glad for the injection of levity into my morning as I was for Gina's success. "I'll give you twenty bucks if you go into his office and pretend like you've changed your mind. Tell him you, me, and Yvette have all decided it's actually a waste to dedicate a whole closet to nursing, when no one is nursing," I whispered. *A whole closet!*

"Nah. I already got my shits and giggles this morning, when I told him I'd solved a problem he said couldn't be solved." She raised her hand to high-five me. "For under sixty bucks."

I'd just reached my desk when Theo called. He sounded awful: his voice strangled and sore. "I'm having a lot of trouble right now."

"What's wrong?" I asked, standing up and looking around for my keys.

"I think this medicine is . . . doing a number on my . . . intestines." He made a groaning sound that lasted several seconds. "And I can't even get to the bathroom, let alone sit down on the toilet."

"You have Justin's number there. On that list, on the side table."

"Justin who?"

I squeezed my whole jaw with my free hand, making my skin pucker out in weird ways. The next few months were going to be even longer than I thought. I reminded him of Justin's offer to help.

He made another one of his sustained and woeful noises. "That would be humiliating."

He thought several seconds. "This is probably how you felt that first time you pooped after the babies were born."

I have to admit I genuinely appreciated Theo's nod to my own experience with assisted bowel movements. "Yeah," I said. "Pretty much, babe."

I settled in quickly at my desk, but my thoughts didn't follow suit. On the one hand, I felt so much lighter knowing Ellen and Dr. M knew my enormous secret and were unbothered by it. And yet it felt irresponsible to let myself be comforted by that, or anything else. Because the events at their lab suggested someone wanted to put an end to their research and would step outside the law to do it. We were dealing with some heavy shit and had no leads to go on; I should've been quaking in my rolling chair.

I leafed through some mail on my desk, trying to look like I was focused on it as I clicked open the browser on my computer and typed *new mole or dried gunk how can I tell* into the search bar. After scrolling absently through the results, I went back to my piles of paper and spied a piece of junk mail with a cartoonish lizard-man logo on it. It reminded me of the whole chimera thing Dr. M and Ellen had told me about, and I pretended to read it as I put my fingers back on my keyboard and typed *Chimera Greek monster ancient modern women*. I glanced around at my coworkers, and when I was sure no one was paying attention, turned back to my screen and hit enter. The first search result was for a Facebook group called "Project Chimera" and I clicked on it, unease rising in my throat. It turned out to be a closed group, based in Idaho. The listing had no public image associated with it, and no details apart from having over three hundred members.

I closed the browser window, shook my head, and flattened my palms on my desk. *Get it together, Harry.* Bret's big game against Bellwether was that afternoon, and I was going to have to focus in order to get my work done in time to go. That realization got me moving finally, as did the prospect of getting to speak with Ellen again. She'd offered—rather generously, given how busy she was—to meet me at the gym once I'd filled her in on the situation with Bret and Coach Sullen. She might've felt she had a second—and bigger—reason to join me, however. Right before we'd parted the night before, I'd told her and Dr. M how I'd threatened Mr. Terrence. They'd exchanged glances and their heart rates had gone up. They must have been worried that my "creature," as Dr. M called it, might try to have a word with one or both coaches at the game.

It wasn't until I got to the gym later on that I remembered Sooby would be there, too. The cheerleaders had come out to support Bret's team in their official Homecoming match, so Satchel would be performing. Her mom was already sitting in the row below Ellen, and I steeled myself as I climbed toward them. Things might still be chilly between Soob and me, but sitting apart would've just been too weird.

"Hey, can you forward me those emails? The ones from your mom?" Sooby asked before I even sat down. Maybe she wanted to break apart any new ice between us, before it could fully form. And to be honest, I appreciated having a ready-made subject to talk about with her. She pulled a laptop from her boat-tote and Ellen pulled her own large handbag onto her lap, to make room for me to sit.

"Uh," I began. I was distracted, having spied the two coaches on the floor with the girls. "Uh—no. Sorry, I deleted them. But I can probably remember the articles they linked to."

"OK, shoot."

I couldn't stop watching Mr. Terrence and Coach Sullen, and forgot to respond to Sooby.

"Harry?" Sooby said, snapping her fingers. "Articles?"

"Oh. Yeah. Let's see," I said, still looking at the men. "The first one was in *The Oregonian*, and it was about rogue waves. It was a few months old, I think."

"OK," Sooby replied, typing furiously. "And the other was about O-P-P, right?"

"Excuse me?" Ellen asked as she looked up from her sewing.

"*Olivia Patchett-Parker* is *such* a mouthful. So I call her O-P-P," Sooby replied.

"Wow. She didn't think through, did she? The hyphenated name?" Ellen chuckled.

"Seriously," I said, smirking. "But yeah, Soob—the other article was about her law-and-order platform. I can't remember which site it was on, or when."

"Not a problem. Just those two? No other emails?"

I slumped a little. "I haven't checked my personal email in a couple of days. But yeah, up to that point it was only the two. Why are you so interested in these, anyway? Is this about that beef you used to have with O-P-P?"

"You told me that you stumbled upon her campaign office on Main Street, right after you got the email. Right?"

"Yeah. And?"

"I just think that's an interesting coincidence. But it might be nothing."

"OK."

"So the one about the waves is really short," she said as she scanned the item. "It says, quote, *A local teenager, Lara Colver, has not been seen since earlier that day when she left the house to attend a weekly surfing lesson, and her family fears the worst. Search efforts are still underway* . . . and then it goes on to say . . . bah-bah-bah, that other missing persons were reported that same day, and the one after."

I didn't take my eyes off the court as she read. I looked from Bret to Coach Sullen to Mr. Terrence, on loop, but I did hear her. "Those poor families," I mumbled.

"That's terrible," Ellen added over a quick pause in her sewing.

The head referee blew her whistle, signaling both teams to return to their bench and prepare to begin the match. Bret seemed to be in her usual, pregame state of mind, so I figured the tension between me and her coaches wasn't affecting her; I certainly couldn't see or smell or detect any stress in her, just nervous excitement.

"Oh, and Soob," I said suddenly, "I just remembered that Patchett-Parker article was specifically about crime in Portland. She had just given a speech or something."

"'Kay."

"What *is* your beef with her, anyway?"

"Our parents used to socialize together. You know that," she replied. She didn't stop typing while she spoke. "They'd go to the cabin. Travel places and stuff. But there was . . . a falling out."

The teams huddled, and late-arriving parents and students made their way into the bleachers, some after scanning the crowd for familiar faces. "See any of our friends with the cowboy hats?" Ellen asked quietly.

"No," I replied, sitting back. "Haven't seen them since the hospital, actually."

Ellen's hands froze. "You saw them at the hospital? Harry, you didn't tell me that!"

I'd opened my mouth to apologize when I spotted Dianne, not far from us, holding the hand of a woman I'd never met. She was assisting her up the bleachers at a slow pace, coming in our direction.

"This is Annika, everybody. She's one of my advanced pottery students," Dianne began, slightly winded. She introduced Ellen, Soob, and me by name. "I wanted her to meet Harry especially, because she just found out she's having twins!"

Ellen *oooohed* for her, and Sooby's hands flew to her cheeks. Annika smiled and put her hand on her abdomen. I started perspiring.

"Have you joined *Multiple Moms* yet?" I asked. Those were the first words out of my mouth. Not *Congratulations*. Not *How are you feeling?*

"Uh, no. I don't know them." Her smile wavered ever so slightly.

"I'll jot down the link for you," I said, rummaging in my bag for a wrapper to write on. "It's a support group for parents of twins, triplets, and anyone else taking care of more than one infant. Their dues are kind of high, but they were a lifesaver for my husband and me. You should download the sample to-do lists from their site."

I took the sudden stretch of Annika's features to mean no one had told her this stuff yet. "*Lists?* Like, plural?"

"Do you have car seats yet? Did you sign up for a training?" I asked, ignoring Sooby's exaggerated sigh.

"What kind of training?"

"On the proper way to install the kind of car seat you bought. There's a lot of them."

"Oh. No, I didn't know about that," Annika said as she pulled her purse off her shoulder and sat down. "Let me grab my notebook real quick."

"Harry," Soob said. "You're scaring this poor woman."

"So, if you're having a shower," I continued, "be sure to ask whoever is hosting to make a sign-up sheet, with a list of dates on it. Then have them pass it around to your guests, and make sure that anyone who's able to make and deliver a dinner for you, in the first weeks after you give birth, doesn't get out the door without signing up." I can see it now, as I write this—that my mind had gone back into the survival mode I'd developed after our twins were born, and I was projecting this onto Annika. At the time, I just thought I was helping.

"Annika?" Dianne asked, resting her hands on the other woman's shoulders. "Is this helpful?"

"Hell, yes," she replied. She was writing pretty fast, her brows at attention, so I kept talking.

"I don't know what your resources are, but if you can afford to hire a 'night doula,' even—"

"Sorry—one sec. A *what*?"

"A night doula," I repeated, pausing for her note-taking to catch up. "So you can sleep through the night. They're really pricey, but if you can afford to hire one for even a night or two, I can't recommend it highly enough. You'll think she's an angel sent down from heaven itself."

"Harry, c'mon," Sooby said. "You're exaggerating. Annika, she's exaggerating. Help me out here, Ellen."

Ellen didn't look up. "Actually, I wanted to just add, Annika, that on your gift registry, you could include a link where friends and family could make a donation to a doula fund. That could be their gift."

Dianne leaned over Annika's shoulder. "Definitely write that down. That's a great idea."

"I wish I had done that," I said. "Shit."

"Saaaaame," Dianne droned.

"Also, start baby-proofing your home," I said, "and get some help from somebody who knows twins."

"Like, *now*? This soon?"

"Yes, now," I replied, leaning toward her and lowering my voice. "They work together, you know."

"Who works together?" Annika whispered back.

"Twins."

"That's it—I'm going to the snack table," Sooby grumbled. She snapped her computer shut and started off down the bleachers. Soon after, Dianne and Annika excused themselves and made their way to other friends.

"How are you feeling, Harry?" Ellen asked when everyone had gone.

"Fine. I'm fine," I replied. She gave me a skeptical smile. "Hey, can you tell me what your costume is yet?" I asked, changing the subject. Her bunches of fabric had grown and bloomed into something more complex since the soccer game.

"No. It's a surprise. So what was Sue-Beth upset about, exactly?"

I let out a huff, partly because I'd failed to change the subject but also because I did, in fact, care that Sooby had walked off in a snit. "She didn't get the responses she wanted from us, I guess."

"Ah," Ellen replied.

"She loooooved being pregnant. And she loooooved having an infant to take care of. She gets testy whenever somebody mentions they didn't enjoy those things or that they struggled. I don't know why."

"You said her mom organized a meal train for you and your husband? Was Sue-Beth around, too?"

"She popped over once or twice in those first six months. She convinced me to bring the babies out to a café one time, too. But she was really busy then, just like she is now."

"I see," Ellen replied. "Do you think it was hard for her, seeing you with two babies?"

"You mean, was she jealous?" I hadn't mentioned that Soob and her husband hadn't been able to conceive again after Satchel—to their immense disappointment—but Ellen had intuited as much. I shrugged. "It's not like I rubbed her nose in it or anything. I was stuck at home with the curtains drawn and my boobs out, twenty-four seven."

Ellen continued to sew while we were quiet a moment. "I just wondered if we'd hurt her feelings, talking to Annika like that. Like I said, I can't afford to alienate people."

"I don't think you alienated her. For whatever that's worth."

"I like to kill people with courtesy, instead."

I laughed. "You *are* super polite."

"Thanks."

"How's Gregory's . . . new project coming along?" I asked.

"Nothing yet."

I told her how I'd Googled "Chimera," and about the Facebook group that came up. "Interesting," she replied. "With no contact information, no details? That's a shame."

"Yeah, I don't think they're connected to a medical or research center. If they are, they've got a really shitty social media intern."

Bret sat on the bench for the entire first game of the match, which Bellwether won. Sooby had returned from the snack table, but there wasn't much conversation. She spent the whole game online, and Ellen focused on her sewing. I stewed over whether or not the coaches had kept Bret on the bench—for the first time all season—as a result of my wheedling into their affairs.

"Where in Hawaii does your mom live?" Ellen asked while we waited for the next game to begin. "I love Hawaii."

"I don't know off the top of my head."

"Kauai," Sooby chimed in.

"Oh, nice. Rainiest place in the world!" Ellen added. "And one of the most beautiful."

"Rainiest? Really?" I asked, turning to look at her.

Ellen briefly crossed her eyes. "I know, I'm a veritable font of useless trivia."

"No, no—not at all. It just surprised me. I'd been picturing her lying on the beach all this time."

The players took to the court again, this time with Bret among them. I guess Mr. Terrence valued a volleyball win more than he did turning the screws on an annoying mother.

"Let's go, Hoffman!" I said. I had a way of clapping my hands that had a real ring to it, which startled Soob.

"See?" she said, turning around to shout out her own encouragement.

"'See' what?"

"Mr. Terrence isn't punishing her. Or you."

I squinted with my whole face; I hadn't mentioned my concerns about Bret's playtime. "Did you find the other article yet?" I asked.

"Yeah. I've been looking for others on the same topics, trying to fill out a broader picture."

"What are you looking for?"

The Hoffman players dominated the second game, and when the third and final one began with a similar lack of tension, I found myself looking over Soob's shoulder as she clicked around the website of *The Rambler*. It was a smaller paper that served the whole region but focused solely on the doings of governments. "A bunch of outlets used this same photo, I noticed. The one from *The Oregonian*."

She scrolled back to the photo in question, which showed Patchett-Parker standing behind a podium. A group of law enforcement officers, all of whom appeared to be men, crowded behind her on a small dais. Something about it made her look powerful.

The photo stayed on Soob's screen awhile, and between cheering for Bret and her teammates—who were on the cusp of winning the match—I peered at the men in the photo. They were out of focus, and hadn't stood in a neat line. The caption didn't include their names. "Can I see your computer for a sec?"

I scrolled around a bit. Each time I tried to dive into the text of the article, though, my eye kept being drawn back to the photo. I didn't know what I was looking for.

When the match ended, we all stood and cheered. It was a decisive victory over a top rival, and all the sweeter for being won as part of Homecoming week. Soob gave a quick wave and went off to chat up some other parents.

"I need to head back for a meeting," Ellen said as we gathered our things. "Think you can stay away from the coaches for the rest of the day?"

I started to throw her an offended look before realizing she was teasing. "Yes, ma'am. This day is for the players." I thanked her for coming, mimed a hug for her—because I knew it made her laugh—and she left.

While I waited for Bret to grab her things from the locker room, I wandered into the gym lobby—the same place where Sooby and I followed the officer after he'd menaced Ellen at PTA. I went up to one of the trophy cases and perused the team photos and other memorabilia, which not only went back decades but included all manner of competitive activities. I had to snort when I came across one of the Science Club—the same one I'd participated in—from the nineties. Glancing around, I found three more photos of the club, along with some trophies and ribbons, all depicting seasons of yesteryear in which Hoffman had won some state or regional title. The Science Club kids—who were all boys in the older photos—wore navy blazers, as other budding scientists would do in decades to come. But the jackets themselves evolved, both to reflect the fashion of the decade and in some cases, to incorporate the logo of a community sponsor. So there were big polyester lapels in 1979. Brass buttons in 1986. And patches on the arm in 1968.

I felt a monster-surge so strong I nearly stumbled backward. *Patches on the arm!* I looked around; there were three parents in a far corner of the lobby, but they were too absorbed in conversation to notice much else. I turned to the case again to look closer at the black-and-white image. The patches were barely discernible; they were of a very dark fabric, and had been attached to an equally dark fabric. I couldn't tell what they depicted, nor make out any letters. But I knew in my bones they were the same patches the men in the Stetsons had on their uniforms. What's more, I felt certain the patch must have appeared in the photo of Olivia Patchett-Parker and all those officers. My monster-brain must have detected it, even though my Harriet-eyes couldn't see it. I was scanning the cases a third time in hopes of finding an actual patch when Sooby called out to me.

"They must really be celebrating down there," she said, referring to the girls on the team. "I think at least half the parents are still here, pacing around."

"Soob, come look at this!" I waved her over.

"Bret asked if she could spend the night, and I said it was OK," she said as she approached.

I turned and tried not to show my displeasure at this. It wasn't like Bret to invite herself over to someone's house, and with all the tension strung between the three of us, it especially irked. "Oh, OK," I said finally. "But come look at the uniforms in this old Science Club picture. They have dark patches on the arms. Does that remind you of anything?"

"No?" she replied with forced amusement, and without taking a second to consider it.

I cocked my head at her and kept my voice low. "The men at PTA, remember? In the cowboy hats? You said that night that they had patches on their arms, but you couldn't read them because it was so low-contrast. Black on black."

"I don't know why you're making a leap between those guys and these cute little boys," she replied as she stepped closer and peered into the glass case. After a few seconds, she clucked her tongue and stood up again. "Oh for God's *sake*, Harry."

"What?"

"Now I know why you made that stretch: You think you see bad motivations wherever Mr. Terrence happens to be."

"What?" I was leaking patience like a sieve, and a bunch of other big emotions swept in to take its place. I jabbed at the case with my index finger, causing it to rattle along the edges. "Soob, Mr. Terrence wasn't a teacher in 1968. This debonair fellow with the horn-rimmed glasses was faculty leader back then."

"Look again, Harry," she replied.

"Mr. Terrence would've been just—" I stopped and pressed my face and hands against the glass again, as requested, and noticed for the first time the square of white paper pinned to the left of the photo. On it, in tiny lettering, were the names of the club members. The last one was *Patrick Terrence*.

"Whoa. That's crazy!" I said. "I didn't notice that, Soob. Seriously. I'd only noticed the patches when you came out of the gym."

"You have no objectivity when it comes to him."

"OK, look: I'd have to be superhuman to set aside *all* my feelings about the man, given the number of terrible experiences I've—"

"You're not helping your case by exaggerating so much."

"*Soob!* What are you talking about?"

"Did you know that I've had to beg some parents to believe me when I say how awesome you are?" she continued in a low voice. "Because I know you put out the fire in the gorge, in the form of that M-O-N-S-T-E-R or whatever—"

"*Excuse me?*" My anger about Mr. Terrence was briefly overpowered by the shock of Sooby somehow knowing my big secret.

She leaned closer. "Yeah. I know all about that, Harry. Because I can do . . . *things*, too. But my point is, I can't exactly mention the amazing community service you did the other night, now can I, when people come to me and complain about how you threatened Mr. T!"

"The *fuck*?" My eyes darted as if trying to follow the barrage of surprises coming at me. *Soob has powers, too?*

"You threatened him, Harry! When you found out he and Coach Sullen were planning to let another player start as setter for one game. Everyone's talking about it."

"How—*what*?" I paused, held up my palms, and said, "Look, I don't know what people are saying. But I didn't threaten him because of Bret playing or not playing volleyball. I threatened him because he refused to do anything about Coach Sullen." I spouted off my list of the ways Coach Sullen had crossed boundaries with Bret.

"So you admit that you threatened him."

I grabbed at my hair with both fists. "*That's* what you're taking from this? Not the fact that your idol insists on keeping a predator on his coaching staff?"

"There you go," she said, throwing up her hands. "Exaggerating again. That poor Annika."

"For the love—"

"Harry, I know you've got a feather-light trigger when it comes to men who aren't there for you in the way you want them to be, and I understand why you're so eager to protect Bret—"

"I want to protect everybody! *Everybody*, Soob!"

"Harry. Harry. *Harry*." she said, her tone doing nothing to lower my hackles. Had she always talked to me like this? Yeah, but it had come across differently before. It had seemed mutual, conspiratorial. Now it felt patronizing. "You've done an amazing job raising Bret. She's not your mother, and *you're* not your mother, either."

The hairs on my arms stood up and I glanced over Soob's shoulders at a group emerging from the gym and found Mr. Terrence among them. His eye caught mine before I could look away. He gave me a squinty smile and raised his hand over his head. I gave him a squinty smile in return.

"See both of you ladies at Scarehouse, I hope?" he called out to us.

Sooby turned and wiggled her fingers, and to my surprise Mr. Terrence stopped walking. He put a hand in its pants pocket, jingled some coins there, and raised his chin; he was expecting an answer. I didn't know what to say but I uncrossed my arms, trying to look as unthreatening as possible. *What a weird state of affairs,* I thought. *I have to treat with kid-gloves the same guy who used to slam desks together whenever he got into a light rage.*

"You know I'll be there," Soob called out to him.

"Running the show, as always!" he replied. "How about you, Mrs. Lime? We have things we need to talk about, I'm sure?"

I tried to freeze my face. Something felt off—in his words, his posture, the whole bit.

"I'm gonna try," I said finally. He tipped his baseball cap at us and moved on. Soob reached out and grabbed onto my forearm.

"Anyway," she said, "Bret's smart, and strong, and she's not going to mess up the way your mom did."

I glared at her. "You think that's what I'm worried about? My mom's 'mess-ups'?"

She smiled and waved to some smiling families who emerged from the gym, arms draped around their daughters. "Maybe you didn't say those exact words, but . . ." Soob whispered to me through a toothy smile.

"You've got it wrong, Soob. What I'm upset about is how people hurt my mother. And yes, I'm worried somebody's going to hurt Bret."

"I worry about that, too. But I don't think it'll be one of her coaches who hurts her," she replied. "They're trying to do their job. I think it's going to be you who hurts Bret, Harry, if you don't stop going around threatening to kill people."

I was seething. "I . . . I gotta go," I stammered, and as I turned away, Bret and Satchel walked into the lobby arm in arm. I'd wanted to put the kibosh on their sleepover, but when I saw them laugh together, openmouthed, I didn't have it in me to quash their giddiness. So I approached them and congratulated Bret, who didn't look me in the eye, then excused myself without another word to Sooby.

3.6 TUESDAY, AROUND 9:00 P.M.

"I know I've said this before, but you really do have the strangest dog," Justin said from his seat at our kitchen table.

"Uh," I said as I closed the back door behind me. I came into the kitchen and stood there in my long coat, glancing around stupidly as if I'd never been there before. It had become nearly impossible to go from one segment of my life to another and still know what to do, or how to feel, when I got there. It had become my new normal, even on days when the monster wasn't in the mix of things. Had my best friend accused me of threatening to kill someone? I had done just that, hadn't I?

"Huh?" I said finally.

"Your dog," Justin replied. He pulled his hand out from a bag of tortilla chips, holding more than he could comfortably hang onto. But Critter stayed in the far corner, laying with her head on her paws, not seeming to care that there was now a 95 percent chance of a snack-fall. Justin threw his head back and popped a chip into his mouth. "I still can't figure her out."

"You know," I mumbled as I shuffled back into the laundry room and hung my coat on a hook, though I heard it fall to the floor as I walked away. I paused in the middle of the kitchen, my head heavy, and rubbed both eyes with the heels of my hands. "Just because a dog doesn't take an interest in you doesn't mean they're strange. You know that, right? Same goes for humans."

"Beer?"

I lifted my head and approached the table, where I leaned over and turned the bag of chips toward me. "Nah, I'm pretty tired," I replied as I pulled out a few.

"I can't figure out what her standards are. She's all over the map. Who or what are you interested in, pretty girl?" he asked Critter.

He got up and went over to her, and scooped her up. She made one of her peculiar whines, nasal but low, and I knew she was annoyed. When he sat down with her on his lap, she tried to push off but Justin was surprisingly quick, and he grabbed hold of her again. He put her back on his lap and this time, locked her in place with one arm. Then he started to pet her. He was thoughtful several minutes before half-whispering, perhaps to himself, "It's been a long time since I could have a dog."

I pulled out a chair and sat down across the kitchen table from him—our gun-happy neighbor who knew I was the monster. I could've used the time to go through my dozens of unread emails. Cleaning the toilets crossed my mind. But by sitting there and noshing with Justin, I could signal my gratitude for his help with Theo, without having to say it out loud.

"Bret was telling me about when you first got this sweet baby. How you took her to the emergency vet because she'd eaten the paper plates in the recycling bin."

"Yep. First weekend we had her," I replied, munching on some chips. "Little asshole."

"Don't you listen to that, baby girl. She doesn't mean it," Justin murmured, smiling with a vulnerability I hadn't seen before. He rested his hand on top of Critter's head, probably because the rest of her coat had the tactile qualities of a wild boar.

"Poor baby. You would eat yourself to death if we let you, wouldn't you, pretty baby?"

Critter flattened her ears in response.

"Actually, she stopped doing that a few years ago."

"She doesn't eat the whole bin anymore, packaging and all? What's her backstory, anyway?"

"She was a stray. Probably for a long time, because she was skin and bones when someone brought her to the shelter. Our vet said that she'd had several litters—"

"But baby's got enough to eat now, doesn't she?" Justin cooed. "Not knowing when she'd eat again was not a good thing for my sweet girl."

"Well, that's part of it. But she also—"

"Thank goodness we're all past that now, right, pretty girl?" When I was quiet for a few beats, he said, "What were you saying?"

I rubbed my forehead. "Mmm . . . I can't remember. I'm too tired to resume my train of thought when it keeps getting interrupted."

He sat upright again, and in his usual voice replied, "Sorry. You were telling me something more about her back story."

I shrugged and shook my head. He squinted at me, then leaned back in his chair. When he draped both of his arms lazily over the sides, Critter was off his lap inside a second. After a few hasty spins, she lay in the same spot Justin had taken her from, then rested her head on her front paws.

"She's fickle, but we love the hell out of her," I said.

He laughed and got up to grab another Bridgeport IPA from the six-pack he'd put in our fridge.

"That's good of you," he replied as he put a bottle in front of me.

"What? You've taken a shine to her, too," I said, munching on a chip. "*Awwwww, da pretty baybaaaaay,*" I said, in an exaggerated impression of his earlier cooing.

He returned to his chair, failing to disguise his amusement with the light frown he put on his face.

"You know why we think she's the bee's knees," I nodded sideways toward Critter, "even though she's an ingrate?"

He crossed his arms and a blurred and faded tattoo peeked out from his shirtsleeve. "No, I don't, actually. She's not cuddly—you're right. Not consistently, anyway."

"Well, you've helped us feed her recently—yes? And you brushed her?"

"It didn't do any good."

"It never does," I replied. "But my point is, we love someone . . . *because* we take care of them."

"Sorry?" he replied, extending his arms wide, as if to stretch out his chest.

"People think they take care of their pet because they love her. But that's backwards."

"So . . . people *don't* actually love their pets?"

"No, no—people definitely love their pets. We just have the cause-and-effect part wrong. We love our pets *because we take care of them.*"

He thought for several seconds. "So, we love things . . . And this goes for people, too?"

"Yup. Kids. Houseplants. Whatever." I scooted my chair back and leaned one knee against the table. "When Bret was about five, we found a bumblebee in the grass out back, and it only had one wing. So we brought her some flower petals and dripped some water into one. Then we watched her while she made her way to one of our raised garden beds, and leaned a couple of sticks against the side of it so she could use them as ladders. And wouldn't you know it—she puttered around in there for like, two weeks! A few days in, she'd even sit on my forearm awhile, doing those strange leg calisthenics that bees do, you know? Bret and I were so in awe and so tickled about it that when she died, we cried our eyes out. Like, sobbed and held each other—seriously. But I *don't* get all drippy like this," I said, pointing toward my face after my voice betrayed a few quivers, "when I come across a random bee who's already bitten the dust. Or if I have to kill a spider. But look at me now, reminiscing about our ol' buddy Bee-a-trice."

"This might come out sounding insincere, but I'm sorry for your loss."

"I just don't believe love is a given. It's not a starting point. Love is a by-product—the happy by-product—of giving away some of your time and attention."

We were quiet for several seconds, me watching him, him watching the table. "So. You don't work at all now?" I asked. "You fully retired?"

"Eh," he replied, moving his head from side to side. "I mean, I do a project now and again. Nothing major."

"What kind of work?"

"I mean, it's not really work. Just, you know, whenever a friend needs an extra hand."

"What are you, some kind of . . . sleeper agent or something?"

He looked down his nose at me. "You don't even know what that means."

"Are you a . . . contractor?"

"Not exactly."

"You're a freelancer!" Now I was just blurting things out. If he was going to be obtuse, I would also be obtuse.

"What? I mean, I guess . . ."

"So you're a freelance . . . sleeper."

"*What?* Harry, that is not a real job that exists."

"I know. If it was, I would have it by now."

He got up from his chair. "Speaking of which, you probably need some sleep. And so do I," he said as he walked toward me. I stiffened without meaning to, because in my muddled state, I wondered if he intended to hug me or something. But he passed me on his way to the sink, where he swished some water inside his bottle before adding it to the recycling.

"Speaking of things that may or may not exist, have you ever seen anyone around here wearing an all-black uniform and black hats—like cowboy hats?"

"A lot of guys wear cowboy hats, once you get a few miles outside Portland."

"I'm not talking about them. I'm talking about a uniform of some kind. Is there any agency, or law enforcement office, where the officers, or whoever, wear uniforms like that?"

"'Officers, or whoever'?" He was throwing some sarcasm back at me now, with a tight smile on his face.

"*I dunno*, Justin! Work with me here. Deputies? Henchmen?"

"Go to bed, Harriet."

"The uniforms have a patch on the arm, I think. But it's hard to see because it's also black. Ring any bells?"

"Good night," he called back as he opened the back door to go home. "I'll come over first thing in the morning."

"Fine," I said. I was frustrated. I hadn't picked up on any bodily tells with Justin—not of fear, uneasiness, or anything else—but I did notice that he'd neglected to answer my question.

"Actually, I do have one other question for you," he said, taking a few steps back. "About our little tête-à-tête last night, out in the yard."

"I thought we were going to pretend like that never happened."

"You said something about . . . George Washington."

I let out a heap of air. "Yeah, I did. The founders. The framers. I was ranting, man. Let's let it go."

"You were talking about . . ." he said, trailing off. "To be honest, I got confused and I just wanted to know what you were saying, is all."

I shook my head and scooted my butt back in the chair. "Nah," I said as I reached for more chips.

"What? It seemed interesting."

I chewed a few seconds. "It *is* interesting. But I'm tired. And Google is free."

"Understood, ma'am." He saluted me, turned on his heel, and left.

I went upstairs, and when I saw that the light was on underneath the door to Bret's empty bedroom, I went over and opened it. Before hitting the switch, I looked the place over, noticing she'd begun taping up pages from magazines, game programs, and so on, on the slanted wall above her twin bed. There must have been twenty of the things, mostly of athletes she admired, and I wondered why I hadn't noticed them before. When was the last time I'd been in there, anyway? I wasn't sure, but it was definitely in my pre-monster days, and the realization hit me somewhere deep—where a patch of my earliest memories remained perennially exposed, like an open wound.

I saw that Bret had made a half-assed attempt to make her bed and had left some clothes slung over the footboard, as there was far too little floor space in the tiny eave to cede to mess. I took a couple of steps inside but stopped short when I spied a trail of sparkles on the carpet: sequins. My old dress was always shedding the things.

I let my forehead fall into my hands as my emotions came like punches, each one hitting its mark: guilt, regret, adoration, fear, grief, and a solid uppercut of self-loathing. Why had I been so nasty with Bret when we'd argued? How, exactly, had I become a person who can't shut up? Speaking your mind comes at a cost, and I was paying for it by borrowing against the love my family and friends had for me. And I wasn't sure how or when I was going to pay it all back.

I wanted more than anything in that moment to pick up the phone and let Soob know that I'd be right over, because for me, fetching Bret and bringing her home seemed like the most important thing in the world to do at that moment. But I fought that urge; she was fine. She was OK. It was our relationship that needed repair—not Bret herself.

3.7   FRIDAY, 7:30 P.M., HALLOWEEN

"We should have left these two at home," I grumbled as I struggled to maneuver the double-stroller along the pitted gravel drive. We'd left the minivan in the designated lot and were making our way to the industrial site that played host to Scarehouse each year. The event had been underway for more than two hours but the kids and I, dressed as characters from *The Wizard of Oz,* were crawling along like we had all the time in the world. Jo and Frankie were flying monkeys—or some new, cuter subspecies of flying monkey, as I didn't have the costuming skills to do justice to the originals. Critter lay curled up inside an old tote bag I'd slung over one shoulder, the real-life Toto to my Dorothy. And Bret was nearly unrecognizable in her witch's hat and green-tinted makeup. I say 'nearly' because the scowl she'd been wearing the past few days gave her away.

I leaned forward, over the back of the stroller. "You guys would've been happier staying home with Daddy and Mr. Justin, wouldn't you? Answering the door for trick-or-treaters?" Frankie and Jojo didn't answer me, either. The clusters of people passing by us were mostly teenagers, which fascinated them.

The line of warehouses on the backside of the property had fallen into deep disrepair, and as the sun went down, their hulking forms cast long shadows over the festivities. Sooby and her team of volunteers had blocked the mostly empty structures off from visitors, which had the added benefit of forming a long barricade that separated our dizzy, spinning fun from the dizzy, spinning water of the Whisper River.

When I glanced at Bret again, she was gazing upward, as if marveling at the decorations.

"The theme's 'Once Upon a Time,' yeah?" I asked, pausing to pull the hem of my dingy, blue-gingham dress out of the wheel well of the stroller, along with some straw that had gotten stuck to it. It was already difficult to hear on account of the rings, dings, bells, buzzes, squeals, honks, and screams coming from the carnival. "It's definitely more of a Grimm interpretation than a Disney one," I added, to no answer from anyone. We finally reached the archway the decorating team had erected in front of the ticket booths. They'd taken bunches of cardboard tubes, painted them in dark colors and connected them, lengthwise, then twisted them together to form a pair of deader-than-dead trees. At their jointure, the face of a green man—also made of recycled materials—loomed over approaching families with an expression of portentous glee.

"Who'll be the first to get spooked by someone's gory costume, do you think? Frankster or—"

"I couldn't care less," Bret replied, speaking for the first time since we'd parked.

"Just try to steer them away from the really scary stuff, OK?" I'd suggested on the drive there that Bret take the twins around the carnival with her, knowing that Sierra and Satchel would be there to help. I told her it was because my back was hurting when really, I was going to meet Ellen, Dr. M, Dianne, Christy, and the other women with special abilities—all of us together for the first time. I was practically bursting with eagerness, and beyond curious to know what Sooby's powers were, too.

We stopped to buy tickets for the games and rides, my brain already inundated by the smells of Scarehouse: elephant ears and buttered popcorn, gas fumes, wet paint. My head was beginning to feel overfull, and I'm sure it didn't help that my body was running solely on the Halloween candy I'd had for both lunch and dinner. And we'd yet to get inside the place.

"You'll stay away from the fun house, right?" I asked as I turned toward Bret, struggling to focus. Now, the flashing bulbs on the rides behind her and the multitude of lights on wires crisscrossing over our heads added to the dizzying mix. It was enough to overstimulate folks with regular human senses; with my extra-sensitive animal ones, my brain felt like it was on some kind of heavy-stains cycle in the washing machine.

I handed Bret some tickets and added, "And—and don't let these two OD on candy."

"Jo and Frankie will be *fiiiiine*. We'll *all* be totally fine," she droned.

The sensory onslaught made it difficult to think of anything except how much I wanted to get out of there. As Bret and I stood dumbly on either side of the stroller, forcing streams of people to flow around us, I realized something unnerving: My monster-faculties were so overwhelmed with data that my brain wasn't lifting out the most important sights, smells, and sounds—it wasn't calling Bret's agita to my attention, for example—because too much info was coming at it, too fast. *Shit.* I sniffed at the air in all directions, but couldn't pin down the locations of Ellen, Dianne, Christy, or the other friends I knew to be on-site, either.

"How about we all play games together?" I blurted out, consumed by the sudden need to stay together. How would I find them when it was time to leave?

"Mom, we have to *go*. Or we'll never make it around the loop," Bret replied. "This stroller is such a clunker."

"Just one or two, before we split up?" I replied, failing to squelch the desperate undertones in my voice. I'd come to rely on my monster-given abilities, and their unexpected curtailment terrified me. "It'll only take a minute."

That's when Sierra floated up behind Bret. "Nice costume, Mrs. Lime," she said, already bubbling with excitement. "You make really good white trash."

I tossed her a boulder of a look. *"Excuse me?"* I was still trying to come up with a response when Bret intervened.

"She's supposed to be Dorothy, Sierra. From *The Wizard of Oz*?" she said in a rush. "I'm the witch, these are the monkeys, and that's Toto." She gestured at my bag.

I turned back to Bret. "So—one quick ring toss, before you go?"

When Bret appeared to deflate before my eyes, I gave up. "You know what? It's OK. You're right. Go have fun."

"OK, see ya later," Bret said as they took off behind the massive stroller. I pressed my palm erratically at my chin—our old "blowing a kiss" gag—but she left without reciprocating. Every sound, sight, and smell reverberated in my head as I turned to survey the scene, a new pang deep in my gut and my shoulders slumped.

The decorating committee had painted larger-than-life scenes from fairy tales and fables on the plywood perimeter. With only one entrance and one emergency exit, fare-hopping was kept to a minimum. But this year, it made me feel claustrophobic.

I bought a cup of red punch and a stack of sugar cookies in the shapes of knights, castles, and such. Critter sat up in anticipation as I polished off a sugar-encrusted ogre, and when I spied Ellen playing the ring toss, I went over. My monster senses weren't necessary, it turned out, to discern that she wasn't in the best of moods, either.

She flung the last of her wooden hoops over the grid of glass bottles on the other side of the table. When it bounced off and away from them, she let out a groan of disappointment.

"This game is a racket," I said over her shoulder. "Who runs this joint?"

"Oh, I don't think so," she replied as she turned and saw me, sounding every bit as glum as I did. Still, she summoned a fleeting smile. "I've never been very good at it."

Critter's tail *thwacked* against the sides of the tote bag, and after reaching down to pet her, Ellen looked me over.

"Are you . . . Dorothy on meth?" she asked. "I mean, down-and-out Dorothy? Or something?"

I frowned. "What did I get so wrong with this costume? Is there something about me that is inherently strung-out-looking?"

Ellen pointed to the new tear in my dress and several stains, half of which had come free with the thing when I'd purchased it at a yard sale. My socks were covered in dust from the parking lot, and when I glanced at the distortion of my face in the metal siding of a food cart, I was surprised at how much of my hair had escaped my pigtails, and how bits of straw caught in my cuffs and hems made for an accidental nod to the Scarecrow. I rubbed at the hastily applied blush on one cheek before realizing I didn't actually care. "I've never been very good at Halloween," I said with a shrug.

She lowered her voice. "I've never liked it, to be honest."

"Halloween? Really? What about that costume you worked so hard on? Wait—where *is* your costume?"

She waved a hand in front of her buttoned-up trench coat. "I've got most of it on under here," she said before lifting an arm holding her oversized bag. "And threw the rest in here. But I wish I hadn't."

"What? How come?"

She heaved a sigh. "I decided I didn't like it."

"*What?* Why not?" It had clearly been an elaborate effort.

"I dunno. I just don't, OK?"

"OK, OK."

I sensed that making and donning a costume in public was a bit like cheering at Brandon's games: She wanted to do it but had innumerable reasons not to, and so far, I hadn't succeeded in understanding.

"Can you tell me who you were going to be, at least?"

Several emotions fluttered across her face as she pulled the strap of her handbag onto her shoulder. Then she shook her head. "Wanna go find the others? I can't take much more of this place," she said.

"Oh, dear God—yes." We entered the current of people moving along the circular path. To our left were the gaming booths, rides, and food trucks; to our right, colossal fairy-tale figures sat in their two-dimensional grandstand, as if watching a jousting tournament. "Where are your kiddos?" I asked, thinking I might as well try and take our minds off how miserable we were.

"Home," Ellen replied, leaning toward me and lowering her voice. I had to read her lips to make out what she was saying. "They got to play a few games, but when they started bickering, I knew I wasn't going to be able to take it, so I sent them home with Gregory. Mama's not supposed to use her powers right now, but I was on the verge of losing my shit, I'm telling you."

"Same," I replied.

"No, not the same at all," she replied in a serious voice. I looked at her and she looked down, her brow furrowed. "You worry a lot less about your kids being mistaken for criminals, all the more so in a dark place and with everyone dressed in weird outfits, feeling jumpy."

I nodded, feeling like an ass. "I'm—I'm sorry. I should have said that I'm also feeling on edge. Claustrophobic-like. And my senses aren't working. *My special senses*," I added in a lower voice. "It's not the same at all, you're right. I wish I'd thought about that—about what it was like for you. Thank you for telling me."

She let out some air. We were shoulder to shoulder with several strangers, inching along in the human equivalent of a cattle chute.

"I feel like what this costume really needs is for me to light up a cigarette," I said.

"Do that, my friend, and I'll feel like showing you one of my precision high-kicks from back in the day."

We looked at each other straight-faced, then snickered together a few seconds.

A moment later something snagged my eye. "Oh, *fuck*. Look at— do you *see* this?" Mr. Terrence was standing against the wall a few yards ahead of us. He was wearing a medieval knight costume. Next to him stood Olivia Patchett-Parker in the garb of a noblewoman. Both wore oversized campaign buttons at their collarbones, and I wondered how they'd become acquainted—or politically allied—and if Sooby had seen them together that night. Patchett-Parker was much farther up the food chain than Mr.

Terrence, being a candidate for Congress and from a wealthy local family. Still, there they were—shaking hands with everyone who passed, causing gridlock. Ellen and I were being herded straight toward them but as we got close, Mr. Terrence pulled a guy toward him to whisper in his ear—one of his trademark moves. Ellen and I moved past them in the herd, and we exchanged a subtle low-five to celebrate our bit of good luck.

After that, the crowding largely dissipated, and Ellen led me to a place in the outer wall that had very little light shining upon it. After waiting for a small gaggle of teenagers to pass, she said a soft, *"Here we go,"* reached past one of the plywood boards, and pulled it toward us. It made just enough of a crack for her to slip through. Then she held it while I followed her into the pitch dark, a shiver running through me as I reminded myself I had no monster-senses at my disposal.

We walked until we reached an alley to our left that ran between the enormous old warehouses. My heartrate picked up, both in anticipation and trepidation, as we entered the rundown portion of the site, rounding the corner of one building and then another before approaching a large door. When Ellen grabbed the handle, I felt I might faint from excitement. It didn't budge, so she yanked it again. "Hmm," she said softly, then rapped lightly.

Suddenly a peephole slid open, revealing Dr. M's familiar green eyes. I could tell by the crinkle between them, however, that something was not OK. The door creaked open.

We followed the brisk pace she set—with my heart thumping harder still—toward a small source of light. Not counting Ellen and myself, a half dozen figures huddled around it: Dr. M was dressed as a character from *The Hobbit*. Soob was dressed as Pris from *Blade Runner*, and I have to admit, it was a killer costume. Next to her stood a tall, scruffy man I'd never seen before, which struck me as odd. Then there was Dianne, in an elaborate zombie costume that included, among other grotesques, a second, smaller head on her right shoulder. She and I waved excitedly to one another. And last of all was Yvette—my work colleague. *Holy cow!* She and I made wide eyes at each other—me shocked, her smiling.

"Sooo . . . Mercury's in retrograde?" I asked as Ellen and I entered their circle.

Everyone chuckled and released some air. I didn't feel any calmer, but now a bigger share of my excitement was of the good kind; these were, excepting the one dude, my friends.

"Everything OK, Dr. M?" Ellen asked softly. I couldn't stop staring at the others.

"The door to the cellar is locked," Sooby called out, answering for her without looking up from her phone. "Not a big deal."

"That's right," Dr. M added. "As you know, Ellen, I wanted to meet underground, to be extra careful and ensure that we weren't seen or heard by anyone. But—"

"We'll be fine up here," Soob interrupted. "Besides, I might have to run out and oversee the fireworks at some point."

"Miriam?" I asked playfully. "Or should we say, 'Balin'?"

Everyone whistled, praised, or applauded: Dr. M had gone all-out with her costume. She had prosthetic ears, two enormous white eyebrows, and a thick, white beard, which would've been enough to make me crack a smile each time I caught sight of her. But she also wore a satin bathrobe the color of oxblood, and underneath it she had some kind of padding wrapped around herself, or maybe a body pillow, to create the illusion of girth.

I turned to the man next to her, and we smiled awkwardly at each other. He was balding a bit and wore wrinkled khaki pants and a blue shirt. He also had a five o'clock shadow and slight potbelly. "I don't think we know each other," I said, putting out my hand.

"Harry, this is our so-called pipe detective," Dr. M said, gesturing to the man. "We didn't feel safe going back to the lab, so we asked her to go in for us and check things out."

"'Her'?"

"OK, you're right. Him. We thought it best if she were a man during the mission."

I was momentarily confused, until the man's features began to morph, and his torso to change shape. He became shorter, too, and his hair became fairer and longer. In a matter of seconds, he was . . . Christy.

"Whooooa," was all I could manage, I was so taken aback at what I'd seen.

"I know. Hi, Harry," she said. Her clothes fell loosely on her shoulders, though she still managed to look stylish, in part by rolling up her sleeves and cuffing her pants in just the right way. "As far as your lab goes, that kind of plumbing isn't my area of expertise. But I talked to a security guy who was on duty the night that sketchy maintenance crew came in. He said only one of them returned his 'hello' and they declined his offer to use the loading dock. He just thought they were rude, but later found out they didn't sign in with his boss and that none of his coworkers had heard of the company."

"When was that?" I asked.

"The lab flooded late the next night," Ellen replied.

"Can I go next?" Dianne asked, bobbing up and down. "I can't wait to show everyone what I can do."

"Sure, sure. Go ahead, dear," Dr. M answered.

Dianne stopped bouncing and held her hands in front of her, one palm facing down and one facing up,. like the chicest of witches preparing to conjure something magical.

"Harry, you might want to close your eyes for this," Ellen said suddenly.

Her warning fell on confused ears, unfortunately, because I did the exact opposite and glanced back at Dianne. A pulpy, pulsing mass, in a hue similar to Dr. M's robe, had formed in her hands, and appeared to be growing.

"Damn it!" she said suddenly, when the thing looked to have collapsed a bit. She walked to a nearby trash can and shook her hands until it slid off and landed in the bin with a thud. "Hearts are so freakin' hard."

"Dianne can grow new organs," Dr. M explained. "And limbs. Show her a limb, would you, dear? You're so good at those."

With a look of disappointment still on her face, Dianne's chest and abdomen started to ripple—and gurgle—and then the tips of some new fingers began to emerge from one of the holes in the artfully distressed tunic she wore as part of her zombie costume. "I mean, this is just novice stuff," she said dejectedly as a hand, then an arm, followed. I was stupefied, but when the others began clapping for her, I eventually joined in.

"OK," I began, taking breaths that were shallower than usual. I leaned on a nearby worktable to steady myself. "OK. So, can somebody tell me why, or how, Dianne can do that? And also about Christy?"

Dr. M lifted both hands. "Let's get to that once everyone's had a chance to show what they can do. Let's see . . ."

"Wait, I have a question for Dianne. What about your second h—" Yvette began.

But Christy cut her off. "Do *not* ask that question. Please."

"I don't want to know the answer to that, either," I added. Yvette laughed.

"Fair enough. Let's continue," Dr. M went on. "I believe we've all seen Yvette demonstrate how she can move objects with her mind, yes?"

Yvette gave me a coy mini-wave, her fingers fluttering near her cheek. "And you thought *you* had telekinesis, didn't you?"

My jaw fell open. "Shit. Was I that obvious? Trying to move those raisins?" I had to laugh with her at my mistake, though I was embarrassed at my self-centeredness.

"I mean, not all objects," Yvette replied. "Stuff that's really big or heavy, or that's more than a few yards away? I'm still working on those."

"Well, that was some impressive writing you did at our meeting," I offered. "You know, with your mind." We shook our heads in shared amazement.

"OK. And Sue-Beth, how about you?" Dr. M said.

Sooby stepped forward and stood quietly a few seconds. She adjusted her wig, then glanced down to inspect a fingernail. I was about to ask if something was wrong when I picked something up in my peripheral vision, near the opposite wall. A new person in a Pris costume—identical to the one Sooby wore—had stepped into view, from behind a large cabinet. The same thing happened again, this time from behind a column, a bit closer. When it happened a few more times, at various points throughout the large space,

I realized these newcomers must be copies, or new versions, of Sooby. "You can . . . replicate yourself?"

She nodded. Glancing around, I noticed each of her twins was repeating the same sequence of gestures—step forward, adjust wig, inspect fingernail, repeat—with each of them at a different place in the routine.

"Do they copy what you say, also?"

She nodded, but I thought there was something unhappy in her mannerisms. "For the most part. So I need to be careful, in case one of them, you know, goes out into the world." The rest of us went quiet, and we listened to her words echo back to us, in a bland and muted disharmony.

"What happens . . . when you don't want them around anymore?" Yvette asked.

"I'm not sure. But they all disappear, eventually. I'm still figuring out how much control I have over them. What I do know is that I don't like being around them all that long."

When I coughed spastically, Sooby quickly added, "Don't you dare say anything, Harriet Lime."

My coughing turned into minor choking, all layered over the laughing I was trying to hold in.

"Also, they sometimes . . . twist my words a bit. And I don't like it," Sooby added. She lost hold of her stern expression then, and as it dissolved into pure amusement, the rest of us allowed ourselves to crack up, too. It was a welcome bit of levity.

When I bent forward at the waist to stretch my back, Critter slid to one side of the tote bag, causing it to tip forward more than I'd intended. She jumped out and motored off, nose to the ground, disappearing behind a pile of heavy-looking junk.

"Critter! Come!" I called. "Critterrrrr?" I was leery of allowing her to wander alone there, since God only knew what kind of weird chemicals or razor-sharp scraps she might uncover. I hadn't lied when I told Justin she didn't gorge herself anymore; she just hadn't totally kicked the dumpster-diving habit.

"She'll be OK," several people told me.

When she wandered into sight again—then back out again, and in one more time—I let her do her thing. "There was never much chance of me getting out of here without a tetanus shot, anyway."

"How about you, Ellen?" Dr. M said.

Ellen shoved her hands into her pockets. "I dunno. I'm self-conscious doing my thing in front of some people."

Several of us nodded. "That's cool. No biggie," I replied.

"Damn neurodivergence," she added.

I kept nodding. I hadn't known she was neurodivergent, but a lot of things clicked for me once she'd said the word. How busy she always kept her hands, the way she abounded in knowledge on the topics she loved, whether from her lab or some sub-subgenre of film. I was also glad she trusted us enough to tell us, and to decline doing things she didn't want to do.

"Well, I had the pleasure of seeing part of it," Dr. M said, "and what I saw was amazing."

"I mean, the headpiece *is* cool. I could just show you all that," Ellen said as she pulled her handbag off her shoulder, then paused. "Actually, I'll just put it all on. It'll look better with the rest of it."

She disappeared behind a large piece of equipment, and minutes later came out with her trench coat off and headpiece on, and she was . . . stunning. We *ooohed* and *ahhhed* at her iridescent beaded bodice, with leather epaulets at her shoulders, her oversized belt—also dazzling in the dim light—and flowing pants. The end of her scepter seemed to glow, too, but it was the headpiece that really wowed—there was a fabric portion attached to several arching bands that gave it structure.

"I'm supposed to be an orisha," she said with a shrug.

"If any of you melanin-deficient folks are wondering," said Yvette, "an orisha is a type of goddess."

"Obviously," Christy said softly.

"An African goddess, to be precise. But I took a bit of license and added some Viking elements," Ellen added, pointing to three pieces—either made of metal, or made to look like it—descended over her nose and the widest points of her cheeks. "Mostly because I wanted the costume to hide who I am. But also because they're just cool."

"Beyond cool," I replied.

She screwed her features hard in one direction, like she was fighting the urge to wave off the compliment. "Thanks. I'm just a little irked that my abilities didn't come with a disguise. Like yours, Harry, and Christy's."

"I like to think that some of us are like Batman," Dianne offered. "We have to DIY that shit."

"I prefer Magneto, but yeah," Yvette added.

"Maybe," I said, "it's one of those abilities that can be developed. I'm pretty sure I didn't have a tail the first time I transformed. And my horns are still coming in," I added, patting my hair.

The others exchanged responses to this theory, some agreeing and others remaining skeptical; a few murmuring to their neighbors and at least one person (Sooby) getting a bit shouty. I marveled; this wasn't the stuff we talked about through the windows of our cars.

"Ellen, I think you're glowing a little more than you were a minute ago," Sooby said in an aside. "Don't you think so, Harry?"

I looked at Ellen sideways. "Maybe."

She rolled her eyes. "Come on. This isn't *Twilight*, ladies. No one is sparkling."

"That reminds me, Soob," I said. "I'm glad Satch is going to wear my spangly dress to Homecoming." I'd made peace with Bret's distaste for my fashion choices.

"No, she's not."

"No?"

"No, she's wearing it tonight. She's some kind of undead prom queen."

I shrugged. "That's one way to rock it."

Ellen looked at her watch. "So before any of us turns into a pumpkin, let's get down to business. How did we all get this way?"

"I don't know," Dianne said with a laugh, "but I think we're going to need uniforms. And a name."

"YES!" Yvette replied, clapping her hands together.

"A *cool* name." This from Soob. "Not a silly one."

"Seriously though, ladies," Dr. M said, raising her hands for quiet.

"I mean, I wouldn't mind making us, like, jackets or something," Ellen murmured while we waited for everyone to stop yammering.

"If we're going to be, like, a team, I need to know," I said, trying to suppress a giggle, "where does everyone stand on butt slaps? Yay or nay?"

"Look, ladies," Dr. M went on, hands still in the air, "Ellen and I have explained that we think this all has something to do with our anatomy, but that's just a theory. We don't know how we got these abilities, or exactly when we got them. We're not sure if it's just us who has them."

"But one other idea we had," Ellen added, "is that this might have something to do with the fact that we all know each other. We all spend time together in some capacity."

I scratched my head. "You mean, like, how our periods get synced up when we live with other women?"

"Well—that old study turned out to be kind of bunk. But we do think it's interesting that we're all acquainted in some way." She mentioned how Christy and Yvette played tennis together, which I hadn't known, including as a doubles team. Ellen and Yvette had met at a march in Portland and stayed in touch. And so on. "These are all meaningful connections."

"Question for each of you," I said. "When you first discovered your special ability, what were you feeling in that moment?"

"Ticked off," Dianne said.

"Overwhelmed and kind of rage-y," Christy added.

"Beyond irate," Ellen replied. "What about you?"

I nodded. "Same. I was pissed."

No sooner had the words left my mouth, than the lights in the building went out.

"Don't worry, everybody. Somebody probably jumped the gun on turning the lights out for the fireworks," Sooby said. One by one, each of our cell phones lit up to illuminate our faces, an effect that only enhanced the eeriness of the unexplained blackout. The light from one phone moved away from the group, toward the wall, as Sooby trotted toward the door and peeked out.

"Do you guys hear that? Some of the people outside are shouting . . ." I said. We went silent, and even without monster hearing, the other women nodded.

"The lights are *all* out!" Soob shouted as she jogged to a far wall, to an electrical panel there. "What the hell?"

"The games have gone quiet, too," Ellen pointed out. Our circle had drawn tighter without my noticing. "No more ding-ding-dings."

Sooby made several *click, click, click* sounds, and when nothing happened, added, "That's weird." The light from her cell phone bobbed toward us again.

"Oh man," I said.

"What is it?" Dr. M asked.

"I can hear a lot better now . . . " I stopped and tried to swallow, but my throat had gone dry and there was nothing to push down.

"What's happening, Harry? Tell us; you're freaking me out!" Sooby said.

"Sorry, I just—" My voice broke. Like a lot of moms, I can't stomach the sound of even one child crying in fear. "There are kids crying out there."

"Then . . . let's go!" Sooby said.

"Just wait! Something . . . something is off," I said. "Something bad's going on."

"Harry, be specific," Dr. M said calmly. "What are you picking up on?"

"I don't know! I'm sorry!" I ran a hand over my forehead, to push back some of the errant hair. "The monster would have better luck sorting through all this."

"NO," came the unanimous answer.

"The monster can't appear in here, Harry. You can do this. Tell us what you're sensing."

"I just—I just . . ." I put my head in my hands. "I have a bad feeling. Something's wrong."

"All right," Ellen said. "I think some of us need to go out there, in our disguises, and get everyone out to the parking lot and help those poor kids find their families."

"That's what I just *said*," Sooby muttered, throwing up her hands. "I'll go. Me and my army. Of me."

"And it was a good idea," Ellen replied in an appeasing tone. "If you don't see us after you've gotten everyone out, come back inside, the way you came."

"I got this."

"Why don't I come with you?" Christy asked. She had turned back into a man without my noticing and was uncuffing her shirt. "It'll be good to stay in groups until we know what's going on."

"And no offense, Sue-Beth," Dianne added, "but folks will listen to, you know—a man."

They headed out, with a band of Sooby's replicants ambling behind them.

That motley crew hadn't been gone more than a few minutes when the crying and shouting began to die down; Soob was good at these things, and Christy could be commanding regardless of her gender. And in the relative quiet, my monster senses fully returned. I had just used them to suss out where Critter was snuffling around when the large sliding door—tall enough for a semi to fit through—opened in a rush and a ghastly screech. In the low ambient light were the silhouettes of five people—all men, laden with a bunch of gear. They trotted toward us in a raggedy line, boots stomping on concrete, the sounds of metal and plastic clicking and clacking against each other. Dr. M called out with a slight tremor, "Hello? Can I help you?"

"Hands up!" one of them barked—the tallest one.

"Huh?" Dianne said quietly as several large flashlights splashed onto our faces. We all froze.

"What the hell . . ." I murmured, squinting. But I knew exactly what the hell—and it was the same reason I'd been uncomfortable moments earlier. "It's the Stetson guys," I whispered to Ellen, on my left.

"Except they're not outfitted for the frontier, it looks like," she whispered before turning and telling the others, in hushed tones, who the men were. It was impossible to be sure, but when the slim rod over his shoulder disappeared from the tall guy's form, I suspected he was holding a gun. I cursed myself for allowing Critter to get away from me and prayed she would stay hidden—and quiet.

"Gentlemen, you need to identify yourselves," Yvette called out in her field voice.

"We're here for the lady scientists," another of the men announced. His voice was marbly and uncertain, in contrast to the display of toughness they were putting on. Still, a chill ran through me.

"Dude—we're moms from the carnival," Dianne spoke up, sounding lightly perturbed in the way one might be when the parent ahead of you gets out of their car at the drop-off lane. "And this is a warehouse. What are you even talking about?"

"Which of you are the scientists?" the taller man shouted. He was more than lightly perturbed; he seemed agitated. "Somebody needs to answer me now, or we'll be taking you all in . . . into custody. Is that what you want?"

"We just want the monster," the guy with the mouthful of marbles said.

"Tim! Shut your face, for fuck's sake!" said a different man, stouter than the others.

I tried not to flinch, but I was beginning to sweat in my dress as my senses all fired and misfired as if my monster-brain was struggling to restart itself. "Oh, *man*," I blurted out. My heart and lungs, too, were fighitng to regain full function.

"Show us some identification, and maybe we can have a convo," Yvette said as she stepped forward. To the last, they raised their guns at her. She put her hands higher and stepped back.

Someone gasped; Ellen stood stock-still.

My eyes finished adjusting to the bright spotlights in the men's hands, finally, and I could see them all clearly for the first time. I noticed how worn their clothes were, and that they weren't uniforms at all. There were a few crisp slacks-and-shirt combos, but also mismatched black T-shirts, turtlenecks, jeans, and cargo shorts, all laundered to differing degrees. The patches on their arms were mostly sewn on by hand—a few of them not all that neatly.

Dr. M cleared her throat. "If I may, let's all take a deep breath, lower our guns, and start—"

"Shut up, lady. We're not here for you."

"He said shut the fuck up! All of you!"

"Put your hands together, in front of you. Jase—zip ties! Now!"

A shorter man pulled something from his utility belt and stepped toward us. "Hands front! *Now!*"

The first hint of perfume—my own perfume, from home—hit my nostrils and gave me a start. My heart jumped to attention, as I knew Bret was wearing one of my shirts that night and it likely held traces of the same scent. But I soon dismissed the possibility it was coming from her; it was an affordable, widely-available brand, and I caught wafts of it at the grocery store all the time.

I sniffed to my right, then left, as subtly as I could, wondering if any of the others owned the stuff. Except they were unlikely to be the source of the smell, since it had only just arrived. "Does anyone else . . . smell that?"

"QUIET! I don't wanna hear another word out of *any* of ya."

The man—Jase—had put zip ties around the wrists of Yvette, Ellen, and Dr. M when I got the second and third hints of the perfume, and this time, it turned the temperature of my blood down several degrees. Because it wasn't only the scent of the perfume that came through my brain, it was also the slight but unmistakable smell of my house, and of my daughter's bedroom specifically.

Jase arrived in front of me just as I turned to face the stairwell—the one that had been unexpectedly locked, and that led to the basement where Sooby had wanted us to meet. That's where the smell was coming from, and now I was inhaling deeply.

"Turn front!"

"OK, OK!" I said as I complied. "Jeez! I'm just, you know, *breathing*."

"Listen lady," The tall guy barked. "I've had enough. Outta all a' you."

Then I smelled fear. Female fear. *Young* fear. I'd come to know these chemical bouquets well and I was certain of it. *"No."* I whipped around toward the door. "I—I gotta go. Someone's down there."

"Lady, what did I just *tell* you?" Shouty guy stomped forward and yanked Jase by his collar so hard that he stumbled three feet backward. I could feel the anger coming off both of them in waves.

"I don't give a shit *what* you tell me," I said in my *Mommy's getting angry, tread lightly* voice. "Someone is locked in that cellar—and I . . . and they're in trouble."

The shouty man rummaged around his belt, dropping a couple of objects and an f-bomb as he went. Jase had finished zip-tying all our hands by then, and I decided not to wait to find out what his pal was looking for. But I'd barely got turned around when the dude finally grabbed a canister and brought it right up to my face, flipped the safety latch, and pressed the nozzle down as far as it would go.

It was bear spray. And I don't think that stuff is meant to be applied at such close range. Nor for that long a period. My eyes felt like they were simmering in the bottom of a Bunsen burner by the time he let up on the stuff. I coughed and spasmed and heard my friends gasp as I fell to my knees, choking. Then I sensed Dr. M and Ellen kneel on either side of me.

"Get back! *Jesus!* Get up, both of you!"

"Let me help her," Dr. M said. Her tone was so calm and soothing that I wanted to hug her and then stay there, maybe forever. "She's hurt—"

"I said: *Get up,* bitch. You, too," he snarled, first at Dr. M and then Ellen.

More gasps—including one from me this time.

"Oh—*oh,*" someone said. I believe it was Ellen. "I don't think so."

"No. No *sir,*" someone else whispered, probably Dianne. "Not your word. Not his word!"

"The *fuck* he thinks he's talking to?" Yvette.

But it was the sound of falling and crashing metal, coming from behind the pile of scraps at our backs, that spoke real volumes to the men. I still couldn't see, but I could sense everyone's movements—thank you, chin hairs, for being my whiskers!—and I could tell that a shadow was forming on the far wall. I also smelled a new sort of anger, something more akin to aggression. What I smelled was Critter.

Now it was the men's turn to gasp, because the shadow was growing rapidly and so was the low, gurgling sound she made—the same one from the night we'd run into Jerry and his owner. Critter was going full-monster again, and the men's flashlights cast her shadow in a way that made her look enormous. I smelled the men's fear—and in at least one case, urine—as her snarling became fully ferocious.

But she didn't attack our aggressors. Instead, she took off running, still growling, out of the source of light. This surprised me at first, and disappointed me a little; but then I realized that with supernatural abilities layered on top of her existing terrier-smarts, Critter might just have been canny enough to lead the men *away* from us. It was a brilliant move, in fact, and I watched in awe as her fuzzy form leapt up a series of junk piles before crashing through a panel of the warehouse's filthy, upper-story windows.

"That's it! Get to the van!" the shouty man yelled.

"GO, GO, GO!" Jase shouted, not to be outdone. They ran back through the still-open door.

Yvette and Diane joined Ellen and Dr. M at my side. "What *was* that?"

"Bear spray." I was glad Ellen said it, because the second I tried to speak, a phlegmy coughing spasm wracked my body. I had so much mucous in my tract I felt like I was going to suffocate. Salty tears slid down my cheeks.

"No—I mean what was that . . . thing?"

"Critter," I gurgled. I think they understood me.

Yvette opened a small folding knife on her keychain and slit through each of our zip ties.

"Hang in there, Harry," Dr. M said as she rubbed my back.

"I'm not getting any signal," Ellen said, looking at her phone.

Dianne yanked her phone from a pocket. "Me neither,"

"Go," I rasped. "Chase . . . them."

Dianne sat back on her heels. "I do have an idea. Of how we could capture those guys."

"Yeah? How?" Yvette asked.

"We'd have to hurry. I can explain on the way, but we need to find a way to catch up to them."

The two of them stood and looked around. "There's nothing but junk here, and they drove off in their van," Dianne said. "We could try running, I guess. They might not have found their way off the site."

"Wait—I got it." Yvette said. "I'll take you."

The rest of us flinched hard when a rusty forklift near the wall suddenly lurched out of its resting place, then came toward us in fits and starts, busting through a series of large drums and causing a whole lot of clanging. Its wheels barely hung on to whatever still pinned them in place.

"Yeesssss," Diane said, sounding gleeful. She and Yvette climbed into the tiny seat, sharing it half-and-half, and they were off. They bumped along, slowly at first, then burst through the door and past Sooby, who had just appeared again. She closed it after them.

"What happened?" she yelled when she saw me, crumpled on the floor like a grown-up rag doll. She ran over. "What's wrong?"

"Some guys with guns came in here," Ellen began. "They had the black patches and everything. They bear-sprayed Harry."

Sooby slowly turned toward me. That was her way of telling me, I knew from experience, that she'd been wrong about something and she knew it.

"Are you OK, Harry? Should we take you to a hospital? I don't have any cell service, for some reason."

"None of us do," Dr. M answered.

I sensed the fear again, from the cellar. "Do you . . . smell that?" I whispered. "Or feel it, I dunno."

Each of them shook their head no.

I planted my hands on the floor and tried to push myself up.

"Sit, Harry," Dr. M said.

"I don't know, Dr. M," Ellen said. "Maybe we should each take one of Harry's arms, and she can lead us to whoever or whatever she's picking up on. "What's going on out there, Sue-Beth?"

"We got all of the little kids to their parents, and some teenagers are still waiting for theirs. Not everyone showed . . ." She trailed off.

I slowly began to stand with the help of all three women. "Is Bret there?"

Soob shook her head no, and I sensed an adrenaline surge in the two other women. "But the twins are with Sierra—they're fine."

"Who else is missing?" I asked. My knees were shaking badly and I was still using the others to support a good bit of my weight.

"That's it, actually. But I'm beginning to think someone cut the power on purpose. Could somebody have cut cell service to the property, too?"

We'd barely turned toward the cellar when I sensed Mr. Terrence emerge from a far door.

"Oh, Patrick—thank God!" Sooby said. "Do you have your walkie-talkie? We've got a medical emergency." I sat down on the floor again, giving the others a break from lifting me.

"No," he said softly. When he reached us, flashlight in hand, I saw that his eyes were wide and his posture slightly stiff. "Did you . . . did you see the monster?"

Soob blinked at him and I sensed her frustration. "No, but can you please go find someone who can call 9-1-1? Harry got maced, and she's bad off."

He noticed me on the floor and started visibly. He took a half-step back. "But . . . is that?"

Ellen let out a rush of air, as if exasperated. "We did see the monster, Mr. Terrence. It was here, and it went that way," she said. She pointed in the direction opposite to the one Critter and the men had gone off in.

Soob, too, was out of patience. "Patrick, is something wrong with you, too? Because we really need you to act now."

"But I heard it," he said, still looking at me. "How can you . . ." Mr. Terrence hadn't stopped staring at me. He didn't so much look like he'd seen a ghost as like he'd *expected* to see one, and hadn't. So it was official: He knew I was the monster.

"That way," Ellen said again. "I think you can catch it if you hurry."

He nodded, still dazed. "OK . . . OK . . ." He trailed off but turned and jogged, in his old-man way, back toward the door, then in the direction Ellen had pointed him in.

"And see if you can call 9-1-1 while you're at it!" Soob called. She turned back to us with her face contorted. "Jesus."

"I think—I think we should take Harry to the parking lot," Dr. M said.

"No!" I said, trying again to stand. "If I could just turn into the monster—"

"You can't, Harry," Ellen said without an ounce of equivocation.

I got up and swayed irregularly on my feet, one hand on Ellen's shoulder and one on Soob's. I sniffed the air again and began limping toward the door. My breath came out in wheezes and I could barely crack open my eyelids, which had swollen to the size of those little pillows they put in ring boxes. But when the light from someone's phone hit Ellen's shoulder and torso, her costume gleamed brighter, suddenly, in a range of gem-like colors that ranged from aqua to pale turquoise.

I stopped dead in my tracks. "Soob."

"Yeah?"

"Was Satchel in the parking lot with the other kids?"

"No, she went home with Philip earlier."

"Are you sure?"

"I mean . . . she was supposed to." We all went cold.

"But she was wearing the spangly dress, which reeks of my perfume—that *Ursa de whatever.*"

"Yes, but she's gone now," Soob repeated. Still, her uncertainty was unmistakable.

Ellen and Dr. M caught on; Sooby did not.

"I'm going to sit down now," Dr. M said as she lowered herself onto a large box. "Sue-Beth, will you keep me company, please?"

"Wait—what's happening?" Soob asked.

"We shouldn't leave anyone alone," Ellen said. "Sue-Beth, why don't you stay here with Dr. M. She needs a rest, looks like."

"Where are you and Harry going?" Soob asked.

"To the cellar," Ellen replied. With her arm across my back and under my shoulders, we tried to hurry.

"Fine," I heard Soob say, then slap her palms on her thighs. "I'll be happy to just sit here."

Once we got to the door, I pulled the handle and as expected, it caught on the deadbolt.

I put my ear up to it, but could hear nothing through the cold metal. Holding onto the handle with both hands, I swung my hip away from the metal door, then back into it with a bang. Pain shot through my pelvis and spine.

"Harry," Ellen said firmly, "let me try." I let go of the door and stepped away.

She came forward, looking even more shimmery than before. "The thing about the placenta," she said, "is that it's not *only* a barrier."

"Huh?" I was breathing heavily now, impatient to get inside. "What, now?"

"The placenta extends for miles—literally miles—into a woman's body, by way of her capillaries and other organs. It invades. It *takes*." She pulled her small fist up to her shoulder and with a single swift jab, punched it through the metal door. She pulled it back out, without a scrape, leaving a hole the size of a softball.

"The placenta pushes *and* pulls. It plays defense *and* offense." I expected her to reach back through the hole she'd made, and turn the lock. Instead she grabbed hold of it by way of the new hole and pried the thing off its hinges. I had to swiftly step out of the way as she set the heavy mass against a nearby wall.

We stepped into the stairwell and started down the steps, the hairs on the back of my neck and up both my arms standing erect. We followed the smell down a corridor and stopped at another door.

I crouched low and put my nose against the crack underneath it, where the air seemed to rush from inside. I took it deep into my lungs, feeling my ribcage expand as I processed the smells. Two humans, for sure. I inhaled again and this time, the results nearly overpowered me. "Ellen," I whispered, my voice trembling. "It's Satchel. With a man."

"You're sure?"

I nodded. "Coach Sullen." I stood up, shaking so furiously that I began to feel dizzy. "Can you get Satchel? And take her up to her mom?" She nodded and we exchanged places.

Ellen ripped the door from its hinges in a single motion and flung it behind us with a *CLANG*. I waited outside while she strode into the room, first shouting at Sullen and then giving instructions to Satchel in a tone that managed to be both soothing and commanding. As I listened, my mom-brain—or rather, my godmother-brain—tossed up a memory from when Satchel was maybe four, and I brought her and Bret to the OMSI planetarium. Satch's little voice was both adorably squeaky and assertive, and to the delight of everyone that day, she kept shouting out song requests as the stars swirled over our heads, as if we were at a Skynard concert rather than a kids' astronomy show.

And I knew, then, that there was nothing I wouldn't do when I got on the other side of that doorway, I was so unbearably angry. Torture. Dismemberment. Murder. Nothing was off the table.

So without leaving my spot, I grew and grew—to my biggest size yet. My head and neck splintered the plastic casing of the fluorescent lights and then the bulbs themselves; my shoulders snapped wires and pushed through pipes; and finally, the curve of my back broke through the structural concrete like a stale cracker. I peeked around the corner, thankful there was no sprinkler system in the old place, and spied Ellen embracing Satchel at the side of the room. Then I went in.

Maybe if Mr. Terrence hadn't dismissed my concerns about Coach Sullen, I wouldn't have reacted the way I did. Maybe if Sullen hadn't been influencing Bret in all those inappropriate ways, I wouldn't have done what I did. But it was all way, way, *way* too much, and I knew then that I'd already waited too long to do something at all. I was fury incarnate as I looked the man dead in the eye and charged him, like a bull.

It only took me a few monster-gallops to reach him, whereupon I stood on my hind legs so that he could see what he was dealing with. I wanted him to be afraid. No, I wanted him to be *terrorized.* Still staring him down, I grabbed him as if he were a filthy rag and after punching around the hole I'd made in the ceiling—to break away enough space—I climbed through it. Back on the ground floor, I nodded to my friends and—*holy hell!*—Bret, too!? She had joined Sooby and Dr. M in the minutes since we'd left them, and now they all stared at the coach and me, mouths agape, as I leapt again, this time through the broken glass of the upper story. I landed on the side of an enormous silo and scurried the rest of the way up.

Sullen screamed and sobbed and begged me to stop. But when I got to the very top, my body once again took its cues from some primal instinct I didn't know I had: My head tilted back. My neck stretched long. And after pulling everything I had from deep inside my chest, I roared—an enormous, beastly *roar* I hadn't thought myself capable of. The sound came barreling out of me, deep and sustained. I heard windows from the warehouses below me shatter, first with a tinkling sound and then a *Pop! Pop! Pop!* as countless shards of glass rained down on the gravel and pavement. It wasn't nearly satisfying enough.

Heaving, I looked down at the pathetic little man in my paw. I pulled my arm back, ready to hurl his body into orbit or more likely, into hell—by way of a very hard landing he did not have the ability—piddly little male that he was—to heal himself from.

But a sudden, loud fizzing and whistling sound, just yards from my head, startled me and stilled my arm. I looked around, confused for a moment, until I remembered that Sooby had planned a small fireworks show for the end of the evening. More of them exploded above and beside me and I glanced down to see Ellen and Dr. M lighting them while Sooby, Satchel, and Bret stood off the side, huddling close. I heard some *oohs* and *ahhs* and realized that a small crowd had remained in the far parking lot, and that they thought I was part of the show. I lowered my arm, noticing that Sullen had gone limp, his eyes glazed over.

I'd find out later that Christy—in her male form—had told the stragglers at the carnival to expect an "extra something" at the end of the night and had stayed with them, keeping them in place, until they all got in their cars and left, satisfied that like the truest of fans, they'd seen a bonus performance that less-devout carnival-goers had not. And I thanked the heavens above for it, because their presence was the only thing that had stopped me from making my first kill.

3.8   FRIDAY, AROUND 8:30 P.M.

When all had gone dark again, I glanced toward where I'd seen my friends—all still in their costumes—and saw that a large black van was approaching them slowly. But my hackles didn't register any danger as I climbed back down the silo and hopped over to them, Coach Sullen still dangling in my hand. He had passed out, overcome with fright.

All of the women were staring at me, and I couldn't blame them. It was the first time they'd seen me as the monster. Soob had Satchel tucked under one arm, her face pressed into her mother's shoulder. Under her other arm was Bret, staring up at me with wide, searching eyes. I pulled the fist holding Coach Sullen behind my back so that they wouldn't have to see him, and when Soob made eye contact with me, I nodded toward a small lean-to shed. She seemed to catch my meaning, and ushered the girls toward it.

Bret glanced backward and scuffed her feet, as if torn between accompanying her friend and leaving our jaw-dropping scene behind. Did she know the monster was me? I couldn't tell; I only knew that I didn't want her to. I still didn't want my family to know my secret, for reasons I didn't yet understand.

"Those horns," Dr. M began, sounding awed. "I thought you said they were small!"

I reached toward my head a bit too fast and pricked a fingertip on the end of one because *yowza*, they'd grown again. Like, a *lot*. I shrugged as the van came to a stop and Dianne and Yvette got out, looking flushed, with Critter—in canine form—on their heels. My ornery little dog and I greeted each other more joyfully than ever before.

"What happened to the men?" Ellen called out.

"We got 'em," Yvette said, beaming. "It was wild, y'all."

"They're in the van," Dianne added. "We zip-tied their hands. And they are *messsss*-y!"

"How did you capture them?"

"Some people might not want to hear this part," Yvette answered, giving me a look. "Because it was SICK! In all senses of the word."

I dropped Coach Sullen facedown on the gritty pavement. Ellen yanked him roughly to his feet and held him up while Yvette zip-tied his wrists and taped over his mouth, then together they put him in the back of the van with the others. Meanwhile, I brought my hands to my ears so I wouldn't catch the gory details of Dianne's story. I did gather, however, that she'd achieved a new level of success in her ability to create new organs. There was a thrilling poetic justice in the fact that our would-be captors—these men who'd threatened and sworn at us and called us bitches—got to see the inside of a uterus for the second time in their miserable little lives.

As I watched the women exchange stories, I couldn't hear what they said but their faces stretched wide with surprise, excitement, awe, and amusement. My heart swelled. I was starting to consider turning back into Harriet when I caught a sniff of Mr. Terrence in the air. I wasn't sure where he'd been since we'd last seen him, but now he was somewhere between us and the river. I took my hands down from my ears and crouched on all fours as a soft growl escaped from me.

"What is it, girl?!" Ellen asked in an exaggerated voice, as if she were Timmy and I was Lassie. Then she cracked up. "Sorry," she said between sputters. "I had to."

"It's Mr. Terrence, isn't it?" Sooby asked, speaking up for the first time. She had passed the job of comforting Satchel—and Bret—on to Dr. M.

I nodded in the direction of the river.

"Running away?"

I nodded again.

Ellen looked to me, then to Sooby, then Dr. M. "I'd like to question him about those guys in the hats now. While I'm still looking fierce as hell."

"GLIMMERY," I said in my gravelly monster-voice, shocking them all—and myself—and literally blowing their hair back. I crouched still lower, so my belly was on the ground and said, "GO FOR RIDE, OKLAHOMA?"

Ellen came over and climbed up, grinning from ear to ear. Once she'd grabbed fistfuls of fur on the nape of my neck, I bounded off in the direction of Mr. Terrence's sweaty, nervous stink.

We got our first look at him when we reached the end of the last warehouse; he was near the far corner of the same building—fifty yards away, at least. The rapids in the gorge were audible from there, even to human ears.

"Mmmph?" I said, unsure if it was wise to chase him.

"HALT, SIR!" Ellen called out. Her voice rang off the walls of the buildings, strong and true. I'm telling you, there's something about using our powers that seems to make them either stronger or broader or something, because I don't think she can project her voice that way when she's at, for example, the deli counter. "WE'D LIKE A WORD—" But after he turned and saw us, he took off.

"Damn it. Mr. Two-Packs-a-Day's got legs."

I grunted in amusement and bounded after him, pausing at the end of the building and looking around. We spied him to our left—standing in front of the fence that lined the edge of the Whisper Gorge.

"WE'RE NOT HERE TO HURT YOU," Ellen called out, trying to be heard over the noise of the river. Then she whispered to me, "Go slow now."

"WE NEED TO ASK YOU A FEW QUESTIONS, THEN YOU CAN GO."

He ran again, this time along the chain link fence. You could barely call it a path, as the pavement was broken up and the ground underneath had eroded beneath the fence.

"I WASN'T DONE, SIR," Ellen said, sighing. I picked up the pace a bit, and when we reached the fence and turned after him, found that Mr. Terrence had chosen to go down a dead-end. He was standing before a taller, electrocuted barrier now, with barbed wire along the top that met with the fencing along the river. There was a lot of detritus and trash in a pile behind him. He had nowhere to go.

There was spray from the rapids in the air, and the ground was moist under my feet. I hoped it wasn't enough moisture to turn me human again. I stepped carefully.

"Just leave me be, OK?" Mr. Terrence yelled to us. "I haven't done anything wrong."

"I don't know about that," Ellen replied. "What do you think, Beast?" she asked, suppressing a smile. I tried smiling with her, but when I bared my oversized hyena-teeth, Mr. Terrence stumbled backward over some broken masonry. "You treat some folks like they're worth less than other people—I know that much."

I took a slow step forward as he got to his feet again. I was starting to worry about his stability. The mud and rock had been substantially eroded, and he was just feet from a big gap at the bottom of the fence— and a nearly vertical drop to the water. But then he had to go and be an asshole. Again.

"How I treat people is irrelevant. Some people rise to the top and others don't. I didn't make it so."

"I beg your pardon!" Ellen exclaimed, clearly as infuriated as I was.

He took a few steps up the pile of rubble then turned toward us, standing on a block of some kind. It rocked in one direction and the other before going still.

"Come down from there, slowly. You're going to fall if you don't," Ellen said. I sat back on my haunches so he wouldn't feel intimidated, then laid my front end down, too, a la the Great Sphinx.

"Sir, we're trying to help," Ellen said, her tone conciliatory. "Even though you think it's OK to treat some people—let's say, for example, *woman* people—like they're less human, and those women have every right to be less-than-human to you in return."

He didn't get a chance to reply because the thing he was standing on tipped abruptly toward the river's edge and he lost his footing. He slipped under the fence and lay facedown with his lower-half out of sight over the edge. He yelped, "Oh dear God—*please help me*," before his grip on the sodden ground gave way and all but his fingers disappeared over the side.

I leapt to him and Ellen slid immediately off my back.

"Take my hand!" she yelled, grabbing a fistful of the loose skin around my neck with one hand to brace herself. I dug all four feet into the earth to anchor us.

He slid further away; now all of him was vertical—and beyond my reach—on the side of the gorge. It was more rock than mud there, and I didn't know if that would improve his luck or not.

"For fuck's sake—just pull me up, will you?"

"NOT AN APPROPRIATE TONE," I said, though I doubted Mr. Terrence would remember the words he'd said to Ellen that night at PTA.

She used my arm like a firepole, sliding down it until she sat in the middle of my palm. "Hold my ankles," she said.

I nodded and pinched them gently with all my fingers as she leaned backward and reached for Mr. Terrence. *Fuck*, she was being so brave for this asshole!

"Take my arm!"

As soon as he removed one hand from the narrow rock ledge, whatever he was clinging to with the other hand gave way. And this time, there was nothing else to grab. He dropped all the way into the water as Ellen and I yelled out to him—or squalled, really, in a jarring chord of fear, desperation, and dread.

I pulled Ellen back up. She'd clapped both hands over her mouth. I grunted and turned toward the water. As was often the case, she knew what I was thinking without me telling her.

"Harry, NO!"

I stepped to the edge and took a breath. Then I looked at her and shrugged. "HARRY SWIM, TOO."

She started to say something, but I was off. I tore the fence like it was tin foil and lowered myself to the spot where Mr. Terrence had lost his grip. I briefly wondered if he had broken his legs in the fall, as this was a far greater height than the ten-meter diving platform at UWV, where I had often goofed off after swim practice with Theo and our teammates.

I knew that something in my legs and arms had given me the elasticity I'd needed to push off the ground and absorb the shock of big landings—not unlike a flea. But I wasn't sure how to translate that to a choppy water surface. I thought the smartest thing would be to dive in, the way Theo had taught me, and the way his parents had taught him.

But first, I channeled my inner flying squirrel. I appreciated, for the first time in my life, that I had some extra skin under my arms as I stepped off the rock and splayed all four limbs out to the side, so that I was briefly horizontal before slowly tilting forward, toward vertical.[41] Just before making contact, I brought my hands in front of me and clasped them together, my elbows soft. Once I'd broken through the water, I immediately spun forward—in as compact a somersault as I could manage—which stopped my forward momentum. It wasn't pretty, but I silently thanked the Lime family, and the Bamfords, and my own mom, too, for a youth spent largely around lakes, rivers, pools, and diving wells. Because I'd survived.

After that, all was chaos. The water churned and tumbled me, and seemed to pull me inexorably downward any time I got close to the surface. I started kicking, and when I took my first stroke noticed that my hands

---

41　This posture slowed my fall. In theory. My heart was a bit skeptical, apparently, because it went absolutely apeshit the whole way down.

had turned human again. I was still trying to right myself when the current yanked me down again and my head struck something, hard, and with an edge to it.

I howled in pain, which caused me to pull water into my lungs and then choke and cough, too. I remember thinking: *This might be how I die.* And also: *For Patrick Motherfucking Terrence, for the love?*

Fortunately, the rock I'd hit was a sign that I'd reached shallower waters, and after floundering for what felt like a full minute, I spied a series of pale lights—the cobra-head kind, which was another clue I was approaching a wider, flatter, slower stretch of the river.[42] I was finally able to pull myself to the surface, where I flattened out on my back and let the water take me while I gulped in air and sculled with both hands. I turned my head to look around, and in a stroke of luck, saw a pale head behind me: Mr. Terrence! I'd passed him, and he was maybe twenty-five yards away. The length of the Bamford's country club pool, albeit far more turbulent. I took some halting freestyle strokes in his direction, keeping my head up and stopping every few seconds to rest and adjust my course in the still-wild water.

When I reached him, I grabbed the back of his collar because unlike me, he was still clothed. I whipped him toward me and onto his back, then leaned onto my own back so that he was nearly on top of me. I put my arm across his chest—over one shoulder and under the armpit on the far side—and did backstroke pulls with my other arm, stopping occasionally to scull for a bit so that I could rest and redirect us toward the shore. I'm not sure how long we floated and swam, floated and swam. But it was cold, and I began to get numb. At some point, I couldn't tell if I was holding onto Mr. Terrence anymore, although he was still there, on top of me, so I guess I was. My head throbbed and my pulling arm was nearly out of juice, but it was in this stop-and-start manner that we gradually approached the water's edge, at the site of a small, well-lit park. I could see figures on the shore gesturing at us and running back and forth.

---

42   Not slow, mind you—just *slower.* By a bit.

Two men in bright yellow helmets stood next to a pair of bicycles, one holding something—a phone, I guessed—to his ear. Once I got close enough, a woman waded into the water and held out what I'm certain was a Quidditch broomstick (I'm not making this up, I swear) for me to grab. She dragged us first onto the slimy rocks that littered the area where the water lapped at the dry land, then onto the soft silt beyond it. The men in bike helmets pulled Mr. Terrence off me and straightened him out on the ground, inches away. They checked for breathing and a pulse while the Quidditch woman—fuck it, let's call her a witch, she deserves it—kneeled next to my head and draped her black cape over my buck-naked body.

I smiled, and Mr. Terrence let out a violent cough. The bystanders helped him roll onto one side—away from me, thankfully—before he began vomiting.

Another pair of faces appeared, first leaning over me and then stepping to Mr. Terrence. They offered each of us a blanket and while they stunk to high heaven, I was grateful for the warmth when the witch helped me skooch the scratchy wool between my bottom and the ground.

"An ambulance is on its way," said one of the cyclists, his concern plain.

I looked up. The moon was especially prominent that night, and I was reminded again of the planetarium show I'd taken the girls to all those years ago, and of something I'd learned there.

"Did you know," I began, my teeth chattering, "that when you're on the moon you *can* actually see the stars? Contrary to what you see in photos. Contrary to what a certain science teacher once told me."

I felt Mr. Terrence roll onto his back again, and one of the cyclists lifted his head onto his lap. He, too, opened his eyes and looked at the sky.

"Yeah?" my witch asked gently. She stroked a bit of hair off my forehead.

"Yeah."[43]

I heard the sounds of an engine, but it wasn't the EMTs who pulled up

---

43   It's true: The stars are visible from the surface of the moon. It's not too bright; it's just that everyone and everything—from the media that covered Apollo to the astronauts to the settings on the old-school cameras they used—were trained and focused on the moon. If you didn't know any better, you'd think it was alone up there. But the stars were there all the time.

next to the park; it was a now-familiar black van, with Dianne's elbow leaning out the window, Yvette and Critter sitting shotgun, and presumably a load of disarmed assholes in the back. When Dianne gestured backward, I saw that behind them was an also-familiar red truck, with Justin at the wheel. *What the fuck is he doing here?* I wondered. When I glanced at the flatbed it appeared empty at first—until Sooby's head popped up briefly over the side. I felt a wash of relief: If my friends and I were in trouble, wouldn't they be in squad cars and handcuffs? And damn it, I had to admit that Justin would know what to do with the men we'd captured.

I lifted my hand a few inches off the ground and tried to wave them on without drawing attention to myself. I thought it best that they keep moving, rather than wait for me and bring attention to themselves. It took a few seconds, but eventually both vehicles drove off. A minute or two later, I passed out.

4

"Look, babe! We match," Theo said in the wee hours of the following morning. He placed his wrist next to mine on the plastic hospital tray. He still had his admission bracelet on from his accident.

"Not 'match,' actually." I pointed out that his bracelet was on his left wrist, mine was on my right. "We're . . . complements."

"Aww." He had to lean on his crutch to lift himself up off the chair next to my bed, far enough so that he could give me a kiss. "That's so poignant, babe!"

"So cheesy, you mean."

"Yeah, but it's a good kind of cheese," he said softly as he sat down again. "Like a Rogue River Blue or something."

"You think?"

"Not a Stilton, though. It wasn't premium or anything."

I chuckled. "Look who woke up on the funny side of the bed today!" I couldn't stop smiling at him. He'd arrived by cab shortly after the doctors finished examining me, and had only stepped out of my room for a bit when Sooby appeared and lost it when she saw me. Theo gave us some privacy as she crawled into bed with me, sobbing. I'd cried, too. We cried for Satchel, for girls everywhere, and for a world that forces its females to be prey for the ill-intentioned males among us.

"I have a confession," Theo said now, his distress plain.

I inhaled slowly. "OK."

"The day of my accident? It wasn't the first time I'd fallen asleep at the wheel."

I exhaled, and I watched his hands come together, briefly, before letting go and then grabbing hold of each other a different way. "OK," I said again.

"The first time, I was driving Bret and the kids back from the school—that night you went for your walking group. The little ones were asleep, so they didn't notice. But Bret did. She had to shake my arm and let me know."

I reached over and slid my hand between his, and he grasped it firmly. "The other night, Bret told me that you don't tell me everything. Maybe that's what she meant."

He nodded and we sat there quietly for a few seconds. The hurt in my head had mostly receded, thanks to whatever painkiller they'd given me. But now I felt foggy, and when Theo blurted excitedly that it turned out the monster was part of this year's Scarehouse festivities, I knew I wasn't in any condition to reveal the truth to him. "Let's talk about this some more when I'm home. And lucid."

A hand grabbed onto the curtain that hung from the ceiling and yanked it to one side. A nurse said there was an agent that needed to see me, and a second later, Justin appeared next to her.

He asked me how I was feeling, and said he wanted to speak to me alone. He helped Theo get situated on his crutches—a quick, two-step process they'd perfected—then held the curtain aside while he hobbled past.

Justin—or should I say *you*?[44]—took the chair Theo had vacated, which felt too close. We'd made a peace of sorts, sure, but that didn't mean I wanted him inside the same circle as my family. When he didn't speak right away, I looked him over, and noticed for the first time that the faded tattoo on his left bicep said "MOM." I wondered how old he was, and whether he was close to the same age as my dad.

---

44   Nah, I'm gonna keep talking to you in the third-person. It's best if I keep pretending this report is simply *about* you. Whenever I remember that it's also written *to* you, I get so much more rant-y.

"They're going to discharge me soon," I blurted out when I couldn't stand the silence any longer. "After a couple more hours of observation." *Please tell me you're not here to arrest me.* I thought to myself. *Or if you are, just out with it already.*

He cleared his throat. "You know, it's a wonder to me how a bunch of unarmed women managed to capture a half-dozen heavily armed men."

"There were only five of them," I said, glancing at the ceiling before turning to him. He was grinning. "But trust: It's a wonder to me, too."

He leaned his elbows on his knees and fiddled with a black baseball cap.

"The lesson here, I believe, is that you should never underestimate a PTA mom. Or her friends."

He laughed.

"What's going to happen to those guys? Where are they now?"

"They're still in their van. I'm going to take them in when I'm done here. Although first, I'm going to drop that Sullen guy off at the local precinct. Turns out he's been wanted for questioning in Pierce for four or five months. Some parents didn't like the way he was teaching yoga after school."

"Pierce . . ." I said, touching my bandaged head. The nurse said they'd had to shave me bald in one spot so they could stitch me up. "Why does that name sound familiar?"

"It's a little place near the coast. Only reason I'd heard of it was because they had those rogue waves last summer, remember? Some folks died."

"Ohhhh, yeah," I said, my eyes going wide. *Rogue waves!* Was it possible my mom sent me that article because it was about Pierce, Oregon, and that's where Bret's coach had been preying on girls before coming to Straussville? But how in the world would she know that? I couldn't figure out how it was possible, and yet it didn't seem plausible as a coincidence, either.

"And the other guys? What are they, a bunch of yahoos who hate women or something?" I asked.

He shifted his weight. "They fit in with a larger trend of armed vigilante groups, made up of people who believe fringe things, much of it not based in fact. Hostility toward one group of people or another tends to bring them together."

I noticed he hadn't quite answered my question. He shifted again, this time to lean on the knee closest to my bedside. He scratched his head in three places before continuing.

"I owe you an apology, Harriet. The night you asked me about the strange officers you'd been seeing? It's true that I didn't know exactly who they were at that time. But it's also true that I'd been assigned to come to Straussville to monitor some extremists, and that they turned out to be some of the same men—"

"I've been wondering how you ended up at Scarehouse!" I interrupted, "Just in time to collect them."

"A few months back, the FBI picked up on some talk online about Dr. Miriam Morris and the type of research she'd gotten funding for. These guys had a problem with it, and a few of them starting showing up in this area from other places, to watch her and Dr. Stout."

"They came in from Idaho, right?"

"They draw from several states. It's not a small group. Anyway, when you mentioned seeing guys in makeshift uniforms around town, I . . . lied to you. I'd been briefed on that by the Bureau but wasn't able to say as much at the time."

"What's their beef with Dr. M, anyway? And Ellen? What's with this Project Chimera business?"

"You know they call themselves Project Chimera?"

"Yep."

He sighed. "They borrowed that name from a local legend. There's this urban myth—maybe you've heard that name before all of this?"

I shook my head.

"Some people believe that there was a secret government agency, back in the early twentieth century, tasked with looking into whether or not women were gaining new . . . abilities. It was, according to believers, in some secret location out here in the Pacific Northwest."

"Oh noes!" I exclaimed. "Women might have '*abilities*'? Lord, save us!"

He shrugged.

"I think you mean *super*-abilities."

"I guess you could call it that."

"I will. Go on."

"At any rate, some people say Project Chimera was a laboratory. Other people say it was some kind of military base. The details vary, as is often the case with these things. But the basic idea was that women were getting very powerful new abilities—sorry, super-abilities—and the government wanted to control and use them for their own purposes. That, as you can imagine, was an idea that stuck around."

"Men wanting to control women? Yeah, that always has legs."

"Fast forward to today, and the guys in this online group co-opt the old name, I think because they, too, are hostile to—and skeptical of—powerful women. It was a good fit."

"And let me guess," I interjected. "They set up a Google Alert for themselves, and when news of Dr. M's research funding came through, they saw that she planned to study fetal microchimerism—which is often shortened to 'chimerism'—and that put her on their radar."

"You guessed it. And when sightings of a strange monster started making regional headlines . . ."

"They must have gone absolutely bananas."

"That's one way to put it, yeah."

We sat quietly for a moment.

"It's so weird," he said finally, looking at the floor with a sly grin. "All this hubbub, all because they saw somebody's Halloween stunt and thought it was a real bogeyman."

"Or woman."

"Yes—sorry." He grinned and stood up. "I don't want to offend any bogeypersons."

"Are my friends or I in any trouble?" I blurted out.

"For what?" he asked as he put his cap on and straightened it.

"For . . . anything?"

"You did a public service, as far as I can tell. So, no—none of you are in any trouble that I'm aware of."

He came closer to the bed, and I froze as he bent forward and rested a hand on my forearm. To my surprise, I wasn't creeped out—just unnerved. "How did you come to live next door to me?" I asked in a rush.

Part of me wanted to know how he'd figured out that I was the monster. And even though we'd just waltzed around the issue like professional dancers, part of me wanted to acknowledge that he knew.

He didn't answer; instead, he nodded to the tray that hovered over my bed, where a small pile of things had appeared. He must have set them down when he leaned over me.

"What's this about?" I asked as I picked up a box that contained a new cell phone.

"That one should be obvious."

I flung him a look. "I don't want any electronic devices from the government."

"Oh, for Pete's sake. It's not from me. Your husband ordered it for you; I'm just the one who remembered to bring it." I picked up the next thing—a notebook.

"That's here because I need you to do me a favor." He smiled. "I know you're very busy, Harriet. But I need you to write an account of what's happened here, since you first noticed something . . . different."

"Didn't we just discuss all of that? Can't you just write up a report?"

"Open the last box, Harry."

I stopped talking and picked up the small box. A ring box. My throat seemed to close when I saw my mangled wedding band inside. When I lifted it out and saw that it had been soldered together again—without much finesse, but still—my eyes began to tear up.

"I can't write this report, Harry. Because there's a hell of a lot that I don't know. But *you* know. And I promise I will keep the information safe."

I sniffled and moved the notebook absently. "I have Microsoft Word, you know."

"Is that Harry-speak for 'Yes, I'll do it, thanks for helping me with the bad men'?"

"What are you going to do with it—my report? Who's going to read it?"

"Think of it as an insurance policy for you and your friends. No one's going to read it—not even me, unless and until someone pulls a similar stunt."

"You mean if someone were to actually capture me or Ellen or Dr. M or any of the others? Then you'll need a record of what happened here?"

"It might be very useful in that case, yes."

I fiddled with my new-old ring, and nodded. I had a gazillion more questions, but when I looked up, he was gone.

While I waited to be discharged, another journalist came in. Unlike the *Willamette Week* writer who'd shown up earlier, this one had a camerawoman and mentioned that she'd already spoken to the man I'd rescued from the water. *Did I know that he'd called me a hero?* she wanted to know. So for a solid three seconds, I looked like a total loon on TV. Because of all the things that had stunned me senseless the past couple of weeks, that one took the cake.

Dr. M stopped by, too, and when they finally discharged me around lunchtime, Christy came by to drive Theo and me home. She'd insisted, though I know she could hardly spare the time.

Back at the house, I saw that Justin's truck was gone, so I couldn't go over and press him for more information about the vigilantes—and bolster my confidence that my friends and I could trust him—though I wanted to. After waving goodbye to Christy, Bret greeted me at the door with a huge hug, and with her mouth in my hair, said she was sorry, over and over. I guess an apology to my hair is as good as any other. I apologized back to hers, and readily agreed when Theo suggested I go straight to bed. He said that he and Bret would take any phone calls—the thing was ringing off the hook—and run interference if anyone came over. I suggested he get Justin to come over and help, as he was still on crutches, so he called and left him a message.

I snuggled Jojo and Frankie for a bit while they watched cartoons, then trudged upstairs and turned the ringer off on our bedroom phone. I napped for several hours, so it was dark when I finally woke up. I went downstairs and leafed through several notes Theo and Bret had written after taking phone calls. One was from Dr. M, inviting me to "another little get-together," which made me smile. I'd had calls from Ellen, Yvette, and Dianne, saying they'd drop by over the next day or so. One from Soob included confirmation that Coach Sullen was in custody and, in her words, "likely to be charged for offenses committed earlier that year, in not one but *two* towns on the coast."

I was eager to see all of them again. But it was the last message, from Marjorie Terrence, that gave me pause. According to Theo, she'd said she wanted me to come over as soon as I felt up to it. No need to call first— just come over. Both she and Patrick, she'd told him, were eager to see me.

"Nothing from Justin?" I called out to the family room, where Bret was doing homework and Theo was doing some new sewing craft.

"Mmm-mm."

"Nope."

"Do you think that's . . . odd?" I asked.

"Nah."

"Not really."

"OK." I put the note about Marjorie Terrence into my pocket. "I gotta run out, OK?"

Justin's truck still hadn't appeared in his driveway. I sniffed the air but got no hints of him, so he wasn't in his yard and probably not at home, either. I walked up to his front door and knocked. When no one answered, I headed back to the minivan and sensed Bret walking briskly up to it from the other side.

"Mom! What are you going to do?" she asked in a voice that was replete with unshed tears—and a pinch of accusation. She folded her arms across her chest and bounced a little too high on one heel.

"Nothing," I said, my voice clipped. She was nervous and so was I. My whole body thrummed with fear—fear that my daughter knew I was the monster. I hadn't changed back to Harriet at the warehouse, and as luck would have it, no one had called me by name while Bret was present. But I wouldn't be at peace until I knew what she knew; and yet I might never be at peace again if she *did* know.

"We're all here now. We're all home. Satchel is home," she said, tucking a bit of hair behind her ear. She let a tear slide down to her chin before wiping it away. "And we're all safe . . . and alive . . . and I just don't want anything to mess that up. Do you?"

I hurried over to her and wrapped my arms around her. She cried harder, into my shoulder, and I rubbed her back and stood still. It occurred to me that she must not have said anything to Theo about me (maybe) being the monster—he would've asked me about it immediately. "We'll talk about what happened," I said after a minute or so. *But will I tell her the truth?* "I promise, we'll talk."

I felt her nod and then wipe her nose on the shoulder of the blazer I'd thrown on—one of my favorites. Dry-clean only. But I didn't care. When she lifted her head up and looked at me, I smiled as I recalled how I'd stood in that same spot not many days earlier. How I'd told her through gritted teeth that we were "not a honking family." Maybe not, but we did occasionally indulge in a good roar.

"Honey," I said with a nod toward the house, "I don't want to mess . . . *this* up either."

"How do you know you won't, even by accident?" Her tone suggested she thought I was the monster, but wasn't certain. Her eyes searched mine.

I thought about my monster then. It had rained the day before, just across the river in the 'Couve,[45] and now our air smelled like rain, too. Maybe the drought was ending. Should I retire the monster now? Would I *have* to retire her, at least for a while, given that we were (hopefully) about to get months of rain? I felt a surge of real grief—for all the things I might have done as the monster if I'd had more time. Plus, I'd miss her desperately. Or miss being her—that power and freedom. Could I give that up? Should I? Could I be a seasonal, summertime-only beast? I needed to talk to my friends.

---

45   A nickname for Vancouver, Washington. The Vancouver that's right across the Columbia River from us.

"No one can know that for sure. But I have a hunch that things are about to get quieter in Straussville again." She turned and trotted back to the door, her bare feet clapping the smooth concrete of the front walk. I drove to the Terrences.

They lived in a tiny bungalow not far from the school, just the two of them. Marjorie answered the door and I thought she might collapse when she saw it was me. But with one hand to her chest, she collected herself and opened the screen door, ushering me in eagerly. She didn't speak, just looked at me and touched my arm, seemingly overcome by emotion. She walked me to their family room, where Mr. Terrence sat in a beige recliner, his feet up and a blanket over his lower half. He was wearing a robe and brushing at something on his lap.

"Look who's here, Patrick! It's Mrs. Lime!"

"Harriet's fine," I said, still trying to make out what this was really about. Were they going to thank me? Was Mr. Terrence going to try and lecture me?

"It's Harriet! I asked her over, and here she is!" Marjorie said, as if she could coax some better manners out of the guy. But I knew better. So did my monster, who gave him the side-eye.

"Hello, Harriet," he said finally, then coughed. He had a slight cold.

"Please excuse me while I grab some snacks, Harriet," Marjorie said, her hands together.

She wore a pink sweater that looked hand-knit, and had tight gray curls. She gave the impression of being older than her husband, but Sooby had told me once that they were high school sweethearts. She went into the kitchen, calling back out to us, "How is it we haven't met before, Harriet?"

Your husband's a total dick, was my first thought. "I don't know," I said instead. I found myself feeling genuine warmth toward her.

She came back in with a tray of cheese and crackers and some juice, her face ecstatic. I think she was expressing her gratitude to me through hospitality. Maybe it was too soon to say the facts out loud: *You saved my husband from certain death by way of frigid drowning.*

"Marjorie, I hear you have one of the oldest book clubs in town."

She sat at the end of the sofa nearest her husband, put her hand on his forearm, and launched into a brief history of her career as a librarian and how it came to be that she inherited the organizing responsibilities of the Straussville Ladies' Literary Review, as they called themselves. When she finally took a second to catch her breath, I jumped in again and asked, "Can my friends and I all join this . . . SLLR?" I asked, pronouncing it like *slurrrr*.

"Marge, sweetheart—I'm a bit chilled. Would you mind getting me another blanket, the wool one we got out in Pendleton?"

She sat up straight. "Oh—oh, I think I can do that. Excuse me, I'll be right—well, it might take me a minute. Some things are still in their moving boxes . . ."

Her words trailed off as she left the room. Mr. Terrence and I looked at each other. His eyes were watery, his skin more wrinkled than I remembered. He looked like he was working hard to hold in some unwieldy emotion. The monster and I took a deep breath.

"Marjorie's *nice*," I said.

"She is," he replied, his voice raspier than usual. To my surprise, he chuckled and added, "Even us bastards get a bit of luck now and then." I thought he might be using the word in its literal sense.

"We do. Just like everyone else," I replied. We looked at each other again.

"Sue-Beth was here, too. Just before you, in fact."

"Oh."

"I wanted to tell you what I told her—"

"That I threatened to kill you if you benched my daughter?" I interrupted. "Bit inaccurate, don't you think?" I waited for my heart rate to kick up, but it didn't.

"I told Sue-Beth that I'd swear on the grave that I did not know Coach Sullen's history. I knew *none* of that." He'd made fists with both hands. Again, he looked as if he were staving off some larger emotion.

"OK," I replied, uncertain if I should believe him. My monster-senses registered him as a good liar, but good liars are like broken clocks—they speak truth on occasion. "Even so, *I* warned you. *I* knew something wasn't right. I brought my experience and intuition to you and you shunned them. But it's funny—you accepted my lifeguarding expertise without any qualms, didn't you?"

He looked down and away.

"How did you find him?" I asked when he didn't reply. "Sullen."

He kept his eyes on the floor. "My buddy Beau Hoffman introduced me a few months back to Ms. Patchett-Parker. She offered to campaign with me, which I thought was a little strange given that she's running for Congress while I'm hoping for county commissioner. But I'm well-known locally, so I thought maybe there was something in it for her," he said, talking more readily now, almost in a rush. "She called me the day after, though, saying she had an assistant coach for me. Said the guy had briefly played in college, and was new to Straussville. I thought it was the least I could do, to thank her for agreeing to make a campaign stop or two with me. And that way, I could pull back on my coaching duties, too."

"O-P-P brought this guy to you?" I asked, not ready to believe it. "She made this happen?"

"Thinking back, she didn't rave about him. Just told me what I told you. I guess I was flattered at her attention, and let my imagination fill in the rest."

"The rest being his qualities as a coach?"

"Yes, but as a human being, too."

"Go on."

"I called her today, but she didn't pick up. Wouldn't take my call. So I tried Beau, who did get back to me. Turns out, Sullen is related to Patchett-Parker by marriage. Some kind of cousin-in-law. And when he got into trouble out in Pierce, she convinced him to relocate."

"She had extra incentive to get it done quietly, given the whole 'law and order' schtick she's campaigning on."

"I bet she gave him some money, too." He crossed his arms and exhaled.

"You two have the same politics, I take it? Campaigning together and all?"

"Of course," he said, his eyes narrowing as if the question confused him.

"Of course," I said, mimicking him a tick. It enraged me to think he held the same extreme positions as OPP. I decided I'd better change course: "What's your connection to Project Chimera?"

He coughed and tried to push himself higher in his chair. "Excuse me?"

"The yokels in black. You know the ones. Your Science Club back in the seventies had the same patches on the arm as the guys who pulled guns on my friends and me."

He shook his head no, and after a few seconds I sensed he wasn't sure what to tell me. "That was Beau's idea. Stupid, fool idea. He was obsessed with the mythology around that . . . supposed agency. When his dad's bank offered to sponsor a trip to the National Science Olympiad, Beau convinced him to let us wear those silly patches rather than put a bank logo on the arm. I think he did the original sketch."

"I see. But what about the guys in the hats? They might not have been official, but they were definitely coordinating with each other."

He sighed. "I'd rather not talk about them."

"What do you mean, you'd 'rather not'?" The monster jumped to her feet inside me. The *fuck* was this guy thinking, acting like he had a leg to stand on?

He was still thinking when I heard a *thump* from another room. "Maybe my new BFF Marjorie knows about them," I said. "Maybe *she'll* tell me."

"Look—Sue-Beth already emailed a letter to the superintendent, insisting he remove me as coach and from the PTA, too, OK? She had all of the board members sign it and when she marched in here—wouldn't sit down, mind you—she dropped every name with any clout in the state judiciary. All right? So I'm out of your hair now."

I studied him for several seconds, happy to watch him squirm. I'd let him change the subject, but only for now; at some point, when he was more recovered, and the kind and accommodating Marjorie wasn't around, I'd pin him to the wall and make him tell me everything he knew.

My next thought—*that I hadn't actually said I wanted him out of my hair*—took me by surprise. The monster, too, raised her brows. But a germ of an idea had taken root in my mind, even if my beastlier half wasn't taking to it.

"Now," he said, clearing his throat, "explain to me how you were at the carnival at the same time that . . . *thing* was running around?"

"I beg your pardon?" The monster and I agreed: This man had some gall.

"I was *so sure* you were that . . . creature. You basically told me so, in the hallway that day."

I held up my hands, feigning innocence. "I'm not sure what got into me that day."

"Then I guess neither of us is gonna get the answer they want tonight."

I stood up. "You know I saved your life last night, right? Here I thought you wanted me to come over so you could thank me or apologize for not listening to me—and for endangering my daughter, for fuck's sake! But all you wanna do is tell me none of it was your fault. Well, you can put that shit right back in the hole you got it from, 'cause I don't want any of it." The monster moonwalked in celebration.

He started to say something but I charged on, "*You*, sir, enabled a predator. I did not. And if you don't drop out of the commissioner race, Sue-Beth and I will do our level best to keep that awful fact on the top of everyone's minds, mmm-kay?" Marjorie returned to the room holding the blanket. "You're leaving already?"

"I am, but . . . " I trailed off, still unsure about my idea. The monster wanted to drop it. I kinda wanted to drop it. But I steeled myself and said it anyway: "I wanna get in on this book club action. Where do we meet, Marjorie, and when?"

Both Terrences seemed surprised by this. Earlier, they must have thought I was expressing interest just to be polite. The monster grumbled, unnerved.

"We meet monthly," she answered finally. "A few of us take turns hostessing."

The monster all but shook me in protest as I looked at Mr. Terrence and added, "Well, I guess I'll be seeing you, too, every now and again."

"Wonderful!" Marjorie replied.

"Hon, would you get me a glass of water?" Mr. Terrence asked after another short coughing spasm. She hurried off to the kitchen again. Meanwhile, the monster informed me she would like a stiff drink.

"You mean you're going to come over here, sit on my couch, and pretend you don't despise me?" he scoffed once his wife was out of earshot.

"'Course not."

He cocked his head at me.

"Sometimes I'll be sitting in that chair." When he rolled his eyes at me, I waved a hand wildly back at him. "Look—not everything is about you, man! I always get to know the new women I come across. It's one of my better characteristics." This was true, if not the whole story. I had a second reason for wanting to join that book club, and put myself in the path of my nemesis and his circle of friends.

"Aren't you trying to—you know—*cancel* me or something?"

I decided to keep it simple, and gave him a partial truth. "You know what they say: 'Keep your friends close . . .'"

He huffed and shook his head. "You're crazy."

I didn't care to explain the matter to Mr. Terrence. I didn't need to tell him that one of my shittier characteristics is that I've too often sat on the sidelines of things—when I showed up at all. That I'd resisted organized gatherings, mostly out of distrust and fear. That I'd done my level best to spend time only with like-minded people, and that that in itself was pretty rare. That these habits had hardly left me with a perfect life.

So I'd come to the decision, right there in their living room, among the plethora of lace doilies and early-American décor, that I would put myself in broader company more. Much more, and I would do it even when I didn't like it much. Isn't that what a lot of families do, anyway? And church congregations? Life corrals you together and *voilà!* You may not love each other, but along the way, you became familiars.

I didn't think about redeeming Mr. Terrence; this was a more selfish endeavor. I knew that entering his orbit now and again would give me an opportunity to expose him and his buddies to *me*, directly. I'd make sure to overshare with them my struggles, quibbles, hopes, fears, schemes, and dreams. They would have to *hear* me, even when I preached on pet topics like the evils of vulvar cleansing products.

And indeed—part of me wanted the chance to keep an eye on Mr. Terrence, even if it wasn't the most magnanimous of missions. What's more, I thought I might relieve a tiny bit of pressure off other moms in Straussville, especially those of color. Lord knows Ellen had already dealt with more than her fair share of Mr. Terrence; it was far past time for her white friends to sort him out and keep him in check.

Thinking of Ellen brought me back to the present, to the conversation at hand. "Since I'll be here cleaning out your cheese drawer every few months," I said with a soft grin, "I assume you'll be less likely to help those cosplay Project Chimera guys the next time they want to sabotage my friends' lab."

"Wait, wait, wait—I never said anything about *that*," he replied as indignance—or perhaps shame—inflamed his whole face.

"It was just a hunch, but now I'm pretty sure it's true. Criminal mischief is a felony, you know. Aiding and abetting it will also get you some jail time."

"I don't know what you're talking about." He was lying at that point, I was sure of it. I'd scared him, and he was off his game.

"Those guys came in from Idaho. And Montana and Washington. They had to have someone local advising them, telling them how to avoid drawing too much attention and so on." I couldn't begin to guess how they'd blocked cell signal at the warehouses. "And by the way: I don't know what's happening with that stupid statue, but you and your building crew should work on repairing the warehouse instead, don't you think?"

When Marjorie emerged from the kitchen with his water, I leaned a skosh closer to him. "I promise not to get too much fur—er, *hair*—on your very nice blanket when I'm here," I whispered, tickled when his expression went from smug to shook. Then I winked and left.

***

When I got home, a commercial van was parked in front of Justin's house. Given the late hour, I wondered if he'd had some kind of plumbing emergency or something. The logo on the side of the vehicle said *Steamy Dean's Complete Clean*, and one of the uniformed men—there were several—getting out of it had a heavy-duty vacuum in hand.

"Hello!" I called out to him. "Is the owner of the house here?"

"No, ma'am," he replied without slowing down.

I followed him a few steps up the driveway and noticed the house's windows and doors were all open. "Are you in charge?"

He glanced over his shoulder but kept going. "You can call the one-eight-hundred number on the side of the van to schedule a service, ma'am."

"No—I was just wondering what happened, and where my neighbor was."

"Nothing happened," he said as he approached the door and set the heavy vacuum inside. "We do move-out cleanings all the time."

"'Move-out'?" I repeated as my knees began to go weak. I pulled out the new phone Justin had given me and called the only phone number we had for him as I walked over and sat on my own front step. But I knew what I would hear before the recording started: *Your call cannot be completed as dialed.* I let my head fall between my knees.

"What's wrong, Harry?"

I yanked my head up. Sooby was coming up the lawn, hands in the pockets of her fleece, her brows looking ready to do battle on my behalf.

"Nothing. I mean, I'm fine. I think." She sat on the step next to me, close enough that our thighs touched. "How's Satch?"

She looked at her lap. "She says she's OK. But I don't know if she knows how she feels yet. We're getting her a therapist."

"And how are you?"

Her voice shook. "I'm . . . heartbroken. I'm guilt-ridden. More than anything, though, I'm enraged, Harry. So fucking enraged."

Finally, I thought. *Welcome to the club.*

"Because what the fuuuuuuck, men?" Her voice cracked, but she kept going as the tears came. "How have we been living all this time, letting all these guys be predatory fucks? Jesus fucking *Christ*."

"I know. Some days, I feel like I could count on one hand the number of men I know who are neither predatory nor wearing blinders about the fact that so many of them are predatory."

"*Fuck* that."

"Fuuuuuuck *thaaaaaaat*."

"We're gonna need some new cuss words for this."

"I hear the Scots have some good ones."

We laughed, but when Soob hid her face in her arms and let out a weighted sob, I put my arms around her and squeezed as hard as I could. Monster-hard. She was barely audible when she whispered, *"I didn't protect my baby, Harry. I didn't protect her."*

I kept hugging on her for several minutes. Then I broke the silence and told her that Justin appeared to have moved out the previous night.

"What?" She turned to look at me.

"And the only address I have for him is the P.O. box where he asked me to send the report he wants me to write."

"Jesus."

I shook my head. "*Fuck*. What if he wasn't even FBI? What if he didn't really take those men into custody, and was lying to us the whole time?"

"Actually, I already called Olivia Patchett-Parker's office and demanded that she confirm whether they were in custody. Which she did."

I looked at her agape. "I still can't believe you called her. What else did she say?"

"Not much. I think she was playing nice because she wanted to suss out how much I know about her role in all this."

"Interesting. I guess there's no way to prove she's connected to the men at the warehouse."

"There isn't even a record of those men *being* at the warehouse."

"Well, it's something we can potentially hold over her."

Sooby nodded. "Yeah. I didn't mention to her that I've already joined her opponent's campaign and plan to absolutely crush her at the ballot box. I don't think Ms. Law-and-Order's constituents will approve of her enabling a predator." She extended her legs in front of her with her ankles crossed. "Oh, and by the way, the Project Chimera Facebook group? Gone. Disappeared."

I picked up a stray piece of gravel and threw it down again. "Fuckers."

"We have no way of going after them, do we? They're gone, and there's no evidence of what they did to us apart from whatever witness testimony the seven of us could provide. And is any of us prepared to go on the record about all of this?"

I tossed a small chunk of broken concrete. "This might be terrible, but part of me is relieved that Justin swept those guys away with no forwarding address."

She snorted. "No—I feel that, too. He saved us, in a way. I mean—can you imagine? Answering cops' questions, or lawyers'? What would we say? The truth? Or would we try to coordinate some big lie among all seven of us?" She visibly shivered. "Anyway, this way I can focus on Satchel."

I nodded. "We can still go after Olivia, though. For covering for Sullen."

"Damn right we can. And we will."

The events at Scarehouse and Soob's visit at the hospital had gone a long way to melt the ice between us, but I still felt a bit weird. There was still so much to say. "I'd like to see her, whenever that's OK. Satchel, I mean."

"Anytime, Harry. That hasn't changed," she said, looking around.

"To be honest, I'm not sure on the etiquette of stopping by someone's house." I paused and took a deep breath before adding, "I thought you'd still come over when Jo and Frankie were born, and it hurt when you stopped. And that you still don't come, to this day. But looking back, I probably never asked."

She turned toward me. "You didn't need to ask! I was just . . . *grieving*, I think is the word. Grieving my inability to have more kids. And the hormones I was still injecting into my ass, for our billionth round of IVF, made me feel like I was losing my mind, Harry! Everything had become too much, and I was afraid if I came over, you'd end up having to take care of me on top of your two new babies, because I was constantly a total wreck. A jealous, hormonal wreck."

"I didn't realize things were that bad for you then. I'm sorry."

"No, I'm sorry. I didn't want to saddle you with it."

"Will you promise me, Soob, to saddle-away in the future? Because I need you to tell me things. No more private pain, OK?"

"Deal. Promise."

"I also need you to stop by my house even though it's a mess. I'm telling all my friends the same thing. No more private pain, no more mess-shame, and no more drive-thru friendships."

"OK. I will. That reminds me," she said, leaning over to pull something from her back pocket. "I got you this gift certificate for a floor cleaning—"

I went to take it, but she pulled it away with her far hand. "But I realize now that what I really need to do is not *care* about the state of your floors," she continued, laughing.

I leaned on top of her and snatched at the thing. "Exactly. Besides, I'm so used to the *eau de urine* thing we've got going on, I might miss it." When I finally nabbed it, I added, "Still, I'll just take this for safekeeping."

She laughed and put her arm around me, then rested her head on my shoulder. I felt closer to her than I had in years. We had more to work out, for sure, but for now, it was so good just to cry and laugh together.

"I'm sorry I didn't listen to you about Mr. Terrence," she said softly.

I kissed her crown. "I know. Apology accepted."

"This old dog can learn new tricks, though."

"If anyone can, it's you."

"It can't be harder than a colicky baby. Not by much, anyway."

"Probably not."

"So what's going to happen to . . . *you* know, your *thing*? Your big, furry thing?" she whispered as she bumped my shoulder with her own. "What should I do with all my . . . acolytes?"

I threw up my hands. "I don't know. I won't be able to go out in the rain, unless I develop resistance to water at some point. But I'm hoping that Ellen and Dr. M's research will tell us something about how and why these things are happening to us."

"Seriously. That'd be nice."

"I wanna know for certain if getting so incredibly angry was the key that unlocked my inner monster, so to speak. If that's what happened with all of us. That's sure the hell what it seemed like for me."

"And why do our powers change sometimes?" Sooby asked, picking blades of grass and then tossing them aside. "Can we cultivate them somehow?"

"So many questions. Good thing we have doctor-friends," I replied. "That reminds me, I asked a nurse to print out my medical record, but I guess she forgot."

"Was that the packet at the foot of your bed when I stopped by?"

"What packet?"

She looked at me. "There was a packet of paper on your bed, in a manila folder."

I closed my eyes and tried to remember the sequence of events at the hospital. Soob came by. Theo came back in, then Justin.

"Mother*fucker*!" I seethed, shooting to my feet.

"What? Who?"

I paced briskly, my hand shaking as I raised it to my temple. I nodded at his house (at *your* house, you motherfucker). "Justin," I whispered, my voice unsteady. "He took the packet. I'm sure of it."

"Deep breaths, Harry," Sooby said as she stood up and reached for my arm. She pulled me toward her so I stopped pacing. "Look at me. How do you know that?"

"I just . . . know. After Justin left, the woman from *Willamette Week* came by, and I remember there being nothing on my blanket because they asked if they could set a piece of equipment there. *Fuck*."

"And you checked around before you left?"

I nodded, and forced myself to take a deep breath. "Christy helped me do a sweep for all my stuff."

She let her hand fall from my arm. "Yikes."

"You know what I think?" I slumped a little. "About the myth that Project Chimera's an actual thing, and a part of the government?"

"Yeah?"

"I don't think it's a myth."

She thought a few seconds. "It would explain a hell of a lot. And yeah, the FBI would have a serious interest in your medical history."

She put an arm around my shoulders and turned me toward the house, squeezing hard. I mumbled "*that fucker*" a few more times as I whipped out my new phone, but couldn't keep from smiling when Soob hooted with joy at the sight of it. I opened a search window and typed, *bad dinner party ideas informal messy no pressure fun.* Then I hit go.

4.2   SEVERAL WEEKS LATER, 7:30 P.M.

I was pleasantly surprised when Theo announced that he'd be organizing semimonthly "poker" nights, and inviting all of my friends' husbands as well as literally anyone else who wanted to join. I was even more pleased when the inaugural gathering turned out to be a hoot—and had almost nothing to do with card-playing.

"So, to recap, the rules of Poker Club will be as such," he began, standing at our kitchen table. He'd had surgery by then—and several pins put into his leg—but had healed fairly quickly and was almost back to his usual activities. "Number one, you don't have to know how to play poker. Or even want to."

There were nods and sips of beers and ciders from the others.

"Number two, there shall be no special house cleanings by the host in advance of Poker Club and if there is, you will be docked ten points."

Dr. M piped in. "And a corollary to that rule, if I may?" She was wearing one of those green visors I'd only ever seen on serious players. "Try not to comment on the state of anyone's house, car, pet, personal appearance, or, most importantly, their kids' hygiene."

"Wait—what are points for? How do we get them?" Gregory, Ellen's husband, asked.

"TBD, Gregory. We'll figure it out. Or maybe we won't! I don't know," Theo replied. He crossed his arms in front of him and I smiled. He was in therapy now, and he was already better off for it. Still, we had a long way to go.

"Actually, I have an idea," Sooby's husband Philip said, raising his hand like a schoolkid.

"Yes—Phil!"

"We get points for bringing frozen Costco entrees instead of cooking or baking something amazing that makes other people, like myself, feel pressured to do the same."

"That's a beautiful idea, sir," Theo said, turning to his white board and jotting it down. "I'd like to suggest a corollary to the Costco rule, and that is: If you forget to bring something one night, or you can't, you will be subjected to multiple rounds of hugs and other consolations."

Everyone nodded. There was even a "Hear! Hear!" Brian looked somewhat confused, but the fact that he'd come seemed like a positive sign for his and Christy's relationship.

Ellen came over and stood next to me; although the "club" was open to all, so far it was all husbands and Dr. M, but I'd begged them to please encourage their wives to come over just to hang out.

"For a person who says she hates groups, you're suddenly joining a lot of groups," Ellen whispered.

"I know," I replied, smirking. "But I'll manage the pain. Somehow."

"Last rule," Theo said, "is that whoever's hosting gets to pick what game to play, and it doesn't have to be cards. Maybe we do Win Lose or Draw one time. Maybe we do some Dungeons & Dragons."

"I'm hosting next," Gregory spoke up again, "and I wanted to do a chili potluck, but my question is, does this violate the Costco rule?"

"Not at all," Philip replied. "We just won't expect everyone to bring chili."

"Got it. Good. Prepare yourselves, gentlemen. And lady."

"How's work lately?" I asked Ellen. "Oh wait—is it OK to ask about work at Poker Club? I'm not sure."

"Totally fine by me," she replied. "Work is . . . getting interesting."

I turned and looked at her, and she was smiling. "You'll tell me if you have some kind of, you know, breakthrough?"

"You'll get briefed at our next gathering," she replied with a sly look, "just like everyone else."

"Just promise you'll text me right away, please, if you develop the ability to reheat French fries so that they taste as great as they do fresh out of the fryer? *Please?*"

She laughed. "Friend, if I or anyone else gets that superpower, I will put it on blast—I promise you."

I twisted my lips at her. "Also, I'm dying to know if there's any more of us."

"Funny you should mention that," she replied with a subtle tremor in her voice.

 "What? Who—"

"I can't tell you any more about that now," she replied. She released all the air in her lungs before adding, "So please don't ask. OK?"

"OK, OK," I said, more curious by the second, especially since Ellen seemed to have qualms about it. *Could it be one of our daughters? Olivia Patchett-Parker? Shit—could it be my freakin' mom?*

My ears pricked up when the sound of a particular diesel engine came within range of my monster-ears.

"What is it?"

"Infa-care," I said softly. "I-5 . . . south, sounds like. Wanna go?"

"Harry, I think folks are still swimming in formula, since the last time we held up a delivery truck," she replied. "Besides, it's drizzling."

"I know, I *know*," I sighed, disappointed. "You're right."

The men around the table burst into laughter.

"What?" Ellen and I both asked.

"We were just talking about 'poker faces,' and I was saying that I have an edge over everyone else here," Theo replied. "Because they might have poker faces but *I*," he said, bringing his hands up to his nonexistent lapels, "I can put on a *Harry* face."

His face went stony—except with big, exaggerated eyes—and he jogged toward me without breaking a smile. I burst out laughing, and had to jog away when he got right up in my grill, still sporting his "Harry face." The more he chased me with that crazy-flat expression, the more I laughed—and laughed and laughed.

ADDENDUM: **Agent Summary**

<u>Threat Assessment</u>

- RE: Mrs. Harriet Lime's understanding of Project Chimera (PC):

  - As of this writing, I am aware of no evidence in Mrs. Lime's possession that supports the existence of a government entity by that name.

  - She is unaware of any connections her mother (Miss Leah Morton) and grandmother (Mrs. Delilah Morton) may have had to an entity calling itself by that name.

  - She and her friends will likely remain hypervigilant of-- and combative to--any civilians who act in the name of PC, or who pose a threat to themselves or their families.

- RE: Mrs. Lime's willingness to destroy property and harm civilians:

  - Any consideration of Mrs. Lime's intent to injure Mr. Sullen, perhaps lethally, should account for the fact that he did seek to harm a minor who is well-known to her at the Scarehouse event. That Mr. Sullen is not facing charges related to his actions that evening is consistent with the usual difficulties inherent in prosecuting cases of attempted sexual assault.

  - Contrary to what Mrs. Lime stated in the preceding report, recent incidents of petty theft have not been limited to infant formula. At least three vending machines in the greater Straussville area have had their front sides violently ripped off in the previous two weeks--and all their "Twizzlers" and jerky products removed.

  - While Mrs. Lime's supernatural outings could intensify again upon the return of drier weather, her husband

(Mr. Theodore Lime) has recently become more engaged in family life, which may impede her. That development would be of benefit to all.

☐ The dog, in all her forms, remains a complete and total mystery to me.

Recommendations

I recommend that Mrs. Lime, Dr. Miriam Morris, and Dr. Ellen Stout each be monitored by no fewer than two undercover officers. I recommend further that coverage of Mrs. Morton be heightened, to account for the increased possibility that she will try to meet with her daughter, or vice versa. Lastly, I advise all Bureau operatives to avoid interfering in the lives of the women involved in the aforementioned incidents, and the lives of their family members. We have yet to witness the full extent of the women's enhanced abilities, and they are not reluctant to use them. Indeed, they appear rather eager.

ACKNOWLEDGMENTS

It took a whole-ass village to bring *Beast Mom* to life.

Editor-extraordinaire Wylie O'Sullivan assisted me from beginning to end, imbuing the manuscript with more good things than I could possibly list here.

Illustrator Maggie Stephenson did absolutely stunning work on the cover art. Bethany Brown and the rest of the team at The Cadence Group worked their magic in helping me prepare the book for publication.

I would not be a novelist without family members buoying me, over many years and in a variety of ways. I want to thank my husband and kids for their resolute support of my dreams and for giving me time and space when I needed to crank. My parents' regular inquiries about the status of the book were also much appreciated. My sister and sisters-in-law provided invaluable feedback and advice.

Also chiming in were my amazing friends—including a number of author-friends. Having Gretchen Grey-Hatton as a writing buddy is a key reason *Beast Mom* got finished.

I want to especially note how the late Helen Anbinder supplied me with regular boosts in confidence and good cheer as I put the finishing touches on this thing.

Many books have influenced me; a few inspired specific elements of *Beast Mom*. Angela Garbes's *Like a Mother: A Feminist Journey through the Science and Culture of Pregnancy* chronicles many of the ways research on women's bodies is less advanced than research on other medical matters. Another source was *All Joy and No Fun* by Jennifer Senior, which is where I first read about the idea that we feel love for someone or something as a *result* of taking care of them. (She offers credit to Alison Gopnik, the author of *The Philosophical Baby*, on this topic.) Lastly, for over two decades, my writerly outlook has been shaped in part by *Bowling Alone: The Collapse and Revival of American Community* by Robert D. Putnam.

ABOUT THE AUTHOR

KIM IMAS received degrees in engineering and urban planning, from Duke and Harvard respectively, before pursuing a career as a writer. Her work appeared in *Boston Magazine* and the *Boston Globe Magazine* before she turned to long-form fiction. Her first novel, a romance, was initially published under a pen name and earned praise from *Publishers Weekly* for its "smooth prose and witty dialogue." A former Oregonian, Kim now lives with her family outside New York and tries to do in novels what Dolly Parton does in song: deliver stories of women's struggles in a way that's too damn delightful to ignore.